I0523845

Printed in the United States of America.

17   16   15   14   13   12   11   10 9   8   7   6   5   4   3   2   1

Werby, Olga

Harvest : a novel / by Olga Werby

ISBN: 978-0-578-50143-7

San Francisco

www.Pipsqueak.com

To my sons, Tim and Nick,
who together combine the passions
for astrophysics with
anthropology and economics.
The results are out of this world.

Table of Contents

Becoming Animals:

Harvest

Olga Werby

ProLog

"The exton controls are not responding!" Marc shouted into his exoskeleton spacesuit helmet.

His exoskeleton was the heavy-duty dirt-and-boulder-mover type. *Move a ton with exton.* Right now, Marc was really just an intelligent bulldozer with life support. But the suit had disconnected from his D-tats, the personal computing device tattoos embedded in his lower arms and jaw, and his directional controls were busted. Now his exoskeleton acted with a mind of its own, moving him away from the construction site and out into the open Martian landscape. He needed to get back to the Malfy—an affectionate acronym for Martians Live Free, a city-sized habitat being built for the next wave of planetary immigrants.

"Marc?" his SB responded from the inside Malfy's operational center. "What's on the fritz this time?" Every contractor working outside was in constant communication with a personally assigned *safety buddy.* "I can't seem to toss the controls over to my side." In an emergency, Marc's SB could take over the controls of his exton and bring him in, even if he was unconscious.

"I've got nothing!" Marc was more irritated than scared. This was his second equipment failure in as many months, and their group of union builders had reported three more to the management since the start of the project about two hundred days ago. It was always the same MO: at the end of a shift, the movement controls failed to respond to their operators' commands, taking the builders out into the desert; and yet, after the rescue when the equipment was checked out, the engineers found nothing wrong with the extons. The first time it happened to Marc, he was even accused of faking the failure to get extra time off for hazardous conditions. As if construction work on Mars wasn't dangerous in and of itself. Fortunately, Marc's supervisor made everyone carry extra oxygen and a spare battery pack after the first few incidents. Just in case. Inconvenient for sure, but it was better than being stuck out of breath without a heater among the Martian dunes in minus 125 degrees Celsius.

"Send someone out to get me," Marc said. "It's an official request."

"Are you sure, Marc? You know if they don't find anything again—"

"I'm telling you, I've got nothing. Everything is dead on my side."

"Yeah, mine too," Marc's SB agreed. "I'll get Greg out there. But he won't be happy. He just got his exton off and you'll be cutting into his three days off period."

"Tell him that I'd go if it was him out here. And tell him to hurry up about it." The earliest he could expect Greg to arrive would be at least an hour, probably more—it took time get these darn things on.

Marc felt funky. His D-tats itched like crazy, probably from all of the energy pushed through them to try to reconnect with his exton. And now his comm was down, too. As soon as he'd gotten over the rim of the crater, he'd lost touch with his SB.

It was lonely out here in the Martian landscape with no one to talk to and all the human structures obscured from view. Marc could only look ahead—his suit didn't allow him to turn his head—and before him stretched miles and miles of nothing but rust sand and red rocks underneath a yellow

sky. Someday this would be paradise, but Marc didn't expect to live that long. Still, it was decent pay, and the benefits were great. And, most importantly, all the construction workers were to be awarded a family subdivision inside the new MLF. Marc looked forward to moving his wife and a new kid he'd never seen out here from Luna Colony. Kids should run around on the surface of a real planet, his mother always said. In a few years, Marc would make his mother's dream a reality right here, on this dusty red rock. And when he did, he would be able to tell his kids that he built this place with his own hands. He would point to a boulder and say, "See that rock? Your daddy placed that rock." It was a satisfying thought...if only the equipment worked right.

He tried to will his suit to obey. Heat erupted around his jaw and down his neck. It took him by surprise—not an emotion he was used to. The off-world building crews went through years of training, and part of that training involved controlling one's thoughts. Spend too much attention on extraneous thoughts and emotions—like surprise and worry—and space got you. Cognition was a limited resource.

This fact about human nature was drilled into Marc, not just during training but from an early age. All Luna Colony children learned to focus and control their attention. Those who couldn't didn't make it to adulthood. It was different there now, in those modern Luna Live Free habitats—Elfys. But when Marc was young...

"Ahhh!" The scream seemed to rip itself out of Marc's throat without his conscious control. Pain twisted his arms inside his suit. He felt himself hyperventilating. Something was seriously wrong with *him,* not just with his exton. The horror of that realization hit him hard as the exoskeleton kept marching him inexorably farther from the base. He smelled cooked meat. It took all his willpower not to think where the

smell was coming from. The life support systems should have noted his elevated heart rate and responded.

Since his D-tats weren't working, Marc tried to blink commands directly into the suit. He drilled down several menus and selected a painkiller injection. He needed to get himself under control. Rescue was still at least thirty minutes away.

Sweat trickled into his eyes. It was difficult to see now. He felt cold and yet heat burned his arms, neck, and jaw. His teeth felt out of alignment. There was a constant buzzing in his left ear, different in tone and structure from the one in his right. But at least it was something he could focus on. He poured himself into the strange, asymmetric tinnitus. Bzzz, bzzz, swish, bzzz, bzzz, swish...

"I found him unresponsive."

Greg sat in front of a board of inquiry. Marc's death was the first among the Martian chapter of the Off-World Builders Union this year. Given that Mars was deemed a relatively low-risk environment, the death had attracted extra scrutiny from both the union leaders and the insurance representatives for the Martians Live Free project.

"Are you saying Builder Mark Kelly's communications were out? Or was he unconscious when you found him?"

"At first it wasn't clear, sir," Greg testified. "The exoskeleton continued to walk into the desert and wouldn't stop until I caught up with it and patched into it directly."

"So the comm was completely out?"

"Yes, sir. I wasn't able to control the exton from a distance, and Marc lost his communication a while before that." Greg wiped the sweat from his forehead. He hated answering stupid questions. Everyone already knew what had happened. Marc's D-tats had fried from some bad connection to his equipment. *Shit happens. Get over it. Move on.*

The interrogation went on for another hour, but at some point, even the insurance representative recognized that Greg had nothing more to add to the report he'd filed with the union. The conclusion was that this was a freak accident caused by improperly implanted personal computing device tattoos a decade earlier. The Luna Colony medical board was granted jurisdiction over the case.

Chapter One

"Sentient life's colonization of the Earth is fractal. Even within a single ecosystem, there are many species that possess intelligence and self-awareness. But only one species becomes dominant."

Professor Volhard took a theatrical pause here. Everyone in the audience knew where she was going with this, but it never hurt to add drama to a presentation.

"Obviously I am talking about humans. We are not the only intelligent, self-aware species on our planet—but we got lucky. We were blessed with favorable initial conditions, and our dominance was almost guaranteed. Lack of luck tends to permanently retard progress. Dinosaurs' loss is our win."

There were a few chuckles from the audience, but no big laughs. Varsaad Volhard sighed inwardly and moved on. She never knew how the lay audience would react, but this was all part of doing the book-selling lecture circuit.

Vars was tall and skinny with short, unruly, dark red hair and glasses to match. She looked a bit like a stick insect in her black pants and black sweater. For the tour, she was trying to dress more interestingly than normal—per instructions from her publisher—and so had added the bright orange scarf that her publisher sent in the mail. The instructions that came with the scarf told her to wear matching orange shoes, but

Vars didn't own any orange shoes, so matching black was as good as it got.

She hadn't failed to notice that the cover of her book— *Luck & Lock on Life & Love: The Human History of Conquest of Resources on Earth, Luna, and Beyond*—had the same color orange titles as the scarf. Her agent or someone in the office was obviously trying. Vars made a mental note to figure out who that was and thank them.

Vars talked for a while without paying attention to what she said—that was a gift that came with giving the same talk for the hundredth time. Fortunately, she was almost at the end of her book tour. Two more lectures and she would be done. She could go back to teaching and research—get her life back. This nomadic lifestyle wasn't for her. But before she got out of there tonight, Vars still had one more surprise argument for these people: a defense of space exploration.

She looked into the dark void in front of her. The stage

lights made the hundred people in the theater disappear from view—a plus for a shy researcher. And she was a true believer in the "what you can't see can't hurt you" principle. Not only had she opted out of vision-correction treatments, she regularly taught without her glasses, leaving all but the front row of her classroom a Monet-like blur. The trick worked well to relieve her agoraphobic anxiety.

"So, what are the prerequisites of space travel?" she asked.

There were a few shout-outs from up in the gallery—the cheap seats usually occupied by students. "Civilization." "Faster-than-light travel." "Aliens." They were on the right track, even if their sources were limited to science fiction movies. But Vars was an evolutionary socio-historian, and that meant she was trained to look both into the future *and* the past. She liked to think that her ideas about possible human future scenarios were well informed by historical precedents and intelligent extrapolations of cultural trends— meaning she wasn't just talking science fiction here.

"Let's start with something simple," she said. "Time." Time was never simple, but people always assumed it was. Everyone had experience with time, so everyone felt like they were experts on the subject. "Humans have a relatively long lifespan for a mammal. And we have the longest childhood of all animals." Well, that was true now. Neanderthal kids had enjoyed a longer childhood, but Vars didn't want to complicate things further. "Not only are we able to learn a lot before we plunge into adulthood," Vars continued, "we also have the time to use that knowledge. I'm sure we would all like to live even longer, but nature has ensured that we live long *enough* to transfer wisdom from one generation to the next, so our species can build on that, expanding our collective grasp of how the universe works. Each generation stands on the shoulders of all those that came before. Without a sufficiently long lifespan to learn and apply that collective mastery, space travel would just not be possible."

Vars tried to peer into the audience to check that they were still with her.

"So why not elephants or whales, you might ask. Both species live a long time and spend a significant proportion of that life as children." Vars didn't wait for answers. "Unfortunately, neither were lucky enough to evolve hands. Even the elephant's prehensile trunk can't compare with the nimbleness of human fingers. And whales have the additional disadvantage of living in an underwater environment. These are significant handicaps to developing space travel. So again, humans got lucky. We evolved to live on land, and we have the right appendages to be able to tinker with objects in our environment. To bend it to our will."

"Language!" someone screamed out of the dark.

Vars smiled. Language came up over and over again at each of her lectures. "Yes, language," she said into the darkened auditorium. "It's been said that language is the ultimate tool of mankind. Its greatest invention." There were sounds of agreement from the audience. "But are we the only species on Earth to possess language? Sure, human languages are incredibly sophisticated and versatile, far more so than those of any other species we have encountered to date. But until a few decades ago, we didn't even believe that there *were* nonhuman languages here on our planet. Now, of course, we know better. Dolphins, elephants, and even some birds have been observed using rudimentary languages unique to their species."

Vars stopped to listen to the audience. There were murmurings of assent, but also a few mutterings of rejection. The idea of animals inventing languages was very new still, but it was no longer controversial among her colleagues. Of course, politics was always way behind science. If humans were to widely acknowledge that dolphins communicated via language, then we might also have to recognize them as having some legal form of "personhood"—and that just wasn't tenable in the current political climate.

The dissent told Vars what proportion of the audience held human-centric views. It was about forty percent or so, judging by the noise. That was about average for this part of the country. In places like Berkeley, California, only one or two people in the audience dared to express such backward opinions loudly enough to be heard on stage. Most dissenters kept quiet, she knew. People were herd mammals, after all, and needed to be surrounded by others with similar views. That was how social echo chambers worked in the age of mass e-media.

"Language," she said, "particularly written language, is essential to passing information from one generation and one community to the next. Written language saved us from having to invent things over and over again—"

"Oral traditions!" someone yelled.

"Oral traditions are fantastic for capturing and communicating culture," Vars replied. "But they are lousy for transmitting technical information. There is no oral tradition of calculus." There was a murmuring of agreement. *Good.* "And before someone brings up apprenticeship, let me just say that I'm a believer in learning while being embedded in a community of practice. We see such educational approaches in species other than our own. Chimps routinely teach their offspring how to fish for termites with specially made twigs. Birds teach their chicks how to hunt and which foods are good and where they can be located. Cerrado, a species of monkey from South America, use giant hammer rocks to break tough palm nuts over carefully selected anvil boulders.

It takes years for the youngsters to learn how to select just the right hammers and anvils and to perfect the technique for bashing open the nuts. So yes, apprenticeship works—but it has its limits. We are the only species on Earth to develop *other* intentional ways of passing on knowledge. Without written information, we wouldn't be in the process of colonizing Mars, or mining the asteroids, or having permanent bases on the moon."

Vars gave the audience a few seconds to absorb this. She wasn't done having fun with them yet. "But before written and oral language traditions, before the apprenticeship form of passing knowledge from generation to generation, there was another way. Nature's way. Evolution's way."

She stopped, giving her listeners a moment or two to guess the answer. Some nights, the audience got it almost immediately; other nights, there wasn't a clue in the house. Tonight, there was only silence.

"Evolution couldn't wait for humans to invent language. Survival depended on passing some information down the chain of generations." *Well? Still nothing?* "I'm talking about instincts, of course. Our drive to mate, to reproduce, to protect our children. Our will to survive against all odds. We've all experienced, or will experience, these instinctual needs. It's in our DNA, so to speak. But that's not the only hard-coded knowledge that we pass along to our offspring.

"I will focus on humans here, because that's what I wrote my book about. Which reminds me: I will be signing copies in the lobby right after the end of the lecture. I'm required to say this by my publisher." There were a few chuckles. *Good.* Vars hated dull groups. It was hard to speak without feedback. "Agoraphobia and claustrophobia, fear of dark places and of heights, ophidiophobia and arachnophobia, instinctual disgust of bodily fluids—blood, urine, pus, feces—all of these are innate for us humans. We are born to avoid tight places and grand expanses. We naturally avoid snakes and spiders even if we've never seen or heard of them before. But we have also learned to overcome these fears. We had to if we were going to go into space. Our spaceships are extremely cramped, and they float in vast expanses of space. Astronauts are forced to recycle their bodily fluids and to no longer be afraid of extreme heights and absolute darkness. Although I may never overcome my fear of snakes and spiders..." She shivered dramatically and earned a few more laughs. "And perhaps, one day, we will meet other explorers out there. And we might have more innate fears to shed."

Vars talked for another quarter hour about the importance of different sensory apparatuses and the need for access to easily extracted raw resources, but it was getting late, and she could feel that the energy had drained from her audience. She was tired, too. She needed to catch a redeye tonight and try to squeeze in a few more hours of sleep before another lecture tomorrow.

Before she was even aware of it, there was hearty applause, and then it was time for smiling, handshaking, and book signing. She'd come to learn that the only people who still bought paper books were the ones who attended these book tour lectures. She was grateful to all of them, and yet she couldn't wait to get out of there.

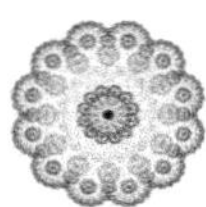

"Dr. Volhard?" The voice was a nice soft baritone. "May I have a moment of your time after you've finished autographing?"

Vars raised her head, a fake smile plastered on her face,

and tried to identify the speaker. There were still half a dozen people waiting, each clutching a copy of her book. But none of those was the speaker. So she went back to signing, and soon enough, like magic, it was done. She rubbed her wrist, which had started to cramp up, and slid the contents of the table—brochures, pens, and leftover business cards—into her bag. She would deal with sorting it all out later.

"Coffee?" the baritone asked again. "I know you take it with sugar and milk. But I wasn't sure of the proportions."

Vars looked up again. A tall, slightly graying man in rimless glasses with a slight yellow tint was standing in front of her, holding a recyclable coffee cup. He was dressed in jeans, a dress shirt with no tie, and a wool jacket—easy elegance, her literary agent would call it. She tried to do something similar for these lectures—approachable, smart, and interesting were her original goals. But at this point in the lecture tour, all she could hope for was clean, awake, and present. Dressing in all black helped.

"I beg your pardon," she said. "Do you have a book for me

to sign?"

"That would have been lovely," the man said, "but I bought an e-version of your book."

"I can sign your data pad," Vars offered. She still didn't take the coffee from his extended hand. And she wasn't planning to.

"What a lovely idea." He smiled. "Do you mind if we talk a bit? I know you're tired—"

"And I have a plane to catch." Vars spoke more harshly than she'd meant to; the man did buy her book, after all.

She tried to go around him, but he wouldn't budge. She looked past him for a security guard at the door. Shouldn't someone be getting everyone out of here? Perhaps escorting her to a taxi? She was getting annoyed and a bit alarmed.

"My name is Ian Rust," the man said.

"Dr. Vars Volhard."

"Of course." He smiled again.

"I really do have to go, Mr. Rust," Vars insisted. She tried to push past the man, her suitcase ready to roll behind her.

"The thing is, Dr. Volhard, we really need your expertise as soon as possible," Rust said.

"Sir, I'm an evolutionary socio-historian. My direct expertise is rarely required on an *emergency* basis. Contact my university office, and I'm sure I would be able to fit you in during one of my ample office hours after I get back."

"Ah, but there are exceptions," he said. "We've read everything that you've published—"

"Everything?"

"Everything. And you have a unique set of expertise that my team at Earth Planetary Space Agency urgently requires." He pulled out his EPSA credentials. "Our car is waiting outside, Dr. Volhard. Won't you please follow me? Do you mind if I call you Vars?"

"Sure," Vars said automatically.

"Then please call me Ian." He handed the coffee to her.

EPSA was the umbrella agency that had taken over for NASA, ESA (European Space Agency), ASA (Australian Space Agency), and JAXA (Japan Aerospace Exploration Agency). So it wasn't entirely "planetary"—China and Russia still ran their own space exploration programs—but it *was* the largest and best-funded agency, and it was the one that was actively pushing the Mars colonization program and comprehensive exploration of the solar system.

Vars had always dreamed of working for EPSA, even as a girl. But somehow, somewhere along the way, her academic career had veered into anthropology, and then evolution, and then…well, here she was. The evo devo diva of anthropology.

And now she was riding down the dark, empty streets in the back seat of a black driverless car, with Dr. Ian Rust, head of the exobiology research team at EPSA, sitting by her side.

Chapter Two

Vars slept on the plane...or tried to. She was too confused, too keyed up to really sleep. That coffee might have been a mistake. Ian said that he couldn't tell her anything until they arrived at his EPSA office in Seattle, which was conveniently her own hometown where she lived with her dad. The man just smiled a lot and talked about how much he had enjoyed reading Vars's new book.

There was a strange edge to their interaction. If Vars hadn't believed Ian's credentials, she would have bailed on him a long time ago. Even so, she felt like she was being kidnapped. And, in a way, she was. She'd had to cancel the last two lectures of her book tour and apologize to her agent over and over again. Ian had promised that EPSA would send an official excuse letter, but Vars still felt like she let her agent and publisher down.

They landed at a general aviation airport, and another black car whisked them to EPSA's headquarters, just outside of Seattle's city limits. She was taken to a conference room on the top floor of the EPSA science building, which Ian called the "tree house." She immediately understood why—it was surrounded on all sides by a balcony planted with a row of trees and some shrubbery. It was quite nice, but Vars couldn't enjoy it; she was simultaneously exhausted and adrenalized.

It was just a matter of time before she crashed.

She must have looked it, too, because someone handed her a very big, very steamy cup of coffee. She sipped it gratefully, completely oblivious to how she came to be holding it. It was still very early in the morning, way before Vars even liked to get up, much less attend a meeting.

About a dozen EPSA people joined her and Ian around the conference table. Vars noticed that several paper copies of her book were laid out; some even looked read, with cracked spines and dog-eared pages.

"So," she said to Ian. "Is *now* a good time and place for you to tell me what this is all about?"

"Now is perfect," Ian said with a big smile. "We are very grateful to have you with us today, Dr. Volhard. This is my exobiology team." He pointed one by one to the people on one side of the table. "Dr. Alice Bear. Dr. Greg Tungsten. Dr. Bob Shapiro. Dr. Saydi Obara. Dr. Evelyn Shar. And Dr. Izzy Rubka."

Vars had heard of some of these people by reputation, of course, but never met any of them personally. EPSA people were a reclusive bunch, tending to mix with their own to the exclusion of others, even with the same research interests. It was one of the reasons Vars always wanted to join the organization—to get access to the best and the brightest minds and a chance to discuss the origins of life over coffee... But the introductions were happening so fast, there was no chance that she would remember how any of these names linked up with faces. Vars doubted she would even recognize these people walking down the street.

But Ian just continued. "And this group," he gestured to two men and a woman, "is on loan from JPL—Jet Propulsion Lab in Pasadena. Trish Cars, Dr. Ron Silverman, and Dr. Benjamin Kouta." Vars gave up on remembering who was

who. "And these two," Ian said, nodding to a pair of identical twins sitting next to him, "are Ibe and Ebi Zimov, our computer science wunderkinds from EISS, European Institute of Space Science."

Ian pronounced their names as *eye-bee* and *ee-bee*; it was the only introduction Vars was likely to remember fully, as the siblings were the most interesting looking pair in the room. They seemed young—Vars guessed not older than twenty—and she was honestly uncertain whether they were male or female or one of each. They were dressed the same—sweatshirts with the EISS logo embroidered on the left, black jeans, black canvas shoes—and both had their hair dyed jet black, shaved on the sides and long on top, falling over their eyes. Vars could see impressive sets of D-tats on the exposed parts of their necks and jaws and peeking out of the twins' sleeves. Other people around the room presumably had

D-tats too, but nothing so obviously ostentatious as these two.

"And before you ask," Ian said, "yes, they are related to Dr. Sergey Aphanasievich Zimov."

That name sounded vaguely familiar, but Vars had no idea who Dr. Zimov was.

She also noted that the other two people present—two men in military uniforms—were not introduced.

"It's a pleasure to meet you all," she said. "Please call me Vars." She smiled at everyone, then turned to Ian. "But once again… Please, I'd very much like to know why I'm here."

"I was just getting to that."

She noticed that he looked tired, too. He hadn't slept much on the plane either. Then again, pretty much everyone in the room looked haggard. Deep circles under the eyes were the norm, not the exception.

Before Ian could continue, one of the women from the exobiology team spoke up. "In your book, Dr. Volhard, you mentioned an example of how robots developed by collectivist cultures would be less likely to kill. Would you mind elaborating on that?"

Vars didn't know what she expected—but it wasn't this. "You flew me out here before dawn to talk about *killer robots*?"

The discussion of robots in her book was just an illustrative example, and a frivolous one at that. It was just a funny way of explaining the differences in value systems between collectivist and individualist cultures. She'd almost cut it from the final draft, but David Gatewood, her editor, had insisted she keep it in.

"Of course not," Ian said. "Robots are just a small part of it. But if you don't mind answering Alice's question…" He gave Vars a pleading look.

"You're serious?" Vars still couldn't believe it. She'd

worked four years on the book, and what had caught EPSA's interest was a stupid joke. *I guess David was right,* she thought. *People, even smart people, grab on to the most flamboyant metaphors.*

"Should I explain the differences between collectivist and individualist societies first?" Vars asked. She looked around the room; she didn't want to assume what these people knew, but at the same time, talking down to the top minds of the Earth Planetary Space Agency was completely unacceptable.

"If you don't mind," Ian said. He composed himself as if awaiting a lecture. In fact, every face in the room had that look of composed concentration that Vars was used to seeing in her grad students.

"Okay." There was nothing to do but move forward. She launched into her introductory lecture on socio-evolution. "While there are many ways of classifying the various human cultures that arose in the last fifty thousand years or so, one division that can be made is focused on the perception of the role of an individual within the group. In collectivist cultures, the group needs are judged *above* the needs of an individual; in the individualist cultures, it's the opposite, naturally."

"Naturally," echoed an older, tiny, dark-skinned woman with bottle-thick glasses and tightly cropped hair, the one who asked the original question. *Alice something.* Vars wasn't familiar with the woman's work. And she hadn't encountered too many people, other than herself...and well, Ian, who wore glasses. In his case, Vars was almost certain it was all about self-image. She wouldn't have been surprised if they were simple tinted glass. But Alice's glasses were thick corrective lenses and far from attractive. Most everyone had their vision corrected in this day and age. So either Alice had a strange affectation or an aversion to treatment. Or perhaps she had a defect that couldn't easily be fixed, which was rare.

"Logic clearly dictates that the needs of the many out-weigh the needs of the few," said one of the youngish-looking men from the JPL team. Vars knew enough popular culture to know he was quoting a character from an old space-exploration series. *Star Trek?*

This is too basic, she thought, and she raised her discourse up a notch. "Let's just jump right into the robot anecdote. Robots designed by collectivist cultures would be less likely to kill. They would have a stronger focus on the *theory of mind*, understanding and taking perspectives of others—"

"Can you backtrack a bit?" Ian asked.

"Sure." Vars thought she now understood the Goldilocks zone she was to lecture to. "Consider guilt. Guilt is one of the strongest human psyche compulsions. We use guilt and embarrassment as tools for social compliance all the time. Guilt is motivational, so to speak. Our social media landscape is full of guilt traps. We finger people who don't pay taxes or contribute in a positive way to our society. We name people who don't recycle or who drop trash on the road or who still use personal transportation vehicles. We social-shame not only the anti-social behavior but even the way people dress and look."

A man in the back spoke up. "We are all familiar with cyber bullying, Dr. Volhard. EPSA is a large, multicultural organization, and we're all required to take classes and workshops in antisocial behavior and sensitivity training."

"I do too, as a university professor and researcher," Vars assured them. "But my point is that social shaming works."

"On robots?"

"I'm getting there," Vars said with a smile. "People from collectivist and individualist societies experience guilt differently. A person from a collectivist culture feels guilt as 'What will people think of me?' While someone from an individualist culture perceives it as 'How will I live with myself?' See the difference?"

"So outcomes vary?" Ian asked.

"Precisely! Consider a criminal," Vars said. "A person who commits a crime in an individualist culture can't escape guilt, for the feelings of guilt are experienced internally, whether anyone is aware of the crime or not."

"Are you implying that in collectivist cultures, a criminal won't experience guilt the same way?" Alice asked.

"That's precisely it, Alice." Vars made herself say the name of the woman to reinforce it in her memory—a simple mnemonic trick. "It's easier to commit a crime if you're convinced that no one will learn of it and you live in a world where it's only the opinion of your group that matters."

"So a murderer won't lose sleep over his deed if he was raised in a collectivist culture?"

"I'm saying that the guilt is assessed differently," Vars said. "And it's always about the extremes of the spectrum: the extreme form of collectivism, the extreme form of individualism. Of course, we live in a world that is both a little collectivist and a little individualist. I'm giving you the very antipodes to make my point clearer."

"Of course, Dr. Volhard," said Ian. "So the robots?"

"Yes, the robots. I'm getting to that, but first one more point." Vars took a big gulp of coffee. It was cold and bitter now, but she needed the caffeine.

She must have made a face, for Ian was instantly on his feet, getting her a refill in a fresh cup. She waited for him to sit back down.

"Thank you, Ian," she said, taking a sip. "Much better."

"My pleasure."

"And this is a perfect example of my next point: the theory of mind. Ian saw my expression when I took a sip from my cold cup and guessed that I was dissatisfied with my coffee."

"It was obvious," Ian said.

"To *you.*"

"I think it was obvious to everyone in the room," he said with a smile.

A few people chuckled.

"That bad? Well, good. Then everyone here has a good theory of mind. You were all able to interpret my feelings, thoughts, and experiences even though you had no direct access to my taste buds. The theory of mind is necessary for higher-order thinking skills. It's necessary for communication, for understanding multiple points of view. Not all animals on Earth have this ability, and even human children take several years to master this skill. Before the age of about four, kids are unable to switch perspectives and understand what motivates others. And even after that age, the theory of mind continues to develop into and throughout adulthood."

"The development of empathy," Alice said.

"That too. Empathy requires that we try to put ourselves in another's situation to understand how they might feel. This is different from sympathy, obviously, which doesn't require such cognitive acrobatics. So a child of five would flinch and hold their hand after observing someone get hit on the hand. It's almost like the pain of another is their pain."

"Are you saying that there's a difference in the development of the theory of mind between collectivist and individualist cultures?" Ian asked. He'd clearly read her book and was now helping his team to quickly get up to speed on the subject.

"Yes. In a collectivist culture, the theory of mind is paramount. The focus of collectivists is on others, so the success of the culture is dependent on nuanced social interactions that require complex cognitive activity and deep understanding of the feelings and motivations of others. In individualist societies, the focus is on the self, so the theory of mind is of less central importance."

"Thus robots designed by collectivist cultures would be less likely to kill," Ian said.

There were murmurs among the people around the table. Apparently not everyone was buying the conclusion about the robots.

"Didn't you just say that in a collectivist society it is easier to commit a crime?" Alice asked.

"Not easier, but with less guilt—and, even then, only so long as the crime isn't discovered by others in your group. In a collectivist society, as long as the crime remains hidden from the group, there are no ill consequences to the individual. But note that committing a murder requires a deep understanding of what others know, how they will react to the crime, and how they will feel about the perpetrator. One would need a deep understanding of the entire web of social interactions." Vars paused. "Again, I'm talking about extremes. But it stands to reason that robots created by collectivist societies would be designed with a focus on the theory of mind, with the ability to analyze problems from multiple perspectives. And such social cognitive flexibility puts more restraints on antisocial behavior than guilt alone."

"So the robots we design are more violent?" Alice asked.

The "we" came up a lot in Vars's classes. Everyone assumed that Western cultures were the most individualistic.

"Only if we design them so," Vars said. "But most of this is discussed in my book, and you clearly all have access to my work…" She trailed off meaningfully. All of this *was* in her book. It didn't make sense to her to be dragged urgently across the country for this predawn meeting. What did EPSA really want from her?

"Ibe," said Ian. "Could you run the short version of our presentation for Dr. Volhard, please?" He turned to Vars. "It's really the best introduction to our problem, and we can fill you in on details after."

The way he said "problem" made Vars uncomfortable.

Ibe and Ebi both got up and set up the presentation. One of them pulled up the oversized sleeve of his black sweatshirt and exposed an ostentatious set of D-tats on his right arm. That twin was a lefty, Vars noted, and a body-computing junky. She'd bet there was another, equally extravagant set of D-tats on the other arm.

She glanced around the room and noted a few other PCD tattoos peeking from people's clothing. Vars heard that EPSA was heavily invested in cyberhumatics—the science of human implant technology and its connectivity with global

networks and robotic extensions—so it wasn't surprising that D-tats were the norm among this group. But Vars had no implants, and it made her feel even more of an outsider.

Dark shades descended over the wraparound windows, cutting off the rays of the morning sun. The lights turned off, and the room was swallowed in a soft purple gloom. Vars yawned into the darkness—it would be so easy just to fall asleep in here, even with an almost full cup of coffee in hand. She heard others yawn as well. Yawning, she knew, was contagious among primates and other empathetic animals.

A 3D projection of the solar system lit up in the center of the conference table. The planets slowly rotated in their orbits. It was a very nice model, but of course it would be—this was EPSA.

"This is our solar system," Ebi said. Her voice pegged her as a girl.

Ibe spoke next. "This is Saturn. And this is Mimas." Based on the timbre of his voice, Vars judged him male. *So not identical twins.*

Using a combination of hand gestures and rapid tapping on his D-tats, Ibe zoomed in on Mimas, Saturn's closest moon. One side of the small whitish moon had a giant crater with a dimple in the center. "Mimas is primarily made of water-ice. As you can see, it's heavily cratered. The big one is named Herschel and is nearly a third of the moon's diameter."

"That's almost eighty miles wide and over six miles deep," Ebi added. "That pimple thing in the center is a mountain that's almost four miles high."

"That must have been some impact," said Vars. Based on the initial questioning, this was not how she'd thought the rest of the morning would go.

"It liquefied the little moon," Ibe said.

Most of the Saturn moons were well explored, and EPSA

was actively working on establishing permanent science stations on some of them. But as far as Vars knew, none of the moons of either Jupiter or Saturn harbored anything more complex than simple bacterial life. Impressive, certainly, but old news now. And not something that an evolutionary socio-historian could help with. Vars's specialty was the development of self-aware cultures.

"A year ago, we detected a signal coming from Mimas," Ian said.

Ibe zoomed in on the giant crater and focused the image on the mountain. The rotation stopped, and the holographic image froze on a close-up. Vars could clearly see something protruding from the ice—a small, dark structure near the base of the central mountain.

Vars inhaled. She was no longer sleepy; all tiredness had been wiped clean. "What's that? One of ours?"

"No," said Ebi and Ibe in unison.

"And that's the main problem of the day," Ian said.

"You mean you don't know?" Vars asked. "It's been what? Twelve—"

"We have been able to divert one of our probes, and it arrived on site a few weeks ago," said of the men from the JPL team. *Ben?*

"So this picture..." Vars said.

"Yes, it's from that probe," said Ben. "We have detailed close-ups."

Ibe zoomed in even further, until the structure occupied most of the conference table.

"Wow," Vars whispered.

Chapter Three

The meeting lasted until late morning, until Vars just couldn't go on. Too tired, too much information, too much. Ian, seeing that Vars could no longer absorb anything new or contribute in any coherent way, insisted on taking her to an on-campus guest suite.

"My dad and I live just thirty minutes away," Vars protested, but Ian wouldn't hear of it. He and one of those guys in uniform—neither of whom had said a word the whole time—led her through the labyrinthine hallways. And without ever setting foot outside, Vars arrived at a small bedroom with a view of redwoods.

"I'll pick you up in a few hours and take you to lunch, okay?" said Ian. He smiled broadly and closed the door.

Vars's suitcase had made it to the EPSA guest room ahead of her and was waiting next to the bed, as was her backpack, which held her tablet and a few copies of her book. Even her raincoat was hanging on a hook by the door.

She took off her shoes and the fashionable orange scarf and thought about everything she'd heard. She still wasn't sure why EPSA wanted to talk with her, although she was thrilled to be included. This was the biggest thing ever. She was thankful for the alone time to process the information a bit. She needed to get a handle on what they were telling her. It was all so…so…incredible!

She pulled up her computing tablet and set it up on a desk by the window. Like her dad, Vars abhorred the PCD tattoos and had never even considered having one implanted. Well, nothing more than an ID microchip, which was required by law anyway. And the personal tablet, too, was an old-fashioned affectation. In her whole life, there had never been a circumstance or a place that didn't provide all of her computing or communication needs at any time she wanted it. Equipment was ubiquitous; in fact, for those who opted to get the new D-tats, it was never farther than their skin. But Vars's dad always used his own computing equipment, and she just picked up the habit.

She needed to get in touch with her dad. Even when work took them to different sides of the world, they talked every night, if only to exchange a few words. But last night, Vars had never gotten around to it, and she knew he would be worried about her. It was just the two of them—Vars's mother had died when Vars was just an infant, and they had no other family left, unless you counted some distant cousins on the other side of the world, in Norway or something. Her dad communicated with them only once or twice a year, and even then only out of a sense of obligation rather than familial closeness.

She considered *versing* with him but, at this time of day, her dad would be out in the field collecting samples. He did research on the effects of microplastics in the environment and tended to spend his mornings dredging through coastal tidal plains. It made more sense just to send him a note. She would tell him about her insane trip to EPSA later tonight when she got home. The idea of spending a night as a guest of EPSA seemed totally ridiculous—she lived just a short ride away.

She recorded a brief *vers*: *Dad, I'm back home in Seattle. Got invited to EPSA! Don't worry. All is good—talk tonight. Love you.*

She hit send. And nothing happened.

She tried again. Nothing. The blinking light on her tablet indicated no connection.

That made no sense. There was no longer a place on the Earth or the moon where communication devices didn't work. Even as far out as Mars, people complained when the services were down. Everyone was fully connected to the planetary network everywhere at all times. How else could anyone function?

Vars tried multiple times. She even restarted her PCD tablet—something she had never done before. But still nothing. Perhaps it was the room? *All those redwoods outside?*

She took the tablet out into the corridor. The man in uniform was standing just outside her door. He smiled. Vars smiled back, but her stomach did a double flip. She told herself that she hadn't been kidnapped, but clearly this man was guarding her in some way. *Holding me prisoner?*

"I'm not getting any connection in my room." She felt the need to explain and immediately got angry with herself. They couldn't keep her here against her will...could they?

"Dr. Volhard." Vars was sure the man was just about to salute her before relaxing his arm again. That was reflexive—years of training taking over. "Dr. Rust asked me to stay with you and help you navigate the facility when you were ready to resume work. Would you like me to escort you back to the tree house conference room?"

"No. I didn't get a chance to rest yet," Vars said uncertainly.

"Is there something I can get you? Coffee?"

"My connection doesn't seem to be working," Vars said again. She lifted her portable PCD to the man's face as evidence.

"Oh. Yes. Dr. Rust mentioned that the connection might not work here."

"Well, I need to get in touch with my father. Is there someplace I can go to do that?" Vars asked. "I didn't see any equipment back in the room." As soon as she said it, Vars realized it was true. There had been no public terminals there, which too was very unusual.

"I was only told to take you to the conference room if you were ready before Dr. Rust picked you up for lunch," the man said.

"I just need to send a message to my dad to tell him I'm okay," Vars tried again. "It's short. See?" She played the brief recording to the man and immediately hated herself for acting like a child who needed permission to talk to her own father.

"I'm sorry, Dr. Volhard. All I can do is take you back."

"Well, I don't like being out of reach like this," Vars snapped. Again she felt like a kid, whining about not getting what she wanted. Not that she had ever been that kind of kid.

Embarrassed, she stepped back into her room and closed the door. Perhaps she was just tired and misinterpreted what was going on.

She climbed into bed and placed her PCD tablet on the pillow. She watched the connection indicator show an error. She blinked. Blinked again.

The next time she opened her eyes was when a knock sounded on her door, four hours later.

"I should have introduced you earlier. This is Major Terry Liut," said Ian.

Vars smiled thinly at the man sitting across the table from her in the small EPSA cafeteria. She recognized the officer as the other uniformed man in the back of room during the morning conference. "Nice to meet you, Major Liut," she said.

Ian smiled. "Terry—we are very informal here—explained to me that you tried to contact your father?"

Tried and repeatedly failed. Even here, in the cafeteria, Vars had no connection on her tablet, and she had yet to see a single public terminal anywhere in the building. Perhaps that was because of EPSA's military component—the agency was a mixture of civilian workforce and the air force of its active member nations. Or perhaps all EPSA employees were required to get a PCD tattoo, so no terminals would be needed.

"Yes," she said. "I just want to let my dad know that I'm all right."

"And we're working on that," Major Liut said. "But you see, we ran into a little problem. We don't have Dr. Matteo Volhard's DNA profile."

Every human had their genetic code registered with authorities the moment they were born—or even sooner in cases of prophylactic genetic testing to identify possible medical problems. After the Keres Triplets asteroid fragments hit the Earth in 2057, wiping out half the human population and ninety percent of all other life on the planet, genetic testing had become a must. Even over a hundred years later, it was the only way to maintain a healthy gene pool.

"I assume it's just some error," Vars said. The Human

Genome Heritage Project was regularly underfunded. Glitches were bound to happen.

"That's what we assumed at first. But it doesn't seem to be a glitch," the major said.

"So...what are you trying to say?" Vars asked. She was getting irritated.

"We ran your DNA sample this morning while you rested, to check it against your officially registered sample—"

"You did *what?*" Anger simply erupted out of her.

Ian raised his hands in a soothing gesture. "Vars, I know you feel like this is a big violation, but—"

"Violation?" Vars felt herself trembling with rage. *First kidnapping, then cutting off all my communication with the outside world and keeping me prisoner, and now this?* "So that's what the coffee was all about!" A dark realization hit her. "No wonder you kept giving me fresh cups. And, like a sucker, I just assumed you were being considerate and nice. All the while you were *stealing* my DNA from me."

"Vars—" Ian began.

"I think we should stick to formal address, Dr. Rust."

"If I may," Major Liut interjected. "Ian was very much against gathering your DNA sample without your explicit permission—"

"But he did it anyway," Vars spat. She needed to get out of here. As she scanned the room for exits, she saw that several other military personnel were stationed around the cafeteria, and all of them were now staring at her.

"He didn't have a choice," the major continued. "When your work was identified as necessary for this project, we had to look into your background. Your father's lack of genetic credentials was flagged."

"I assure you that was in error," Vars said.

"And *I* can assure you that EPSA doesn't make mistakes,"

said Liut. "At least not in this area. By law, we have to track all of our people's genetic material. We are charged with creating a genetically diverse population for off-Earth colonization. We take genetic diversity seriously."

"And I think you might have made a mistake this time," Vars said quietly.

"The only way a citizen of Earth, or of any off-world colony, would not be part of the Human Genome Heritage Project database is if he or she was born in one of the human seed vaults," the major said. "Are you aware of any information that might lead you to believe that your father might be a former Seed?"

Vars felt her head spin. There were several human seed vaults on Earth, one on the moon, and one planned on Mars. There was talk about establishing yet another one in the outer reaches of the solar system. The establishment of the Vaults was one of the governmental responses to the cataclysm that followed the Keres Triplets asteroid strike. As the nations of Earth recovered, they worked together to build the Vaults partly in order to ensure the genetic diversity of humanity. Individuals were selected by a secret set of criteria and spirited away into underground catacombs that were supposed to be impervious to all disasters. That was almost three-quarters of a century ago. And, in each year since, a genetic lottery had been held to deposit a few more babies into the Vaults.

The Seeds, as the humans who grew up in those communities were called, developed an almost monastic lifestyle. All were required to donate sperm and eggs to the outside world. The resulting embryos were highly prized by those interested in embryonic adoption. Seeds who reached the age of maturity at about thirty years old or so—Vars wasn't too familiar with their secretive ways—were allowed to make a choice to leave their society and join the general population or to stay and spend their entire lives below ground. Vars had heard horror stories of Seed children and adults being exploited for their unique genetics. She found the whole system detestable.

Now these men in front of her were hinting that her father was a Seed. That just couldn't be.

"My dad would have told me," she said. But even as she spoke, doubt wormed its way into her heart. No close family except for the "distant cousins" who lived in Norway, which just happened to be the location of one of the Vaults. *And Dad's extreme aversion to public communication terminals and D-tats...*

The major and Ian sat quietly, waiting. Furious as she was, Vars still appreciated the space to think. Would EPSA have a reason to lie to her? *They are the good guys, right?*

"I need to talk to my dad," she said finally.

"I figured as much," said Ian. "We've sent a representative to talk with him."

The major added, "And we would also like to run a blood test on you."

"You didn't get all you needed from my coffee cup?"

"We just want to be sure," Ian said. "I...we want you on our team, Dr. Volhard. You have a tremendous contribution to make to our understanding of how to even approach what we're dealing with. This genetic thing," he glanced over at the major, "will be straightened out, one way or another. If you could just overlook this very...this awkward start to our relationship, I'm sure you will find working at EPSA very rewarding."

"Are you offering me a job?" Vars asked.

"If we can straighten out this genetic mystery," said Major Liut.

Ian glanced sharply at the man and said, "Yes."

"I see," Vars said. A job at EPSA was what she had always

wanted. *It's just...*

"And I would like you to start immediately," Ian added. "My department will smooth everything out with your university—"

Everything was happening too fast. Vars felt confused and conflicted. "I still have a few classes left to teach this semester," she said and realized that she was agreeing to the offer.

"That won't be a problem," Ian assured her. "We need you, Dr. Volhard."

"Where do I go to take the blood test?" Vars asked. She noted that as soon as she said it, not only did she feel better, but Ian seemed to relax. Even Major Liut's face was drained of some of its tension. *They really do want me.*

"If you'll follow me, please, Dr. Volhard," said Ian.

"We can go back to Vars."

"Perfect! Thank you, Vars."

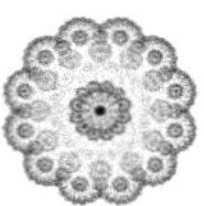

The test didn't take long, or at least the top-level pass at the results didn't. The more detailed analysis would take a day or so. Vars felt herself holding her breath as they stood around the display in the medlab. It read:

The paternal haplogroup is E-M5021—a relatively common haplogroup, associated with Ashkenazi Jewish ancestry.

The maternal haplogroup is U5a1—a very old mitochondrial haplogroup that was part of the initial human expansion into Europe after the retreat of the ice sheets, 30,000 years ago.

*Top-level analysis of potentially
problematic variants:*

- *increased risk for age-related
macular degeneration*

- *hereditary hemochromatosis variant detected*

- *lactose intolerance*

- *less likely to be a deep sleeper*

- *wet earwax variant*

- *variant for a high number of freckles*

- *dark red hair variant*

- *light skin pigmentation*

- *likely to taste a wide range of bitter compounds*

- *likely to consume more caffeine*

It continued on, but Vars stopped there. She'd never paid much attention to genetic testing—she always figured if there was something truly problematic, her dad and her pediatrician would have fixed it or kept track of it. At a minimum, she would have known about it. She did note that the list of traits didn't explain her slight epicanthic eyefold—but then who really cared?

"Your results are excellent," Ian said.

"And they match your genetic ID profile," added Major Liut.

"In fact," Ian said, "there's nothing there that would preclude you from going on an outer planetary mission—"

"Wait, what?" Vars was taken aback by the suggestion. Sure, she had always been interested in participating in some space program mission, *theoretically.* But to hear it said so casually…

"We've already obtained your health records, and you are in fine physical shape for your age," Ian continued.

"You obtained my health records?" Vars felt violated all over again. How could her personal doctor hand over medical records without her explicit permission? There were laws against that.

"Your agreement to employment at EPSA—we have the recording of your assent for legal purposes—gave us permission to initiate a full background check on you and your father," the major said. "Medical records were obviously part of that."

Had she actually agreed to take this job? Vars wasn't sure she had, at least not without ambiguity. She never actually came out and said she would take the job offer...she didn't think. Then again, she knew she wouldn't turn down a chance to be part of Ian's team—and potentially go *into space* to investigate the strange alien artifact. Yes, of course she was taking the job. She just hated how all of this was being handled.

"And my father?" Vars wasn't sure what she had agreed to with regard to her dad.

"Once we explained the situation to him," said Major Liut, "Dr. Volhard volunteered to take the genetic test."

"When did you even have a chance to talk to him? No, hang on. You're saying he *volunteered*?" Her dad was a very private man; that would had been very unlike him to agree to genetic testing.

"Once we told him we realized who he was..." Ian said.

Who he was? "Do you mean to say that my father admitted to being an ex-Seed?"

Neither man answered the question. "We have his preliminary test here," the major said. "Would you like to see his results?"

Vars could only nod. This was all happening too fast.

The major typed a few commands on the D-tats embedded into his left arm, and the medlab display lit up with genetic information for Dr. Matteo Volhard.

The paternal haplogroup is E-M5021—a relatively common haplogroup, associated with Ashkenazi Jewish ancestry.

The maternal haplogroup is U5a1—a very old mitochondrial haplogroup that was part of the initial human expansion into Europe after the retreat of the ice sheets, 30,000 years ago.

Top-level analysis of potentially problematic variants:

* *increased risk for age-related macular degeneration*

* *hereditary hemochromatosis variant detected*

* *lactose intolerance*

* *less likely to be a deep sleeper*

* *wet earwax variant*

* *variant for a high number of freckles*

* *dark red hair variant*

* *light skin pigmentation*

* *likely to taste a wide range of bitter compounds*

* *likely to consume more caffeine*

"Something is wrong," Vars said. "This is identical to mine."

"At the top level, yes," the major said. "We will, of course, do a complete analysis of both of your DNA profiles. In the meantime, would you like to see how similar your genetic profiles really are?"

"Major, are you saying...?" Ian didn't finish. He looked as surprised as Vars felt.

"Dr. Varsaad Volhard and Dr. Matteo Volhard share over 80% of their genetic traits, according to preliminary DNA profiles," the major read out from his report. He looked Vars in the eyes. "Dr. Matteo Volhard is both Varsaad's father and sibling."

Vars felt her head spin. Her vision tunneled as she lost all of her peripheral sight to darkness. Someone kept repeating her name, but that was all she was able to process.

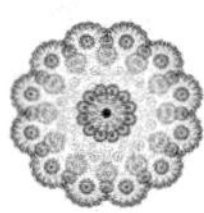

"Vars? Vars?" A woman's voice. "It will be okay. Here, drink this."

Vars felt cold water trickle past her lips. She took a real sip and swallowed. It felt good going down her throat. The cold spread into her chest.

She slowly opened her eyes. She was lying down on a hospital bed, still in the same medlab where she'd learned of the genetic results. The thick-spectacled woman from Ian's team, the exo-biologist, stood beside her. There was no one else in the room.

"Alice?" she said.

"I got here as quickly as I could." Alice had a look of real concern etched on her gentle face. Why had she come here? Why did she care how Vars felt?

"I'm okay," Vars said. "I'm just tired. No sleep. The stress of the book tour. The artifact you found. And now all this."

She waved her hands feebly in the air. She wasn't sure how much Alice knew. "Did Ian tell you he offered me a job at EPSA?"

"Yes. And that you've accepted."

Vars sat up, picked up the glass of ice water, and finished it. Dehydration was never a plus. "Do you know how complicated my genetic relation is to my father?"

Alice flicked her eyes up to the ceiling in a gesture that Vars somehow understood. *She's telling me that they're*

recording us. Vars double-blinked to indicate that she'd received the warning.

"I know about you and Matteo," Alice said in answer to Vars's question. News certainly got around fast at EPSA.

"So...do we need to call someone in order to leave the medlab?" Vars asked. They clearly couldn't talk about anything here—not privately, anyway. And she wanted to learn more about the Mimas artifact. She wanted to know why Ian thought she could help. And she wanted to know why Alice seemed so invested in her well-being. She needed to know if she could work here.

Chapter Four

Alice took Vars back to the tree house, where the others were already assembled, waiting. Trays of sandwiches and coffee carafes were arranged on a table along the wall. Vars eyed the cups with suspicion—but what was done was done. She had made a decision to work with these people.

"Welcome back," said Ian. Vars thought she detected a forced note of excitement in his voice. "Thank you, Alice, for guiding our new team member back here. Vars, I was just updating everyone on your new status as a senior scientist in charge of understanding alien motivations."

"What?" Vars froze in the middle of grabbing a turkey and cheese on sourdough.

"Well, in our group, you have unique qualifications to deal with solving the mystery of *why*," Ian said. "So far we've only been focusing on the *how*—how the artifact got buried in a crater on one of Saturn's moons and how it managed to free itself and send a message."

"We're also looking at its age, power requirements, and abilities," said the youngest-looking member of the JPL team, the one who had joked about *Star Trek*. Thankfully, everyone was now wearing nametags, and Vars was able to read his name: Dr. Benjamin Kouta. He saw her looking at his tag. "Call me Ben," he said with a smile.

"And I'm Trish Cars," said the woman from the same team. "No honorifics."

"That's because she's smarter than everyone in this room," Ben joked. "Present company excluded, of course." He glanced at Vars, turning slightly red.

"Only for the time being," said Trish. But Vars saw that the woman was just joking. This was just a friendly rivalry, nothing toxic. That boded well for Vars's ability to fit into this group. "We're also focusing on where the message was sent," Trish continued, "what it was, and whether there may have been any previous messages."

"As you can see, we have a rather full agenda," Ian said. He gestured toward the food. "So please, everyone eat so we can start up again."

Vars took a seat and began to eat, and the other scientists got up and got food as well. So they hadn't been waiting for her long. *Good.* She noticed that Major Liut and his partner, the one who kept her jailed in her room, had taken up their same positions in back as before, observing but not eating. As she looked at the major, Vars felt her indignation well up again. She hated the feeling of being trapped. She wondered what precisely they had said to get her dad to "volunteer" his DNA sample. It had to have been something very persuasive. *Or very threatening.* Vars vowed to find out.

When they had all finished their sandwiches, Dr. Evelyn Shar—"Please call me Evi"—spoke up. "This morning, Vars, you made a distinction between collectivist and individualist cultures." *Was it only this morning?* "Would you mind elaborating on how social groups might evolve into such different cultures?"

Vars nodded. "I assume for now you're interested in just the general brush strokes?"

"Yes, let's start there. We can dive into the details later."

"Keep this concrete, Vars," Ian said. "We're all used to data-driven science in this group."

Vars didn't think he intended this as an insult, though it certainly sounded like one. Physicists, biochemists, and engineers—the hard-science types—tended to feel superior to practitioners of the soft sciences like sociology. And Vars, with her expertise in evolutionary socio-history, must really seem an odd duck to these people. What hard-science types didn't always understand was that she was just as data-driven as them—it was just that it tended to be rather difficult to conduct controlled studies on groups of people who had died thousands of years ago. Even experiments on people alive today were frowned upon. So, in many ways, the job of a "soft" scientist was the more challenging one when it came to data analytics.

"Despite any belief to the contrary," Vars said, "we evolutionary socio-historians do rely on real hard facts to drive our theories."

"Of course you do," Ian said. But Vars could tell that none of them were convinced.

"I will focus on *Homo sapiens* for now," Vars said. "We can use examples from other species once we've covered some basics." She took a deep breath. "When we talk about evolutionary history, it is important to zoom out and to look on a grand scale, ignoring the small perturbations of individual personality-inspired events that tend to even out over eons of human evolution. Hitler, for instance, might have been very consequential to the history of the twentieth century but, in the grander scheme of human evolution, he's a minor bump. While the Keres Triplets were even more devastating, it took us only a century to rebuild the Earth's population to pre-impact levels. In the macro view, it was a minor event too."

"I wouldn't exactly say that Keres was a minor event,"

objected Alice. "It radically changed the psyche of the human race. It pushed us beyond the Earth."

"And yet there have been many other events during our deep history that have been just as influential," said Vars. "The Keres impact devastated our most important nest of genetic diversity—Africa—but it was far from the first time that the human population experienced a genetic bottleneck. Compared even to other great apes—gorillas, for example—humans are genetically monochromatic."

"Thus the Human Genome Heritage Project," said Bob Shapiro.

Vars noticed that Alice gave him an odd sideways glance. So they all knew about her heritage. Well, it was better that way. Secrets like that tended to fester and impede communication within a group. These people needed to accept her into their team, if they were to work well together.

"DNA propinquity is a problem," Ian said, "but please, Vars, go on with your explanation for the rise of cultural differences."

"If we date modern humans to about 150,000 years ago, then we can consider behavior and environmental conditions on that time scale," Vars said.

"Why environmental?" Ian asked.

"Behavior and the environment are tightly linked. Just as gene expression and the environment are. It's nonsensical to talk of one without the other." This was a point that confused most of Vars's students early on in her class—before it became obvious to all of them. "Let's talk food. The type and availability of food are dependent on the environment, which is in turn dependent on location. Some early humans were luckier than others.

"Consider, for example, the animals humans cultivated for domestication. There are animals associated with food goals—the main staples are goats, pigs, cows, sheep, water buffalo, yak, reindeer, ducks, geese, turkeys, and chickens—and there are animals mostly associated with tool goals—horses, donkeys, camels. These are not exhaustive lists, of course. And I'm setting aside our canine companions, since humans and dogs coevolved together. Anyway, as you can guess, the ancestors to these domesticated animals were not evenly distributed among ancient human settlements."

"The Americas got stuck with llamas, alpacas, guinea pigs, and ducks," said Dr. Izzy Rubka. "So no wheel carts. Tough luck there." He must have read at least parts of Vars's book.

"Yes," Vars agreed. "What's the point of inventing the wheel if there are no workhorses to pull them? So, in this way, the animal availability in the environment influenced the behavior of humans—our inventions, our way of life, our culture.

"The same applies to plants. There are only a few plants on our planet that meet the criteria required for domestication. First, seeds need to be large enough for easy cultivation. Too small, and the effort to gather them isn't worth the caloric energy they provide. Second, nutritional value. The goal here is great-tasting, calorie-rich, nonpoisonous, easy-to-process plants. Alternatively, or in addition, different parts of plants could be useful as tools—rope, clothing, building material. Third, a reasonable growth season. Consider oaks. Acorns are large enough and have rich nutritional value—"

"They're bitter as all hell," Izzy interrupted. Based on his features, Vars guessed the man likely had some Mesoamerican ancestry. Perhaps his elementary school teachers made him eat acorn mush as part of some cultural enrichment curriculum, teaching him the wrong lesson.

"It's true," Vars said, "most acorns are very bitter and unpalatable. But a few oak trees carry a mutation that lacks the bitter agent compound. The acorns from those trees are quite palatable, tasty even. But even those trees, however, aren't suitable for domestication because of their extreme growth season. It takes a full human generation for oak trees to mature; and that makes cultivation highly impractical. When a tribe discovered a good oak in the neighborhood, people partook of its harvests and even made sure to plant some acorns, sure—but that's quite different from domestication."

Ian summed up. "So the Earth always had an unequal distribution of plants and animals with good domestication properties; and the direct result was an unequal growth potential for the humans living in different geographic regions. Some humans won the domestication lottery; others lost it."

"Exactly. Australia, for instance, got the short end of the deal," Vars said. "It's hard to build a high-tech civilization without being blessed with great initial conditions."

Ian nodded. "And this would also apply to natural resources, like the easy availability of copper, iron…"

"And even good river clay," Vars agreed. "There's a very good reason why the Dordogne Valley in France is one of earliest birthplaces of pottery: the clay there is particularly conducive to making it."

"Would this also be true on the scale of planets and whole star systems?" Ian asked.

Vars stopped to think. "Well, it depends on what resources are necessary to support advanced civilizations. We know what those are for humans…"

She didn't need to finish the thought. It was obvious to everyone that the aliens that had built the communication device on Mimas would have their own unique needs.

Ian looked around the room. "I want everyone to think about the lottery that our alien friends had to win in order to get their artifact into our solar system. Please consult with

Dr. Volhard—Vars—and let's get some theories going. We want to be more prepared to tackle this when we get there."

"Get there?" Vars felt herself sink into the chair.

"Our departure date is scheduled for early next month," Ian said. "I know it's a very short notice for you, but we're hoping you'll be able to catch up on our side of the project while we're en route to Saturn." He turned to Alice. "Would you mind helping our new colleague get up to speed?"

Alice smiled. "Certainly."

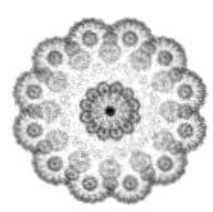

Vars didn't even notice when the room finally cleared. Even Major Liut and his partner left. Only Vars and Alice remained.

"Come," the woman said and gently guided Vars out of the room. "Allow me to show you around a bit."

Vars let Alice take her by the arm and walk her out of the building into the surrounding redwoods. Spiral stairs wound their way between the giant tree trunks and down onto the forest floor below.

"Where are you taking me?" Vars asked.

"We should talk, no?" Alice said. She gestured to a narrow path among the trees. "In private."

Vars noticed again how short Alice was—barely four and a half feet tall. Shorter, if the woman took off her shoes. Yet Alice didn't have any obvious dwarfism characteristics—everything was well proportioned—but it was still extremely uncommon for anyone to be so short in this day and age when every child was carefully screened and all genetic abnormalities were dealt with…one way or another. Perhaps the woman had some Pygmy ancestry? After the Keres Triplets, however, not much of Africa had survived.

As they walked into the forest, Vars spotted a small drone following them. "Alice?" She nodded toward the flying machine.

Alice pulled up her sleeve and activated something on a strap-on tablet. Apparently she didn't have any D-tats either. The drone changed course, flew ahead of them, and then rose up into the canopy. "It helps to be important," Alice said with a smile. "Now. We have only a few minutes of privacy. Let's use it well."

"I need to talk to my dad," Vars said. "He must be frantic—"

"I've already sent a message to Matteo."

"You know my father?"

"We've met," Alice said cryptically. "But the important thing is that he now understands what's going on, and he knows not to expect a communication from you in the near future."

"But I *want* to talk with him," Vars objected.

"He knows that. But it can't be helped. The EPSA freaked out when they found out your dad was a Seed."

"*I* didn't know! He never told me."

"Of course he didn't," Alice said. "It's not something we like to broadcast to the world."

Vars stopped dead in her tracks. "We?"

"I'm surprised you hadn't guessed yet."

Vars looked at Alice again. The woman was obviously a genetic outlier. Vars finally put two and two together.

"It's called a *Green Beard* effect," said Alice, gesturing to Vars to keep walking. "Markers or signs that identify an individual as belonging to a group. You can instantly identify an athlete, right? You can probably even identify the sport. Lean and short are probably marathon runners. High jumpers are tall with very long legs, similar to basketball players.

American football players are built differently from the athletes that succeed at the other type of football. We've been playing with sports genetics for some time, with predictable results."

Vars noticed that Alice's voice never rose nor fell. Vars found it soothing—it turned down the volume of her own emotions. Her dad did that too, she realized. He was also good at controlling his emotional responses and presentation.

Alice raised an eyebrow at Vars. "I'm not saying I'm an athlete—obviously. But have you ever seen someone, anyone, who looks even remotely like me?"

Vars never had. She shook her head.

"My body screams that I'm a Seed," Alice said.

"I never..." Vars felt embarrassed to even to be discussing this.

"Most people don't," Alice went on. "We've been civilized not to pay attention to such gene expression." She waved her arms over her body to point out her obvious Pygmy traits. "But you would have guessed, if you ever thought about it."

Vars *had* thought about it—but the whole "Seed" concept simply wasn't something she had ever given any thought to prior to today. "So as soon as you found out about my dad, you reached out to him?"

"No. I already knew your dad. From our time in the Vault. His Seed-sibling, Phoebe, was my teacher back then."

Vars almost tripped over her own feet.

"Regardless of what you've heard and read in the tabloids," Alice continued, "Seeds that leave their Vaults do well in this new world. We're all well educated and are very well connected to each other, forming a web of support in every field and on every continent. Aside from Africa, of course." It would be many centuries before Africa was habitable again.

That made sense to Vars—these people were orphans

who had grown up together in tight, closed communities. As a result, their loyalty to other Seeds was probably far greater than to any other organization or state. Her dad must have been in constant communication with his home Vault. The thought hit Vars like lightning. *Those distant cousins? Must all be Seeds like him.*

"What about me?" Vars asked. "Why did Dad have me?"

"Actually, he didn't know about you until he discovered you abandoned by the Vault door."

"What?"

"I don't know the particulars. I never saw you as a baby," Alice said, still in the same calm, even voice. "I only know that once you were discovered, Matteo left and took you with him."

Vars wasn't sure how to take all this. It was a lot to absorb. The whole day had been a lot.

"What's my dad's Green Beard?" she asked.

"Not all Green Beards are as obvious as mine," Alice said and laughed.

Vars immediately felt self-conscious about her lack of social graces.

It must have shown, because Alice smiled and said, "See? You're very well trained. I can tell you don't even feel comfortable asking. I bet you didn't even let yourself notice how short I was, not right away. Not until it was so obvious that you had to bend your head down to talk to me."

"Yes. Even then it took me a while," Vars admitted.

"Civilization is meant to keep us civilized," Alice said. "And Ian brought you here to help us overcome some of those learned deficits."

As they walked among the giant sequoias, Vars realized that the trail was like a long noodle, bending in and around itself, never crossing, but tracing a very convoluted path through this man-made forest. And now the EPSA headquarters was once more looming before them between the trees. Their private time was almost over.

"When Ian found out you were a Seed, he immediately petitioned to hire you," Alice said. "EPSA knows the value of genetic outliers. One way or another, he was going to make sure you joined our team."

"So I never had a choice?"

"Do you not want to be part of the team that investigates the first alien contact?"

"Yes, but—"

"Then you are exactly where you need to be, Dr. Varsaad Volhard."

"And they all know you're a Seed too?" Vars asked.

"I'm sure they do. It's obvious. Although no one ever asked or even raised the possibility. And you and I won't be discussing it again. Now listen to me, as our time is almost up: I will find a way for you to keep in contact with your father. But please, for now, just go along with the program. We all have a lot to learn."

Chapter Five

"Thank you for meeting me in person, Alice."

Matteo Volhard helped the elfin woman down into a boat tied underneath the pier. It was a Friday night, and the seafood restaurant on the pier was packed to capacity. It was noisy above and dark below—perfect for a private conversation.

"Thank you for arranging something that would work," Alice said as she slid into one of the two seats on Matteo's runabout. "We were all encouraged to visit our favorite places to eat before takeoff. But I don't think I was followed. "

"Of course." Matteo piloted the boat away from the pier and into the darkness of the open water. "How is Vars?" he asked as soon as they were far enough away not to be picked up by security cameras.

"She's handling it as well as can be expected," Alice said. "I'm more worried about you, Matteo. How are you holding up?"

"As well as can be expected," he parroted back. "I've heard that EPSA managed to get my DNA sample. I didn't volunteer it, you know."

"I didn't think you did. But that's old news now, right?"

Matteo just nodded. There was nothing to be done. It had been an unexpected luxury that he had been able to keep this secret for as long as he had.

"Did Elder Alaba inform you of my discovery?" he asked.

"No, but after he shut down all deliveries and canceled all new Seed inductees and M-Seeds exoduses, we knew something was up. It takes a lot to halt a world treaty like this. I don't know the particulars, though. Almost at the same time, Ian informed me about the Mimas artifact and the signal. My freedom of movement had been restricted since I joined his team." In truth, Alice's freedom had been worse than restricted—it had been almost entirely removed altogether. The dispensation to visit a restaurant was an unexpected comfort. But she wasn't here to complain, especially since she managed to use her visit to meet up with Matteo. Sometimes being a Seed was convenient—there was a strong network of support that allowed little luxuries like dropping off Major Liut's radar...for a short while.

"Yes, the timing is just too striking to be coincidental," Matteo said. He spoke softly, as if, even out here in the middle of the inky black waters of the Puget Sound, he might be overheard.

"I don't know how much you know of my work," he began, and Alice shook her head—she knew nothing, really. "Okay, then," he said. "I've been working on micropollution since I left the Vault. Elder Alaba arranged for Vars and me to get Canadian citizenship and secured work for me at a research facility in the Pacific Northwest." Matteo talked and maneuvered the boat farther and farther from shore. "We couldn't have been placed better. The job allowed us to travel safely all around the world, collecting water samples for micropollution analysis, and it gave me unprecedented access to the sites that were quarantined after the Keres Triplets and the subsequent nuclear exchange between South Asia and Africa. It also made me well known among the external Seed community. I was able to easily carry information and small deliveries to our people all over the world.

"But I also loved the work I was doing. It felt meaningful. As my library of micropollution samples grew, the companion database became the world's research standard. About ten years ago, just as Vars started her studies at the University of Washington, I was asked to head the lab here in Seattle. It allowed me to stay close to her and still do my research. And I felt I could protect her. Silly how that need to keep your child safe just never goes away." He looked away, unable to hold Alice's gaze, obviously a little self-conscious about his attachment to his adult daughter. Alice didn't see a problem with that—most Seeds learned to forge strong ties within their community. In Matteo's case, his relation to Vars was even stronger by the strange circumstances of her birth.

"Then, a year ago, I stumbled on my first nanobot," he continued. "It was right here in these waters. I watched as this impossibly small, incredibly able bot gathered microscopic bits of plastic, sorted them by type, and assembled them into structures. It happened fast, right before my eyes. That single nanobot was able to build what looked like a small engine. When I saw how far it progressed overnight, I froze it in nitrogen. I didn't want this thing to complete whatever it was creating.

"But it didn't stop there. In my other samples, there were other microscopic bots, building other structures. Fast. In hours—sometimes even minutes—assemblies went from microscopic to macroscopic.

"Starting about ten months ago, *every* sample I collected had at least one of these machines. Every one. From every location around the world." He shook his head as if to shake off a bad dream; Alice saw fear in him. "That's when I went to Elder Alaba. I tried bringing him one of my frozen samples—the microassembly stops at minus 150° C—but the wardens wouldn't let me within even a few miles of the Vault.

"And then, when I got back to my lab, a message was waiting for me from Seed Phoebe. She told me to test my own blood. I almost fainted: it had never crossed my mind to look inside my own body, Alice. But of course, we all knew that microplastics in the environment travel up the food chain and end up in the bodies of the top consumer…us."

They sat in silence for some time while Alice tried to digest the implications of what Matteo had told her.

"So every human on Earth has these alien nanobots scrambling around in our bodies?" she finally asked.

"All but the Seeds. The Vaults mostly produce their own food, and the Elders enacted isolation protocols after my discovery. Nothing goes in or out of the Vaults…at least on Earth.

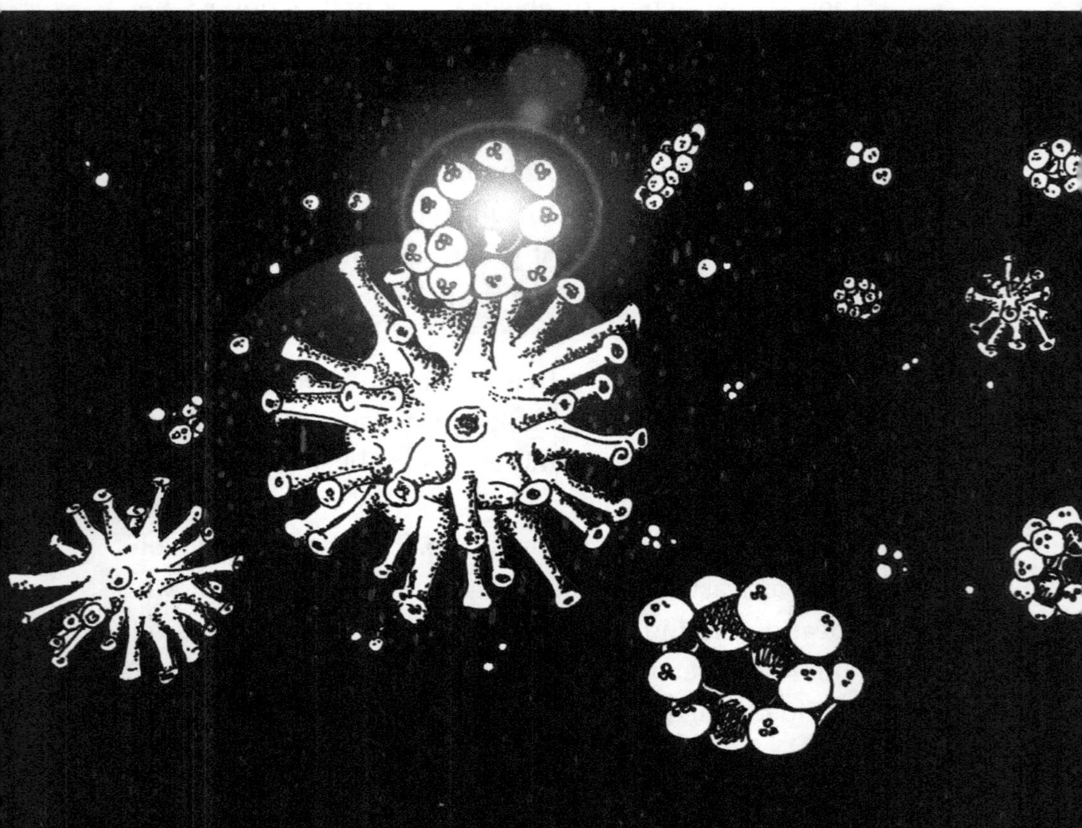

Obviously on Lunar—"

"And now we're about to go and investigate the alien artifact orbiting about Saturn *while* infected with alien nanobots." Alice shivered.

"Yes."

"Did you try killing them?"

"So far, the only things that have worked are extreme temperatures—cold and heat. But obviously we can't cook or freeze live humans."

As Alice sat and watched the black waves rhythmically hit the side of Matteo's boat, she realized that her feelings toward the waters had changed. Before, she'd always had this sense of awe while watching the churning of the Earth's oceans. Now she felt dread. She shivered and rubbed her arms.

"And one more thing," Matteo said, watching her. "The D-tats seem to be particularly vulnerable."

"What do you mean?" Alice suddenly felt her own PCD tattoos itch like crazy. She'd resisted getting the implants for years but had finally been required to get them just a week ago in preparation for the upcoming voyage to Mimas.

"I've surreptitiously tested some of my grad students," Matteo said. "The nanobots seek out the implant sites and attach to some of the bio-wiring."

"And no one's noticed this but you?" Alice couldn't believe this wasn't common knowledge. She vowed to rip the things from her body as soon as she got back on land.

"No one picked up on the nanobots in the waters either," Matteo said. "They will, of course. It's just a matter of time. But I want you to make sure that Vars doesn't get the implants, you hear me? Please, Alice. Make sure my girl doesn't get compromised further." He was terrified for his child.

Alice saw the dread in her fellow Seed's eyes. She shared

his horror, feeling the alien plague maneuver freely in her own body. It was beyond horror...

"Take me back. Take me back now," she ordered, her voice shrill. Matteo started the engine and reversed course. "Did you try blood-cleansing devices?" she asked after a time. "Surely they can be modified to filter out these things."

"I've tried. Elder Alaba put Phoebe on the project. The problem is that everything we consume is contaminated, so it doesn't last. The only place we've achieved one hundred percent success was in the Vaults...well, our Vault. They've stopped all food shipments, even baby formula. And as you know they've stopped receiving new Seeds altogether; the milk wasn't—"

"So the only humans that aren't contaminated by alien technology are all locked in the Seed Vaults?"

"Yes. But only here, on Earth. The Moon colonies have a problem. They still rely on shipments from Earth for life support, and the nanobots must have been imported that way. Elder Alaba was able to communicate with his counterpart at the Luna Vault and confirm the infection." The way he said the word *infection* made Alice's stomach lurch. "They're currently working on finding ways of cleansing their Seeds, but we're guessing that these things will be present in any person exposed to supply shipments from Earth as of approximately ten months ago. For all we know, these things will also be found on Mars and—"

"Who's 'we'?"

"Seed Phoebe, Elder Alaba, and most of the scientists at our Vault."

"How come I wasn't informed?" Alice asked. The Vaults maintained good communications with their ex-Seeds. Alice should have been notified as soon as the danger became obvious.

"The bloody things were discovered just a few weeks ago. And then Vars disappeared. And then..." Matteo looked around; they were pulling up to the pier. "I arranged to talk to you as soon as I could," he added quietly.

"I want these things out of me."

"What about the rest of the EPSA team?" he asked.

"We all have the implants. Most had them already—those who didn't were required to get them. I'll make sure we remove them from the Mimas team, but...will that even help? We'll still have these things floating around our bodies. And all of our supplies for the mission would be coming from Earth. Everything will be contaminated..."

"I know. But for now, removing the implants is the best we can do."

He lifted Alice up onto the ladder to the pier. Once she was secure, he squeezed her arm goodbye; she felt the sick tingling of her D-tats where he touched her. She inhaled deeply to drive away nausea and climbed up as fast as she could.

Chapter Six

The next weeks at EPSA were a blur for Vars. She didn't even have time to spend with the team or Alice—her days were entirely taken up with training for the space voyage. Since she had never expected to leave Earth—evolutionary socio-historians didn't tend to do that kind of travel—Vars had never taken so much as a basic course in space safety. She now found herself cramming like a grad student in an effort to pass an endless array of required tests before the team left for Mimas.

"How's progress, Vars?" Ian asked. He had come to take Vars to lunch. He tried to do so every few days.

"I haven't done so much memorization since I was a student. And the physical training..." Vars complained light-heartedly. The truth was she found it all very interesting and wanted to be as ready as she could be. Yet despite the many hours of drills and testing, she realized that in a real emergency she would be a liability. She hoped Ian's team knew it too. They must—she was sure all her progress reports and scores were shared with Ian and the rest of the Mimas group.

As if reading her mind, Ian said, "I looked over your progress reports. You're doing amazing! Just amazing."

"Thanks."

She started to turn toward the cafeteria, but instead Ian

gestured toward the door leading outside into the redwood grove. "Let's go outside today. I figured it would be nice to experience a bit of sunshine, a touch of nature, before we take off."

Vars realized that Ian was right: once they left, it would be a very long time before she walked outside again without protective gear.

Ian took her to the gazebo with a table big enough for at least a dozen people. It had all kinds of built-in tech for meetings and outdoor lunches. The food was already laid out: a coffee dispenser, cheeses, lunchmeats, fruits, and a giant basket of fresh-baked breads and pastries. EPSA didn't skimp.

"This is all very nice of you, Ian. But I really don't have time for a long lunch." Vars was feeling overwhelmed with the amount of work she still had to finish before departure.

"Yes, you do. I'm giving you the rest of the day off. You—*we* need this."

Ian pulled out a chair for her, then sat next to her. Vars noticed that there were three other settings and wondered who else from the team would be joining them. She hoped Alice would; Vars hadn't talked to the woman since their walk among these trees a few weeks back.

Ian poured both of them an iced coffee. He grabbed some bread and salami and assembled a sandwich on his plate. "Sandwich?" he asked. "We have turkey and veg."

"I think I'll just have some of that fruit salad and a Danish," said Vars. "I can't imagine we'll get a lot of fresh apples, citrus, or fresh pastries out in space."

Ian laughed. "You're right. Although we will have some basic lettuce and such from the hydroponics. And the coffee sucks up there too, so drink up now." He helped himself to some fruits, charcuterie, and a croissant in addition to his sandwich.

As Vars drank her iced coffee, the twins, Ebi and Ibe, joined them. Both piled their plates high with pastries. Either they, too, were worried about the lack of freshly baked goods in space, or they both had a sweet tooth.

"Ebi. Ibe," Vars said. She tried to quickly slide her eyes off each, pretending to recognize who was who—which she still couldn't do reliably. As always, the siblings were dressed nearly identically, as if trying to make it even harder on her. Vars was sure that after several months of traveling in very close quarters, she would have no problem. But now... "It's nice to see you again," she added with a smile.

"We've been working on variables to consider when determining whether a species has what it takes to become spacefaring," said one of them without any preamble.

That's Ebi, Vars thought. Even as her speech mannerisms were identical to her brother's, her voice was just a tad higher. As long as both of them were together and spoke first, Vars thought she would be able to tell them apart. But she was sure the twins played pranks on people all the time. She vowed never to guess the sender of a versing message from them. Sound was just too easy to manipulate.

"We used your notes and references to start our list," added Ibe.

"And included a few other ideas," said Ebi. Vars would bet that they routinely finished each other's sentences.

"I would love to see what you came up with," she said. "I'm not sure my humanity-focused ideas were useful—"

"Oh, you've made a great start," Ibe said while stuffing his face with a whole Danish. It came out a bit patronizing, but Vars didn't think it was on purpose. The twins were... different.

Vars took a big bite of her own Danish. Mimicking was a great way for primates to forge trust; and she wanted the twins to trust her.

"So, first and most obvious," Ebi said, "individuals who build star-faring civilizations need a long lifespan. It's either that or a more efficient transfer of knowledge from generation to generation."

"You did read my book," Vars said. She had written several chapters on technologically advanced societies and the prerequisites that were necessary for their development and sustainability. She'd specifically noted that it would be hard to develop technology if one's life expectancy hovered in the mid-twenties. That's why the improvements in hygiene and agriculture yielded not only longer lifespans but also the Industrial Revolution. Improvements in human condition functioned as a feedback loop—longer life gave people more opportunities to study and invent new ways of doing things, including advancements in life-extension therapies. Yet this feedback loop was subject to disruption and collapse. Human history was littered with ruins of once grand civilizations. "To sustain longevity, you would need plenty of opportunities to acquire knowledge, new and old. Life-long learning is a must for successful civilizations," she added.

"Of course! That's on our list," Ibe said through the side of his mouth, which was mostly occupied trying to reduce the giant pastry into swallowable bits.

"And we also need a civilization that makes invention profitable," Ebi said. "There would need to be laws that protect inventors. Patents or something similar. So then we would need a centralized, global government to enforce those."

"Strong individualism with a personal expectation to reap rewards from one's accomplishments," Ibe added. "Risk-taking—that has to be encouraged too."

"Don't be too human-focused," Vars managed to say between the twins' back and forth. "What about a hive mind, for instance?"

"Of course, of course," Ibe said. "That's just one possibility, though."

"And it would have to be a science-focused society," Ebi continued without a pause. "No science, no space travel. Naturally."

"Naturally," Vars repeated. It was interesting to hear which parts of her book the twins had taken to heart. She hadn't heard anything about the need for compassion or community yet. All discussion of collectivist versus individualist societies dissipated. *People focus on only those parts of discussion that match their own sensibilities.* Vars was witnessing selective information processing; she had to remember to pop those bias bubbles continuously...including her own. It mattered more than ever now.

"And, of course, the species would need plenty of resources and a climate that doesn't require too much struggle for survival," Ebi said. "Space travel requires leisure. If everything is focused on survival, then there's no time or resources left for big projects. Survival trumps exploration. And, of course, big projects need low-cost labor—slaves, or a caste system, or technology—"

"Or an inferior race that can provide for the needs of the scientists and explorers," Ibe finished.

Vars noted how "scientists" were included in the twins' conception of the elite social class. In her own work, she had found that researchers tended *not* to make it into the top tier of human societies. But the twins' perspective was heavily informed by their perception of their own position in the human hierarchy. Bias always led to more bias.

"Inferior race?" Vars questioned. She wondered where they were going with that.

"Sure," said Ibe. "It would obviously be convenient to

have some other entity do the unpleasant work. We still use animals, even very intelligent animals, to do work for us. And for a long time, most human societies had slaves. War is a great way of subjugating the losing side."

"I wrote about tolerance of diversity as one of the necessary traits for the flourishing of an advanced science-driven civilization," Vars said. She didn't like how the twins had jumped straight to the basest of human traits. "Acceptance of novelty and new ways of doing things are prerequisites for scientific thought—*and* for the fruits of new research to take hold and spread among the population."

"Yes, of course," Ebi replied. "Without diffusion of innovation, there's less technology and more tech abandonment."

Ibe picked up the thought. "Technology begets technology. It's an autocatalytic process—a self-increasing positive feedback loop. Really, Vars, we've read all of your book—practically memorized it," Ibe assured her. "But per your words, knowledge and technology are spread three ways: borrowing, trading, and taking. When we go and research the Mimas artifact, we hope to borrow all the tech we can understand—in order to reverse-engineer it—and take all we don't."

"And if, or when, we contact the Mims," began Ebi, "we'll—"

"Mims? We've named the aliens?" Vars interrupted.

"Just a working name," Ian cut in. He had been listening quietly during this whole exchange.

"As I was saying, if we contact the Mims," Ebi began again, "we'll do our best to establish trade, of course."

"If we have something they desire," said Vars.

"Well, they *did* come to us," Ian pointed out.

"And if we can't find something they want or if we are not willing to make the trade they desire, then what?" Vars asked. "Are you prepared to start an interstellar war?" She couldn't believe she'd even said such a crazy thing out loud, but the way the conversation was going, she wanted to know. How far was Ian's team willing to go? What would be the parameters of this interspecies negotiations? Who made the ultimate decisions?

"War is a very ugly word," said Ibe.

"War is ugly," Vars agreed.

Ian spoke soothingly. "Ebi and Ibe were tasked with creating the first rough draft of what we could expect from the Mims. But that's all it is—a rough draft. I'm hoping that once we get on the way, we'll all work together—under your guidance, Vars—to refine these ideas."

"Yes, we definitely need to work on your preliminary set of variables," said Vars. She hoped it wasn't too late to steer Ibe and Ebi and the rest of the team into a more peaceful frame of mind. Diplomacy stood a better chance at succeeding if they knew the boundaries they were not willing to cross.

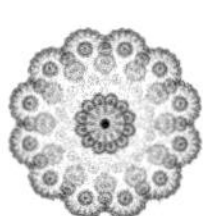

Alice arrived at Vars's EPSA-assigned quarters late that evening just as Vars was getting ready for bed.

"Alice?" Vars said. It came out more of a question than a hello, but then again, it was late. "What can I do for you?"

Without a word, Alice stepped inside and practically collapsed into a big reading chair. She held her arms to her body and looked to be in a lot of pain.

"What's wrong?" Vars asked, suddenly concerned. "What did they do to you?"

"I had them rip it all out," she said. She pulled up her sleeves. The bandages started at her wrists and disappeared under her clothing.

"But why?" Vars was about to have D-tats implanted herself—Ian had made it a condition of her going into space. She rubbed her own arms in sympathy; it felt like ants were marching up and down her veins. And this was *before* the surgery.

Alice made a small, pitiful sound, and Vars jumped to get her some water. She didn't know what else to do; what other comforts could she offer the woman?

"Thank you," Alice said. She tried to pick up the glass that Vars placed by her side but couldn't do it. Her arms were shaking too much.

"Why, Alice? Why did you do it?" Vars asked again.

"I had a bad reaction," Alice said, but the way she looked at Vars made Vars think it was something else.

Vars looked about her room. She hadn't seen any surveillance equipment in her room, and Ian had assured her that EPSA didn't do that kind of stuff. But Alice was clearly acting as if it wasn't safe to talk here.

"Should we go outside and get you some air?" Vars asked. "Sometimes, after surgery and anesthesia—"

"That's a wonderful idea." Alice started to stand up but swayed a bit. Vars rushed to her and offered aid. She wasn't sure where it didn't hurt to touch, so she just provided her arm for support. "Thank you, Vars. Outside, in the fresh air…"

Vars grabbed the extra blanket at the foot of her bed and escorted Alice out.

It was cool but not yet cold. It was damp, and Vars worried that the fresh air might actually hurt Alice. But the woman kept pulling her deeper into the artificial woods. The redwoods had been planted to resemble a natural tree dispersal, and only a few yards in, the buildings were obscured from view. A few yards in, it actually felt like wilderness, even though they were in one of the most well-developed and technologically advanced areas on the planet.

"Pull out my tablet," Alice said, turning to show a large jacket pocket.

Vars pulled a mini personal computing device from the pocket. It was a newer model than Vars's.

It took Alice a few tries to get her biometrics to unlock the device. "My fingers are still a bit clumsy," she said. "Can you take over? I had all my work transferred back to this. Just pull up security and…"

Vars quickly navigated to the appropriate controls. All the PCDs were standardized, so it was easy, but Vars saw that Alice had a few additional features on her tablet.

"Alice PCD," Alice said, using her voice command to authorize further use. She gestured for Vars to hold the device in front of her, and Alice managed to swipe and click a few times. "Okay, that should do. We'll have a few moments of privacy."

"Is there something wrong?" Vars asked. She was still supporting Alice by the elbow and could feel the slight tremors that ran through the woman's delicate bones. She threw the blanket over both of them, using her own shoulders to support it and allowing the resulting shelter to protect Alice from the late evening chill.

"I've seen your dad," Alice said. Before Vars could respond, Alice continued. She very quickly summarized everything Matteo had told her—about nanobots, wide-scale contamination including human bodies, and the as-yet-undetermined effects on the D-tats.

"So *that's* why you had yours removed," Vars said.

"The timing is just too coincidental," Alice said. "We discover the alien artifact just as it sends a message out into space, and at the same time Matteo discovers alien nanobots all over Earth, Luna, and we have to assume Mars. And these bots are in every ecosystem, including our bodies."

"And there's no question that they're of alien origin?"

"None," Alice said.

"You believe these things are linked?"

"We have to assume that, right?"

Vars considered it, then nodded in agreement. "So what should we do?"

"You have to refuse the D-tats."

"Ian said it was a deal breaker—no D-tats, no going on the mission."

"Ian talks tough, but he'll let you go. If need be, I'll come up with a medical excuse for you."

"Would that be enough?" Vars didn't think it would be that easy.

"It worked for me," Alice said. "I induced an allergic reaction. They pulled mine out as I was going into anaphylactic shock."

"You could have died!"

Alice shrugged. "I couldn't think of anything else. But I'll insist that they test you first. Most people get their first implants before puberty. We're both adults, so it's plausible that we might face higher risks of rejection."

"Wouldn't it make sense to just tell them the truth? Don't we want everyone else's D-tats removed too?" Vars asked. It just didn't make sense...

"Oh, it's just a matter of time before someone else discovers the nanobots," Alice said. "And then all the D-tats will come out. But first we need to learn what the bots are about. On the journey, we'll be in an isolated environment, so there's no harm. Not right away. It'll be our chance to study—"

"Alice, this is crazy! If these bots are crawling through our bodies, we *have* to remove them. All of us."

Alice sighed. "Matteo doesn't think that's even possible.

We've been consuming the microplastics for decades as part of our food and water. And they're self-replicating. These things are everywhere."

"Are we...are we under invasion?" Vars couldn't believe she'd just uttered these words. First interstellar war and now this. *But what else could this be?*

"Yes. Or, at least, that's the consensus among the Vault Elders."

Vars was having trouble taking all this in. "Did my dad agree with this? He wants to keep the nanobots a secret too?"

"It's only for a little while, Vars. We want to see what these things do once we get close to the artifact. If this *is* an invasion, we need to know their objectives. We need to understand what their goals. Otherwise how do we stop them? But obviously, Matteo doesn't want you to get the implants."

Vars shook her head. "No. You're both nuts. I have to go tell Ian." She turned to leave, but Alice grabbed her wrist.

"Vars. There's more. D-tats are addictive—you know that. My tats were recent, so it wasn't an issue for me. But the twins have been tatted for practically their whole lives. Can you imagine what would happen to them if they had theirs removed? They wouldn't be able to go on the mission. They probably won't even be able to function. I'd bet neither of them ever stoop to using tactile interfaces. They do *everything* via direct neural commands through their implants."

Vars didn't think it was one hundred percent accurate—she had seen the twins touch their wrist implants—but it was close to the truth. The twins flaunted their proficiency with implant technology. It was a matter of pride somehow, too. Removing D-tats would amount to hand amputation for them...or worse.

"And it's not just them," Alice continued. "Ian would have to postpone the mission, probably gather a new group of scientists. It would put us back years. Do you think we have that much time? If this is a prelude to an alien invasion, we have to get out there and figure out what we are facing. We don't have a choice. We can't wait. You see that, Vars, right?"

"I...I don't know."

"Once we're out of here, we can 'fumigate' our ship and perform whatever extractions and purifications are necessary," Alice said. "But until then, you can't say anything about this."

The intensity in the woman's voice frightened Vars. She didn't have time to think this through. She had to rely on the conclusions of her father and his Seed Elders; they had deliberated for a long time, it seemed. And Alice was so smart.

"But why can't we at least tell Ian?" Vars asked. "He should know."

"Because he'd have to report it, and we'd be stuck in a morass of panic and bureaucracy. I expect our mission would be turned into a military operation, and you can just imagine what that would mean to scientific exploration and decision-making."

"The nanobots would be considered an act of war," Vars said, understanding. "But it might *not* be war."

"Precisely," said Alice. "If we wanted to explore another star system, wouldn't we send nanobots first? Perhaps just a few self-assembling units?"

"Something to explore the environment and report back," Vars speculated.

"Right. And it's not a given that these aliens—these Mims—were even aware that we'd be vulnerable to these bots. Matteo believes that if it weren't for the microplastics in our water systems, the bots wouldn't have spread as widely as they did; they wouldn't have invaded our bodies."

"So it could all be just a huge mistake," Vars said. She

thought back to this afternoon with the twins. They were already talking war. She had to stop the team from assuming the worst prior to gathering the facts.

"Or, let's not kid ourselves," Alice said. "It could be a full-blown invasion. We don't know. But if we tell Ian and the military gets involved, they'll assume it's an all-out invasion, and that'll be the end of that."

Vars looked at the small woman who was still barely able to stand after her brutal procedure. "I understand now. I just...I'm sorry I reacted the way I did, Alice. The idea of having bots crawling around inside me..."

"I was furious with Matteo when he told me," Alice confessed. "I wanted to rip my implants out right there and then. Fear clouded everything. Then I spoke to Elder Alaba, our Seed Vault's senior member, and he made me understand." She smiled. "He's an amazing man. He was one of the original Seeds. Back then, he didn't even have the choice to leave the Vault like I did—being sent into the Vault was a life sentence. But Elder Alaba embraced his duty to raise a generation of humans that could bounce back after a catastrophe. He helped design the Vault systems, figured out the politics and psychological solutions to Seed internment. We couldn't have succeeded without him."

"You sound as if you almost miss it," Vars said.

Alice laughed. "In a way. I mean... I left the Vault as soon as I could. I couldn't have lived down there my whole life, even though I had the best education, the best teachers, and a very supportive community. But mostly, I'm just glad the Vault is there. It's comforting to know that there's a backup for humankind. Just in case something happens, there *is* someone ready to pick up the pieces and start over."

Vars realized she had no idea what it was like to be a Seed. What it had been like for her dad. What might it have meant for her, if she had stayed. Even after she found out that she was a Seed, she hadn't tried to figure it out.

"There's a taboo in our culture that arrests the desire to know more about the Vaults," Alice said, as if reading her mind. "All those stupid stories about Seed prostitutes? The tabloid nightmares and horror movie fodder? Those are just something the Elders came up with to keep the Vaults safe. Because in a time of plenty, there would be a desire to dismantle the whole system. People are quick to forget the past."

Vars knew Alice was right. If there was an open debate today, people would choose to end the Human Genome Heritage Project. The fear engendered by the Keres Triplets was gone...well, greatly diminished, now that asteroid sentinels and guidance systems were in place to remove dangerous rocks from Earth collision orbits. People felt safe.

"So," Alice said. "We make sure you don't get the D-tats. We move forward with the mission as planned. And once we're far enough away from the Earth's influence, we tell Ian and the others about the nanobots."

"Unless they've already discovered the bots by then," Vars said.

"Then it will be a moot point," Alice agreed. "In that case, our job will be to keep the mission from falling under military control."

"I understand and agree," Vars said.

They returned to the EPSA dorms with Vars practically carrying Alice. Behind them, Vars thought she heard soft footfalls on the thick carpet of redwood needles. But perhaps she imagined it.

Chapter Seven

Matteo huddled next to a large heater. After decades of living in a relatively mild climate, he found the harsh Finnish winter difficult. His bones ached, and he felt out of sorts.

Of course, it might also have been because Vars had left for Mimas and he hadn't even gotten a chance to hug his little girl goodbye. But Elder Alaba had insisted it be done this way. Nothing was to slow down that mission. Nothing.

Matteo had a mission of his own now. He had taken a leave of absence from his lab in Seattle and moved to the remote medical research facility in the far north that exclusively served the needs of the Vault, his former home. Elder Alaba had made him the lead investigator on the nanobots, their effects on human tissues, and their integration with D-tats.

What do these aliens want? Matteo asked himself over and over again. *What would I do if I could infect billions of humans with nanobots that could interface directly with implanted devices that plugged into the planet-wide information and communication network?* The possible answers to these questions kept him up late into the night and drove him out of bed early every morning.

"Matteo? Are you awake?" A tall, thin, redheaded woman placed a hand on his shoulder, and Matteo jumped. "Sorry!"

she said.

"It's okay, Phoebe. I guess I'm just not used to the quiet ways of the Seeds. Not anymore." He looked up at her. "Had a good first night?"

He knew she hadn't. Phoebe was a lifer by choice; she had never wanted to leave the Vault. But Elder Alaba insisted she joined Matteo's team here at the facility. Phoebe was Matteo's Seed-sister—as babies, they had been "donated" to the vault in the same year. She was born to parents who "won" the Vault lottery, while he was born in another Vault and transferred into Elder Alaba's care as per Seed custom. Neither of them remembered their birth parents. Seed families tended to cause friction inside the Vault and were rarely allowed to stay together. Seeds were required to make regular deposits of their genetic material, just not to have children...but for another extinction-level event. As Seed-siblings, Matteo and Phoebe grew up together, studied together, worked together. Phoebe was the first person Matteo turned to when he discovered Vars as an abandoned baby outside the Vault's door many years ago. She was really the only one, other than Elder Alaba, that Matteo had kept in personal contact with all this time. More importantly, she was a brilliant biologist—and that was what had gotten her attached to Matteo's team, against her will.

Phoebe must have read the expression on his face. "Don't blame yourself for my being here," she said. "This was the only way." It gave Matteo the creeps to know that little nanobots floated freely inside his body. It made him feel even worse to know that now Phoebe had them, too. "Elder Alaba promised me I'll get cleaned and allowed back in someday," she added.

Matteo doubted that would ever happen—no one who left the Vault had ever returned. But he didn't say anything. If Phoebe needed to believe that she would be let back in, he would let her maintain that fantasy for a while.

"Well," Matteo said. "I guess we'd better get to work." He stood up with fake enthusiasm. His body creaked audibly—damn, he was getting old. "I've been working on putting together the lab we need. I have shipments coming from all over the world."

"So I was told," Phoebe said.

She followed him into the working wing. Given the punishing environment of Northern Finland, the facility was mostly underground. In this way it was similar to the Vault, and Matteo knew that it gave Phoebe some level of comfort. She wasn't used to open spaces, a sky overhead, great expanses of land. Those things frightened her as if she had a bad case of agoraphobia. Matteo knew she felt that way because he remembered feeling that way himself, in the early days of life after the Vault. Even now, he felt it some. It was one of the reasons he was so comfortable inside ocean submersibles.

"Don't you think we're being a bit too paranoid?" Phoebe asked. "Wouldn't it have been easier to just to have everything we need built at one place and shipped here?"

"I subcontracted that bit of paranoia to the Elders," Matteo said. "I'm freaked out enough about the bots without considering greater implications."

"When will our first group of *volunteers* arrive?" Phoebe asked. She stumbled on the word—she was "volunteered" too, but Matteo hoped that she would have chosen to come and help even if she wasn't asked. She knew he needed help.

The scientists joining them here were mostly Seeds who left their Vaults years ago plus a few individuals that they'd vouched for and who had passed whatever hurdles the Vault Elders had thrown their way. In addition to competent researchers, the unspoken truth was that Matteo and Phoebe needed access to test subjects if they were to learn how nanobots evolved and reacted to different environmental conditions. In a way, they were all to be scientists and subjects of their own research. It wasn't something Matteo wanted to dwell on.

"The first three arrive later today," he said.

They entered the newly repurposed lab—a huge underground room partitioned by structural glass into several distinct areas.

"Shiny," Phoebe said.

"These are all environmentally isolated, of course," Matteo said, gesturing. "We'll set up a surgery area in the far corner there, with Seed Sophie in charge. She was *volunteered* from the Australian vault." Sophie's work was all about developing advanced cyberhumatics, and she was a good surgeon. She also had some ideas on panspermia—the theory, now verified, that life originated on Earth and spread throughout the solar system via dirt fragments launched into space by large meteoric impacts. Matteo needed her expertise.

"You should stop calling her 'Seed Sophie,'" Phoebe said. "You might accidentally slip." Unlike the Vault, their lab could theoretically directly maintain ties with the outside world. It wouldn't help their interactions with "civilian" scientists if they announced their origins too loudly.

"You're right, of course. Elder Alaba yelled at me, too. We are to call him 'Dr. Alaba' now." It was just an extra precaution; communications beyond the immediate team were not very likely given how 'Dr. Alaba' felt about their work. "I'll do my best with Sophie," he added. "Please feel free to kick me if I mess up."

After years of feeling like an outsider, Matteo cherished every moment he would get to work and live with fellow Seeds. It was especially good to be with Phoebe again. He just wished Vars were here to meet his Seed-sister.

"Missing your daughter?" Phoebe asked. She could still read him like an open book.

"For so many years it was just me and her," he said.

"It must have been hard," Phoebe said. "I remember that until Vars came along, you weren't sure if you even wanted to leave the Vault."

"I would probably have decided to go eventually," he said. "I wasn't like you."

"Like me?"

"Well, I mean to say, I always knew you'd stay. You were a scientist from the earliest moments I can remember." He looked her in the eyes. "I know being here is brutal for you. I'm so sorry about that. Thank you for helping, Phoebe. It means the world."

"You survived it," she said. "And I will too. And it's really not too far from home for me. We'll be in close contact with the Vault. Compared to what you lived through, it's nothing." It sounded like a mantra.

Matteo showed Phoebe around the rest of the lab, including her new workstation and the machines that he'd managed to unpack, if not set up, before she joined him. The real work would start when Sophie and the other "volunteers" arrived. The plan was to test the nanobots directly in the subjects' bodies. Rats first, but humans too. They needed to know what to expect before Vars's mission got in trouble.

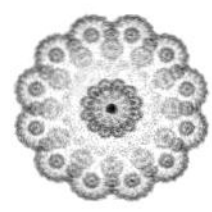

"Look, I don't bite," Sophie said.

Sophie was a six-foot-three Amazon of a woman, with wheat-blond, almost white hair that was closely cropped, making the D-tats implanted on both sides of her lower jaw and neck all the more noticeable. She wore a sleeveless top, and her long arms were also heavily covered with cyberhumatics gear. Matteo would bet that she probably had a few other D-tats underneath her clothing. She might not bite, but she looked scary as hell.

"If it becomes a problem, I'll deal with it," she said when he pointed out that it might be dangerous for her to be so connected. *What if the bots take over?* "I'm implanted with a kill switch. All Australian Seeds have one. We aren't stupid, you know."

"I've just never..." Matteo raised his hands, trying to signal that he meant no disrespect. Different Seed Vaults had different cultures. He understood that. Sophie's Vault, the Australian Vault, was the only Earth-based one where the Seeds received implants.

"Your Vault went your way," she said, "and we took a different direction. Come on, let's get this show on the road. I was told we're under extreme time pressure."

Matteo nodded. He was only reluctantly in charge of this operation. He had argued for Phoebe to take over that role—after all, she was the head teacher and the lab director back at their Vault, as well as being a natural-born leader—but she had refused, on the basis that she had no experience with the outside world. So Matteo was stuck in command, not where he was comfortable operating.

"You're right," he said. "Let me show you what Phoebe and I managed to grow last night."

Matteo ushered Sophie over to the shared biobench. In the middle of a smooth metal surface sat an isolation chamber with lights pointed at it. Inside, easily visible without any special magnification, was a metallic-looking structure with an irregular Menger sponge fractal pattern. It was made from what looked like hundreds of

Rubik's Cubes—three-by-three-by-three cube structures—with every central cube removed and then repeated a few hundred times, preserving the structure at every magnification. Each cubic building block was an exact miniature replica of the whole structure. And the whole thing shimmered.

"Is it...moving?" Sophie asked.

"Yes," Matteo replied. "The structure continues to grow and repeat. Not perfectly; there are slight variations."

"Some sides progressed farther and have developed a bit of lopsidedness," Phoebe chimed in. "But the process is ongoing."

"And you said this thing has been under construction since last night?" Sophie asked.

"Just over nine hours now," Matteo said.

"And it's photovoltaic?"

"Yes." Matteo shut off the spotlights. The slight coruscating of the working nanobots stopped. He turned the lights back on, and the structure returned to its seething activity.

"What spectrum?" Sophie asked. She had apparently gotten over her initial shock. Matteo noted that she was nervously scratching at the D-tats on her arms. His own arms itched, and he didn't even have any cyberhumatics...just the free-swimming nanobots in his blood.

"UV works best," Phoebe said. She had been testing various frequencies of light while Matteo worked to put together Sophie's workstation. "But all frequencies provide some energy."

"But the bots you discovered in our blood, those can't be using photovoltaics."

"No, we assume they derive energy directly from the bio-processes in our bodies," Phoebe said. "We don't know much yet. We look forward to working with you on that."

"But so far, you haven't seen anything destructive, right?"

Sophie asked, still rubbing her arms. "These things don't *do* anything?"

"Not yet," said Matteo. "We don't know more than what I sent you."

Matteo had sent a package of information to Sophie's Vault. Her Elders' reply had been to send Sophie. He didn't know what other measures they were taking to protect themselves, but he was sure that the Australian Vault was working on developing serious precautions against the invasion. The mission of *all* Vaults was to survive and revive the human population should the unthinkable happen. Methods varied, but the objective was the same.

"Well then, let's get to work." Sophie looked excited to get going, but Matteo heard a note of panic in her voice. He looked over at Phoebe, who gave the slightest of nods—she'd noticed it too. Sophie was good at hiding it, but she was scared.

In the next few days, Matteo's lab grew several structures, all following a similar program of building. But they were no closer to figuring out what these structures were for.

"Are you telling me we've been using the same sample all this time?" Sophie yelled in exasperation.

Her temper was explosive. Matteo didn't understand how she'd managed to live inside a Seed Vault all her life; she seemed temperamentally unfit for it. But Phoebe pointed out that Sophie's exuberant emotions might stem from the novelty of the environment she now found herself in. Phoebe, too, found it difficult to cope, although she didn't go around scaring the other researchers. There were three additional members on their team now, bringing the total in their lab to six.

"I have samples from all over the world stored in the freezer," Matteo replied. "It just seemed prudent to figure out what we can get out of one before we moved on."

"Keep as many of the variables constant—" Phoebe began, trying to show support, but Sophie cut her off with a wave and stormed off to get another sample from the freezer.

Phoebe turned to Matteo. "She can't just run over everyone like this," she whispered. "We have to be systematic or we'll never figure out what's going on."

"I know," Matteo replied. "Perhaps she'll calm down in a few days." He scratched his chin. "Do you believe that the nanobots would be different in different parts of the world? Because even under magnification, they look identical to me." The truth was that he'd been using the same sample, the one from San Diego, not only for the sake of experimental control, but because he didn't think a different sample would yield different results. They didn't when he grew out a few samples back in his personal lab in Seattle. Growth times varied a bit, but the structures were surprisingly similar—all followed the same fractal pattern...well, in the short time frames he allowed the nanobot growth to proceed, all grew some version of a 3D box fractal. The results could differ over longer time frames. They just hadn't gotten around to testing...

"Computers from the same batch series look the same, but that doesn't mean they run the same program," Phoebe said. "Consider genetics. It's not enough to do a complete genetic profile. Genetic traits can only be understood in relation to a particular environment. The more different environments are tested, the more heritability can be shown."

Matteo had considered that. "We've already tested the San Diego nanobots under different light waves," he said. "Differences were slight—mostly just in the speed of construction."

"Yes, but there *were* differences. And Sophie is right—different samples might have evolved differently, depending on the environment they found themselves in."

It wasn't that Phoebe's or Sophie's points were invalid; but Matteo still felt like arguing. Sophie was making him edgy. He needed to set a research agenda or they would all just run around doing their own things. "We don't even understand the dispersion pattern—how did these bots get to be so ubiquitous so quickly?" he said. "Was there one event that introduced a group of nanobots on Earth and then they spread? Or are we being continuously bombarded with these things?"

"What makes you think the bots dispersed quickly?" Phoebe asked. "What if they've been here for eons, hidden like the Mimas artifact, and they only recently came online because of some signal or some environmental trigger?"

"We don't know that the artifact has been hidden for eons," Matteo said.

"Alice said that the albedo of the substructure around the Mimas artifact looks like clean ice, very different from the surrounding dirty-snowball landscape. All other data seem to point to the alien artifact melting out of the Herschel Crater, too. And that giant impact on the little moon is old."

"I read her report too, but perhaps not as carefully as I should have," Matteo admitted. Alice had sent a detailed analysis to the Elders before the Mimas mission departed. Matteo had spent days familiarizing himself with Alice's thoughts about the project, but it was a lot of material, and he had also been busy setting up this lab. There was just so much to do, and no time to get it all done. There was no excuse, but he felt stretched to the limit. He knew Phoebe wasn't blaming him, yet Matteo still felt defensive for some reason. And he was worried about Vars having to deal with these bots out in space, where help wasn't just a few minutes away. *Where I can't help her,* he thought. *That's really my problem. My baby is in trouble and I'm not there for her.*

"We'll figure it out." Phoebe gave him a quick hug. She could always tell when he needed a bit of emotional support.

"Are you quite done over there?" Sophie called from the other side of the room. "Come check this out."

Matteo and Phoebe walked over. Two more test stations had been set up in addition to the isolation chamber holding the San Diego sample nanobots.

"This one is from the east coast of Africa, from the Tanzania Radiation Flats," Sophie said, pointing. Matteo remembered spending weeks in a decontamination facility after gathering those samples. Vars was so angry he had put himself at such risk. "And this one is from the northwestern coast of Australia." Sophie's Vault wasn't far from where Matteo had collected that particular sample.

"I gathered that one up right among the dying stromatolite mounds," he said. "But barely a year before, I was at the same location, just around the corner from the Hamelin Pool on Australia's Coral Coast, and that sample had nothing. No nanobots and even a limited microplastics count."

"Well, the bots are there now, and they're building," Sophie said.

They leaned in to watch. The Tanzania sample appeared to be set on overdrive—assembling at least ten times faster than the bots from the San Diego sample. Structures practically exploded into existence. And these were different structures, nothing like the perforated cubes. These resembled twisting snakes. So much for Matteo's assumption that identical nanobots built similar structures. And these nanobot creations moved, not just changing shape, but actually roaming around the enclosure, seeming to probe the walls.

"These containers are bot-proof, right?" Phoebe asked.

"In theory," said Matteo. "We do have a freeze switch if things feel out of control."

"Good."

Sophie was bending over the containment cube for the Australian sample, peering through a magnifying loop. "There are no structures here."

"Not yet," Phoebe said. "But we now know that the rates of construction between the sample vary widely, even under the same wavelength setting."

"And we also just learned that the structures are different," Matteo said. "Sophie was right: we should have been looking at various samples all along," he added. The Australian Seed didn't react to his apology. She was hyper focused on the experiments.

The snake-like assemblies of Tanzania nanobots fused and started to resemble mycelia, the slender root-like structures that formed the underground portion of mushrooms. Mushrooms were a staple food in the subterranean human Seed Vaults, so every young Seed recognized these structures. In fact, many of the Vault walls were covered with a bioluminescent version of mycelia, developed especially for the underground cities, flooding the deep passages with a dim green glow.

The nanobot-assembled mycelia soon covered the entire walls of the isolation chamber. Suddenly the whole thing shuddered and moved slightly on the table.

"Shut it down!" Phoebe screamed.

Matteo pulled the switch.

The walls of the chamber became etched with ice. The nanobot structures pulled away from the outside surfaces and shriveled.

　　"I want these things under constant surveillance," Sophie said. She was clearly shaken. They all were.

Chapter Eight

Saturn was between eight and a half and ten and a half times farther away from the sun than Earth, depending on their orbital positions. At the moment, Earth and Saturn were just over one billion kilometers distant—meaning it would take four months for the Mimas EPSA group to get there.

The entire team Vars met at EPSA was on the flight: Alice, Greg, Bob, "Evi," Izzy, Trish, Ron, and Ben Kouta. And, of course, Ian and the twins were there. Major Terry Liut led the military personnel onboard their little spaceship. There were eleven of them in addition to the major. Some were pilots, technicians, engineers, and other people who kept the ship going, but Vars suspected a few were soldiers.

The ship was shaped like a cigar with lots of extra bits tacked on. The living quarters were in the top half and engines and fuel in the bottom. The first two weeks were devoted to gaining the acceleration needed to get to Saturn, and the ship maintained its basic shape. It was difficult to get anything done while still under acceleration. The scientists stayed in their cabins and worked strapped into their sleeping pods, trying to find accommodation with their stomachs in freefall. Vars found the practical realities of weightlessness a lot more discomforting than the theories she learned in her space prep classes. These first weeks off Earth made Vars reconsider her decision to come along on this expedition many times.

But once the engines cut off, the ship broke up into two cylinders that pulled apart and started to rotate around their center of mass, creating simulated gravity. It was weak, but it made a huge difference to the lives of scientists with little experience in space flight. Personal grooming and other body-function necessities were all more familiar and the slew of continuous embarrassments were behind them...literally in most cases. Vars felt like she could finally focus on the mission...in between smashing her body against every doorframe and corner of the ship. The force of impact in space was still mass times acceleration. Vars found acceleration very easy, pushing her body along the walls and floor of their little ship with muscles used to Earth's gravity. Unfortunately, low gravity didn't mean low mass.

A thin corridor connected the two halves, making the ship look like a spiky dumbbell; the transit between was not for the faint of heart. The closer one got to the center of mass, the less "gravity" one felt. Fortunately, those who were not directly involved in running the ship didn't have to make the passage...not on a regular basis anyway. Even thinking about that transit made Vars break out in cold sweat. She would bet she was not the only one. So while the rotating dumbbell configuration was great for bodily comfort, it resulted in a unfortunate separation of scientists from the military crew that ran their spaceship, all of whom were veteran space travelers and far better trained for a space voyage of this length and difficulty.

Everything served at least double duty on the ship. The cafeteria had a giant screen embedded into one of the walls, making it an ideal place for "gazing at the universe" as well as projecting data, research notes, and graphs during meetings.

And this room could also easily transform into additional exercise space just by folding away tables and chairs. The biolab was also a medlab and came equipped with multiple "showers"—personal steam pods, really. Most people shared cabins, but Vars was fortunate to have her own personal quarters and even got a chair and a small desk—she was expected to host subgroup meetings in her room. Alice was assigned a sleeping bunk in the medlab as the most qualified medical technician onboard; at least she got shower priority. Some of Liut's people slept four per room, but they slept in shifts. Liut also had the advantage of military discipline; scientists tended to be an unruly, individualistic bunch.

It was not until their third week in space that most of Ian's people settled into routine life and work on board. That left eleven uninterrupted weeks to think and work through what they would need to do once they faced the alien artifact and two more weeks of freefall under maneuvers to decelerate, get into orbit around Saturn, and then land down onto the surface of its little moon. Considering how widely Vars's and the twins' views on how to approach the Mims diverged, Vars felt overwhelmed with the amount of education she had to impart in so little time. Not just to those two, but to the whole group. All were opinionated, all were doctors of their respective disciplines, except for Trish Cars, who was announced on day one as the smartest among Ian's group of brainiacs. And all of them have been working the problem back on Earth while Vars crammed the basics of spaceflight survival. Now they needed to form a team, become of one mind on how to approach these Mims.

And there was also the major. Liut had been a constant feature at all of the science team's meetings even before they left for Mimas. He never missed a meeting in space. There was just no getting rid of the man. Vars was not a fan, but it wasn't her job to like people. Her job was to make sure that this mission of first contact didn't turn into a prelude to war...a war that she didn't believe humans had a chance of winning.

Vars had a feeling that, in a crunch, Ian's scientists would be no match for those under Major Liut's command. And she wasn't even sure that the scientists would oppose the military, if it came to that. Alice, of course, would be on her side. And Ben, probably. Because of his constant references to *Star Trek*, Vars assumed his point of view on aliens was strongly

informed by that old series' optimistic outlook on relationships between star-fairing cultures. Ian, too, might be on her side. And perhaps Trish. But if Vars was dividing the crew of the ship into "us and them," it didn't bode well for the rest.

Vars felt her blood itch and rubbed her arms. Finding a way to force everyone to cutout their D-tats and scrub their blood to remove all of the alien nanobots was high on her agenda, too. But Alice was the lead on that. Eleven weeks was a *very* short time to get it all done. And she needed to do it without alienating anyone...

Ian's team gathered in the largest space on the ship—the cafeteria. When everyone finally managed to get comfortable, Vars started on her first prepared lecture.

"Tasmanians were isolated from all other human societies by ten millennia and a hundred miles of water," she said in her teacher's voice.

"Vars? Maybe you could pick a topic a bit more relevant to our work here?" Ian said. Others also grumbled. Even back on Earth, everyone hated when Vars started out by making a point with ancient history. But she needed to give these people exemplars that were relatable and yet not too familiar—it was a very fine path to thread.

"Just cut to the chase, Vars," Trish said. "We'll catch up. Really."

"I find that giving concrete examples helps distill ideas and makes them more memorable," Vars said. "So please indulge me. You might even learn something interesting."

"I'd settle for useful," she heard someone whisper loudly from the corner. Vars turned to look, but her movement was too forceful, and she hit her knee on the side of the table... again. She was learning to be more graceful, but everything took time to learn. *Everything.*

Vars saw that the twins were already on their D-tats, probably looking up all the relevant information on the ancient Tasmanians so they could sneer at her in disdain and correct her on any detail she might get wrong. But she didn't care—if that's what it took for Ebi and Ibe to learn the material, she was happy. She had a feeling that they were the key. If she could get them on her side, then she would have won the battle for the heart and soul of this expedition.

"Go on, Vars," Ben said, giving her a very obvious wink. "We all want to hear about the clash between the hunter-gatherers and the British Empire, which obviously didn't abide by the Prime Directive."

Ron and Trish groaned. Ben's *Star Trek* references got old quick.

"It's true that the British Empire had no qualms about exploiting native populations," Vars said. "Neither did the Spanish, or the Portuguese, or the French."

"Or the Dutch," Ben added.

"Let's not forget the Germans, the Italians, and the Belgians," said Alice.

"And the Chinese," said Evi. "And the Russians."

"And the Mayans and the Aztecs," said Ben, happy to point out the less obvious.

"Yes," Vars said, putting a stop to a discussion that might become the airing of ancestral grievances. "When a technologically advanced civilization comes in contact with peoples who took a different socio-evolutionary path, those with high technology and plentiful resources tend to decimate the native peoples and their cultures."

"Obviously," Ibe said in a loud whisper again. *So it was him.*

"Are you trying to point out the technological differences between us and the Mims?" Ian asked.

"Not all advanced civilizations will necessarily destroy those who are less advanced," Ben said. "I can think of two arguments against this. One, this could be a human issue. Humans as a people could just have this nasty trait of distrusting strangers and choosing the path of war over cooperation."

"While that's a valid point..." Major Liut spoke up for the first time. It seemed unusual for him to speak at all during these meetings, virtual or otherwise. "We have to assume that the aliens are hostile until proven otherwise. We can't risk thinking this is a benevolent encounter."

Not for the first time, Vars noted that Liut wore a

long-sleeve shirt. Everyone typically went sleeveless for easy access to their D-tats. And the ship was temperature-controlled, so he couldn't have been chilled. *Did he have his D-tats removed? If so, how did he know?* She felt the hair stand on her arms and tried to remember if she saw any implants on other military personnel onboard.

"Vars?" Ian prodded her to go on.

"Yes, sorry," Vars said and continued. "It's easy to start thinking in terms of us versus them." *Scientists versus soldiers.* "Humans are wired for it. But—"

"That's my point," interrupted Ben. "And my second point is that there might be an evolutionary stage of development, which humans haven't reached yet, where this kind of thinking drops away. We can't just automatically think of the Mims as the enemy. We have to give them a chance."

"That might be," Vars conceded. She certainly liked Ben's attitude better than the major's...or her own. "But I'd like to get back to the Tasmanians." Ibe groaned. Vars stared him down. "By the time Tasmanians rejoined the rest of humanity, ten thousand years had passed. And we know the history of their first contact."

"So you are saying we *have* to think of the Mims as evil?" Ben said. He clearly hated the direction the discussion was turning, per Liut's comment. Vars thought that was good—she wanted their prejudices to come out early. It would be best if everyone laid out their deepest fears. Until they had been aired publicly and in person, it would be hard to overcome them. And it wasn't just the scientists she needed to convince, but also the military, both here on the ship and back on Earth. That would be far more difficult, especially lacking the face-to-face contact so necessary for reaching shared understandings and mutual agreements. Diplomacy was always an in-person activity. Perhaps it was good that

Liut made the effort to join them, although he made reaching consensus among scientists more difficult.

"I'm saying that ten thousand years is not such a long time," Vars said. "At one point, the people who colonized the small islands of the South Pacific were some of the most technologically advanced people on Earth. The people who became Tasmanians were among humanity's earliest explorers. They built boats that could cross hundreds of miles of open ocean. It would be thousands of years before Europeans could match that feat."

"But they did all that, and then they stopped," Evi said. "Why would they not continue? Why not use their boats to go back and forth to the mainland? Why didn't they keep in contact with their ancestors?"

"All good questions," Vars said. "They had advanced technology and used it to go where no man had gone before." She winked at Ben—she had to use all tools available to bring cohesion to this group. "And then they threw it all away and settled down in isolation."

"That's crazy," Liut said.

"But it happened. We may not know *why* Tasmanians lost their technology and their drive to explore, but we do know it did happen. Technology, once acquired, needs to be maintained. Maintenance and progress need expertise. And that, in turn, requires continuous, intergenerational knowledge transfer—an educational system. Historical events have to be evaluated not only by their place in the time flow of civilization, but also by the average lifespan of individuals and by the length of the intergenerational stretch. Humans live for close to a century now. A present-day generation is approximately thirty years. Both of these measures have been extended by a decade or more in modern times."

"So your theory is that Tasmanians didn't effectively pass

on the expertise and enthusiasm for exploration to the next generation after their initial settlement?" Liut asked. Vars got him to participate, to ask questions—a small win.

"That's one possibility," Ian said. "Their lifespans could have suffered a decline after the initial resettlement. The first few generations could have lived just a few years longer than the intergenerational distance." He looked to Vars for confirmation. "It's like Tasmanians suffered through a technological Dark Age."

"Humans do tend to suffer those over and over again," added Ben. "It could have easily happened to us after the Keres Triplets."

"The point is," Vars said, "the Mimas artifact remained buried under the ice for many millennia before melting out of its tomb and sending a message. What might have happened to the people who sent it in all that time? We are not the same people we were two thousand years ago...or even a century ago."

Liut frowned. "So even if we figure out what the artifact is all about, it might not have anything to do with modern Mims or their motives right now?" he asked.

"I want us to have multiple time perspectives," Vars said. "There's the here and now. But there's also deep time."

"And deep space," said Ian.

"Which are the same really," Ben added.

Vars sought Alice out in her medlab. She wanted an update on news from Earth. Alice had an encrypted communications link with the Vault's warders' station and thus indirectly to her dad. Vars also needed to find out if anyone else on the ship had their D-tats removed prior to the voyage. Since Alice was their medical officer, she might know the answer from a routine interaction with the crew. But if Alice knew, why wouldn't she have told Vars about it right away? It just didn't make sense. She trusted Alice…she had to.

"Hey Alice, did you see Major Liut—"

"Terry," Alice corrected her. Like Vars, Alice never really expected to go off on interplanetary mission. Even as she had longer to prepare for this voyage, the woman was nearly as bruised-up as Vars. Vars could see a bloody gash above Alice's right eye. Mass didn't change in space. Vars wasn't the only one to learn that lesson over and over and over again. "Stick with the program, Vars," Alice said grumpily. "First names only. Team cohesion and all that."

Vars nodded. "Why is *Terry* wearing long sleeves now?"

Alice raised an eyebrow and winced. "Are you saying…" She paused. "You think he had his D-tats removed? But why would he? He shouldn't know about…" She didn't finish. She didn't know. Vars exhaled—she didn't even know she was holding her breath.

They looked at each other. Even before leaving Earth, they both agreed that talking openly about nanobots before it became common knowledge was not a good idea. There were cameras everywhere on the ship, even if no one was supposed to be monitoring private conversations from the bridge. There was an illusion of privacy on board, but only that. Vars moved to get closer to Alice.

"Shouldn't," Vars agreed carefully. She finally managed to get around the lab equipment and get herself into a chair without banging up her knees. Knees and elbows were the worst…followed by head injuries and sprained wrists from trying to grab on to the handholds in the corridors and door jams. But now Vars was close enough to Alice to speak without being overheard. "Back at EPSA Redwood Grove," she said, "when you came to me after your surgery, I might have heard someone following us in the shadows of the trees."

"And you didn't say anything at the time?" Alice said, her voice inching up. "Or later?"

"I wasn't sure." Vars felt overwhelmed with information at the time...and Alice was barely conscious. Still, neither was an excuse. "I'm sorry, Alice, I should have."

"So now you think it was Terry?"

"I don't know," Vars said quietly. "I just wonder if he removed all of his...before leaving Earth."

"I haven't heard anything," Alice said. It should have been in the medical records, but apparently not. "I'll keep an eye out."

"Any word from my dad?" Vars could hear anxiety in her own voice.

"Just that they're testing *subjects* from various sites. Nothing concrete yet," Alice said.

"Why is this not all over the news yet?" Vars fretted. "We should be working on removing all of the...from everyone on the ship." It was hard not mentioning the nanobots or D-tats. "Even if we scheduled out the surgeries now, it would be tight. We'll reach Mimas in just thirteen weeks."

"You, of all people, are jumping to conclusions?" Alice said pointedly. "We don't know the why of anything. There might be a perfectly benign explanation, as we've discussed." She gave Vars a significant look, and Vars felt her cheeks flush. "If we wanted to explore an exoplanet in another star system, we might have thought of something like...like what your father is studying..."

"Yet you don't believe that," Vars said, glancing at Alice's arms. She still wore long sleeves every day to cover up the scars.

"No, I don't. But it's in my nature to think the worst. And it's *your* job to make us see positive alternatives."

"I'm afraid my nature is similar to yours," Vars said.

"Either way, you're doing a good job of opening up the field of possibilities." Alice patted Vars on the arm. "Go work. I'll tell you when I have something."

Ben poked his head into Vars's quarters after they broke off for the day to work on problems separately. "Can I come in?"

"Sure." Vars moved over to sit on her bed to give Ben the only chair. The man slid into it with unexpected grace. *Space experience.* "What can I do for you, Ben?" she asked.

"I just wanted to let you know that not all of us are unappreciative of the stuff you're trying to teach us."

Vars smiled. "And who's 'we'?"

"Well, at least Ron, Trish, and myself."

"The whole JPL contingent."

"We've known each other longest," Ben said. He was fidgeting with the rim of the little desk, running his fingers up and down, tracing the edges and corners. Vars was very familiar with those—her body found a multitude of ways of exploring the corners and edges in her room.

"Was that all you came to tell me?" Vars asked. "I mean, I'm very appreciative, but..."

"I wanted to share some of our ideas," Ben said, "based on the Mimas probe's close-up views of the alien artifact."

"I'd love to know what you think."

Ben became animated, all shyness gone. "Well, first of all, we've assumed that the artifact was old."

"But you guys did the analysis of the surface, didn't you?"

"Yes, from orbit, obviously. The ice around the perimeter of the artifact is new."

"So this would indicate that this thing erupted from the crater only recently, right?"

"We still think so. But—" He turned to the screen on Vars's wall and manipulated his D-tats. *Having those is incredibly convenient,* Vars thought. "See here?" He pointed to a bright patch on the photo. "This image was taken when the probe just got into orbit around Mimas. And this one," he pulled up another image and overlaid it on top, "was taken a few hours ago."

Vars looked. The images didn't match. It wasn't just the shadows, which were different—it was the shape of the artifact and the size of the "fresh" ice around it. "Did more of it come out?" she asked.

Ben pointed to other details. "This section over here? It has moved to the other side. And this thing?" He was drawing with his fingers directly on the image, leaving traces for Vars to keep track of all he was showing her. "We think it twisted, and now part of the structure is under the ice again."

"You're saying it's changing? Moving its bits around?"

"More than that. This whole part? The one that looks like some kind of broken crystal? It's completely new. It's like it grew from nothing."

"Or from the materials available on the surface," Vars said. She heard the awe in her own voice. She had been preparing herself for examining an ancient artifact, an old machine. One that did manage to send out some message, but a message from the past. What Ben was showing her was something very different. She shivered. "Do you think it's getting instructions for transmutation of its features?" she asked.

"We haven't intercepted anything, but we don't know

what to think yet."

"Does Ian know about this?"

"Of course," Ben said. "But we're worried about making this public—sending it back home or even showing this to Major Liut—before we can frame it as something less threatening than it seems at first blush."

"You don't want Major Liut to jump to conclusions." Vars noted that Ben called him Major Liut, too. There was no doubt about the existence of a split between the civilian and military personnel on board. It was dangerous. And if they were being monitored as Alice believed...

"When you talked about war..." Ben didn't finish, but Vars knew what he meant. There was a future path where they could really blow this first contact. It would be all too easy to get frightened, to make decisions based on fear, to take a wrong guess. One miscalculation could lead them to an unwinnable war.

"Thank you for sharing this with me," Vars said. She turned her attention back to the screen. "If you don't mind, can you zoom in on the new section?"

Ben rotated the image and zoomed in on the newer fragment of the artifact. It looked like a series of Rubik's Cubes with the center piece taken out of each face. There were hundreds of these at different sizes, stacked together.

"It's like a fractal," Ben said. "It repeats at every scale of magnification."

"And you guys have no idea what that could be for?"

"None." Ben sat back and watched as the image slowly rotated, showing off various views and sections of the artifact. Vars noted that he was rubbing his D-tats. In fact, they looked very red and irritated.

"Can I take a look at your arm, Ben?" Vars asked, keeping her voice level and hands steady.

"Oh, you mean this?" Ben held up his left arm. Red lines radiated away from the cyberhumatics. "It's nothing."

"Did you show it to medical?" Vars asked. In addition to Alice, onboard AI kept track of all of their health.

Ben shook his head. "But everyone is having the same problem. It's just something about being in space."

"Everyone?" Vars felt terror grip her body. It took a lot of effort not to show her panic.

"Well, Ron and Trish both complained. And I've seen Ian scratch his until I thought he would pull the whole thing out. He couldn't use the D-tats on his left arm for a few days. And Evi mentioned something, too, now that I think about it. Huh." Ben finally looked concerned.

"Do you mind coming with me to see Alice?" Vars asked.

She didn't wait for Ben to say yes. She just dragged him behind her. It was time they stopped playing games and pulled this nonsense out of the whole crew.

Chapter Nine

The quarantine order came the day Matteo discovered three of his research assistants dead in the lab—three out of his team of six to date; half of his people gone in one blow. Actually, it was Sophie who found them first. They lay on the floor, their bodies threaded with thousands of filaments that weaved a complicated web, attaching the fingers of one to the eyes of another, linking heads and legs together, binding bodies and hair and nails. It was difficult to see where one individual stopped and another began.

Even now, an hour later, Sophie was still barely keeping her hysteria at bay. The dead researchers had all come from her vault in Australia, so she knew them well. All Seeds from the same vault knew each other well.

"These webs are made of human tissue," Phoebe said from behind a microscope. "But the bots obviously built them. Their bodies…they're just teeming with bots."

Like Sophie and Matteo, Phoebe was wearing a hazmat suit, with warm clothes underneath. In order to depress nanobot activity in the lab, Matteo had lowered the temperature in the whole facility to almost twenty below.

"Should we try to separate them?" Sophie asked. "It feels wrong to just…to just stuff them in a freezer like this."

"No," Matteo said. "There's too much risk. I'm sorry,

Sophie." He felt bad about it, but their situation was dire as it was, and he couldn't add to the risk. And there might come a time when they would need to dissect the bodies of the dead researchers to learn nanobots' plans for the modifications they inflicted on those bodies...just not now....not when everything was so raw. Matteo shook his head and added, "We'll just have to try to disinfect this facility as best as we can, so we can continue working."

"Continue working? You can't expect us to continue after this!" Sophie screamed. Earlier, she tried using her kill switch to turn off the cyberhumatics in her body, but absolutely nothing happened. She had Phoebe try to access the switch remotely, still nothing.

"We're here to do a job," Matteo said. "Nothing changed." He tried to sound soothing, but Sophie was practically hyperventilating. He caught her staring into space every few minutes—he guessed she kept trying to turn her D-tats off. Sophie's cyberhumatics would have to be surgically removed, ASAP.

Sophie backed away from them and practically collapsed into a chair against the far wall, as far away from the corpses as possible, hugging herself for comfort. Matteo let the woman fight her grief. He and Phoebe could do the cleanup without her, giving Sophie space to come to terms with what happened to her fellow Seeds...and her own body.

"*Everything* changed!" she shrieked. "We're under attack! Every human on Earth will end up like...like...like that!"

"Not everyone," Phoebe said softly when they moved out of Sophie's hearing range. And Matteo knew just what she meant. The dead researchers had PCD implants, which made them particularly susceptible to the alien nanobots. The Seeds from the Vaults that eschewed D-tats would be better protected...theoretically, anyway.

"There's no choice; we can't quit," Matteo said. "We can't leave this facility—we're under full lockdown. No more additional resources, no more assistants, not even food deliveries. We are on our own." Fortunately, they had received resources for a much larger group—it would be many months before food became a problem.

While Sophie rocked her sorrow and panic in the corner, Matteo and Phoebe put away the specimens. They would keep those in deep freeze so that the bots couldn't remain active. While the nanobots stopped all motion at -120° Celsius, at -200° Celsius they lost their coherence and fell apart. Even warming them up again didn't trigger regeneration. It was one of the first things Matteo learned—how to kill the alien bots. Deep freeze was a method to completely destroy the nanobots—though not applicable to living hosts. The bodies of Slev, Viktoria, and Weehun were a different matter. Those needed to be frozen solid...as one thing. Matteo allocated a full freezer, now a morgue, just for those. He and Phoebe worked silently to maneuver the large mess of strangely entangled human tissues into cold storage; he tried not to think...not about these dead. *Are there more out there? No.* He stopped himself. He had to focus on what he could do for his little girl. Every problem he solved here on Earth gave her a chance to survive out there in space.

The bots' reaction to cold was also a clue to their initial transport into the Solar System and eventually Earth. The temperature of interstellar space was -270.45° Celsius, so the nanobots' delivery vehicle had to generate at least seventy-one degrees of heat above that to keep the bots from falling apart. That or send instructions for manufacturing the bots once they arrived at their destination. Either way, the nanobots weren't just floating in space like interstellar dust. This was one bit of useful information Matteo managed to pass on to the Elders already. *Not enough, but something.*

After about an hour, Sophie recovered herself enough to help. Still, it took all day to clear the lab and another full day to disinfect. They froze different sections of the building in succession—first the storage areas, then the main lab, and lastly the living quarters. Matteo's lab was designed like a spaceship—sections could be completely cut off from each other, and the whole facility could be sealed off from the outside world, much like the Vaults. Most of the tech in the lab was Vault-built. The Elders must have foreseen the possible need to completely isolate Matteo and his people. Though no one could have known it would happen so soon, leaving only three researchers to do all the work. They had initially planned on having over twenty scientists in total; those plans were now scrapped.

Matteo, Phoebe, and Sophie stayed in hazmat isolation suits at all times. Even as they cleansed the lab, they took time to filter each other's blood in their extra-corporeal plasmapheresis suite and to repeatedly disinfect the suits.

The blood filtering worked well enough to get the free-swimming nanobots out of their bodies, but those that clustered around Sophie's D-tats were more problematic. By the time they were done with disinfecting the lab, the most abundant source of the nanobots remaining was inside Sophie. Without discussion, they immediately began preparations for her D-tats removal surgery.

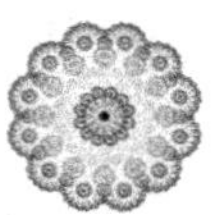

"It's been two days, and we haven't heard anything more from the outside, other than to go on lockdown," Sophie fretted.

Matteo knew she was just nervous. The surgery was very risky. He'd heard how badly it had gone for Alice, and she'd only had the D-tats for a few days. Sophie had them for years.

"Elder Alaba didn't even send an all-clear for the other Vaults," Sophie said. "My Seed-family might be in trouble."

"He might not know," Phoebe said. She was readying herself to perform the surgical procedure—between her and Matteo, she had the most hands-on experience. "But I'm sure the Australian and Luna Vaults are doing everything possible to free their Seeds from the nanobots." Luna-based Seeds had opted into D-tats from their very founding. Life in space was hard enough as it was; they saw D-tats as a necessary adaptation.

"Slev, Viktoria, Weehun." Sophie had been reciting the names of the dead researchers like a prayer, over and over. "What's the point of all this? What do these aliens *want*?"

Matteo knew it was his job to find those answers; and his daughter's job was to find solutions. He wondered what she knew. What messages had her ship received from Earth? He had notified the Elders about the deaths in his lab right away; had they in turn told Vars and Alice about what the nanobots had done to his researchers? Had they passed on the information about nanobots and freezing temperatures? It would be easy to freeze the bots out in space—just push them out of the airlock. Well—you'd still have to get them out of the people first.

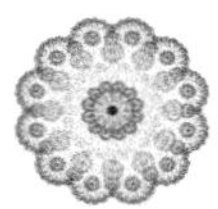

Sophie's arms were restrained and packed with ice, and her blood was continuously churned through the scrubber and cooled—not low enough to neutralize the bots, but enough to slow the buggers way down. They hoped that by taking these precautions, they would be able to keep ahead of bot regeneration. Keeping the body on the verge of hypothermia also reduced the chance of brain damage during surgery.

"Matteo!" Phoebe called out almost as soon as her laser knife penetrated the first layer of Sophie's left jaw implant. They had chosen to remove the D-tats on her neck first. As that was the most delicate operation, Phoebe wanted to be fresh for it.

"What?" But one glance told Matteo why she'd cried out. The boundaries of the cyberhumatics were enlarged and significantly deepened. The nanobots had attached and built upon the original D-tats, greatly expanding the implanted cybernetic material around Sophie's jaw. No wonder the kill switch didn't work—it was gone!

"I don't know how deep to go," Phoebe said, her voice breaking.

"You go as deep as you have to," Matteo said. "We have to take it all out."

"She'll be disfigured for life."

"It can't be helped."

Phoebe sighed. "I don't even know if I can get it all. There's so much."

"Then get all that you can. We'll try to freeze or burn the rest."

Matteo monitored Sophie's vitals while Phoebe cut and burned. As soon as she removed a chunk of circuitry, Matteo deposited it into an incinerator—extreme heat was just as effective at destroying the bots as extreme cold. Periodically, he also emptied the nanobots that had collected in the blood scrubber; he burned those too. But the ones that were stuck around the implant sites were more difficult to get. Phoebe obviously didn't want to make the incision too wide—she worried about damaging or even killing Sophie. And the bots were like cancer cells; some metastasized around the implant sites and others floated around the body looking for new places to start building.

It took over an hour to remove the left neck/jaw set of Sophie's D-tats. The right side went faster, but Matteo could see Phoebe was getting fatigued already.

After a while, she pulled back. "Check the first site," she said. "I think I need some coffee."

While Phoebe sipped the warm liquid caffeine through a thermos straw, Matteo moved the imager back over Sophie's left side. Even before he was able to get a clear focus, he could see something was wrong. All along the edges where Phoebe had scraped off the cyberhumatics, new structures were forming.

Phoebe leaned over to look for herself and cursed under her breath. "No! There was nothing there. You saw it—it was a clean excision. Matteo—"

"I know." Matteo was sure she was right. Phoebe had taken everything out. She was careful. She'd left a clean site. He saw it. But now it was teeming with nanobots rebuilding new...alien cyberhumatics connections, using Sophie's own flesh as building material.

"They're not recreating her old D-tats," Matteo said after a few moments of inspection. The structure that was forming right in front of their eyes had started on the same repeating pattern they'd seen in the lab a few days ago—a fractal arrangement of boxes within boxes.

"What do you think they're building?" Phoebe asked.

Matteo noted that her hands shook slightly; it was the first time he had ever seen his Seed-sister so freaked out. Even when they had discovered the fused bodies, Phoebe had regained her calm almost instantly.

"Whatever it is, we're putting a stop to it," he said. Matteo grabbed some dry ice and applied it directly on Sophie's skin. His own hands shook, too, and he dropped some crystals on the ground.

"Careful, or you'll destroy her healthy tissues," Phoebe said. Her voice was even once more. She was amazing like that.

"I don't see any other choice. If she lives, she has to do it bot-free." Matteo moved the scanner to the other side, where Phoebe had just been operating. There, too, the bots were returning. He layered more solid carbon dioxide over the area. Then he looked down at Sophie's arms. "I suggest we move more quickly. Let's get the big chunks of D-tats off her, and then see about icing the rest."

Phoebe went back to work. She was still methodical, but she moved faster and her excisions were bigger. Sophie would be severely disfigured and impaired at the end of this, but it was the only way to ensure her nanobots were exterminated.

Each time Phoebe moved to a new region of nanobot infestation, Matteo set to work freezing the last area with dry ice. At -78.5° Celsius, it still wasn't cold enough to kill the bots, but it sure slowed the ghastly things down. And a significant portion of the dislodged nanobots got sucked out with the scrubber. The result was fewer nanobots on the whole. He had to hope they were making progress for all the pain and damage they were inflicting.

After forty minutes of cutting and freezing, Matteo became convinced they were gaining an upper hand on the bots. There were definitely fewer of them now. Phoebe remained laser-focused on her work, which wasn't surprising; she'd always had incredible focus. *And that's why she was able to stay in the Vault so easily,* thought Matteo. Even if Vars hadn't been a factor in his life, Matteo knew he didn't have the temperament to live out his life in a closed underground community, in isolation from the rest of humanity. But Phoebe thrived in there.

The thought reminded him of their quarantine. The truth was he was locked away right now, isolated even more than he had ever been in the Vault. He felt panic rise up, and it took all he had to remain in the moment and to continue to help Phoebe cut away the alien-infected cyberhumatics.

Phoebe suddenly swore—this was twice in a row now. Not that he was counting, but it was very unusual for her.

"What now?" Cold sweat dripped down Matteo's back.

"The structures on her left wrist are just too thick. If I remove it all, she'll lose all function in that hand."

"Keep working on it," Matteo said, but he saw what she meant. The nanobots' constructs went deep into Sophie's flesh, to the bone...*into* the bone. There was no removing them all. Not without...

"Just cut the whole thing off," he said.

"What?"

"You said she would lose function anyway. Cut it off. To the elbow." Matteo hoped he was making a reasoned decision and not just letting his fear drive him. It comforted him to know that Phoebe wouldn't follow stupid directions unless she agreed with them.

Which apparently she did.

She took off Sophie's left hand, then started slicing up the arm, looking to see how far the alien structures went. "It just keeps going!" she said. "It must have formed connections with her neck implants." She cut more. And more. And... "No, wait. We have... Bring the tissue imager. I think it ends here."

Matteo pushed the imager over the incision area. It was clear. He exhaled.

"So they were *trying* to make the connection," Phoebe

muttered. "They just hadn't made it far enough yet." She continued cutting. When she was done, Sophie had lost her left arm up to three inches above the elbow.

"She still has her right arm," Matteo said. He meant it as encouragement, though whether it was for himself or for Phoebe, he wasn't sure.

"Freeze the stump," Phoebe said. Matteo applied the full -200°C to the final cut. "At least she's free of them on that side."

"The right side doesn't look too bad," Matteo said. "The nanobots are no longer swarming there."

"I don't think they can replicate at these temperatures," Phoebe said.

If that was true, that was another discovery they could use to fight these things, these invaders. Something else he could give to Vars.

It was many hours later when Phoebe made her last cut, sat down, and surveyed Sophie's mutilated body. They decided to keep Sophie on ice even after the surgery. It would slow down her recovery, but it would give them a chance to observe the nanobots' reaction. And the low temperatures might actually help stabilize her, prevent her from going into shock.

They both watched the scanner as Matteo rotated the views from Sophie's left side of the neck and jaw to her right side and then to her right arm and the left stump. There were no new formations. The blood scrubber whirled and whizzed, and there were fewer and fewer bots. The surgery had been a success…if you could call what they had done to Sophie a success.

As Matteo continued to monitor the scanner, his mind wandered randomly between thoughts. But there was one thing that kept bothering him. *Why are we on lockdown?* That thought swirled continuously just below his awareness, popping up now and then with a shock. It couldn't just be the deaths of the Australian researchers. Their research was far too important to be hampered even by such a horrific event. The Elders would have insisted on getting more researchers into the lab—individuals without D-tats. Frankly, given the nanobots' obvious threat, the Elders should have sent even more people than originally planned. There was just too much at stake.

Something must have triggered a worldwide nanobot attack, Matteo thought. *Perhaps the bots reached a critical mass? Like what happened to Sophie's left arm? Or perhaps they were all activated somehow by some signal?*

Matteo wished he knew more about what was happening on the Luna and Mars colonies. Most living in Elfy projects and the builders of Malfies were heavily implanted with cyberhumatics. *What is happening to those people? And what about the ships in space? Are any of the remote EPSA probes acting funny?* He had no way to know. *What's the purpose? Why now?* But most of all, Matteo worried about Vars.

He felt himself losing control over the direction of his thoughts—a sign of an impending panic attack. Panic attacks were common among the entombed kids until they learned how to control their minds and emotions. Matteo now did what he had been taught to do back in his Vault as a small Seed: he tried to meditate. He focused on his breathing, slowing down his heart rate. He was always told that if he did it long enough, he would feel better.

Twelve hours passed.

Matteo stopped the scrubber when it indicated three consecutive passes without picking up a single nanobot. He didn't fool himself into thinking that Sophie was bot-free now, but he had to stop the process at some point. In a few days, he would make them all go through the scrubber again. It would be like dialysis—do or die.

Without the blood-cooling, Sophie could be brought back to consciousness—slowly, of course. There was no rush now. They were in full isolation and had no outside connection to the world; the Vaults and their wardens' stations went silent. And they had a job to do. Matteo had Phoebe, and with luck, Sophie. As long as there were at least two of them, they'd have someone to monitor while the other underwent a de-botting procedure. If they dropped below two…well, he'd come up with something.

"How's Sophie?" Phoebe asked. She had slept right there in the lab and was now getting together some food rations. Unlike regular humans, Seeds were comfortable with using survival rations indefinitely.

"She should be coming around soon," Matteo said.

Phoebe sat beside him next to the operating table. "What do you think they want?" she asked.

Matteo knew who she meant. "What would you want if you came across a habitable *and* inhabited planet?" he countered.

"It depends on what I was looking for. If I was looking to find companionship, I would try to send emissaries and make inroads into friendship."

"And if you just wanted resources?"

"Only bad science fiction posits intelligent creatures ready to plunder worlds for resources across interstellar space."

Matteo nodded slowly and sucked his coffee through a straw—he wasn't ready to take off his bio-isolation suit yet. Phoebe was still wearing hers too. *Better safe than sorry.*

"There are many potentially habitable worlds," he said. He always believed it was good to think out loud. "Based on our observations, we've guesstimated about ten billion terrestrial planets across our galaxy. Of those, about fifteen hundred are within a fifty-light-year radius of Earth."

"You're assuming that aliens only care about terrestrial planets," Phoebe said.

"These seem to." Matteo glanced at Sophie's bio-indicators; she was warming up nicely. "The nanobots are here on Earth, which means they were looking for planets similar to ours."

"Perhaps that was only because *we* were here. These aliens figured out that Earth had a potentially intelligent species, so they sent representatives to meet us. Scouts."

"That doesn't seem likely," Matteo said. "Setting aside for the moment the fact that the nanobots are doing real damage to us, we've only started showing a real potential for intelligence and technology about three thousand years ago. And that's if we assume the Egyptian pyramids were seen from space. More likely, our first signs of intelligence would have been our radio and TV signals. Then we're talking just about the last two hundred years really."

"So? The aliens noticed the strange signals and sent a probe to investigate," Phoebe said.

"Except the Mimas probe is thousands of years old based on the ice strata analysis, according to Alice."

"Okay. Then let's say they saw the pyramids. Or who

knows? Maybe they saw signs even earlier."

"Maybe," said Matteo. "But it's more likely that they didn't. Which means they spotted a planet that was teeming with life, but without obvious *intelligent* life. And in that case, we must assume these nanobots weren't sent to contact us, because the senders weren't even aware that there was anyone here to contact."

They sat for a while in silence. Aside from some gentle hum from the machinery and heaters, the lab was quiet. Perhaps too quiet.

"She'll wake up soon," Phoebe noted. Sophie's vitals were growing stronger.

Matteo was still working through their conversation. "The Mimas probe sent out its signal a year ago," he said. "Why only then?"

"Perhaps that's when the aliens finally noticed us," Phoebe said.

"Is that bad or good?"

Phoebe didn't answer.

Chapter Ten

News of the nanobot attack on Earth and the colonies came right after Alice finished an emergency excision surgery for Ben's D-tats. Ben had a sudden allergic reaction—something caused the nanobots in his blood to swarm the site of his implant. Fortunately, he had only one basic cyberhumatics on his lower left arm, and it wasn't too difficult to remove.

The news from Earth was hazy at first, with precious few details about outcomes and damage. Major Liut immediately ordered everyone on board to have their D-tats removed. That meant all the researchers—aside from Alice and Vars, of course, and now Ben. Surprisingly...and fortunately, none of the military crew chosen for this mission had any. And it turned out that Major Liut had his removed back on Earth prior to taking off for Saturn, as Vars had suspected. Still, Alice had a lot of surgeries ahead of her.

The surgeries were scheduled out over fourteen days—one procedure every other day or so to ensure that Alice wasn't too exhausted by the job—but eventually Alice managed to remove all cyberhumatics from every member of their science team...except for Ebi and Ibe. The twins' implants were so complex that Alice didn't think it was possible to strip them away without doing life-threatening damage. As a result, the siblings were placed under constant surveillance. It didn't seem fair—they hadn't done anything wrong—but humanity was under attack, and who said life was fair?

"Did he really spy on us that time in the redwoods?" Vars asked. She and Alice were having lunch together after a long morning in the medlab.

"You mean Terry?"

"I saw his D-tats back at EPSA headquarters. He had a fancy, military-type set. How did he know to remove them? And why weren't we told?"

"Your dad told us," Alice said. She sounded tired, perhaps too tired for this conversation.

"My dad told *you*," Vars said. "But how did Major Liut know?"

"Please, just call him Terry," Alice said. "It's not worth the aggravation not to." She rubbed her head.

Vars knew it had been a very long two weeks for Alice. It hadn't been easy on Vars, either. As the only other scientist who didn't need the excision surgery, she had assisted Alice with all the procedures. Liut...Terry didn't allow any of the military crew to help, citing tight scheduling or some such. Vars would bet he was worried about exposing his people to aggressive nanobots.

"Not a single military crew member had D-tats. It's proof they knew something that we didn't!" Vars pressed. Tired as she was, she didn't have the energy to keep her emotions under control, and with Alice she felt like she didn't need to hide so much. She stopped fretting about surveillance on-board the ship too—they had bigger things to worry about. They needed to work as a team. "We don't have equal access to information!" she protested again. Without that, how could they make sound decisions together?

"Are you really surprised?" Alice said. "Somehow *they*

knew."

And here it was—us versus them...the wrong *us* versus them. It should have been humans versus aliens. And perhaps not even that. Vars rubbed her eyes—she had so much convincing to do.

"That's probably why we had so little trouble convincing them not to give you the implants before the mission," Alice continued.

"If that's the case, then why not have everyone—"

"Vars, we've already talked about this," Alice said. "Requiring everyone to undergo removal surgery back on Earth would have pushed out our departure. There clearly wasn't time. Ian's team had to go, and all of his people had implants...except us."

There was nothing to say to that. "What do you think will happen to Ebi and Ibe?" Vars asked.

She couldn't say she had developed a rapport with the twins, but it bugged her that Ebi and Ibe no longer had freedom of the ship. Even when they attended the science meetings, there were two burly crewmen stationed just behind their seats, as if to catch them in a traitorous act. It was crazy. And what about those tight schedules that Liut used as an excuse to avoid help with surgeries? Still, there was no evidence that the nanobots did anything more than attach themselves to the D-tats. And sure, that was bad, but did it give Liut the permission to take away the twins' freedom? Vars didn't think so. Unless Liut wasn't telling them something. Unless something else had happened back on Earth...or on Luna or Mars.

There were rumors that back on Earth some people developed so much additional cyberhumatics growth that they looked almost encased in nanobot exoskeletons. But even that didn't make Ebi and Ibe a danger to others...not yet.

"The twins will just have to wait until we get to a full medlab facility on Mars," Alice said. That was the closest location, and it was far behind them now. They were way past the orbit of Jupiter. "I'm hopeful that in the meantime, they'll be fine. There's so little freedom on a spaceship anyway, that practically, Terry's restrictions on their movements mean very little. Frankly, I'm more worried about Ian. The loss of arm control will impair his ability to function. It's bad now, but once we get to Mimas? There is no way that I can clear him for an EVA on the surface. He'll fight me on this. And it gives Terry the upper hand, so to speak."

None of the surgeries had been free of complications. There were numerous complaints about loss of sensation, painful scar tissue, and disfigurement. But Ian's arm suffered a lot of neurological damage. He would require extensive reconstruction surgery after they returned home. Except the standard treatment in such cases was to implant cyberhumatics to restore function while supporting the healing of tissues. So perhaps Ian was stuck with a bum arm for a while.

"You did great," Vars said. "The scars and most of the cosmetic issues can be addressed when we get back."

"I know." Alice gave her a weak smile. She didn't look convinced.

"Have you by chance heard anything from my dad?" Vars asked.

"No. Total blackout. I'm not getting anything from the Vaults or the wardens."

"Something crazy must have happened back there. I don't understand why the mission control isn't giving us all the information available. We need everything they've got if we're going to figure what these Mims want from us." She didn't believe that Liut was stupid enough to keep things from the scientists. What would be the point in that?

"But you've been thinking about it, Vars, right?"

A soft noise came from just outside the door. Alice looked questioningly at Vars.

"Yes," Vars said, both answering the question and confirming that she believed someone was listening in on their conversation. Not that it mattered. They were all on the same mission, on the same team. And to succeed, they needed to act like it.

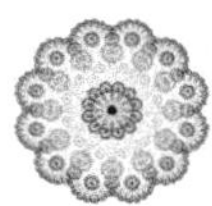

Ian assembled his science team in the ship's cafeteria, their all-hands-on-board meeting room. Most had bandages and synthetic skin on their arms and in some cases their necks and jaws as well. All looked like they'd lost weight.

"We've had a rough few weeks," Ian said. "But we have to get back to work. We're about to begin deceleration maneuvers. In only two weeks, we will enter into orbit around Saturn and then Mimas."

There was a sense of unease in the room. The news blackout from home cast a dark spell over the team. They had started out on a voyage of friendship and greetings to a new civilization; now they found themselves in the middle of what seemed to be a prelude to an invasion.

"So let's get back to what we know," Ian continued. "Vars?"

Vars had became the de facto leader of these team discussions, at least on the background research part. "What do the aliens want?" she asked the room. It finally dawned on everyone that in a first contact situation, it would be the sociologists and anthropologists, diplomats and lawyers that would take the lead. Those in the "hard sciences" didn't have enough grounding to extrapolate interspecies communication or alien motivations even to begin these negotiations.

"I want to start with listing resources," Vars said. She had given this a lot of thought and needed to get everyone on the same page. "We've already discussed that space travel requires advanced technology—"

"So do the nanobots," Ebi said. It was obvious that she had been scratching her arms and neck—the skin around her D-tats was red, raw, and angry. Vars felt bad for the girl; aside from prescribing some inflammation creams and some cold compresses, there wasn't anything Alice could do to help her or her brother, not out here.

"Yes," Vars said. "Nanobots require advanced tech as well. So we have three direct pieces of evidence that the Mims possess high-tech development: the nanobots, the artifact, and the fact that both are in our Solar System and thus managed to travel interstellar distances."

"And we know that both come from the same technological base," said Ian.

"We assume that, but we don't *know* it," Trish pointed out. "Though I think it's a fair assumption," she quickly added.

"We've already discussed time as a necessary resource," Vars said, "but I'd like to break it down in more detail, without putting a human spin on it." She had her notes on her personal tablet, like everyone else in the room now. "Time needs to be assessed at multiple scales. First, there needs to be enough time for life to develop. Then complex life, followed by intelligent life—by no means a given at any point. And only then can a highly advanced civilization arise—not a necessary outcome, but a necessary condition in this case."

"Obviously, we are constrained by the age of the universe and the distribution of heavy elements," Trish said. Vars was pleased that the woman had taken her suggestion so seriously and started with the basic givens. "So if the universe is just about fourteen billion years old—and to keep it simple, let's just say the Milky Way is about the same age—then we still need to roll through several star lifetimes to fuse enough heavy elements and release them via supernovas into the interstellar space for the formation of complex life."

"There is no organic chemistry without carbon," Ian said, nodding.

"Our sun is just over four and a half billion years old." Ben picked up on time line derivation analysis. "We have an abundance of carbon, oxygen, nitrogen, and so on. The first stars after the Big Bang would have been mostly hydrogen, some deuterium, a bit of helium..." Trish shook her head and Ben moved on to his main point. "Since Mims are using heavy elements in ways that resemble ours, we have to assume that their star system is not very much older than ours. I'd put the earliest date at about six billion years. Of course, their system could also be younger than ours. There's no reason to think their evolutionary path was as long as our own."

"Yes," Vars agreed. "Life on Earth had several setbacks. If not for the asteroid that hit the Yucatan Peninsula sixty-five million years ago, the descendants of dinosaurs could be sitting here instead of us, arguing why the Mims' nanobots are attaching to their cybernetic implants. We owe our ascent as a species to the Chicxulub impact."

"So we've now established a lower bound...kinda," said Ibe with a smirk. On the wall viewer beside him, he was pulling up artists' renditions of the dinosaurs' last days in all of their glory and with all of the gory details.

"Thank you for the visuals," Vars said. "The amazing thing about life on Earth is how fast it came to be. Fossil records demonstrate signs of life as early as a few million years after the planet's formation."

"Are you saying that's strange?" Evi said. "For this is our

area of expertise." She motioned to the group of six scientists, including Ian, who sat on her side of the room.

"Are you saying it's normal?" Vars countered. The speed of life emergence was a hot topic of debate in her community. But Evi and her colleagues were the obvious experts at this gathering.

"We don't have anything to compare it to," Evi said. "The life we found on Mars is just spores that found a way to drift from Earth—"

Saydi, another member of the exobiology team, cut in. "Or that could be the other way around. We could have evolved from Martian spores."

Evi brushed the remark aside. "The point is that everything living or life-building that we've discovered in our solar system so far had a single point of origin. We've all developed from a single spark of life."

"But only Earth managed to get beyond single-cell life forms," Alice pointed out. "And since life on Earth has been documented as far back as four billion years ago, it makes sense that Earth is the source of all life in our star system."

"All good points," Ian said, stepping in, "but it's not an argument we will resolve here today. I want to hear what Vars has to say. I believe you were talking about time?" Even impaired and on medications, Ian was better at controlling this group. Vars exhaled but went on; she wanted everyone to get on the same page. It was the only way to move forward... together, as a team.

"Yes. Let's assume that an almost immediate rise of life is typical in a planetary system capable of supporting it," Vars said. "Then we are talking about life that could have started around six billion years ago, right?"

"Approximately," said Ben.

"Approximately," Vars agreed. "A common ancestor of

all modern humans lived in Africa, approximately two and a half million years ago, by conservative estimates." With Africa all but wiped out in the Keres Triplets Event, there was no longer a possibility of furthering research in that area, not until radiation levels were back to safe levels...in a few million years...if humans lived that long. "*Homo sapiens* diverged from *Homo Neaderthalensis* some seven hundred thousand years ago." No one challenged her on this; she was back in her territory now. "Language, as we think of it," Vars continued, "was probably widespread by fifty thousand years ago, although it was very different from what we use now. Ten thousand years ago, humans started to grow their own food and domesticate various plant and animal species, including themselves."

"Humans domesticated humans?" Ben asked.

"That's one way of thinking about it," Vars said. "Like other domesticated animals, modern humans are products of arrested development—our heads stay huge, we take a very long time to mature, we need decades to learn the foundation of knowledge that would make us productive citizens. I could go on, but I would like to stay focused on the timescales."

"Please," said Ian. He looked impatient...and he wasn't alone.

"Our biggest technological spurt," Vars went on, "occurred only in the last three hundred years." Ben opened his mouth to speak, but she cut him off with a look. "And I know you can point to examples from previous centuries. But we are painting with very large brush strokes. The point I'm making is that—"

"If Mims were one of the original life forms in our galaxy, they could have almost two billion years on us," Ibe said, jumping right to the conclusion as usual.

"That's one possible timescale," Vars agreed.

"Okay," said Ben. "So we can look at the star systems within some reasonable distance from our solar system and see which are likely candidates for life."

"Distance is time," said Ibe and Ebi, almost simultaneously.

Ian ignored them. "I know you guys have already made a potential list of candidates," he said.

"Yes," said Ron, "but to narrow it down, we were hoping for something more useful from Vars than a two-billion-year head start." Ron hardly ever talked, so Vars turned to take a good look at the man. In his late fifties, he was the oldest member of the JPL team. His head was shaved now. Ron was balding before, as Vars recalled, but still wore his hair in a ponytail back on Earth. But long hair was a pain in space, so he must have shaved it all off for practical reasons—he wasn't vain, at least not about his appearance. He was tall and spindly, folding in on himself, perching rather than sitting next to the end of the table. Ron always looked as if he was getting ready to leave. Both of his arms were bandaged, and Vars remembered how badly his right arm ended up being perforated during the excision surgery. *Like Ian, Ron too must be in quite a bit of pain.* Yet the man hid it well.

"There are a number of different timescales," Vars repeated. "There's the life of the universe. The life of a star system. The age of the planet and when first life arises. The time span of the intelligent species. The age of the techno-logically advanced civilization. And then there's the lifespan of an individual."

"We've discussed this before," Ian snapped. His impatience was growing. Unfortunately, he was not the only one.

"Yes. But there are multiple ways of passing knowledge to the next generation," Vars said. "Coevolution of an intelligent species with a large stratification of cognitive abilities would provide for slave labor and would free up time to develop technology faster. On Earth, *Homo sapiens* exterminated all other hominids, but on other planets things could have evolved differently."

"What a shame. We could have used all those Neanderthals and *Homo floresiensis* to do our dirty work," said Ibe in a loud whisper.

"Oh, there were probably many, many more species of hominids than that," said Vars. "And yes, if they were around, they would have suffered the fates of the great apes and whales. We humans have a weakness for thinking ourselves superior."

"So we would have developed castes of workers or soldiers, leaving the intellectuals to push the boundaries of science," said Ian. "Specialization reduces the total resources necessary to train each potential member of the society, allocating more resources for exploration and further sub-fragmentation into skills-focused guilds. But are you saying Mims are like that?"

"I'm trying to make sure we're not making assumptions based on our own evolution. There are many paths to a starfaring civilization," Vars said. "We use cyberhumatics. But we've only begun on what's possible when it comes to augmenting human intelligence and memory capability. I'm sure you've all felt bereft of your implants. Those must have felt like part of your own intelligence, providing an instant access to all recorded human knowledge with just a thought."

Vars looked around and saw she'd hit a nerve. Back on Earth, unimplanted Seeds and augmented humans tested very differently on basic memory tests. As always, it was a case of use it or lose it. "If not for the nanobots," she went on, "we could have pushed and pushed cyberhumatics until we managed to compress the transfer of knowledge from one generation to the next into an ever shorter time period. We were on that road already." Ebi and Ibe were clear examples of a generation of humans that were enhanced practically since birth.

"Having knowledge that's easily accessible is not the same as being able to incorporate the individual data points into a coherent worldview," Alice said. She had been quiet up until now. Vars knew Alice felt that the others hadn't forgiven her for cutting them up the way she did. Maybe she was right about that. The others weren't overtly hostile, but everyone seemed to sit just a little further from Alice, positioning themselves so as not to actually look at her. It was difficult enough to forge a team without awkward antipathies. Vars stifled a sigh.

"True," she agreed with Alice's comment. "But cyber-humatics do give a big boost. Each generation stands on the shoulders of all who came before, and digital memory implants could significantly shorten the cycle of scientific discovery. Just imagine an instant informational update for the whole human race when a useful discovery is made. Or digitally implanting the memories and skills of each guild—"

"Now you're just spinning science fiction," Ian interrupted. "There's no evidence that Mims do this."

"Except the nanobots," Vars replied. "And we know that these bots come in flavors. Alice managed to grow out a few 'colonies,' for the lack of a better word, from various implant sites. Not all bots grew the same structures, although the box fractal is the most common pattern of growth."

"Like the diversity of structures we're seeing on Mimas," said Trish.

"So," said Ben, "let's imagine we have a super advanced civilization that sends a probe to our solar system. Would it send something big? No. It would send a small probe full of self-replicating nanobots."

Ian nodded in agreement. "Our own Mimas mini probe drones will gather samples for us. Same idea." They had several ready to launch when they arrived at the Saturn's moon.

"I don't think it's a good idea to bring anything from Mimas on board," Alice said.

"Our ship is teeming with nanobots, and so far it hasn't been a problem," Ron said.

"So far," Alice echoed. "But *something* triggered the behavior of the bots back on Earth and the colonies. Would bringing a sample of the artifact into the ship trigger another set of unforeseen behaviors?"

"How long have you known about the link between the signal and the nanobots?" said a voice from the doorway.

Everyone turned to see Major Liut standing there. Vars wondered how long he had been listening—but then again, it wasn't as if what they were discussing was a secret. All meeting notes were shared and posted for everyone to read or watch. Vars also noticed that Alice was facing the door—she knew Liut was standing there the whole time. Was her question for his benefit?

"As long as you, I assume," Alice answered.

Ian looked from her to Liut. "Terry? Is there something you would like to add? We're working on a very compressed time schedule. We won't have the luxury to blue-sky like this once we land on Mimas."

Liut stepped forward. "Thirty-two years ago, Alice, your Seed Vault sent out Dr. Matteo Volhard and his daughter to study microplastics across Earth's ecosystems." Everyone looked to Vars. She sat stone-faced; she didn't know what Major Liut wanted from her or Alice. They were all on the same side in this—humans versus Mims—they needed to start acting like it too. "And you left the Vault just a few years after that," he said to Alice. It sounded like an accusation.

"More than a decade later," Alice corrected him. "But Ian knows all about my history."

"Isn't it a strange coincidence that you and Vars and Matteo just happen to work on the most important project to face humanity?" Liut pushed.

"What are you saying?" Vars asked. "That…that we somehow knew of the aliens and didn't mention it?" It was preposterous.

"Did the Vaults know?" Liut asked.

"Of course not," Alice said.

"Then why is Dr. Volhard made to work in the lab in the far north of Finland?"

"What?" Vars asked. She knew of no such thing. "My dad went back into the Vault?"

"Of course not," said Liut. "No one goes back into the Vault. And all the Vaults must be on lockdown on Earth and on Luna. They would have placed themselves into total isolation. And that only supposed to happen during an extinction-level event." He glared at Vars.

Ian got to his feet. "Do you have more information about what's going on with the nanobots back on Earth, Terry?" He said the name Terry like a slap. "Because if you do, we need to know it *now*."

"We just got a report from Mars," Liut said. "They're having problems with their extons and other equipment."

"What does that mean?" Ron asked.

"There've been deaths," said Liut. "So if you know something and aren't telling us…" He looked menacingly from Vars to Alice.

"Matteo came to me with information about the nanobots just before liftoff," Alice said.

"You knew?" several scientists exclaimed at the same time.

"Only that the bots existed," Alice said. "Matteo didn't want his daughter implanted. And I made my own decision to have the cyberhumatics removed."

"Anything else?" said Ian, frowning.

Alice thrust out her chin. "The Vaults didn't know about the Mimas artifact—I'm sure of it. But they *were* worried first about microplastics pollution and then about nanobots and the danger those bots might pose, even if at the time there was no proof of any risks. And the fastest way to get going on this mission was to keep the existence of the nanobots a secret. The Vault Elders knew that it would only be a short time before everyone knew." She turned to face Major Liut. "But it's obvious *you* knew about the bots before we left Earth."

"I wondered why none of your crew had implants," Ben said, as if just seeing the connection. "But of course it's obvious. You knew! What else do you know, Major Liut?"

"I came to ask you the same question," he protested.

"Alice? Vars?" Ian said. "Do you have anything else to add?"

"We haven't heard from the Elders since communications with Earth went down," Vars said.

"And before that?"

"Just that my dad was working with various nanobot samples. Alice got a few basic updates from the Vault Elders and shared those with everyone here. The temperatures at which nanobots fell apart came from him. But I had no idea that my dad went north or was in some kind of secret lab. The Elders never mentioned anything, and we were never in direct contact with my dad." Vars took a deep breath. "Is my father okay, Major Liut?"

"I don't know," he said. "We lost contact with the Vaults a while ago." Vars gasped. "But then we've lost contact with our mission control, too. We're flying blind." Every face in the room reflected the shock that Vars felt. This was worse than Liut hiding information...much worse.

"Then I think we're all in the same boat, so to speak," said Ben. "We all have to work on solving the Mims problem. No secrets, right?" He looked at Vars and Alice. They both nodded. "Right?" he asked Liut.

"I hope not," the major said. He sat down, joining the meeting. "If this is an invasion, we're on the front line. It's our job to solve this." He sounded tired.

After Liut joined them, the meeting devolved into accusations, the twins started to scream, and Ian put an end to it by asking everyone to work alone or in small groups for the next day or so until the tensions had a chance to die down. Emotions were just too raw. Not for the first time, Vars regretted not coming clean about nanobots right away. It might have slowed down their departure, but it would have made them into a more cohesive team. And the excision surgeries wouldn't have resulted in so much damage if performed back on Earth. It was one of the reasons Liut's people were in much better physical and emotional shape than Ian's. And that made the division between scientists and the military crew even deeper. The damage from all this mistrust was difficult to calculate.

Vars suspected Ian was going to need to negotiate hard with Liut for control. Who was in charge of this mission now? Who got to make the ultimate decisions now that they were cut off from Earth? She was worried that Ian might be mistaken about his own position within the command hierarchy onboard their ship. But then if this was an invasion, Liut and his crew *should* take over as the military representatives of Earth. It would be hard to argue that was inappropriate. But were they at war? It was too easy to jump to conclusions. And they were all very jumpy...

"Were you really a Seed?" Ben surprised her as he joined Vars on her way back to her stateroom. Vars tried to turn to face the man and overcompensated, smashing her head on the ceiling. "Are you all right?" he asked.

Vars only grumped in return, stopping herself from rubbing the newly developing bump on her head. The corridors of the ship were equipped with hand and foot holds to help people move around in low gravity. One "step" was really a long jump, and Vars had more cuts and bruises than she cared to remember from hitting the walls and scraping the various storage compartment handles as she bounced around like a crazy ball in a marble maze.

"I'll just walk you back to you room," he said with a smile. Vars turned like a sack of potatoes and, without answering Ben's original question, pulled herself farther along the corridor. She didn't know why Ben was following her. He was certainly better at navigating the turns than her, although far from graceful with his arm in a sling—the surgery made him a bit clumsy too.

"Here we are," Vars said. "Thank you for seeing me safely back to my quarters." She was tired and cranky and wanted to try to contact her dad via the Vault again, regardless of the futility of trying. If he moved into one of the Vault-run facilities, there should be a better chance of establishing communication with him than if he was back at his civilian lab in Seattle. The Vaults knew why they were going to Mimas, knew the need for communication. How long ago did he move? Why didn't the Elders mention something to Alice?

"Do you mind if I come in?" Ben asked.

Vars was so taken aback by the unexpected request that she just waved him inside, her social norms winning out. Ben slid in and closed the door. Vars looked at him expectantly.

"Look, I don't know if our rooms are bugged or anything," he said. Vars nodded in acknowledgment—she didn't know for a fact, but it was a safe assumption they were all being monitored. She wasn't even sure that was a bad idea, given the nanobots and all. "But it doesn't matter, not anymore," he finished.

"Why not?"

"Well, if we're really under attack by a superior alien force, then we'd better all work together."

Vars was silent. She still didn't know what Ben wanted of her.

"Do you mind if I sit?" he asked and slid into the only seat—Vars's desk chair—before she had a chance to answer. "Let me get straight to the point. I want to work with you, Vars."

"What do you mean?" Bigger than most, her cabin still felt very crowded.

"Like Ian said, we're to break up and work in small teams. And I think we'd make a good team." He beamed at her.

Vars sat on her built-in bed pod. Her plan had always been to work with Alice. She knew and trusted the woman; they got along, whereas her communications with Ben had been limited to group meetings. Well, that and playing nurse when his D-tats started to act up.

"I see you're uncertain about this," he said. "So let me convince you."

"Please." Vars inhaled and settled down for his sales pitch.

"Look, I think when we all get together, we never actually get to the point you're trying to make. And it's not you," he waved his hands when Vars was about to cut him off, "it's the room. We're just a bunch of know-it-alls who've worked together for years and now resent having to listen to some stranger with a soft science background and a *seedy* past." He smiled a crooked smile. "You are a Seed, aren't you?"

"Technically?" Vars said. "Not really. And I've only learned that my dad was one when Ian kidnapped me from my book tour." She ignored the soft scientist jab—she was used to that one, even back at her own university.

"Well, all of us have a tainted past. For instance, I went to Caltech."

"I've heard," Vars said, but she found herself smiling. Ben was easygoing and kind. It was difficult to push him away.

"So I think we can do great things together. Mix it up a bit. Because if we stick to our own groups, we'll come up with the same solutions over and over again. That was the reason Ian brought you in, Vars—to shake things up."

"Did Ian suggest you work with me?"

"Nah, Ian doesn't get credit for that. This was all my idea. Besides, one can only take Trish for so long." He imitated the scientist's high-pitched voice: *"I'm the smartest person in this room."*

Vars laughed.

"See? It would even be fun."

Vars knew when she was beaten. "So when do we start?"

"Right away, of course. Now!" Ben pulled out his personal computing pad, and his demeanor changed from playful to serious. "What were the other points you were trying to make today?"

"Okay, now's as good a time as any, I suppose." Vars pulled out her own pad and gathered her notes. All just random streams of consciousness at this point, but Ben seemed willing to listen and help shape her thoughts. She needed that help. "I've been thinking a lot about the why question," she said.

"Why the Mims are here?" Ben asked. "Well that's the million-dollar question, isn't it?"

"There has to be a good reason. Travelling interstellar distances takes so long that it doesn't make sense to send species representatives just to go out exploring. It's too costly. It requires an enormous investment of time and resources."

"Agreed—space tourism works only in the movies. Which is why the Mims didn't come themselves. They sent a probe and nanobots."

"That is cheaper," Vars agreed, "but it still requires planning and patience that spans thousands of years."

"If not more."

"If not more. So why bother?"

"Curiosity," Ben said. "We'd do it as soon as we're able. Go where no man has—"

"—gone before," Vars finished. "Yeah, I get that. But that's us. Humans. We're driven by curiosity. Not all species have the same motivation."

"Okay, so let's say an advanced species is looking to spread itself across several star systems," Ben said. "We'll be doing that too. We've already moved beyond Earth—all eggs in one basket and all that wisdom."

"Which saves us from some freak asteroid impact."

"Always fighting the last battle, right? But it doesn't protect us from some stray stellar encounter or a speeding orphan planet zooming through our solar system, disrupting every planetary orbit, or a super nova in our galactic neighborhood, or a bunch of other freak cosmic mishaps. Humans *have* to spread into the stars in order to ensure our survival."

"Would that be common wisdom among other civilizations? Would Mims think the same way?"

"They'd be facing the same galactic hazards, wouldn't

they?"

"Okay, let's take that as our starting position," Vars said. "Any civilization advanced enough to be capable of crossing from star to star would use that technology to ensure its own survival by starting colonies."

"I'd say that's a sound assumption. It would probably make sense to talk about stellar neighborhoods."

"Keeping the colonies within communication distance?"

"Well, it would still be difficult to communicate between colonies even if they spread within just a hundred-light-year radius."

"Yes, and so we come back to the Tasmania problem," Vars said. "At such distances, it's easy to lose touch with far-flung colonies. And then there's divergent evolution problem—once the populations split, it's just a matter of time before the colonies would speciate."

"Point taken. So after just a few thousand years, if the colonies survive, they'll become something else."

"And cultural evolution—and divergence—will progress even faster," Vars said. "Think how fast human language split up."

"And how equally fast it came back together," Ben noted.

"That too. Societies evolve to take advantage of their circumstances."

"And yet some traditions stick. We still put up a Christmas tree in my family every year. Isn't that a pagan tradition?"

"It is," Vars agreed. "But the point I'm making is that time makes a cohesive star-faring civilization difficult. The Mims's artifact is thousands of years old."

"Perhaps twenty-seven hundred years. At least, that's our best guess at the moment. We'll refine that estimate once we get our hands on it."

"I still think that's a bad idea," Vars said. She stood up

and started pacing or as close to that as one could get in a low g and cramped space environment. The trick was to keep her head and limbs from smashing...

"Don't worry, Vars. We'll figure out a way to test the artifact without bringing it on board. Ron is working on a solution with Liut's people, Ziva and Jay from engineering."

That made Vars feel a bit better—not only that people were looking into solutions but the fact that scientists and crew were working together on something. She stopped pacing...bumping. "Okay. Let's assume, just as a starting point, that aliens live about as long as we do. Let's call that one hundred years. Twenty-seven hundred years would be twenty-seven lifespans. And over a hundred generations."

"Good point. Twenty-seven lifespans ago, we were in the peak of Hellenistic civilization. The Roman Empire had yet to rise and fall," Ben said. "Which means we're not thinking about this the right way."

Vars liked that he got her thinking so fast, without too much explanation. "Exactly! So why would an alien civilization send a probe to another star system, wait for almost three thousand years, and then attack the dominant intelligent species of that star system on its homeworld and colonies? What would be the point?" A wave of exhaustion hit Vars so hard that she swayed and had to settle back down on her bed pod.

Ben noticed. "And that's why Ian put you on the team, Dr. Volhard." He smiled at her. "It's been very productive talking with you. Shall we pick this up again first thing tomorrow morning?"

"Sure," she said. She was asleep within moments of Ben leaving her stateroom.

Chapter Eleven

"So what's our goal now?" Sophie asked from her hospital bed. She was still too weak to be of much help in the lab, and she would require a lot of reconstructive surgery when... if they ever got out of this place.

"Now we try to grow out these beasts," Phoebe said. "I want to see what they can become, understand their true purpose."

"Aside from taking over every human?"

"I don't think that's their true purpose. If you sent a probe across the galaxy, would you want to take over the dominant intelligent species at the end of your destination?"

"Depends," Sophie said, trying to get out of bed. The woman was unsteady but determined. One had to admire that...

"You can give yourself a few days," Phoebe said.

"We don't have a few days," Matteo muttered. "Vars will be on Mimas in just a week."

"Does it matter? We have no way of communicating with her ship," Phoebe said.

"Us? No. But the Elders do. By now, Alice would have removed all of the cyberhumatics from the team—"

"How do you know that?" Sophie asked.

"The Elders told the military about the problem before

they left. So even if Alice didn't get a chance to push for removal early on, the top officer on the expedition would have ordered it once they were far enough past Mars for the mission to proceed regardless of the condition of its members."

Phoebe glanced over at Sophie. She hoped Alice had done better with her crew than she managed with the Australian Seed. But of course that was a given—Alice had known she would need to perform the excisions; she had practiced. Phoebe, while a trained surgeon, had been unprepared. Others were to bring those skills into their lab...others that never made it here. Everything happened too fast.

"So let's get this done," Sophie said. She used her IV pole for support as she walked over to the lab side of the room. "Show me."

Matteo carefully explained the experiments he and Phoebe had set up in the week Sophie spent on ice. Once again they were using isolation chambers to grow the various structures from the different samples of nanobots—excluding the one sample that had gotten out of control. Then Matteo walked Sophie over to a thick glass wall. There, behind the glass, he and Phoebe were working on an ethically unsavory experiment. The lab had several rats, and Phoebe had implanted them with simple cyberhumatics. The rats were then exposed to the various "species" of nanobots.

The truth was the Elders had wanted them to use primates or even human volunteers for this experiment. Back then, Phoebe had flatly refused. Somewhere out there, she was sure, other labs were experimenting with humans, but she wouldn't do it. The thought made her skin crawl. *For now, just rats. And later? Well, there are only the three of us left in here.* Still she found it unsettling that the first four volunteers sent into their lab were heavily implanted with cyberhumatics. Coincidence? She didn't think so.

"We've discovered that nanobots evolve," Matteo was saying. "Here's a rat infected with the nanobots from Northeastern Australia." Phoebe noted his use of the word "infection"—which wasn't how she thought of it. "And here's one with the nanobots we removed from your body."

The rat with Sophie's nanobots was almost twice the size of the other specimen. It had grown a carapace that shielded all of its back and part of its head, with several protrusions coming off the top. The nanobot-created structure was still flexible enough for the rat to sit up on its hind legs, but the animal didn't move much. Could it if it wanted to? Phoebe had no idea. Imaging internal organs and skeletal structures, i.e., exposing the ray to X-rays, could change the behavior

of the nanobots. Thus, imaging was saved for later analysis. They did leave food and water two feet away from the creature—when it got hungry, it would have to move. But for now, the rat monster just sat there, passively observing them. *Unnerving.*

"What are those for?" Sophie asked about the protrusions.

"No idea," Matteo said. "We've just been allowing the various growths to take form and tracking the differences."

"They *are* very different," Sophie said.

Phoebe noted that as Sophie was examining the modified rats, the woman started to turn a nasty shade of green. Perhaps Sophie was just doing too much...or perhaps she was experiencing the same reaction Phoebe had looking at these nanobot-modified rats: fear. Deep-seated, elemental fear.

Phoebe rolled a desk chair under Sophie. "Here," she said. "Sit." Sophie collapsed into the chair. "It gets easier with familiarity," she added. And that was almost true. Phoebe could now force herself to look at the rats with a degree of scientific detachment...almost.

"Would I have..." Sophie didn't finish, but Phoebe knew what she was asking. *Would I have grown into something like that?*

"It's not what happened to... You know," Matteo said and turned away.

Phoebe had noticed that Matteo couldn't really talk about the three research assistants who died. They both knew they should have dissected them and looked for clues, but... Well, some things required getting used to, and some were beyond even that.

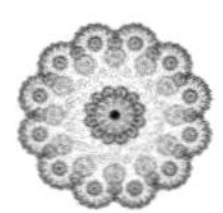

Even under total isolation from the world outside, Matteo and Phoebe decided to continue their work in the lab. They would get the results out somehow. And Sophie was getting strong enough to start contributing significantly to their work. It was good to have another pair of hands and a brilliant mind applied to the problem. The regiment of blood-filtering that each of them needed to endure took a lot of time. It was exhausting, draining.

They infected another two rats with Sophie's strain of nanobots and allowed them to interact in the same enclosure. These rats' carapaces grew twice as fast, and soon they started to fuse together into one super nanobot-controlled organism. It was sick, and Phoebe couldn't wait to destroy them…it.

"Why? What's the purpose?" Matteo muttered as he went around the lab recording data for a report to the Elders.

"Are we ready for dissections?" Sophie asked.

"Are you sure you're up for it?" Phoebe asked. Sophie was more qualified with the cyberhumatics, but her left hand was gone, and her right was extensively damaged. She was having problems feeling her pinkie in that hand, and there were tremors. The AI-assisted surgical arm would compensate for a lot for Sophie's difficulties, but would that be enough?

"I'm perfectly capable of using the controls with my right hand," she said defiantly.

"Yes, but—"

"I've had years of experience with this, Phoebe. If there's something worth noting, I'll note it," Sophie snapped at her.

Phoebe helped Sophie get into her biohazard suit, then tucked away the left sleeve so it wouldn't get in the way. She felt this was a mistake, but Matteo had said it would be good for Sophie, a way for her to regain some control over her new reality. And with just the three of them, they couldn't afford to baby her. Not that Sophie would let them.

When Sophie was ready, Matteo opened the airlock doors. He'd set up a double-door system with a passage that could be flash-heated to kill any nanobots that escaped the rat lab. It wasn't enough to completely keep their living area free of bots, but it helped.

As soon as Sophie stepped into the lab, Matteo closed the door remotely behind her. There weren't many precautions for getting through the airlock on the way in—just close the first door and then proceed to open the next. It was only on the way out that they first blew super-refrigerated air into the airlock to slow down any nanobots clinging to the hazmat suits. The suits were then removed and left in the airlock when the person exited, whereupon the airlock would be sealed again on both sides and the temperature would go up high enough to fry the bots. The suits could withstand the heat.

Inside, Sophie went straight to the enclosure and slipped her right arm inside the control glove for the robotic arm. Manipulating the glove with tactile commands, she grabbed the pair of freshly fused rats and transferred them into the dissection chamber. She injected them both with a tranquilizer cocktail; there was no point in hurting the animals.

Even as the rats lost consciousness, the nanobots continued to build. If anything, the speed of construction accelerated. At the rate that the bots were repurposing the rats' tissues and chemical components, there soon wouldn't be any rat organs left.

"What are they building?" Phoebe said to herself for the umpteenth time. She and Matteo were watching Sophie's actions on the monitors, as well as looking directly through the glass wall.

Sophie placed the rats belly up, carapace down. Before their eyes, the limbs disappeared, consumed by the bots.

Then the tails went, too. What had once been two distinct rats was now a mass of undifferentiated tissue that was slowly being sucked into a fractal shape.

Sophie used the magnifying eye to zoom in, and Matteo and Phoebe leaned in to see the image on their side of the lab. At that range, the nanobots took on the quality of an artificial beehive. There was buzzing and purpose, and yet it was all seemingly random, to the eyes of the human observers, anyway.

Matteo spoke into the microphone. "Try cutting into it."

Sophie instructed the robotic arm to begin the dissection protocol they had programmed earlier. This was the same robotic arm that Phoebe used in Sophie's surgery, and it was fully capable of doing microscopic work, even removing one nanobot at a time. But at the moment, they just wanted to see if the structure had any differentiated layers like outer skin, organelles, connective tissues, or the equivalent. Were the nanobots mindlessly transmuting everything into a single, ever-repeating pattern, or were they truly trying to create something new? And if so, what?

Light, pincers, and scalpel descended into the seething mass. Sophie's right arm plunged with exaggerated movements around the rat enclosure, and the robotic arm translated her big gestures into micro precision cuts. It was clear that Sophie was very adept with this equipment, even without relying on cyberhumatics. There was elegance to her movements, like a dance. With just one arm, Sophie was better at this than Matteo or Phoebe. It had been the right decision to assign this job to her.

Snip, plunk, swish. Another snip. Sophie removed layer after layer of nanobots. The merging of the flesh and the nonbiological material was amazing, nothing like the cyberhumatics, which functioned as separate components with an interface to the body. These structures were fully integrated.

"We can learn from this," Sophie said. She opened up the rats like they were some Hieronymus Bosch flower, one hellish petal after another.

A screech reverberated through the whole building, like microphone feedback but louder—piercing and painful.

Phoebe and Matteo clamped their hands over their ears.

The sound stopped after a second, but then Sophie's robotic arm started to vibrate. She took a step back from the dissection chamber, her arm still inside the controls. Suddenly, the robotic arm got pulled into the enclosure, and then just as suddenly it sprang free. Sophie was tossed around by her right arm. Without another arm to stabilize herself, it took a moment for her to get to her feet.

"It's gone," Sophie said, looking into the rats' enclosure. Her voice had a hint of hysteria.

"What's gone?" Matteo said. "Step away, Sophie, the cameras aren't tracking right. We can't see."

Sophie took a step to the side, and Phoebe and Matteo were able to see the now-empty enclosure through the glass wall. Where the rats had been there was now nothing.

Sophie pointed to the robotic arm. It was still moving, but it was…different. There was a new bend to the robotic appendage.

"Sophie, get your arm out of it! Let go!" Phoebe screamed.

Sophie tried, but her arm was stuck in the machine. Phoebe saw her say something but couldn't tell what it was; her microphone, like the cameras, had just stopped working.

"We have to get her out of there!"

Matteo was already suiting up. "Get her to stay away from that thing," he said as he jumped into the airlock.

Phoebe looked back at Sophie, who had stumbled and fallen to her knees, her biohazard suit ripped. The nanobot structure was already growing from the robotic arm controls directly onto Sophie's shoulder and neck, around the bandages—into the area where Phoebe had cut off all cyberhumatics just days ago. Phoebe felt dread. She lifted her eyes and met Sophie's. Sophie started to yell, but her throat was immediately swarmed with nanobot structures.

"Matteo! Don't go in there! It's too late!" Phoebe screamed.

He heard her. Through a combination of effort and extreme fear, he stayed inside the airlock. His knees buckled. From the floor, both arms on the inside door, he watched Sophie being consumed by nanobots.

Phoebe punched the lock to open the airlock door back into their side of the room. She was confident that the door to the nanobot enclosure on the opposite side of the airlock would now be locked—everything was set up so only one door could be opened at a time. That was a standard feature of all biohazard lab junctures.

"Matteo?" she called softly. "Please. Come back." She stepped into the airlock and gently guided him out, locking the second door behind them. She felt better with two doors between them and whatever was left of Sophie.

She helped Matteo out of his suit. And then they went back to watching the grotesque transformation of their colleague on the other side of the safety glass.

Chapter Twelve

For the next week, Vars and Ben were inseparable, spending all of their time brainstorming the *whys* of Mims. It was a good thing they had paired up too, since it had fallen to Alice to minister to all of the recovering scientists—she was the most qualified medic on board—leaving Vars without her usual research companion. And the kind of work Vars was trying to do—Gedanken experiments on the nature of galactic alien civilizations—required the back and forth of a deep dialogue. Ben was good at this. Almost as good as Alice…or Vars's dad.

"I want to get back to your ideas about available resources," Ben said. He and Vars were in his quarters this time. Ron, Ben's roommate, was working with engineering crew most of the time now, and Ben and Vars had free run of his space during the day shift. Variety was important to creativity. The nearly identical rooms weren't ideal for that, but Ben's did have two bed pods instead of one—something. "If we evolved in a star system with only one planet," he continued, "our resources post-Keres Triplets would have been dismal."

"We might have looked to developing space stations," Vars said. She sat on the floor on a big square pillow that Ben had managed to scrounge from somewhere. "We started with space stations before building permanent Elfies on the moon."

"Yes," Ben said, but with impatience in his voice. Vars had learned by now that when he got like this, it meant he had a brainstorm and wanted to share something with her. But Ben never just came out and said anything outright. He preferred the Socratic method of interaction, where he asked Vars pointed questions until she reached the same conclusion as him. It was maddening sometimes, especially because Vars had a similar style of discussion and they were only days from reaching Saturn. The ship was about to reassume its more maneuverable configuration, folding back into one rigid mass propelled by multiple engines. That meant the loss of what little pseudo gravity they maintained via rotation. It was all necessary for slowing down and landing on Mimas; and Ian was riding Vars and the rest of his group hard to present their ideas before that happened.

"So are you talking mineral wealth?" Vars asked. Without access to asteroids for metals and comets for water, it would have been difficult to colonize the solar system as much as humans had done in the last hundred years.

"Not only," Ben said. "I'm also talking about real estate. To expand into the stars, a civilization would presumably need to begin within its own star system. So systems with just one planet would be at a disadvantage right from the start. Sort of like what you were discussing in your book about domestication of animals and plants: people who lived in areas with a variety of good options for domestication—the wild ancestors of goats, cows, horses, rice—got ahead a lot faster than people in poor resource areas. So luck is critical to developing a star-faring civilization."

"I see your point," Vars said. "Our system is rich in planets and resources." Not to mention, human science exploration would have suffered from lack of examples of other planetary bodies to study. Variety was important for spurring invention,

Vars knew.

Ben pushed on. "Alice was talking the other day about the wealth of our DNA heritage. The sheer diversity of life on Earth, and to a lesser degree on Mars, on Jupiter's moons, and even on Titan, is extraordinary, don't you think?"

"Alice is a Seed. She grew up thinking about DNA diversity in this way," Vars said. "But yes, we do have an abundance of evolutionary solutions to living in extreme environments and to generating energy—"

"Yes! And motion. We use biomimetics all the time. It's the go-to solution on my team." Ben's eyes twinkled with excitement. He'd once told Vars that his expertise in solving robotic motion problems by studying animals' movements was what had gotten him a role on Ian's team in the first place. With Mims, his job was to extrapolate backwards, to reverse-engineer from the movements of artificial specimens to the possible biology of their makers. "We had an army of different AI-controlled miniature robots to build our colonies on Mars and on the moon. They were all designed based on our observations of nature. Our machines slither like snakes into the crevices of asteroids, swim like jellyfish in the oceans of Europa, crawl like crabs on the surface of Mars. And it's not just the engineering solutions. Alice talked about splicing DNA to create life that would someday make Mars more like Earth. We have an abundance of riches here."

"It's always easier to steal than to start from scratch," Vars agreed. "Are you saying that alien civilizations would covet our star system for its biodiversity and lucky configuration of planets?"

"I'm just extrapolating from what you wrote in your book about civilizations on Earth. We had winners and losers. And it had nothing to do with native intelligence or ability. Unlike the other great apes, humans have very limited genetic diversity. The winners and losers were predominantly determined by their initial geographic location. So wouldn't the same be true on a galactic scale? Too close to the center of the galaxy, and the chance of being exterminated by some violent gamma ray event in a neighboring star system or some stray orphan planet becomes too high. Too far out on the edges of the spiral arms or galactic halo, and the distance between neighboring stars is just too great for colonization efforts. Distances, energies, and densities are all parts of the fates of interstellar life."

"So not only is Earth in the Goldilocks Zone of our own planetary system," Vars said, "but our sun is well placed in relation to the galactic neighborhood. Am I getting it? In which case, I'm guessing you and your team have created a list of other star systems that are advantageously positioned?"

"Wait on that, Vars. I want to get back to that *why* question. Why would someone send a probe to our star system, wait a few millennia, and then attack us?"

"If you're saying that our solar system has intrinsic value, then you've answered your own question," said Vars. "Mind you, I'm not agreeing, not yet." She liked Ben when he got this super enthusiastic, but it was hard to argue with him at these times. She'd learned just to nod, give gentle encouragements, and wait for Ben to share his ideas in a systematic way.

"I know, I know." Ben was up and circling the cramped space of his room. Vars had to duck under his windmilling arms now and then. "But resources are everything. It's really your idea, Vars. I'm just repeating it. We barely survived the human-ending event of 2057. And we refocused our energies on spreading human seeds—sorry for the reference—as wide as we can. But if we only had the one planet, our options would have been much more limited."

"If the 'human-ending event' was one of the things you

mentioned before—a stray orphan planet disrupting our system, a supernova event too close, or a million of other cosmically horrible events—then having a well-stocked star system wouldn't be enough," Vars said.

"Yes. And that's why humans' long-term plan has to be to go to the stars. To ensure survival, we need to spread far and wide."

"That's a distant future."

"Yes. For now. But we're talking about a two-billion-year range, right? Mims might have had time to plan that far."

"So your theory is that Mims are here to take over our solar system for their colonies?"

"If humans think this way, wouldn't other intelligences? And it never worked out well for the indigenous populations of Earth when technologically-advanced and resource-rich colonists arrived and took their lands."

"It's a leap, Ben. Remember when we talked about human nature? It was *your* point. Humans bear their evolutionary baggage of millions of years. But other civilizations will have their own natures, their own evolutionary paths. Comparing the base motivations of humans to aliens doesn't make sense."

"It's not about their nature, Vars. No one wants to go extinct because the universe BURPS."

"Burps?"

"BURPS—it's an acronym. B is for Burned by stellar evolution. The sun will turn into a red giant and swallow up Mercury, Venus, Earth, and Luna. This is just a matter of time; we have this on our schedule.

"U is for Undone by a cosmic cataclysm. A supernova, a gamma ray burst, or some galactic center event that burns away our atmosphere and singes all life across Earth and its solar system colonies. Again, it's just matter of statistics: sooner or later something will blow up too near to us.

"R is for Ripped by a stray stellar bullet. The solar system rips apart by coming too close to some other galactic inhabitants. We set up the Asteroid Hunter Program after the Keres Triplets event, but if a whole planet, or a star, or a black hole were to swing our way, we'd be helpless to stop it. The only way for humans to survive such an event would be to have a colony in another star system. Hopefully far enough away to remain unaffected by the loss of our home world.

"P is for Poisoned by our own hubris. Plagues, wars, evil AI, ecological disasters. We were almost there once. In fact, the Triplets might have saved us from this particular destiny. But in a few centuries, we're bound to forget and start tinkering all over again. It might be part of our human nature.

"And finally, S is for Stagnate through lack of advancement. Humans get bored and die out." Ben sat back down. "That's BURPS."

"I see you've given this a lot of thought," Vars said. "But dying of boredom, Ben, really?"

"I would," Ben said with a smile. "Wouldn't you?"

Vars allowed herself a chuckle. "So allow me to summarize your ideas."

"Not just mine."

"Fine. Any civilization that survives to acquire space flight would need to plan on expanding and exporting its people to the stars to ensure its own survival."

"It's how it has to be," Ben said. "The one thing we've learned about life—granted, only in our own solar system—is that it strives to survive. It mutates and pushes the boundaries and takes over ecosystems, but it refuses to die."

"And once that life acquires intelligence—"

"It puts its mind into survival."

"And you believe Mims want what we have."

"That would be one interpretation, but not the only one,"

Ben said.

"What are some others?"

"That's where you come in, Vars. You're the expert." He leaned back and smiled smugly at her. Sometimes, Vars got a sense that this was all unreal to Ben—fun and games, all an intellectual challenge. It's like he was able to forget that the world was hanging on the balance. And when Vars was with him, he made it easy for her to forget too, to get carried away in these conversations. It some ways, Ben made it easier for Vars to think beyond the horror of the moment. Sometimes, when she considered what was really happening, she just wanted to curl up and give up.

"Are you sure Ian didn't assign you to me?" Vars asked. She could see Ian doing just that.

"Nah, it was my idea. And really, I'm just spurring you on and giving you another perspective on your own work. Didn't you say that if not for a cosmic accident, it would be dinosaurs and not us?"

"So basically you're saying that in just a few years, we might be the ones sending probes full of little robots to explore other worlds?"

"It's in the works already."

"Where? Where would you send the first probe?" Vars asked, getting pulled back into the *what if* game.

"Well, it's still up for debate. But it's just a question of time and resources. In 2017, the National Aeronautics and Space Administration—"

"I know of NASA."

"NASA announced the discovery of Ross 128. It's a single-planet star system with a well-behaved star—"

"Well-behaved?"

"Quiet, not a lot of eruptions of radiation, small flares, basically a nice and steady source of light, heat, and energy.

Perfect for our type of life. The planet, Ross 128, is a just a twinge larger than Earth and lies right inside the habitable zone. Perfect."

"But only one planet," Vars said.

"Yes, that's a big downside. Before I met you, I would have voted for that world. But now? Now, ideally, we want a rich star system, full of planets. Something like Trappist-1. The name came from the telescope that discovered the system: Transiting Planets and Planetesimals Small Telescope. Anyway, it's an ultracool dwarf star with seven Earth-sized planets orbiting at good distances for life. The fourth, fifth, and sixth planets in that system lie completely within the habitable zone."

"That's perfect!" Vars ignored the importance that Ben had placed on her thoughts. She didn't feel that influential. She was barely keeping up...

"Yes. Based on some preliminary observations of seasonal variations of atmospheric methane on the sixth planet, we're pretty sure there's at least primitive life there. Of course, after 2057, all of the Earth's resources were focused on our immediate survival. It's only in the last decade or so that we've returned to searching for potential exoplanets to colonize."

"So is Trappist-1 on the list for human colonization?"

"Well, no. Unfortunately, this system is forty light years away."

"So it's interesting long-term perhaps, but not for an initial colony," Vars said.

"Precisely."

"And Mims, presumably, would think along the same lines."

"Presumably. Alas, the speed of light is still the law of our universe."

"It's not like *Star Trek*," Vars said with a smile. "So Mims sent out a bunch of probes into their immediate stellar neighborhood to look for potentially good locations for their colonies."

"The smaller the probe, the less flexible the technology within, the cheaper the investment per probe…which means the more systems Mims can afford to visit."

"Right. So let's say they find a couple of good locations. Then what?"

"It's very costly to send a real colony ship. As you've said, it's not like *Star Trek*. The real colony ship would be a one-way trip for its passengers."

"So you have to prep the place," Vars said.

She thought about Spain and Portugal sending ships across the globe in the fifteen and sixteen hundreds. At the time, it was a total leap of faith, a jump into the unknown, into the blank places on the maps where dragons lived. Mims would have had it a bit easier—they'd have the technology to identify which star systems were promising and presumably even discover something about the exoplanets as well: atmospheric composition, existence of organic compounds, possible oceans of liquid water. Still, that wouldn't be enough. Not to colonize.

"They would send probes to terraform the potential planets to meet Mims' needs," Vars said after a few moments of consideration.

"Like the nanobots," Ben agreed.

"But is that what those things are doing? Terraforming Earth for Mims' needs?"

"You tell me. Wouldn't the meaning of 'terraform' be different for every civilization?"

"When the Europeans came to America, they brought seeds to plant the food they liked. They brought horses and cows and pigs. They brought their technology and tools."

"They brought all they needed to survive," Ben agreed. "I assume Mims would too."

"Across interstellar space? How long would it take us to send a ship to our nearest star neighbor?"

"Alpha Centauri A is about 4.3 light-years away. If the ship travels at half the speed of light, then it would take a little more than eight years to get there. That's of course from the ship's reference frame; we're talking relativistic velocities, so there'll be Lorentz contraction, shortening the distance the ship would need to traverse. But from Earth's point of view, it would take closer to ten years. But then there's acceleration and deceleration times—"

"Relax, Ben. I'm just looking for an approximation. So if we wanted to send a probe to Alpha Centauri, we could get it there in a decade or two?"

"Probably longer, but not much longer. Of course, a colony ship would require a lot more energy to accelerate to those speeds, so it would take significantly longer."

"Still within one generation."

"Yes. But it would be a one-way trip. And no help once the colonists got there; just whatever we could do to prepare the place for colonization in advance. Just like with the Luna colony and Mars, we sent advanced probes ahead of time, full of things we needed to survive."

"Food, water, air, shelter, energy," Vars said.

"Yes. The basics." There was a lot to think about.

Saturn took up most of the view from the bridge of the ship. And it was breathtaking. The gas giant's cloud tops churned with top-level atmospheric storms, and occasionally a vortex created a window into a layer below through the eye of the storm. Like a kaleidoscope, Saturn was continuously evolving and yet unchanging. Slowly the view shifted, and Vars found herself looking down on the surface of Mimas. The pilot fired the engines and moved their spaceship into the little moon's orbit.

"Welcome to Mimas, ladies and gentlemen," said Major Liut.

Everyone, military crew and scientists, had squeezed in to watch the approach. This was the first time anyone would see the Mims's artifact with their own eyes, out the window, as opposed to through instrument-collected imagery. No one wanted to miss this.

The bridge had four crew stations and a captain's chair. Major Liut took the command position, and his people staffed the navigation, flight control, and engineering posts. Ian sat in the other crew chair, though not to operate any controls;

he just needed a place to sit. After the surgery, he had lost a lot of stamina, not to mention the use of one of his hands. Getting around the ship during the few days of weightlessness with just one arm put additional strain on the man. Vars would bet Ian was covered in bruises...she was.

Vars positioned herself right behind Ian's chair, with a full view of the window. Ben was beside her. Alice, due to her short stature, was pushed to the front and now floated right in front of Liut, bracing herself against the foot and handholds of the bridge. Even sitting down, the major towered over the diminutive scientist.

Mimas floated below them. It was the first Saturn moon large enough to assume a spherical shape. The other mini-moons, closer to the mother planet, were really just big rocks, shepherding Saturn's rings. And while Mimas was way

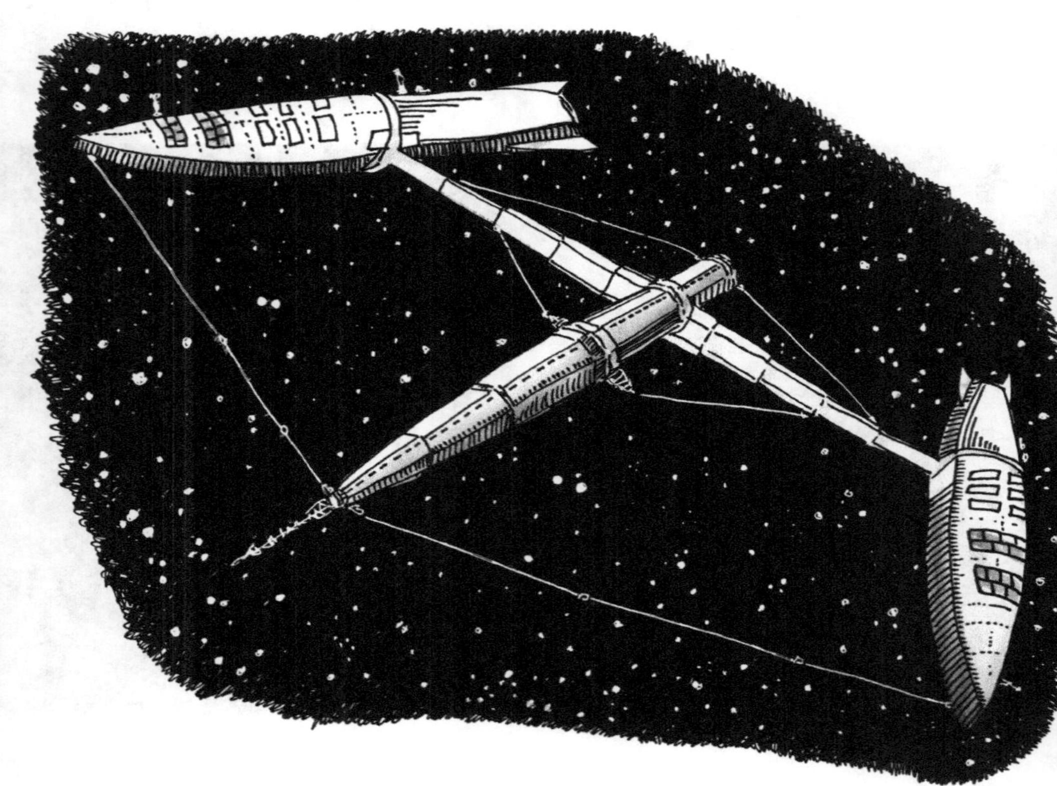

beyond the F ring—the last well-defined ring of Saturn—it was still within the haze of the E ring, a diffuse collection of dust and ice that titrated as far out as the orbit of the next significant moon, Enceladus.

Aside from the giant circular impact scar with a central dimple, the small Saturn moon looked a lot like Earth's moon: gray, heavily cratered, not particularly interesting. But unlike Luna, Mimas was mostly made from water ice, and below the pockmarked surface of thick dust and dirty ice, there lay an ocean. For years, there had been speculation that life could survive, even thrive, under Mimas's frozen surface crust. And twenty years ago, a drilling probe dropped from an unmanned ship did in fact find single-celled organisms deep under the ice.

Of course, by that time, it had been discovered that every possible solar system object that could harbor life did so. It had been the same story probe after probe: drill down, take samples, get the same type of hardy extremophile zoo. All were single-celled, and all used the same method of transforming nutrients into usable energy via cellular respiration: organic compounds plus oxygen oxidized into carbon dioxide plus water and energy. The same adenosine triphosphate molecule, ATP, had been present in every life form discovered across the solar system. This was further evidence that all life in the solar system had evolved in the same location and spread, quite early on, to every planet, moon, asteroid, and planetoid capable of supporting it. All life discovered to date had the same Last Universal Common Ancestor, LUCA, as all life on Earth. But only Earth had evolved past the single-cell stage to host life in such a wide variety.

"It's massive," Vars said as the Herschel crater floated below them.

"There! On the south slope of the central mound," said Liut, pointing. "It's partly in shadow now, but you can just see the glint of the Mims structure."

Sure enough, halfway up the bottom slope was a collection of cubes, seemingly randomly scattered. They were larger than Vars had expected, even though she'd seen dozens of images taken by the probe in orbit around Mimas.

In the last few days, she and Ben had spent a lot of time discussing the different types of probes one might want to send to another star system. Given the vast distances, stellar exploration couldn't proceed the same way as a planetary system survey. For one thing, communication with the home world would be so slow and cumbersome that a star probe would need to be smart enough to operate without guidance for many years, perhaps decades. And such probes would need to be cheap and redundant. The objective would be to send a lot of probes to each location, in the hope that some survived long enough to complete their mission and send back data.

A "scout" probe was one possibility—send something small and use it as a listening post, picking up radio waves from neighboring objects and transmitting a positive signal back home via a narrow-focused beam. A "toehold" probe was another option—a medium-sized probe that could establish a communication hub as well as collect some data. Such a probe would be large enough to have resources to make decisions once it reached its destination. It might set down on a planet or put itself into orbit around one. But a larger probe would be more expensive, so one might imagine sending out a lot of *scouts* but only a few *toeholds*.

"It's the size of a decent Malfy!" said one of Liut's people.

"It's certainly bigger than a scout," said Ben. "Why would Mims send such an expensive ship thousands of years before humans were even detectable?"

"You mean our radio signals?" Liut asked.

"Yes, but also the changing composition of our atmosphere due to the Industrial Revolution. That could be detected remotely via spectroscopy."

"But that was still just in the last few centuries," said Vars. "On the scale of a few thousand years, it doesn't change the calculation much."

"Which means this wasn't the first probe the Mims sent," said Ian. It would had been just too expensive to send something this large right away without earlier smaller reconnaissance probe. "But of course we knew that already," he added.

"They wanted our star system," said Evi. She'd had the bad fortune of getting stuck in the very back of the bridge, halfway into the hallway, floating by the ceiling. "Vars said that we have an unusually rich system. All these planets and moons and asteroids. Who wouldn't want to colonize all this?"

"That wasn't Vars," Trish grumbled quietly but loud enough to be heard.

"This is a community effort," Ian said. "We're all here to solve the same problem."

Vars noted that Ian glanced at Liut as he said it. Things were still tense between the scientists and the military crew. Ian thought it was completely Liut's fault. Regardless, they all needed more communication and sharing, less suspicion and accusations.

"Where do you think their first probe went?" Liut asked.

"Earth," said Vars and Trish almost simultaneously.

"If we were Mims," Trish said, "we would send a probe to the most promising planet. And that would be ours."

"All planets in our solar system are *ours*," Liut said.

"True," Ian agreed. "But Earth will always be our home planet."

"It's the most promising to our kind of life," Vars said. "We don't know what Mims require yet."

"Maybe Mims sent their nanobots to multiple planets," said Alice. "We know they were found on Earth, Luna, and Mars, but that could be because we brought them with us from Earth. Terry, have we gotten confirmation on whether the Luna and Mars nanobots are the same as the ones found on Earth?"

"That information is still unavailable," Liut replied cryptically.

This was not the first time Alice had raised this particular question. And Liut had yet to give her a straight answer. Perhaps he truly didn't know.

Despite strong objections from Ian and his team, Liut insisted that they land right inside the Herschel Crater, less than two miles from the artifact.

"We need answers," he said. "Stop pussy-footing around." Then he closed all discussion on the matter. If the scientists had any delusions that they were in charge, they didn't any more. Vars certainly didn't.

Not that Vars disagreed on that point—obviously they had to find out what Mims wanted from them—she just objected to Liut's approach. And, if she had to be honest with herself, she was scared of the prospect of being marooned on a moon of Saturn with an artifact from a potentially hostile alien civilization. For that's what they were going to be if they landed: marooned. A slingshot maneuver around Saturn could still bring them back to Mars. If they sat down on Mimas's surface, they had no way of getting back up, and they had enough provisions to survive for only six months. The plan had always been that they would be resupplied by other ships that would soon follow their departure. But given the situation on Earth, they had no reasonable expectation that another ship was going to show up and deliver additional fuel and supplies. Things felt grim...unless Liut was holding back information. Vars wouldn't put it past him.

With the crew getting ready for landing, the scientists were sent back to prepare in their own cabins. Having a bunch of people floating around the bridge, getting in the way, wasn't wise. Ben and Vars returned to their blue-sky jam sessions in her room—there wasn't many other ways they could contribute just yet. Evi insisted on joining them.

"So," Evi started. "Let's assume the probe was sent to

our star system to listen and report back when, or if, the life forms on one of the planets became intelligent enough to generate complex content and beam it out into space via electromagnetic signals. That would be 278 years ago. I'm discarding the early experiments with sending radio signals to synchronize clocks across Europe in the 1850s and the telegraph communication of the same era. I'm putting the start date at 1904, when the Eiffel Tower started to broadcast French radio service."

"That signal wouldn't have been strong enough to be picked up on Mimas," Ben said. "Although if they had listening station directly on Earth... But I get where you're going with this, Evi. And not too long after that, the signals grew stronger. So let's say 250 years ago the Mims first heard our broadcasts and figured out they were listening to another intelligence."

"At which point, they probably sent a message home," Evi said. "That message takes time to get to them—depending on how far away they are. And when the Mims receive that message, they send a return message—with some instructions."

"They might have taken time to debate what to do," Vars said. "But yes, a message would have to get there and back. Which would place the Mims at a maximum of 125 light-years away from us."

"We picked up the latest signal sent from Mimas—a lucky coincidence since we landed our life-seeking probe on that moon just two decades ago," Ben said. "And the timing of the alien signal is very close to your dad's discovery of nanobots all over the world."

"We've been going on the assumption of just one signal, but that's just a guess," Evi said. "The artifact could have been beaming information home for millennia."

"But still just one signal in the last twenty years," Ben

said.

"What of fresh ice?" Vars asked. After the signal was detected, the alien artifact was finally spotted on Mimas's surface because in was in an area of an unexpectedly high albedo. The fresh ice was far more reflective than the gray muck found everywhere else on the surface of Mimas.

"That's new," Ben agreed. "But who's to say that they needed to have their probe come out from under the ice to send data home?"

"But there *was* a change," Vars argued.

"Yes, there was," Evi agreed. "But do we understand it more now that we've talked about this endlessly?"

"Of course it helps to talk about it," Ben said. "We help each other understand what's going on through these conversations."

"Well," said Evi, "this time tomorrow we'll be down there, and perhaps we'll be able to do more than just rehash the same ideas over and over again."

Vars didn't know why the exobiologist was in a particularly foul mood—but everyone was on edge. Vars was stressed too. She felt a strange mix of high anxiety and thrill of landing on a new world and coming in direct contact with another sentient species in their galaxy. Moment by moment, fear and excitement alternated as the top emotion. It was a psychological roller coaster ride...and they were not all riding in the same car...or even on the same train.

When their small meeting broke up, Ben pulled Vars aside. "Ian injected himself with medical cyberhumatics last night," he whispered.

"What?"

"He was complaining about feeling useless because of his arm. Evi said something about the healing kits in the medlab. So he went and injected himself to get some use of his arm before we land. He wants to be part of the team that goes out and inspects the Mims's artifact in person."

"That's crazy," Vars said. But it did explain why Ian looked particularly tired back on the bridge. It took energy to bond with cyberhumatics. "Does anyone else know?"

"Just Evi," Ben said. "She told me that Ian is starting to get some sensation back in his hand. But would you tell Alice? She should check on him—just in case he picked up an extra dose of nanobots as part of his regenerative package." Of course, everyone on board had nanobots in their systems—no amount of blood filtration removed every single alien bot—but without the cyberhumatics sites, no one showed abnormal nanobot clustering. Not yet. Ian was a fool.

Chapter Thirteen

Phoebe and Matteo huddled together on the floor of the lab in a little nest of blankets and equipment covers. From their position behind the barricaded airlock door, they could watch the bio-enclosure where Sophie and the rats lived. It had been two days since Sophie had become trapped inside. By now she had grown a new arm. Well, it was really just a nanobot-constructed *skeleture*, but it worked, and the fingers wiggled...under Sophie's control, hopefully.

"What do you think?" Sophie said over the speaker system.

Phoebe flicked on her microphone. "Very impressive." The newly-made arm really *was* amazing. It was far superior to any human-made medical cyberhumatics used to restore function in damaged limbs.

Sophie went around her enclosure, collecting the new batch of nanobot-injected rats. She worked methodically but didn't explain what she was doing.

Matteo spoke softly, as if to himself. "To send a spaceship full of these things would require a society with a large enough economy to dedicate significant effort to a venture that provided no immediate rewards. That means large surpluses of intellectual and natural resources. Capital."

"Mathematical and computational literacy," Phoebe

added softly.

"Desire to explore. Natural curiosity about the world."

"Ability to focus the energy of the entire civilization on a difficult task."

"Not necessarily," Matteo said. "In the years before the Keres Triples, the British aristocracy, for instance, routinely just up and decided to find the source of the Nile or…or went on an expedition to the South Pole. The Royal Navy's West Africa Squadron patrolled the Atlantic and stopped sixteen hundred slave ships, saving one hundred and fifty thousand Africans—and that was just an act of one people: the British. They didn't require the whole planet to get behind their endeavors. The British just passed the Slave Trade Act and devoted the resources to put it into action."

"Granted," Phoebe said. "All that's needed is desire, ability, and enough resources to pull it off."

They sat in silence, watching Sophie graft a rat onto her shoulder. The animal was already encased in a carapace of nanobots and "melted" into Sophie's body with remarkable speed, adding flesh to Sophie's new nanobot-bones.

"Why?" Matteo gestured at Sophie's enclosure.

"To see that it's possible?" Phoebe said.

"To see for whom? Sophie or the bots?"

"Well, that's the question, isn't it?"

After a few more minutes, the rat was completely absorbed into Sophie—ratty body, carapace, and all. It was as if the rat had never existed. Sophie flexed her new arm, wiggling her newly skinned fingers. They looked human…from this distance anyway. She picked up another rat.

There was a low hum in the lab—the generators kicked in again. It must have gotten dark outside. During the few hours of daylight, the lab facility mostly worked on solar power; at night, the batteries discharged all the energy that

they'd managed to capture, and the generators picked up the slack. This far north, there wasn't enough daytime this time of year to subsist purely on solar.

Phoebe shivered.

"Cold?" They kept the temperature low, both to control the nanobot spread and to conserve energy. Without a guaranteed resupply, they had to conserve everything.

"I'm good," Phoebe said. Frankly, she wasn't sure if she had shivered because of the cold or because of fear.

They continued to watch Sophie. Every once in a while, she would turn toward the glass partition and smile at them. The freaked panic that she had shown when the nanobots first overpowered her was long gone. She was back to her usual competent, confident self. Except...different.

"What else?" Matteo asked.

"What do you mean?"

"What else are we missing?" he said. "Why are these things here now? Why are they doing this? What's their purpose? What are we missing?" he asked again.

"Well, let's start from first principles," Phoebe said. "What do we really know that's true?"

"Fourteen months ago, I found the first nanobot in a water sample gathered around San Diego. The nanobots are remarkably compatible with our planet's biologicals. They're able to attach themselves to cells and hijack the energy structures within to power themselves up. But you know this—I've shown you all my work."

"Yes. But we're going over it again. Do you have something better to do while Sophie sucks up all the rats?"

"No, sorry. I just hate feeling so powerless...so isolated."

"That's because you left the Vault system. Isolation is where I thrive." Phoebe gently squeezed Matteo's hand underneath the blankets, like she used to do when they were just Seedlings.

"Thanks, Phoebe."

"So…" Phoebe tilted her head toward Sophie. "However creepy that is, it's also amazing technology."

"Not even a gray whisker out of place," Matteo agreed. "The bots just took the tissues from the rats and rearranged them to make a human arm. As I've said, they're remarkably compatible with Earth's biology. To an insane degree."

"Perhaps they're just really good at bioengineering."

"No, I think it's more than that. These bots were *meant* for us."

"You mean the mammals of Earth *are* their targets?"

"Not just mammals. The first bot I found was right on the surface, attached to a phytoplankton. The diatom was generating enough energy via photosynthesis for both its own use and that of the nanobot. I went on to find protozoa, bacteria, even mycoplankton all actively supporting nanobots. The bots knew just how to interface with a variety of Earth organisms. So why would an alien civilization send nanobots to another star system and hijack the energy generation pathways from our life forms?"

"I assume the energy vampirism is just a side effect," Phoebe said. "Just a way of powering their little machines. The real question is what they need those machines *for.*"

"But that's just an assumption. It could be the intended effect. If you wanted to take over another star system, wouldn't it be easier if all the life that could protest or wage war against you was conveniently removed?"

"They're not killing Sophie," Phoebe pointed out.

"No. Just the rats. But we have no idea what's going on the outside. What's happening to people all around the world? The Lunar colonies? Mars? On Vars's ship?"

They had tried to get in touch with the Vaults and with

Matteo's own institution back in Seattle, but all they'd gotten was static. Either the world suffered a catastrophic failure or their lab was purposely being shielded. The second alternative was of course preferable to the first, even if personally unpleasant.

"If humans wanted to colonize another star system, what would we do?" Phoebe asked.

"We would identify a good candidate for colonization—a stable star, a planet in a habitable zone, not too far away from Earth—and then send a probe," Matteo said.

Phoebe had come to the conclusion a long time ago that Seeds would make the best long-distance colonists. Not only were they fit psychologically for the long confinement of the voyage between stars, the Seeds had the genetic diversity required to start a stable colony. "And when would we send the colonists?" she asked.

"Only after we were sure our people would be able to survive out there on the new world."

"Exactly! We wouldn't send them right away. We'd wait for the probes to verify that they had found someplace suitable for us. And then we would send ships with the supplies our colonists would need when they got there. Only after that would we send people."

"That's what we did with Mars," Matteo agreed. "But when we're talking about colonizing another star system, we'd need more than just a supply ship or two." He pointed to the window separating them from Sophie. "It's possible that we might need to send...bodies."

On the other side of the lab, Sophie had stripped off her clothing, and underneath, her entire body was now covered in a fine mesh-like suit—nanobots in yet another form. She was watching Phoebe and Matteo, unblinking, unsmiling, expressionless.

Phoebe felt herself tremble again. She turned the intercom back on. "Sophie? What's going on now?"

"Check this out," Sophie said. She picked up the metal lab bench with one hand and held it out with her arm extended all the way away from her body. "And this." She set down the bench and picked up a metal pipe. Effortlessly, she twisted the three inch thick steel into a pretzel. The nanobot suit had given her capabilities similar to those of a construction worker's exton.

Phoebe killed the intercom. "Can she break the glass?" she whispered to Matteo.

There was a soft hiss and a slight whine, and Sophie's voice came over the speakers again, even though the switch was still off. "Of course I can," she said. "But there's no reason to freak you guys out more than you already are. We're all scientists in here, just trying to do our jobs."

"What's your job, Sophie?" Matteo asked.

"I'm here to understand, just like you," the woman said with the same flat expression. Phoebe worked hard to control her breathing.

Chapter Fourteen

Vars was tethered to Ivan Kroffnic, one of the more experienced crewmembers. Ben was also there as an expert on biomimetics, linked up with Trish Cars. Their expedition to the surface was rounded off by two of Liut's officers, Ziva Yarr and Glen Kabukicho. The officers' job was to do reconnaissance, ensure safety, and, Vars guessed, to keep her and the two JPL engineers from doing anything stupid…like dying or injuring themselves.

On the flight to Mimas, there had been surprisingly little interaction between the military crew and the scientists. But they all used the same cafeteria, so Vars at least knew all the names of Liut's people. Ziva and Glen were young and athletic. Ivan was also very fit, but older. Perhaps Liut had decided Vars, the least experienced member of the crew, needed someone more mature to keep an eye on her.

It wasn't clear to Vars who'd made the decision about who would be the first people on Mimas outing. She could only guess that she was assigned to the team either because she was completely expendable or too troublesome to keep around. Or maybe it was because Liut didn't trust her. Whatever the reason, she didn't care. She was walking on the surface of another world. Who cared why she was allowed to do so?

The reconnaissance team members were data-linked to each other and to the ship, mostly via versing only—video feeds were unreliable due to interference from Saturn's intense radiation—but the crew of the ship could watch them out of the windows and on the ship's external cameras and follow via audio. The plan was to bring detailed close-up images and other readings collected from actual contact with the Mims's structure back for thorough examination by the whole team. Ziva and Glen also rolled cables and set up a few external cameras to enable better communication between the people walking the surface and their ship in the future.

There was no atmosphere on Mimas to obscure the view. Saturn hung over their heads on full display, with its rings edge on, appearing to cut the gas giant in half. At about twenty degrees from Saturn's poles, aurora was playing among the churning clouds. Here and there, monstrous lightning strikes set the gas giant's atmosphere aglow. It was hard to look away from the full glory of the spinning spiral storms in Saturn's upper atmosphere.

"Remember to breathe, Vars," Ivan said almost at the same time as her suit started to blink angrily at her. Vars hadn't realized she'd been holding her breath. The view was literally breathtaking.

"Thank you," she said. She looked around again, this time focusing on the surface of the moon and not on the view above it. Mimas was a tiny moon, composed mostly of water, both frozen and liquid. It was a million times lighter than Earth; one only had to "jump" at the speed of 360 miles per hour to get off the moon altogether—the escape velocity. If Mimas had an atmosphere, any old jet would have been fast enough to fly off this small ice ball.

The shape of the Herschel impact crater was partly due to the moon's low mass. It was a solidified version of a raindrop

hitting a puddle of water. The difference, of course, was the scale of the impact features. The crater was just over eighty miles in diameter, ringed by mountains. The central ridge was as tall as Earth's Mount Everest, with its sides almost vertical. Weak gravity allowed for sheer walls. Many had remarked how Mimas, with its Herschel Crater, resembled the Death Star—the space station from a two-centuries-old science fiction story.

The crater's central mountain had a double peak. At the base of the smaller one, about four hundred feet above the flat plane of the crater, was the Mims's artifact, glinting in the reflected light from Saturn. It had clearly grown in size since it had first been spotted by one of the telescopes in orbit around Earth, extending about five hundred feet up the slope.

"Magnificent, isn't it?" Ben said. "Like some alien beehive."

"Well, it *is* alien, and nanobots have some aspects of a bee swarm," Trish said, with more sarcasm than the moment deserved. Vars assumed it was her coping strategy. None of the scientists on this mission had ever been this far from home... or so close to an alien construct, nanobots not withstanding. "And it did act like honey to lure us in," Trish added.

Ziva and Glen slow-hopped ahead of them. Distances were deceptive here. Everything was equally sharp, whether close or far away with no atmosphere to add that bit of haze that assisted distance-perception. But Vars knew their spacecraft had landed a few miles from the sharp slope of the central mount. That was just a few hops and skips for the athletic Glen and Ziva. It was taking Vars a lot longer. Ivan hung back with her.

Still, soon enough, they reached the slope, and Vars found herself holding her breath again. She suddenly had the overwhelming sense that the artifact in front of them was full of intent. She just needed to figure out what that was.

Glen and Ziva were already bouncing up the steep slope of frozen ice like mountain goats. At the base of the artifact, they stopped. Observations from orbit had shown that the artifact was mostly hollow and that there was an opening at the top. The plan was to climb up and take a peek inside. Sure enough, within moments, Ziva had spooled out her tether and started to ascend. Glen took the spotter position below. The cube-within-a-cube construction formed a natural ladder. The gravity was so low that it seemed that Ziva could practically jump all the way to the top of the alien structure. She made it look easy.

"It's a very sturdy construction," Ziva said as she made her way up. "The outer layer looks completely structural. But through the cutouts, I can see a lot more…activity."

"Activity?" Ben asked.

"Yes. It's like little fireflies zooming inside. But not random—there's a pattern to it. Even if I can't understand it…yet."

"Would you say the outer surface is old, weathered?" Vars asked. Mimas was orbiting through the outer ring of Saturn, and just a few months of moving through all this dust would have eroded the outer surface of any structure if it wasn't being continuously rebuilt. All this particulate material bombarding their own spaceship was a cause for concern, too, which was why Liut planned on implementing the JPL team's suggestion of coating their shelter with a layer of ice for additional protection against weathering. It wasn't like they were leaving Mimas any time soon…or even had the capability to do so if they wanted.

"Surface looks new," Ziva said. "Come and see for yourselves." She waved them up. "I've tried to break off a sample, but it didn't work."

"You tried to get a sample?" Trish practically yelled. "Do you know what bees do when their hive gets attacked?" She was running, or what passed for running in super low gravity, toward the artifact. Ben was practically pulled along. "Crazy jarhead," she groused.

"Ziva, Glen, please restrain from doing any more damage to the structure," said Ben. "We come in peace, remember?" Vars could hear the strain in his voice; he was having trouble keeping up with Trish.

"Right," Ziva said, with more than a hint of sarcasm.

How hard is it for everyone to work on the same team? Toward the same goal? Vars sighed and tried to walk faster. Unlike the rest of the team, she didn't have much experience wearing an exton; she had to pay attention to every step, every move. The grips on her soles required careful positioning and just as careful release. Theoretically, the suit made walking on ice easier, but not for Vars. And every time she sped up, her safety buddy held her back.

"Just take your time, Vars," Ivan would say, reducing the length of their tether. Vars didn't even get angry with him. It was obvious she was struggling. *Who knew that a few miles could be so far?*

"Okay, I've made it to the top opening," Ziva announced. She waved down at them from nine hundred feet above the floor of the crater. The central mount towered thousands of feet above her. "But this thing doesn't end here. It continues inside the mountain, boring up and into the ice."

Vars still huffed and heaved to the base of the artifact. Ben was already climbing it, while Trish stayed below as his safety buddy. Ziva secured a bunch of ropes to the sides of the structure by tying them to the cube clusters at regular intervals, making it easier to climb. Vars wished that the woman showed a bit more reverence for the artifact, but then again, Ben *was* making full use of her lines. He managed to reach the top in much less time than it took Ziva to scale it.

What's the rush? Vars wanted to say. But instead she said, "What do you see, Ben?"

"If I had to make a wild guess," Ben said, "it would be that we are looking at a power generating station. A battery, essentially."

"What is it powering?" Trish asked.

"Good question," Ben said. "I'd like to get a look inside, but...it's too narrow for me. It looked bigger from orbit." He leaned into the opening. "Who knows? Maybe it *was* bigger."

"It's too small for me, too," Ziva said. "If we were just a tad smaller...or didn't need these extons..."

"We should send in a drone," said Ben.

Liut spoke up into their head speakers; he was quiet all through the walk and climb, not offering any suggestions or opinions...so not like him. "No," he vetoed the drone idea. "Sending machines into that thing is a last resort." Vars actually agreed with him. The Mims's nanobots were just too good at taking over human tech. "Isn't Alice a midget or something?" he asked.

"She's Bambuti," Vars patiently corrected the major. What was the point of getting irritated by that man? He obviously knew who and what Alice was. He was trying to get a rise out of her. "Of Pygmy heritage," she added anyway.

"That's what I meant." Surprisingly, there was a note of contrition in Liut voice. "Would Alice fit?"

"She actually might," Ziva said. Ben agreed. Even encased in her exton, Alice was the size of a child.

"Okay. Alice will come on the next EVA," Ian spoke from the ship. Even with his new cyberhumatics-driven arm—or perhaps because of it—Liut had barred him from leaving the ship or going anywhere near the Mims's structure. But Ian still monitored all actions and conversations closely. Vars assumed that both men were on the bridge scowling at each other. *One team...*

"I'll use the lasers to take measurements as far as I can," Ben said. "I'll also lower my camera into the opening. I have enough tether for at least a few yards. That'll give us something to look at back on the ship." He peered over the edge, down at Vars. "So Vars, now that we're up close, what do you think of it?"

What did she think? She had stopped *thinking* a while ago—she was now all emotions and impressions. At least the rest of the EVA went smoothly enough...and fast. Time had a way of contracting when one was having *fun*.

Alice did indeed fit through the opening. Ziva and Glen lowered her into the structure via a tether until her feet hit the curving floor of the tunnel. She was wearing a stripped-down version of her exton and was connected to the rest of the team by a video link. Establishing the direct feed to the control room was the one concrete thing they had accomplished on their first EVA: Ziva and Glen had laid out several kilometers of data cable between the alien artifact and the ship.

Ben stood at the base of the artifact with Trish, Vars, and Ivan. "Clearly it must, at a minimum, gather and transmit data," he said. "If I were sending a mission to the stars, I would want to get as much data back as possible."

"Would you be willing to wait a century?" Trish asked.

"Me personally? Heck no. But I mean the entire civilization. When we sent early probes to the outer reaches of our solar system, many researchers didn't expect to live long enough to see the results of the experiments they'd launched.

We explore because that's what people do."

"We explore because it greatly increases the long-term survival of the human species," Trish said.

"That too," Ben agreed. "But on an individual level, we explore simply because we're curious. I just want to see what's out there. And if by my curiosity I advance the survival chances of the whole human race, so much the better."

"So now you think it's a giant antenna?" Ian chimed in from the ship. "I thought you said this structure was for power generation."

"It can do more than one thing," said Ben. "And we have to assume there are sensors and data storage in there somewhere, too. Sensors that collect data, a transmitter that sends that data home, and power to make it all work—the basic trifecta of long-distance exploration."

As they talked, Ben set up his portable instruments for examining the nanobot-constructed cubes: a field microscope, a small heat and power tracer, and an X-ray spectrometer. Ben's field microscope came with several flashlight-type illumination sources including one in ultraviolet spectrum, helping to expose and identify the assorted micro-components on the surface of the artifact. The heat tracer analyzed variations in infrared output and created a heat map of the section of the structure it was focused on. Nanobots gave off different heat signatures depending on the work they were doing, at least back on the ship when Alice studied them in her lab. In addition to heat, this tracer created a visualization of the artifact's magnetic envelope on a granular level. As electricity flowed inside the alien structure, it generated corresponding magnetic fields. The power tracer gave a glimpse of where and how much electricity the Mims's systems used. Ben's third portable instrument was the alpha particle X-ray spectrometer, which gathered information on the alien structure's chemical composition. With these tools, they could begin to understand the configurations the nanobots assembled, make guesses at their possible functions and power requirements, and produce a list of the components from which they were constructed. Back on the ship, Ron Silverman, the other member of the JPL team, was set to compare Ben's findings with the nanobots native to their ship. At least that was the plan when they left the ship this morning. Reality always had a way of intruding on the best-laid plans.

"Interesting," Ben said after a while. "These bots are constructed from the minerals found in the surrounding ice—the dust from Saturn's rings, essentially. They're distilling the ice and gathering materials to create more nanobots. The fresh-looking ice here? That's just a byproduct of nanobot replication."

"So instead of emerging from under the ice, the artifact grew out of it?" Liut asked. Vars was surprised when the major declared that he would not be going on any EVAs personally. Instead, he carefully monitored everything from the bridge, never surrendering the control of the ship. All data gathered by the EVA team were shown on the ship's screens in addition to the multiple views from the surface stationary cameras as well as everyone's body cams. In some ways, the bridge crew was getting a more complete picture of the alien artifact than the people on the ground.

"It would seem so," Ben said after a small hesitation. It was hard to work the equipment, move, and talk at the same time. At least Vars found it so. Ivan was very insistent that she did things one at a time, serially, no splitting attention between tasks.

"What triggered the growth?" Ian asked. He too was on the bridge.

"That's the question, isn't it?" Ben said. "While we were

wrong about the origin of the fresh ice, the trigger would be the same, no?"

"The signal," said Liut.

"We don't know what came first, the signal or the growth," Trish pointed out. "Let's not confuse coincidence with causation. There was a trigger, but I don't think we've found it yet."

"But our ideas about *scouts* and *toeholds* probes are no longer relevant," said Vars. "If these things can multiply using local resources and build out whatever structures they need from that, then the original interstellar probe could have been just a small package of a few specialized nanobots capable of expanding their local presence via replication. The first alien ship to reach the solar system could have been a simple set of instructions, really. Cheap to make, cheap to send."

Back on the bridge, Evi joined the conversation. "We've talked about radio signals from Earth's first broadcasts as a possible trigger. That would have been about two hundred and fifty years ago. If this artifact was already here on Mimas back then, it could have picked up those signals from Earth and sent a message to *its* home world."

"Then when it finally received a response," Ben continued, "it sent *another* signal and started to build all of this just over a year ago."

"So you think the trigger is evidence of intelligent life?" Liut asked. "But haven't humans been building structures visible from space for several millennia? The Great Pyramids, the Great Wall of China..."

"Perhaps these things were blind to that," Vars said. "Perhaps communication of information over the electromagnetic spectrum is what they were sent to sniff out."

"And then attack?" Liut asked.

"Why would proof of intelligence merit an attack?" Ian asked. "That doesn't make sense."

"I don't think we're thinking about this right," Vars said.

"Well, it's *your* job to make sure that we *do*," Liut snapped. She didn't understand what that man was trying to do—stress her out? She was there already. They all were.

"I can no longer see Alice directly," Ziva announced. "She has now crawled into a curved part of the tunnel."

"Should we get her out?" Ian asked. "Alice?"

"All is good," Alice replied. "I'd rather keep going." Her voice was even if clipped. Alice showed no signs of anxiety, despite her limited experience with the EVA equipment and the stress of crawling through the alien artifact.

Vars envied her friend's ability to control her fears. Personally, she was having a hard time just breathing and thinking at the same time. Ivan had to continually remind her not to hyperventilate or to stop holding her breath. Vars's normal autonomic body functions were disrupted by insane novelty of it all.

"Alice looks safe," Ziva said. "Her heart rate is stable. The head cam shows identical formations all through the walls of the tunnel. No change at the turn. If fact, it doesn't even look like the Mims are aware of us. I'm getting no interaction between the nanobot structures and our equipment at all. Even the patterns of fireflies haven't changed. "

"Well," Ben said, "I'm interacting down here. I've, uh… I've accidentally broken off a piece." He sounded guilty.

"I hope the bees don't come stinging," Ziva said smugly.

"Nothing yet," said Ben. "Should I take the piece back to the ship?"

"Nothing goes into the ship," Liut ordered. "We'll monitor it, but I want it stored outside the ship, isolated. If it stays inert for a while, we can revisit this decision again then. How did it break off?"

"Frankly, it just fell off when I trained the X-ray

spectrometer on it. Perhaps it's not happy with high-energy radiation?"

"That would be a useful discovery," said Liut. "The cold doesn't have the same effect on these bots as it does back on Earth, per Dr. Matteo Volhard's observations." The temperature effects on nanobots back on Earth was one of the few bits of useful information Alice managed to receive from the Elders before communications were disrupted.

X-ray effects were interesting, but Vars was having trouble following the team's chatter; her focus was Alice. "Alice?" she called. "How are you doing? Alice?"

Almost half a minute went by and the woman didn't answer, but the sounds of her heart remained steady. And now, everyone was concentrating exclusively on the feed from Alice's helmet-mounted camera. Per the tether, she crawled seventy meters into the side tunnel; and the walls still looked exactly the same as the outer walls of the structure. *Why is she not responding?*

"Alice?" called Ziva. "Can you please respond? Just a word would do. Someone check the audio feed—"

Ron's voice cut in. "Sorry to interrupt you guys," he said from back onboard ship. "But I think Ziva is wrong about those lights. They're not the same. Look at them at a higher energy. From one of the stationary cameras at the base of the artifact, I'm picking up a few stray sparks." Of course Ron was watching the lights—he and Ben had spent the previous night fruitlessly trying to decipher the patterns.

"Ben?" Vars said. "Use your scope to look into the opening at the fireflies in UV and higher. Alice? Can you hear us? You need to answer. Now!"

"There's definitely something wrong with her audio feed," Ziva said. "But we are getting good visuals of the inside and Alice's bio signals are strong. The tether is taut..." She sounded unsure.

"Give her a few dozen meters more," Ian said. "Alice would have signaled for help, if she needed any. There's no change in the tension pattern of the tether, is there? Still the same creep pattern?"

"No change," Ziva answered. Vars tried to force herself to relax. They were getting great data, and Alice didn't take stupid risks. She would have signaled if there was something...

Ben and Trish grabbed their equipment and slowly started to climb to the top of the structure. The low gravity and extons made it very easy to lift even the heaviest objects, but while the instrument packs felt light, they were still massive and thus unwieldy. In the time it took for Ben and Trish to make it to the top of the opening, Alice had moved another twenty meters farther into the alien tunnel. Her slow progress was steady, unchanged in pace. The video feed showed the same jerky motion based on her crawling movements. Her audio remained silent.

Ziva and Glen helped the scientists set up their instruments, and soon they were all looking at the data output. Ron was right: there was another layer of activity at UV, and still another in the low X-ray range. How did they overlook monitoring the fireflies at all frequencies?

"When did you notice the change?" Ben asked Ron.

"As soon as I saw it, I spoke up."

"Time to get Alice out of there," Ian called. Vars couldn't agree with him more. Liut didn't object either.

Ziva and Glen started reeling in the cord connecting them to Alice.

"It's too easy," Ziva said just after a few moments. Vars heard worry in her voice. "The tension is about right, but we should be getting more resistance. Even if Alice set her exton to trace her movements backwards and is just riding out, there would be snags and bumps..."

They pulled faster, and past the turn in the tunnel the cord rolled without a struggle or even a tug. With a gasp and a flick, Ziva pulled out the camera that had been mounted to Alice's exton.

Just the camera. No Alice.

There was a collective cry of surprise and horror.

"When did we lose her?" Ian asked. "You guys saw her through the top just minutes ago." His voice was unsteady. "We watched her every move on the screens here..."

"I'll go in after her," Ziva said. "I'm the smallest. I can make it."

"No," ordered Liut. "We wait and try to contact Alice in other ways."

"You're too big to fit anyway," Glen said softly. "We should send a drone." Or did he say "should have sent?" Vars wasn't sure.

"Alice! Alice! Do you hear me?" Ian called, but Alice was no longer physically connected to them—the tether had all of the data cords embedded in it. Ian's audio calls were only traveling as far as Alice's discarded head cam. She couldn't hear them, and they couldn't hear her.

Vars wasn't staying at the base of the artifact any longer. She started to climb. Ivan followed, keeping a close eye on her.

At the top, Ben, Trish, Ziva, and Glen were all peering into the opening.

"How is it that you didn't notice the camera had detached?" Ivan asked.

"There was no change in tension pattern," Glen said. "And the head cam didn't show Alice herself, it just focused on the tunnel walls. The video continued down the tunnel, and then, when we reeled in the tether, it moved back. We even continued to get her vital signs." Those had cut off as soon as Alice's camera was pulled out of the side tunnel.

Glen and other Liut's people were clearly upset, but they retained their professional calm. Vars wasn't even try-ing—they'd just suffered their first casualty on Mimas. *We lost Alice!*

"Let's assume they got her the moment the fireflies changed their tune," Ivan said. He was all focus now.

"We keep making these assumptions about what sparks Mims to act," Vars said. "Let's just say that she was gone from the moment we lost direct visual contact."

"Either way," said Ivan, "it seems likely we lost her *before* we started reeling her in. That means the camera, without Alice attached to it, was crawling down the shaft."

"It even maintained an appropriate rhythmic jerkiness," Glen said.

"And even the heartbeat," added Ziva. "Damn, I would've sworn..."

"We're sending in a drone to look for Alice," Ben said firmly. "Tether it, and stack it up with multiple cameras, like beads on a string, so none are ever outside of our view. Each camera monitors the one in front and the one behind, as well as all others that are in its field of view."

"It'll take time to assemble that," said Glen.

"Then we'd better get started."

Glen nodded. "Let's pool all of our personal cameras. We'll all stay where we can be observed by our safety buddy. Complete direct visual contact at all times."

They all removed their head-mounted cameras and passed them on to Glen and Ziva, who attached them to a cord at regular intervals. Vars was impressed at how fast the thing came together—these guys were pros at improvisational engineering in space. It was the first time she had truly appreciated the team Major Liut had put together. She'd always known they were good pilots and mechanics, but this was different. Space deployment field readiness...

"Ready," Ziva said.

"Let it drop," said Ivan. And they all settled down to watch the cam-views and each other.

One of Ben's scampering drones pulled the assembly down the hole. Each camera shot forth several little gears that engaged with the walls and allowed the drone to pull it along.

"They all can do that?" Vars asked.

"Cameras are made to mount on different locations and to different devices," Glen explained. "It's easy to keep the attachment gears engaged in a makeshift drive mode. The assembly could go a hundred meters deep."

"We won't be able to make them go that far," Ziva disagreed, "but hopefully we won't have to."

A hundred meters didn't seem far enough. The Mims had gotten Alice. Vars didn't understand how, but she felt certain of it. The question was what were the aliens planning to do with her? With all of them?

The camera train moved slowly around the curve in the tunnel. It showed the same thing that they'd seen earlier through Alice's camera. Vars would bet it was a perfect match frame by frame…and then the drone bumped into a wall. The tunnel into which Alice had turned was blocked. The drone tried to push through. Once. Twice. Then it sucked in its gears, and so did all the cameras behind it. There was nowhere to go.

"That wasn't there before," Vars said.

"Did we miss a turn?" Ivan asked.

"No," said Ian. "We've been comparing the footage from Alice's cam with the view from the centipede cam. This is definitely the same tunnel."

"Or an identical tunnel," Ben said. "We *are* looking at a fractal construction."

"But there wasn't any other way to turn," Ziva said. "This was it."

"Except there's no Alice," said Vars.

"No Alice," Ziva echoed.

"Leave the cam centipede inside," Liut said. "Glen and Ziva, you stay there. The rest return to the ship. We'll take turns watching for Alice."

He didn't mention that she had only four hours of breathable air left. He didn't have to. They were all thinking the same thing.

Chapter Fifteen

"Understand what?" Matteo asked.

Sophie was addressing him through the glass window. Her arm was completely regenerated, though there was a slight gray tinge to her skin now.

"I've studied the effects of upper atmosphere turbulence on sending genetic material from Earth into space...to populate the other planets in our solar system with life," said Sophie. To Matteo, it came across as a non sequitur.

"We know," he said. "That was one of the reasons the Elders sent you here. Because of your...Sophie's work on panspermia."

Phoebe whispered into his ear. "Is she talking as Sophie or as someone else?"

He just shrugged—what did it matter at the moment? They were trapped underground, in an isolated lab, out in the remote northern wastelands, without communications with the outside world. If Sophie—or whoever this was—wanted to talk, there was nothing for it but to listen.

"But I've been thinking small," Sophie said. "Life can drift in interstellar space for millennia before hitting fertile ground."

"That's a very old hypothesis," said Phoebe.

"Old doesn't mean wrong," Sophie countered. She

stretched, moving each of her muscles in turn in a strange wave. It was still easier to think of her as Sophie...for now.

"Did she just get taller?" Phoebe whispered.

"Maybe," he whispered back.

"We no longer think it's strange that Titan's subsurface oceans have the same life as Earth," Sophie said.

"I don't think anyone thought that was strange," said Phoebe. "Not since we discovered life on Mars and found that it was identical, biologically speaking, to ours."

"But would you think it strange if life was the same on Rigil Kentaurus's system?" Rigil Kentaurus was the A system of Alpha Centauri.

"Alpha Centauri is only 4.37 light-years from us," Phoebe said. "So perhaps not *very* surprising."

"What if we learned that life was the same throughout our galaxy?" Sophie pressed.

"That would be surprising," Matteo said. "The first life on Earth evolved about four billion years ago. And the stuff we're discovering on the moons of Jupiter and Saturn is based on much later, more evolved Earth forms. Most even have mitochondria—"

Sophie interrupted. "Using a conservative estimate, a mitochondria-capturing endosymbiotic event occurred around two billion years ago. Prokaryotes, of course, are even older." Prokaryotes—"before the kernel"—were simple organisms that lacked structured nuclei and other cell organelles. Life forms discovered all over the solar system had examples of both prokaryotes and eukaryotes, which had membrane-bound organelles including mitochondrions. It was still an open question if there was one late-stage panspermia event that carried both kinds of life off Earth or multiple events that dispersed life across the solar system at different stages of evolutionary development. "Even if we say this endosymbiotic capture was more recent," Sophie continued, "say, a mere one and a half billion years ago, that's still a lot of time."

"Who's to say Earth was the birthplace then?" Matteo said. "Wouldn't that be just too Earth-centric? Haven't we moved away from 'We are the center of the universe' thinking by now?"

"Good, good," Sophie said. She popped a few new joints. The sounds made Matteo shudder, and Phoebe squeezed his hand. "So lets assume for the moment that life in our star system was seeded from elsewhere. What does that mean?"

"Not much to us, really," Matteo said. "Evolution still took place here on Earth. Perhaps the spark came from elsewhere, but we're here now."

"But how convenient would it be, for us, if we could travel anywhere across the Milky Way and never run into food we couldn't consume or atmospheres that were not too chemically incompatible?"

"Then we would be living in a *Star Trek* universe," Matteo said. "What are you driving at?"

"The universe is relatively young," Sophie said. "Life as we know it could have begun only about six billion years ago. Biology needed enough time to forge the heavy elements inside the stars and disperse them across the galaxy."

"Still older than the Earth and the sun," said Phoebe.

"But there had to be that first time, right?"

"There's always a beginning," Matteo agreed.

"Spoken like a true Seed," said Sophie, and Matteo felt like she was mocking him...yet she was a Seed too.

"What are you saying?" he asked again.

"I'm saying, imagine a civilization that arose from the earliest seeds of life."

"Those people would have a few billion years on us," said Phoebe.

"Precisely," Sophie agreed. "And what better way to spend that time than seeding the galaxy with life?" She moved around on her side of the glass, rearranging Matteo's nanobot samples.

"Are you saying that these bots are life spores from some super advanced civilization?" Matteo said.

"Oh, no." Sophie laughed. It was a carefree, gregarious sound. She sounded just like the same old Seed Sophie that had shown up at Matteo's lab just a few days ago. "The cosmic gardening was done eons ago. The nanobot incursion is just the final preparation for harvesting."

Matteo and Phoebe watched in horror as Sophie pulled the emergency metal shutter down on her side, blocking out their view of her lab partition. Apparently, the conversation was over.

They spent the night on the floor of the lab again, but Phoebe couldn't sleep. Her mind raced with questions. What were the nanobots doing to Sophie? They had clearly taken over her body—had they taken over her consciousness as well? Was there still a *Sophie* in there somewhere? And what was going on outside the lab? Were similar stories playing out all across the planet?

Phoebe slid out from underneath the blankets. It was so cold. She pulled up the collar of her jacket, if only to feel more protected inside the cocoon of her own clothing. Quietly, so as to not wake Matteo, she crept toward the lockout controls that separated their space from Sophie's. She activated the mechanism to lower the shutter on their side of the window. If they couldn't look in on Sophie, she shouldn't be able to look out at them either.

Feeling a bit better, she went over to the communications station and tried calling the Vault again. Whatever was happening outside, the Vaults would be the last to fall. Or at least she hoped so.

"Elder Alaba? Elder Alaba?" she called gently into the darkness, but there was nothing but static on the feeds. The connection must had been cut, the communications cable physically severed.

She considered going outside. At this point, what, really, did they have to lose? They had limited supplies, so it was never a matter of *if* they would go outside; it was only a matter of *when*. And per Sophie, the invasion was happening. Or about to happen. Either way, there was no way to stop it from inside this lab.

"Phoebe?" Matteo called. "What are you doing?" He stood up, wrapped the blankets around himself, and walked over to her. "I tried contacting the Elders just a few hours ago."

"I couldn't sleep," she said.

He wrapped one side of the blanket around her shoulders and pulled her close. It was nice.

"I was thinking," she said. "That we should leave."

"I know."

That wasn't the answer Phoebe expected. "I just don't think we'll learn more from Sophie. She seems…"

"Not Sophie anymore," Matteo finished her thought. "And she is not willing to tell us more. We are no longer in control of the lab, so there doesn't seem to be a point to staying. I think we should try to head toward the wardens' station. I don't think they'll let us back in the Vault, but perhaps we can at least establish communications with the Elders, tell them what's happened here, find out what's going on out there."

"That's thirty miles from here," Phoebe said. It would take several days to walk that distance, and the cold of Finland's winter would fight them all the way. "But we can make it," she added after a hesitation.

"Of course we can," Matteo said.

They were both silent for a bit, each lost in their own thoughts.

Then Matteo spoke. "I've been thinking about the last thing Sophie told us—about 'cosmic gardening.' Why wait so long before…'harvesting,' as Sophie put it? The Earth has been habitable for years. Why now?"

"You mean what's different now as opposed to the time of the dinosaurs, for example?"

"Yes. We've used up a lot of Earth's natural resources. We've polluted the hell out of our planet, created radioactive wastes. We've built things. We've traveled to other worlds and built there. We've gotten stronger, and we don't want to surrender our planetary system. It's ours. Why wait until there's a dominant, sentient life form? Why wait until we're strong enough, established enough to fight back?"

"Perhaps that's precisely what they've been waiting for," Phoebe said. "Perhaps it's not just about the real estate. Maybe they need us too."

"That's what I'm thinking, too. Perhaps they want to do to us what they did to Sophie."

"But why would they need a bunch of strange nanobot-human hybrids?"

"What's the easiest thing to send between stars?" Matteo said. He didn't wait for her to answer. "Information. And consciousness *is* information, in a way. We are each the sum of everything that happened to us, everything we've ever experienced and learned, all that we've thought and felt. All of that is just information. Our consciousness is nothing but software riding the hardware of our anatomy."

Phoebe felt a rush of fear. "Are you saying they want to install new software into our bodies?"

"Wouldn't that be the easiest way to move people between stars? Information travels at the speed of light. And when it arrives, all it needs is a good receptor. A *compatible* receptor, right?"

"So your hypothesis is that they planted us—or they planted the seeds of life that would one day evolve into us. And when we appeared on the scene—when we grew advanced enough to meet their needs—now they're coming in to take our bodies for their own?" Phoebe found Matteo's hypothesis revolting. She was desperate for a different theory to fit the facts...as they knew them. "That's crazy, Matteo. Information is part of consciousness, but only a part. Human consciousness evolved with human bodies: the wetworks are a necessary ingredient to making us *us*. You can't just stick another piece of software into our brain. It doesn't work like that." Phoebe spoke with more conviction than she felt. "I've studied biology all my life, and every living thing is bound by what it is—its structure, its form, its function. Even genes don't determine who we are—they require the environment to shape them. How can something alien just come in and commandeer our bodies, our brains?"

"All of that is true, Phoebe, but...what if you had two billion years to work on that problem? There could be a solution. And if there is...it would make sense to address their survival directive by turning the whole galaxy into a garden for their essence."

Matteo was clearly excited by the idea and didn't notice the look of horror on Phoebe's face. She wanted to stop him from hypothesizing further...but what if he was right?

Chapter Sixteen

Vars, Ben, and Trish were back on the ship, placed on an enforced rest period. Ron and Evi were now out on the surface with Liut's people, who apparently didn't require as much down time as the "pampered" scientists. Ron had cobbled together a drilling kludge with a low X-ray pointer to give the drone a way to break through the closed-up wall, and Ziva was presently busy attaching the mechanism to a drone. Liut himself was still on the ship, directing the rescue operations from there. Or perhaps Ian was directing the activity—each man seemed to think he was in charge.

It had now been over three hours since Alice had descended into the hole in the artifact. She had only fifty-three minutes of air left. Vars wished there was a way she could help, but there wasn't; she could only watch and wait. The personal inability to do something constructive to help Alice was driving her crazy.

They all gathered on the bridge to watch the military-trained crewmen try to retrieve Alice. While waiting, they talked. They felt like they had to keep talking, keep thinking, or their minds would slip down the well to Alice... Surprisingly, Ebi and Ibe had joined them, though they only observed quietly from the farthest corner of the bridge. The twins had been practically mute since the PDCs were removed from the rest of the scientists, ghosting through most interactions on board. At least one of Liut's people was always around to watch them...just in case. Vars felt a strange mix of sympathy and distrust toward the twins.

"War leads only to *limited* space exploration." Vars began the old argument again. "It doesn't support a sustained effort. Ultimately, widespread violence and conflict takes resources away from such scientific pursuits."

"It's only war if both sides engage," Liut said. He always seemed to listen to Vars's discussions, even as he was focusing on other tasks. It was as if he didn't trust Vars to recognize when she realized something important. It was unnerving. "Was it really war when the Europeans came to New Zealand?" he challenged. "Or even to the New World?"

"It's war to *us*." Ian was quick to answer. His voice seemed flatter than usual. Then again, Vars realized she was hyper-sensitive about everything Ian did or said ever since he had reinserted his cyberhumatics. She had become certain that the bots had him. Liut was obviously suspicious of Ian too now—she never saw Ian alone any more. There was always someone from Liut's crew around wherever Ian happened to be. Like Ebi and Ibe, he must be compromised. The three of them felt like a dark presence, a heaviness. Vars tried to pretend they weren't there. But how could she avoid listening to Ian? And wasn't he the one who pushed for Alice to continue even after her audio feed went dead? Vars wasn't sure anymore...

"In asymmetric engagements like these," Liut replied to Ian, "it's irrelevant what *we* think. Maybe we won't win the war, but we can find other ways to resist."

"The natives always do," Vars agreed.

"Or we can be assimilated," Trish grumbled. She cast a quick glance at Ben. "And no, I'm not talking about Borg here,

Ben. I'm talking about aborigines, the locals who didn't have a choice but to be conquered, to be assimilated into someone else's culture."

"So we just roll over for these Mims and give up our home? Earth? Our solar system?" Ben asked.

"If that's what it takes to survive?" Trish said. "Yes."

"I think we're jumping the gun here," Ian said. "Let's get back to what we know and work from there. Perhaps we're in a middle of mass miscommunication, a misunderstanding of astronomical proportions."

Vars didn't have to look to know that Trish was sneering. The woman's opinions were well-known—she never held back. And yet Trish, and everyone one else, turned to Vars for answers. For some reason, they all looked to her to make it all better. She felt the pressure of their expectations like a physical weight.

"Ben and I discussed the riches of our star system," Vars said, trying to focus on the problem, pushing Alice running out of air out of her mind...for just a few minutes, just to give herself room to think on the problem of Mims. "We're well-positioned within the galaxy," she continued, "and we have a nice stable star..." *It was Ian.* She was sure. Perhaps she could play back the ship recordings to double check who said what and when? Vars glanced at Ben, willing him to keep the discussion going.

"We're rich in planets and asteroids." Ben picked up the argument, and Vars felt grateful. The guilt of not giving her full attention to Alice's plight was like a thick mental fog, making intuitive leaps or even recalling basic facts almost impossible. But Ben kept talking. "Even with a million stars in a practical colonization radius to choose from," he lectured, "our solar system would be desirable real estate. If we were advanced enough to colonize our galactic neighborhood, we would certainly choose a system like this one."

"Even if it's occupied?" Ian asked.

"As Vars has illustrated, human history has multiple examples of technologically advanced groups taking what they need, without concern for the presence of indigenous peoples."

"I would hope we would outgrow our grabbing tendencies," Trish muttered.

Vars was with her. *Wouldn't we choose the path of light in the end?* She forced herself to focus on the discussion. This was what she could do to help. She could think, theorize, reject bad ideas, argue against jumping to conclusions…conclusions that could lead to interstellar war. *It's what Alice would have wanted me to do.*

"We aren't talking about hopes," Liut said. "We have to assume the Mims would take what they want. We need to assume the worst-case scenario."

Vars turned to face the man. Liut seemed more open to engagement than usual. Perhaps now was the time to ask about Earth. "Terry," she said. "What's happening back home?"

The whole room stilled, waiting to see if Liut would answer this time. He hesitated, then shook his head in resignation. "I don't know."

Vars believed him. "Well, then we're all working in the dark," she said. "So let's do our best not to make too many assumptions. We have no choice but to speculate, but remember that's all it is—speculation."

Liut nodded.

Vars continued. "We've established that our solar system is blessed with physical riches. But that's only part of what we'd be looking for if we got to another star system. Ben has also talked about biomimetics."

Ben's eyes lit up and he started to speak, but Vars stopped him with a hand. She had an idea and wanted to pursue it before it slithered away from her.

"Back on Earth," she said, "we set up the Seed Vaults to preserve humanity's biodiversity. And before that, we did the same with our botanical heritage. There's talk now of setting up embryo cryo-vaults to collect and preserve animal diversity. Why? Because biodiversity has value. Because, as we have learned after 2057, biodiversity—not just among humans, but among all life—is crucial to our survival."

Vars saw comprehension blossom on Ben's face and felt herself on the right track.

"Which is what makes Earth so special," she continued. "We've explored the biomes of Mars, and Titan, and Europa, as well as Luna; and in all cases, the biodiversity index was low."

"Luna doesn't really count," Trish objected. "And Mars is barely on the edge of the habitable zone. You wouldn't expect biodiversity there."

"Mars *was* in the habitable zone though," Ebi said softly from her corner, "in the early days of our solar system, when the sun was younger and brighter and put out more heat."

"And yet there are only a few bacteria found in its soil," Vars said. "Nothing more, not even as fossilized remains."

"Titan has more," Ebi said. "But I get your point: only Earth has the incredible abundance of biomimetic solutions available for the taking."

"Yes," Ian said slowly. "What we have is valuable. It's like a vast library of life functions."

Everyone sat and contemplated the idea for a while.

Liut finally broke the silence. "I hear what you're saying, Vars: they want our DNA. Our plants, our animals, all that stuff. But wouldn't any advanced civilization have a similarly rich genetic history? And who even says that they use DNA like we do?"

"Their bots *are* conveniently compatible with our chemistry," Ibe said.

"Probably because they had thousands of years to adapt," Liut said.

"If they existed only on Earth, that hypothesis might be valid. But the bots here on Mimas are the same, almost, as the ones found all over Earth. And *we* didn't bring Earth bots here—these bots were here before we got here." Ibe looked around the bridge. "These bots didn't *evolve* to be compatible with our chemistry—which means they were *designed* to be so from the start."

The drone failed to break through the wall of the fractal structure. Ron and Evi tried to come up with some workaround, but eventually Liut put a halt to the rescue mission. The clock didn't lie: Alice's oxygen had run out thirty minutes earlier. He didn't have to make a formal announcement of what everyone already knew.

Alice was dead.

"We should hold a service," Ben said.

"I don't think she was religious," Ian said. "Seeds tend not to be."

Vars barely even heard them. *Alice is dead.* It was as if her mind had become stuck on that one thought and couldn't get past it.

It took her a second to realize that everyone was looking at her. Someone must have asked her a question.

"What?" she said.

"What kind of service would Alice have wanted?" Evi asked. "What do Seeds do?"

"I...I don't know." Vars was trying very hard not to cry. The pain in her throat was strangling, making it difficult to focus on anything or anyone. She sucked in air and pushed her way out into the hallway. She wanted to be gone, away from everyone. Grief was a private thing for her. *It probably is for Alice too*, she thought. *Was.*

"Let her go," someone said. And then she was free to run, to escape into her cabin, into her personal hell.

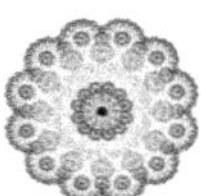

Vars shut the door and wished, not for the first time, that there were locks on the ship's private cabins. She had never been a "people person," and spending so much time in such tight quarters so maddeningly close to so many was hard. Agoraphobia and claustrophobia were the bane of space travel. Vars was feeling both. She was so far from home, so far from her dad, so pressed by everyone to find answers.

She curled up on her bed and half cried, half slept. Alice had been her one link to sanity. And now she had nothing. No one.

"Vars?"

Her door slid open. *Those damn locks...*

"Vars?" Ben walked in and sat on the bed next to her. He was kind enough to close the door...just not with himself on the other side of it. "Ian wanted me to check on you."

"Why? What is he worried about?"

"You and Alice were close," he said. "You were both Seeds—"

"I was never a Seed, Ben," she snapped. "I never even

had a clue. I have no memory of any Vault or—" She stopped herself when she saw Ben's twisted face. He was hurting. The truth was, he had known Alice much longer than Vars had. Much better. She softened her tone. "I'm sorry."

"Me too," he said. "We should have sent the drone first."

"Ian insisted, didn't he?" Vars tried to remember again whose idea it had been to send Alice.

"I'm not sure. It could have been Liut. Does it matter?"

"I think Ian is compromised."

Ben nodded. "But aren't we all?"

But some more than others, Vars thought.

She noticed that Ben was rubbing his implant site, an unconscious gesture. All the others did the same—they rubbed, scratched, or just made micro gestures like a brief twitch or a flick of a finger. The scars were a constant source of irritation, but Vars suspected the touches were more related to habit. The scientists had relied on their D-tats for years, and the loss was difficult to overcome. Surprisingly, among Liut's crew, he was the only one who showed any signs of D-tats bereavement. With others, there were no hints of overcoming cyberhumatics privation. Could the people Liut picked for this mission never been implanted? Was it another clue? And if so, what did that mean?

The door slid open again, and Trish walked in. "Mind?" she said.

Vars suppressed a sigh and slid over a bit, making room on the bed for the woman to sit. Ben moved to the only chair.

"I didn't really like Alice when I met her," Trish said without preamble. "She struck me as too stuck up, too good for us. She acted like she always knew better than everyone else. And the worst part was, she *did* know better than us. She was always right. It was insufferable."

"We'll all miss her," Ben said. "She taught me the current

thinking on panspermia, you know. Apparently the Seeds in Australia are all over that—"

"Why are you here, Trish?" Vars asked, interrupting Ben's nervous chattering. She didn't want to talk about Alice; she didn't even want to think of Alice. She wanted to rest... needed to. "Both of you. Why are you here? In my room?"

"It seemed like the place to be," Trish said. "Ben just got here first. Grief is easier to bear when the load is shared." She scooted over, pressing Vars into the wall, and patted a spot on the other side of her. "Come back, Ben. Join us."

To Vars's surprise, Ben returned to sit on the bed next to the two of them. It was uncomfortably cozy now.

"I will really miss Alice," Trish said, "whether she's truly dead or...something else."

Vars hadn't allowed herself to even think in that direction, and here Trish just blurted it out.

"She's dead to us," Ben said. "That's all that really matters. She's gone, and we need her."

"And I don't trust Ian," said Trish. At least they agreed on that. "Or Liut."

"Or the twins," Ben added.

"The list is getting long," Trish agreed. "But you're fully human, Vars, and...I guess maybe that's why we're both here. You're a pure Seed. A link to our humanity. When in doubt..." She took Vars's hand and held it. It wasn't unpleasant, just unexpected, unaccustomed, different. "I want us to work together," she said. "I know you've been working with Ben. And I want in." She squeezed Vars's hand lightly. "Ben has never been my type," she added quietly. "And you've never declared yourself."

Vars jerked her hand out of Trish's and wrapped her arms around herself. She wasn't following. Was Trish...propositioning her? Here? Now?

Seeing Vars's reaction, the woman said, "Relax. Who has the energy for that?" She looked embarrassed. "I just feel so... so alone," she added in almost inaudible whisper.

"Why don't you stop freaking out our host and tell her what Alice taught you about the biological quirks of life in our solar system?" Ben said. "Vars is all about evolution and historical trends, but she's all soft science. She's not even a biologist. And Alice is no longer here to fill her in."

Vars didn't react to the slight—she'd heard worse from Ben, especially in the early days. And besides, she wasn't feeling much of anything right now. Just tired. Still, she missed the first few words Trish said.

"—basic organic chemistry. Life uses organic molecules to pass information from one generation to the next," Trish started. "I'm sure you've heard of DNA—" Vars groaned and Trish smiled. "Of course you have. Even a soft scientist like you—"

"Trish, please?" Vars asked. It just wasn't the time. She didn't have the energy to deal the woman's smugness.

"Right then," she continued. "So if you think of DNA as a life's writing system, then our system has just four letters to get all of the required information down."

"A typical human DNA molecule is almost five centimeters long," Ben said. "That's not very microscopic." He used his fingers to show the distance. "This long...all twisted and folded to fit inside each and every microscopic cell in our body."

"Right," said Trish. "But why use only four letters, you might ask? Why not more or less?"

"I don't know," Vars said. Her dad had tried to teach her this stuff, but she was an uncooperative student at best.

"All life in the solar system uses a four-base system to encode information," Trish continued. "Thymine, cytosine, adenine, and guanine are the letters of our DNA code. Like other languages, there are rules—some letters go together, some don't. So these four molecules—thymine, cytosine, adenine, and guanine—combine to form two groups of bases. The pyrimidines are composed of thymine and cytosine, with a single six-member sugar ring. And the purines are composed of adenine and guanine, with a double ring of sugar—one with five atoms and one made from six—attached on the side." Trish used her fingers to demonstrate the molecular chains forming the rings of the organic molecules. She wiggled her thumbs and pinkies to indicate the attachment points.

"Trish, I'm grateful, really," Vars said, "but organic chemistry has never been my strong suit, and now is not the—"

"It's easy, really," Ben said. "Just four nitrogenous nucleotide bases that form the letters of the DNA code. Well, five really, if you consider methylation—"

"Ben..." Vars pleaded.

"I'm just saying it's not as complicated as it sounds." He made finger rings and wiggled his own fingers. *Alice probably would have done the same,* Vars realized. She decided to just let the two of them talk. *Grief is an idiosyncratic thing; everyone does it differently.*

"Nucleotides in the DNA are pretty simple," Ben went on. "There's the phosphate group that sort of looks like a four-spiked star, a five-carbon sugar ring, and a nitrogen-containing base. It's the nitrogen bases that come in four varieties—"

"Five," Trish corrected him. "And we are up to ten artificial possibilities."

"Yes, but only four are found in nature," Ben said.

"So only four letters of the genetic alphabet across the entire solar system," Vars said. She understood that much. The four-base code was something she knew a bit about...in *very* broad strokes.

"That's right," said Ben. "So again, why four letters and not two?"

"Are you asking me?" Vars said. Though she was utterly confused, she appreciated the conversation. Somehow, talking about the chemistry of life with these two goofy scientists was making her feel better. And Ben was beginning to look less sour. Trish too. It was good to talk about stuff that took up one's whole concentration. There was no room for anything else.

Ben smiled. "Okay, I'll explain. DNA is a double helix, as I'm sure you know." Vars nodded. "But amino acids that our bodies need are produced by the genetic code of the messenger ribonucleic acid, mRNA."

"And that's about as far as I got in organic chemistry. Sorry." Vars smiled shyly.

"—so this makes for three nucleotide bases per codon." Trish pushed on regardless of Vars's protests. "Making a total of sixty-four possible combinations," she said as if the conclusion was self-evident. It wasn't, not to Vars.

"Uh..." Vars felt lost and her focus slipped. Apparently there *was* still room in her mind for distraction after all.

Trish rolled her eyes at her. "Four to the third power?"

"Yes, yes, of course. Four times four time four. Sixty-four." Vars felt like kicking herself for missing...whatever it was she had just missed.

"But if there were only two base pairs—two letters in the life's alphabet," Ben jumped in, "then it would be just two to the third—two times two times two—or eight possible combinations. So it would require longer strands of DNA to get the same information across. It's like a coded message—the more symbols you've got, the easier it is to communicate. Got that?"

"I think so. Four letters, sixty-four combinations," Vars said. "Two letters, only eight. Got that. But wouldn't more be better? Didn't you just say there were ten possible base pairs?"

"Theoretically," said Trish. "Or synthetically, I should say. Alice managed to create artificial base pairs in her lab back in the Vault. It was one of the reasons Ian hired her." Vars didn't know that.

"That woman is brilliant," Ben said. "Or—was…"

Trish gave him a dirty look—*don't go there.*

"Yes. Sorry. So, to get back to coding genetic information," Ben said. "Two was not enough—it takes huge strings of DNA to code the necessary proteins of life. Just think of an alphabet with only two letters—any little bit of information written with only two letters would take a ton of room to express. Books would be enormous; scientific papers insufferably long…" Trish kicked him to stop. He smiled sheepishly and continued. "This means it would be easy to mess things up—mutations or transcription errors would be more common. Six letters is better for the density of information transfer, but difficult to set up. Too complex for life. So four—"

"Is the Goldilocks number," Vars said. A familiar principle, one she'd seen over and over again.

"It's all about replication, information transmission, and error rate," Ben said. "The more bases, the longer it takes to replicate, the more information is passed, the higher the error rate. A four-base system, using thymine, cytosine, adenine, and guanine, is almost forty percent faster than an only thymine-adenine base system and one hundred thirty-three percent faster than an only guanine-cytosine base system. Which means that evolution would have taken a billion years longer for a thymine-adenine base system and over two billion years longer for a guanine-cytosine one, assuming a four-billion-year history of life on Earth. That's a *huge* difference."

"Huge," Trish repeated.

"Evolution requires the information to be passed on from one generation to the next," Vars said to show that she was following. "It matters not only how many letters but which letters are used to pass this information on."

"Precisely," Trish said. "And a cool thing that Alice explained in one of our early meetings was the reason behind homochirality—our life's preference for a left-handed versus right-handed configuration of amino acids."

"Wait. Did I miss something?" Vars asked. "I thought we were talking about the DNA code letters."

"Trish likes to jump around," Ben explained. "Especially when she has an interesting tidbit of science that her audience doesn't know but might find fascinating."

"More mind-blowing than fascinating," said Trish. "But you tell it, Ben. You explain it better."

He sat up a bit straighter. "Before Alice, our group always discussed the handedness of the molecules as the result of the *founder effect*."

Vars knew that principle. It essentially stated that the first population possessed various traits for unknown reasons—perhaps for arbitrary or temporary reasons—and that those traits became the de facto standard in subsequent generations, for no reason other than that's how things started out. Like the tendency of most mammals to have five digits on each limb—something in deep prehistory had five bones, those bones gave rise over millennia to five fingers. "The founder effect is all about the initial conditions," she said to demonstrate that she knew what it meant.

"That's it. But there *is* a reason for the homochirality observed in life," Ben said. "It's because our galaxy rotates in one direction," he said dramatically, "thus creating a chiral spin and a certain magnetic orientation. So the Milky Way's dust particles polarize starlight in one particular direction. This polarization causes preferential degradation of right-handed molecules over left-handed ones. There are still right-handed molecules around—in fact, some bacteria are known to use right-handed amino acids—but it's not the norm. Humans rely only on left-handed amino acids—"

"And the nanobots preferentially bond to those," Vars said, sitting up straighter. "They're left-handed too."

"Yes. And because life in other star systems would have had to deal with the same galactic conditions..."

"The same chirality for the entire galaxy."

"And one more thing," Trish said. "Even though gravity, electromagnetism, and strong nuclear forces don't have a handedness—they are achiral—the radioactive decay of the weak nuclear force is chiral. Beta decay creates electrons that favor a particular spin, which in turn are preferentially more damaging to the right-handed amino acids. Again, the left-handed amino acids win."

"Well, you're right about one thing," Vars said. "My mind is blown." And she truly felt a better. A little bit of Alice stayed with them. The Mims didn't take away all of Alice's insights. There was comfort in that.

Vars woke up to a low but insistent hum. It resonated throughout the ship but wasn't one of alarms that they were all drilled on, signaling life-or-death situations. It sounded like a bad microphone switch somewhere out in ship corridors. Vars sat up and found Ben on the floor curled up with Trish. Both had fallen asleep right there after their late-night discussion. Carefully, so as not to disturb them—let them rest until she knew more—Vars slipped out of her room to investigate the sound.

There was something about being inside a spaceship, even grounded, that reminded Vars of her stomach—she heard random noises, none that she definitively recognized the source for, but they all seemed relatively benign if rather off-putting on occasion. Either way, humans were very good at ignoring even the strangest things once they became common. So in no time at all, Vars stopped hearing the bangs, clacks, pings, and groans onboard their ship. They became background noise. This persistent hum was different. She didn't recognize it. It was new.

The corridor outside her cabin was dark; lights turned to sleep mode. But Vars knew there was always someone on duty, even if just to monitor for any possible messages from Earth or Luna. The scientists were allowed a looser schedule, but Liut kept his people on a steady duty rotation.

She walked-slid to the bridge, keeping one hand on the rails at all times. Mimas's low gravity required everyone to use handholds to avoid bumping into walls and ceilings. She was covered in bruises, learning the hard way that proprioception required a lot of experience before it became automatic. All of Vars's experience with how to move her body through space had to be relearned, first for the journey here under the simulated gravity and then for the tiny moon's gravity.

She encountered no one in the corridor. *Perhaps everyone is asleep?* she thought stupidly. Her heart rate ratcheted up, and the sweat on her hands made the handholds slippery.

The door to the bridge was wide open. The lights inside were set at full brightness, as always. Vars propelled herself forward.

There was no one there.

Chapter Seventeen

Northern Finland and Norway were more populated than one would expect, given their inhospitable climate. This was especially true along the coasts, and more so after the Triplets Event. Still, a good portion of the population was seasonal. Away from the moderating effects of the coast, some winter days were colder than the surface of Mars, after accounting for wind-chill. Minus forty degrees wasn't a rarity, but an expectation.

Then again, it was easier to get around when the land was frozen solid. All those bays and fjords and thousands and thousands of lakes and ponds—even simple puddles, swamps, and bogs—they could all be traversed directly when frozen over, saving days of roundabout travel. This meant that if Matteo could get their snowmobile to work—if it wasn't too cold for the battery and the fuel didn't turn to jelly—he and Phoebe would be able to get to the wardens' station in a day. But if they had to walk or ski… Hypothermia was a real threat this far north. It all depended on the weather, and they had no way of getting forecasts at the moment. They just had to take their chances and hope that there wasn't a big storm brewing out there on the day they chose to leave the lab.

From the wardens' station, it was just a few more miles to the seed vault. Unfortunately, there were no roads between the two locations. The wardens were careful to take a different route every time they made a delivery, to ensure that no permanent trail developed. This was both for the Seeds' safety and to keep them isolated...sometimes against their will. But Matteo had made that journey on foot once before, with a small child in tow besides. If they could get to the station, he was sure he could get them to the Vault. But he hadn't made up his mind yet as to whether they'd go that far. One thing at a time, as Elder Alaba would say.

He crawled under one of the lab desks, using the blankets for cover—he didn't want some stray camera to catch on to what he was doing—and wired another explosive into the net of charges he and Phoebe had been setting up over the last several days. The explosion might not be hot enough to destroy all the bots in the lab, but it would be big enough to collapse the structure and expose everything inside to the outside temperatures. And perhaps the combination of heat and cold would be enough to at least neutralize the Sophie-bot long enough for them to escape.

There was no moment when either Matteo or Phoebe spoke about the plan to destroy the lab and potentially kill their fellow Seed—they just both started wiring explosives more or less at the same time. They'd always had a preternatural ability to synchronize their thoughts and goals.

"Oh, good," Phoebe said loudly. "The light works now." She demonstrably turned a desk lamp on and off. "I'll go check the lights in the bathroom." Her voice was a bit theatrical, but perhaps the nanobots wouldn't notice how fake she sounded.

Matteo crawled out from under the desk, pushing boxes of lab supplies behind him, obscuring the view of the charge he had just set. Just one more, and they would be ready to leave. The explosives were on timers, allowing them thirty minutes to get away after they got past the main door. Any more and he worried the Sophie-bot would get suspicious and come to investigate. For good measure, he'd already physically damaged the security doors between their halves of the lab, figuring any extra time gave them that much higher chance of getting out alive.

"It's my turn to get supplies from up on top," he called out, again just for the Sophie-bot's benefit. He zipped himself in multiple layers of clothing. With so many missing researchers, he and Phoebe had more Arctic survival gear than they could use at one time. Underneath the blanket Phoebe was wearing as a cape, she too had managed to put on several layers already, not all at once though and casually complaining of getting a chill the entire time.

"I'll help," she said, walking out of the bathroom. "Let me just grab my coat." She slipped into one of the dead Seeds' snowsuits—hers was a bit too small with all the extra layers she had on—and grabbed a backpack already filled with bedrolls. "Don't you need something to carry the provisions in?" she asked innocently. She didn't lift his pack herself—it was heavy, and the idea was to make it look like it was mostly empty, ready to bring back supplies rather than take things out.

Matteo lifted his backpack with exaggerated effortlessness and walked out. The last two full explosive charges and a detonator were in his pocket. This was the weakest part of their plan. The snowmobile was stored in the maintenance building that had been left to freeze over the last few weeks—they'd shut off the heaters to conserve power and to slow down the spread of the bots. The accumulation of snow on the roofs and walkways could be several feet thick by now, and the doors could be frozen solid. But the explosion would take care of some of this problem. They just needed to get out of range for now, and then come back and try to get the snowmobile to work. If it didn't, they would ski out of here under their own power. There was snow equipment up above, on ground level.

They walked up several flights of concrete stairs with only a small flashlight for illumination. The security cameras could see in infrared, but still there was no point in giving the nanobots any help. Matteo was familiar enough with the lab's layout, and Phoebe held on to one of his pack's straps. The ascent reminded him of running the stairs back at the Vault when he was a kid. Except here, the walls didn't glow green with bioluminescent bacteria.

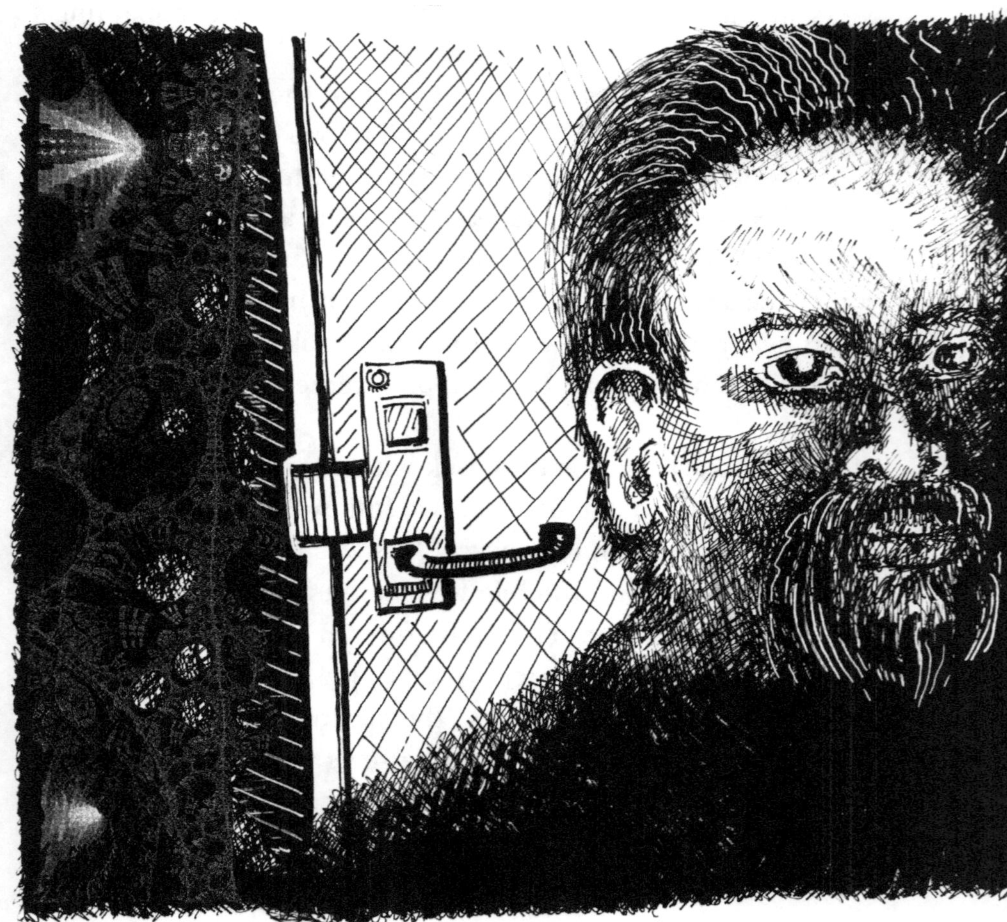

They made it to the top underground floor without any problems. Matteo set his pack on the floor beside the lock panel on the blast-proof security door. Well, it was blast-proof if the explosions were on the outside.

"Give me a hand, would you?"

Phoebe held up a big flashlight to blind the camera over the lock while Matteo used his tools to pull out a small monitor. "I'm not sure I remember my personal password," she said for the benefit of the security camera, pretending to fumble to remove gloves and mittens she'd put on earlier just for this purpose. "I know you made fun of me for wearing all of these, but my fingers just don't seem to get warm any-more. I should have grabbed some of those chem warmers maybe." She fumbled some more, making a lot of noise, even dropping her gloves a few times, all the while keeping the flashlight swinging around, away from Matteo. He hoped it was distracting enough.

After removing the video plate, Matteo pulled it out as much as the wires allowed. He slipped the explosive into the resulting cavity.

"Need help with the lock?" he asked. That was the signal to let Phoebe know he was done with his part.

"Almost," she said. She typed in the code, ensuring that the security camera caught her password. The door was never meant to keep people inside, just to protect them from would-be intruders. Getting out was supposed to be easy. But Phoebe had done a little reprogramming of the locks earlier. Sophie's codes no longer worked, and if Sophie-bot and her nanobot army tried to use Phoebe's password, the whole thing would blow, regardless of the time delay Matteo set. They didn't want to take a chance of anyone—or anything— getting out.

"All good now," Phoebe said.

"Then grab your pack and let's go get some supplies."

They walked out of the lab, clicking the door closed behind them. They now had thirty minutes to get to safety.

The main lab was built into a rocky hill, with five stories below ground and one above. They were still one level deep, so they ascended one more flight of stairs to ground level. Matteo tried not to rush—they had to preserve the appearance of unhurried calm. He was sure they were being watched. He would watch, if he was being left behind.

They weren't even outside yet, and the air was so cold it already felt like it was filled with sharp little needles. It was difficult to breathe. Matteo pulled up his facemask; inhaling air at these temperatures wasn't recommended. He felt like he needed to cough.

They arrived at ground level. This part of the building was designed to look like a welcoming vestibule of sorts. If any strangers happened to appear on the lab's front doorstep, they could conceivably come in and spend the night without ever knowing there was a secret facility built underneath it. There was a fire-burning stove, some foodstuffs in perpetual refrigeration, a dry chem toilet—it wasn't warm enough to keep the pipes from freezing up—as well as first aid, a radio, and ski equipment. Everything a wayward traveler might need to survive a day or two, but not enough to inspire a desire to linger.

Matteo walked directly to the radio and tried to reach the Vault, or the wardens' station, or anyone outside at all. Anyone.

"Matteo?" There was a slight edge to Phoebe's voice. "Let's get the supplies from the warehouse—"

"Just thought to give it try," he said. He felt it would look suspicious of them *not* to try.

"Well, I'm getting the skis—it looks like the path is totally gone," Phoebe said, peeking through the frosted-over window. This was all for show. She couldn't see a thing.

"Yes, of course," Matteo said. "In and out. Before we freeze to death out there." He grabbed some skis too and walked with them to the outside door. He pushed—then pushed again. The door didn't budge.

The outside door was never locked. Benevolent hospitality in an inhospitable environment was the unwritten law of the land. A stranger trapped outside might not survive, so the outer door was kept unlocked. The door to the lab, a story below ground, was where the real security lay.

Phoebe pushed too. "It's frozen shut," she said, her timbre slightly higher than normal.

Matteo looked around the room. They could start a fire, but it would take too much time to warm the room enough to thaw the door open. Spotting an iron poker next to the stove, he picked it up and tried to use it as a crowbar. But the door was closely fitted into its opening, leaving no space to pry for leverage.

"Well then," Phoebe said. Her voice had returned to normal, without even a tremor to indicate she was scared. "I think we should break the window, don't you? We still need those supplies..."

Matteo examined the small double-pane window by the door. It was no more than a foot and a half square—no one installed view windows out in the Arctic—and would be a tight fit. But they had no choice. He swung the poker and hit the darn thing as hard as he could. Again. And again.

Finally it cracked, but it didn't shatter. A thousand little bits were still held together. "Tempered glass," he said.

"Obviously," said Phoebe. "Use the rod to clear the opening."

Matteo quickly swirled the iron around the window's

perimeter, and the glass finally fell from the pane, mostly in one crushed piece. He shoved their skis through the hole, then lifted his Seed-sibling and pushed her through the opening, feet first. It was a tight fit even for her. He pushed their packs out after her.

"Your turn," Phoebe said from outside. "Take your coat off first." He stripped off one coat, then another, pushing them outside to Phoebe. It was cold. Damn cold. "Put your head out first and wiggle your shoulders through. I'll pull on you from this side."

Matteo pulled a chair over to the window, stood on it, and slid his head and one arm through the opening, turning slightly to give his shoulders the maximum diagonal space. As he did, he saw that a camera was pointed directly at him, at his face. And at that moment, he was sure of one thing: it...they knew. The bots and Sophie knew this wasn't about getting supplies. No one broke windows and tried to squeeze through just to get more lab supplies.

He turned his face toward Phoebe. "They know," he mouthed.

"I know, I know. Just push." She grabbed his shoulders and pulled. He wiggled and snaked his upper body, trying to help her help him. He wished he could use his arms, but they were pinned, one in, one out. Phoebe was wrenching his shoulder out of its socket, and the pain was amazing, but Matteo ignored it. He needed Phoebe to get going, to get safe. Ten minutes left.

"I won't leave you," she said as if reading his mind. "So you'd better get yourself through this damn hole." She had him by the jacket, her feet braced against the wall, legs straining. "You might come out of this pants-less," she said with an evil smile.

"As long as I come out..." The chair fell to the floor with a

thud. He lost his leverage. It was all on Phoebe now. "But I'd prefer you didn't see me so exposed."

"Save your breath," she puffed.

Finally one of his arms—the first out—was free to help her. Matteo grabbed the side of the window and pushed. His shoulder screamed. He might have popped or ripped something.

"That's it," Phoebe was saying. "Keep pushing. Almost out."

Finally, Matteo popped through the broken window and hit the ice and snow face first, taking Phoebe to the ground with him.

"Come on," she said. "Three minutes and counting."

From inside, they could hear pounding on the door one level down. Sophie-bot had apparently discovered that Phoebe's password no longer worked. She was clever enough not to try her own. She...they understood...

Phoebe put all four skis down on the ground, draped Matteo's coats on top, dropped the two backpacks on the makeshift sled, and began pushing it down the hill—slowly at first, then faster. "Get on!" she cried and jumped on top of the bags.

Matteo kept pushing for a little while longer. When he felt it had enough momentum to carry them both down the slope, he put his feet on the skis and held on to Phoebe's shoulders.

They got just beyond the bottom of the hill before the explosion ripped the air around them. Matteo was knocked off his feet and rolled through ice and snow. Then everything went dark.

"Matteo. Matteo."

The voice kept repeating his name. He had to make it stop. "What?"

"Finally," Phoebe said. "Time to go. I've checked you over, and nothing's broken—bloody nose notwithstanding."

"Are you okay?" Matteo asked. He tried to move, and a sharp pain seared the back of his head. *A concussion?* He stifled a groan; no reason to stress Phoebe any more than she already was. With luck he had just taken a bad knock, no more.

"As okay as possible under the circumstances." Phoebe

helped him sit up and then roll over onto his hands and knees. He cried out as he put weight on his shoulder. Something was definitely ripped. The pain was nauseating...or perhaps that was his head injury?

"Cold," he said instead of vomiting. Cold actually helped a bit.

"No shit," she said. "Get your coats back on."

Matteo did as he was told, moving his head and shoulder as little as possible. He saw that Phoebe had tried to keep him warm by piling the coats and blankets on top of his body while he was unconscious. And still he was freezing. "Damn, it's cold," he said as he dressed. "How long was I knocked out?"

"Not long. Five minutes tops." That was a vague answer for a Seed. Seeds had an excellent internal time-sense—an ability honed by living in a place with no diurnal cues. If Phoebe was uncertain, she'd probably been stunned by the blast as well.

When Matteo finally had his layers of clothing back on, he looked around. Their stuff was strewn about. One of the skis was broken, and the others were nowhere in sight. Parts of the building were scattered quite a ways in all directions. They had thought the blast door would have kept the damage to the top of the building to a minimum, but obviously it didn't. After scanning the destruction around them, Matteo spotted his bag; the iron poker was sticking out of it like a spear. *That was close.*

"We don't have much time," Phoebe said. She started to gather the blankets and restuff the backpacks. "Two hours of daylight, at most."

As Matteo picked up his pack, he started to toss away the heavy iron poker but reconsidered, deciding to keep it. *Might come in handy.* He patted the pocket of his coat. The last explosive was still there, together with the remote detonator they didn't have to use.

He pointed to the broken ski. "Any signs of the others?"

"Just part of one over there," Phoebe said, gesturing to a something sticking out of a snowbank.

"Well then, that settles it. We're getting that snowmobile." Frankly, he didn't think he could walk to the wardens' station in his condition.

Matteo heaved the bag over his good shoulder; the nausea was receding a bit; so perhaps no concussion. He walked back up the hill to the separate structure that housed the vehicle. In the summer, the warehouse roof served as a helicopter pad, but now it was a dome of snow pockmarked with debris from the explosion. Matteo tried to remember which side of the building had the door. It wasn't obvious under all this snow.

"South," Phoebe said, anticipating him.

Of course—always put the entrance on the opposite side from the prevailing wind.

They walked around the building. Surprisingly, there wasn't as much snow on that side, and the door was easily accessible. *Too* accessible. Someone had cleared it recently.

Matteo entered the master administrator code, shielding the numbers with his glove.

"Do you think that's still necessary?" Phoebe asked.

Matteo just shrugged and opened the door. Just inside was a brand new snowmobile, all prepped and ready.

"This is...awfully convenient."

"Very," said Phoebe. "But I don't care. Let's get out here. We can speculate when we get to the wardens' station."

Matteo pressed the start button, and the machine grumped to life. "Get on," he said as he secured his bag to the rack at the back.

"I'll sit in the back for a while," Phoebe offered. That

was the seat that was both frigid and dangerous—the cold winds would whip her, and her back would be exposed to any threats. Front was the preferable position. The glass shield protected the driver from wind chill and sleet.

Matteo considered her offer. The gentlemanly thing to do was to decline. But his shoulder was hot with pain, and his head was ringing. "Okay," he said. "But only for a while."

He got on first, and she saddled around him, holding his back. She still wore her pack—it was another layer of protection from the elements...and other things. He patted the heavy iron bar at his side.

The world felt peaceful and quiet as they rode away—or perhaps Matteo had just lost some of his hearing in the blast. The landscape was almost flat and completely desolate; there was nothing around for miles and miles. For the first time in weeks, Matteo felt himself let go, releasing some of the tension. He made his mind hush and focused only on the ground, looking for the best possible route through the ice and snow.

Chapter Eighteen

Vars looked around the bridge again, making sure she hadn't missed something. There was clearly no one here. Some overhead screens showed technical readouts and some views of the far and close-up images of the alien structure, all devoid of any human activity. One monitor showed the view of the ship itself as seen from a camera staked into the ground a few meters away from their landing site. It all looked normal, or at least as Vars expected. Liut hadn't initiated the icing procedure yet. If it weren't for the strange hum and the empty bridge, nothing would seem amiss. So Vars left to explore the rest of the ship.

The public spaces—at least the dining area, medlab, and the corridors—were all empty. Vars didn't remember a time this whole trip when she didn't run into someone outside of her room—the ship wasn't that big and there was always someone on duty.

"Okay," Vars said aloud just to hear her own voice. "People could all be asleep. Perhaps no one else noticed the sound." But even as she said it, she knew it was just desperation talking. Something had happened. Something was very wrong.

She practically ran back to her stateroom...well, more like hopped-swam in the low gravity of Mimas. "Ben!" she shouted even before she opened the door. But her room was empty too now. Neither Ben nor Trish was there. The blankets and pillows they had been using were neatly folded back on her bed.

What was going on? Where *was* everyone?

Vars almost pinched herself to make sure she wasn't still asleep. She wasn't. This was all too real.

She made her way back to the bridge and transferred the feeds from all onboard and external security cameras to the main viewing wall. She saw no one, not on any of the feeds. Every single crew quarters was empty. As far as she could tell, she was the only person on board the ship.

Then she spotted movement—*outside* the ship. Two figures in extons were walking toward the Mims's artifact. Ben and Trish. It had to be them.

For a split second, Vars considered running after them. But she stopped herself. Somehow, the Mims had summoned Ben, Trish, and the others. They hadn't summoned her. If they had, she would already be walking toward the artifact, like an automaton. She was sure of that. Whatever was happening, she couldn't stop it. Not out there. All she could do was sit, wait…and hope for a miracle.

It took two hours for Ben and Trish to get to the artifact, climb it, and lower themselves inside. Vars watched them every step of the way. Just before Ben entered, there was a moment when he turned back to look at the ship, and his hand almost went up in something like a wave…before diverting its action to a helmet adjustment. And then he followed Trish inside.

Vars was now alone.

Now what?

She considered her situation. Everyone was dead? She didn't know. But she was still here. The Mims didn't take her… not yet. She felt strangely numb. She was stranded here on a tiny moon of Saturn, unless help arrived. On the plus side, the ship had resources for twenty-five...which would now last her quite a long time...an ugly, selfish calculation. She might survive to be rescued. If rescue arrived. If she could manage to hold herself together until then. If the Mims let her live that long. If she wanted to live that long...

Too many ifs.

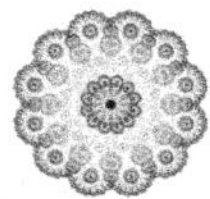

Days passed. Vars moved all her stuff onto the bridge, so she could watch the data feeds at all times. She slept there, ate there, and only left to relieve herself. She kept the communications channels open. If Earth or Luna or Mars or even Mims wanted to talk to her, she was ready. And if they didn't... well, she talked to them anyway, keeping the mike on all the time. The possibility of contact was the only thing keeping her sane...keeping her from just walking out there into the cosmos and never coming back.

"When you're deep in it, it's difficult not to focus on details," Vars said into the microphone. "It's the forest and the trees thing. Did I already talk about this? Well, it's important to repeat." She was seated in the captain's chair, wrapped in blankets, drinking coffee. She had managed to move the whole coffee station to the bridge, where it belonged, goddamn it. She took a big drag of the stuff. It was cold, but still drinkable. Her standards had long ago slipped—nothing tasted right in space. "Science and discovery have never progressed linearly through time. There have always been reversals and turnarounds and blind alleys. This is especially true when a scientific field becomes well established, respectable. Respectability comes with traditions. At best, no one likes an upstart. At worst, you get Copernicus. Well, I guess it could be a lot worse than that..."

She swallowed another cold sip. "It always starts with observations. Those observations turn into descriptions. Descriptions are fitted into a system that explains the observations. Any new observations that don't fit the system become ignored. Belonging to a community of practitioners in a well-established science discipline is a little like having blinders on: we're primed to see only what we expect to see, what our peers *approve* of us seeing. If we can't explain something within our sanctioned scientific system, we simply drop that data point...or points, or entire data sets. That's just the easiest, safest thing to do, career-wise.

"Think back to the environmental wars over global warming. Or the Earth being the center of the universe—that'd be Copernicus again." She paused, trying to remember how he'd died. Was he burned at the stake? That didn't sound right. Natural death? That felt wrong too. Vars's mind was spinning in circles. She drank more coffee and returned to her soliloquy.

"Or the whole silly evolution debate. Or the expansion of the universe deniers. Or even the retroviruses and the memory debate—that whole thing about the Arc protein and how it started as a viral infection and then became a necessary part of brain chemistry and memory formation. Whole academic careers were ruined over that discovery. Lives are constantly destroyed over ideas that don't fit neatly within the system of the world we're comfortable with or were conforming to at some point in our history. It's crazy.

"We might not do any of this consciously—in fact, most researchers would probably freak out at me even suggesting such a thing. But I've seen it. We've all seen it. How does it feel to be laughed at as you propose plate tectonics when the establishment believes in the unchanging earth theory? Poor Alfred Wegener. It probably didn't help that he was a meteorologist infringing on the geologists' turf. 'Continental drift that, Mr. Wegener.'"

Vars made an obscene gesture and barked out a bitter laugh, spilling some of the coffee over her blanket. It wasn't her first stain. Perhaps when she finally ran out of coffee, she could brew her blanket.

She contemplated the view from the ship. Saturn was always rising—Mimas was in total tidal lock to its master planet, always facing Saturn in the same orientation. But the rings, seen edge-on from Vars's perspective, changed continuously—Saturn's reflected light backlit the dust and ice particles making up the rings. The bigger, rotating rocks in the rings bounced light in random directions, creating a breathtaking light show. *Just for me,* thought Vars. There was an inexhaustible majesty to the view of Saturn, bisected by its own rings, forever breaching the rim mountains of Herschel Crater. *Spectacular.*

The storms, in all of their fractal complexity, raged on the surface of the gas giant, easily seen at this distance and with no atmosphere to obscure the details. Vars loved the beautiful swirls that changed slowly over time and as Mimas followed its orbit about Saturn. Within the storms, there was an almost constant staccato of lightning strikes. Each flash highlighted the deeper structures inside the raging clouds.

Vars had watched the celestial show continuously...almost every waking moment since moving onto the bridge. It was awe-inspiring every time she looked up. And it took away some of her loneliness and fear somehow—it was hard to focus on self-pity in the face of the glory of the universe revealed out of her window...at least that's what Vars kept telling herself.

"Hmm, what was I talking about? Oh yes—the beautiful diversity of life on our home world." She paused to visualize herself as a girl walking on a beach with her dad. All that life hidden behind every grain of sand. And what a life it was. Even at those tiny scales, life was teeming with energy. So much of it. At all levels of observation. *Another fractal complexity...*

"But what if we were unique?" she mused into the microphone. "I know, I know—we aren't supposed to think of our world as unique. The universe doesn't revolve around us—poor Copernicus again. There are billions of planets in our galaxy alone. It's the height of presumption to think of ourselves as special. But allow me a bit of hubris here. What if we were? What if we had more than everyone else? More diversity? More unique evolutionary solutions? Ben's work on biomimetics... What if mass extinctions, which jump-started evolution over and over on Earth, were not a common universal phenomenon at all?

"Mims reached their technological potential well ahead of us—by billions of years, maybe. That could only be if life on their world didn't get periodically whipped out, requiring a do-over...and over, and over, and over. Could this mean that Earth, as a result, has more? More of everything? Is this why Mims want us? Is this why? I'm asking you, Mims. What do you *want*?"

Vars stopped when she realized she was screaming. She hadn't intended to raise her voice. She took another sip of coffee. It was now ice-cold.

She suddenly remembered talking about God with her dad. Why had the idea of a deity come up over and over during human evolution? Wouldn't some *Homo sapiens* tribes have gone a different way? Evolving into humanists, for example? But no—every single human population from the dawn of time had believed in something bigger than itself. Anthropologists even used ritualized burials as a way to mark the transition from animal to human. Not that it was a valid marker—even animals interned their dead sometimes, and they certainly mourned their loved ones—but something about the ritualization of death suggested a stark divide between the lower- and higher-order beings. And it was this incessant pattern of deification and believing in life after death that formed the cornerstone of all religions. That's what her dad had said, anyway. He also said that Seeds studied religion as a tool to manipulate the political narrative of the world beyond the Vaults.

"Did you plant the god instinct in us and other animals?" Vars asked, looking out at the Mims's artifact. It had grown. And she'd noticed that it periodically vented some gas. Saturn's light occasionally caught the plumes coming off the top of the structure. Like right now. What were they venting? Human remains? The plumes reminded Vars of a crematorium chimney for some perverted reason. She shook away the imagery.

Vars no longer even considered going out there to the artifact. She *had* considered it—quite a lot, actually. She wanted to look for the others. For Alice. For Ben. For Trish. For all of them. But she didn't have the training to be out there alone. She could barely get around the ship without serious injury. *And what would I do if I made it all the way out there, anyway? Stand at the base of the artifact and shout out names?*

"Alice?" Vars said quietly. "Are you still there somewhere? Alice?"

She must have slept. There was a theory that said dreaming was the brain's attempt to train for disaster—in the safety of a dream. It was a learning though previsualization kind of argument. Vars dreamt of her dad. She hoped he was okay. She hoped that the radio silence from Earth was just some strange technical failure, perhaps a bad nanobot-human technology interaction. A hitch in broadcasting. Perhaps the problem was even here, on Mimas. Didn't Liut say something about interference caused by Saturn? Yes, it could be that.

"Vars."

A single failure here, on their ship, was much more likely than a total equipment failure on Earth, Luna, Mars, and all of the rest of solar system-wide communication satellites. That was just too improbable...

"Vars."

But it could be something more sinister. It certainly felt like it. If *she* were taking over another star system, she would disable communications first. That's what humans did when they tried to wage war against each other—they cut off the flow of information, kept the enemy in the dark, took away situational awareness.

"Vars."

It was an effective tactic. Humans were inherently social animals and didn't function well in isolation. Even Vars. If this experience had taught her one thing, it was that she didn't function well alone—despite all those years believing herself a loner. She laughed bitterly at her lack of self-awareness. People were always delusional about their own capabilities, strengths, and weaknesses.

"Vars?"

She looked outside once more. The Mims's artifact had stopped venting, and she could see the sky-encompassing vastness of Saturn without that obstruction. And the rings again. The tumbling rocks and dust would be here long after—

"Vars!"

"What?" Vars said in a small voice. She was hoarse from screaming earlier.

"Vars!" It was a man's voice. Scraggly, sick-sounding. "Vars? Is that you? Vars!"

The voice alternated between using Vars's name as a question and a call. Or perhaps a prayer.

"This is Dr. Varsaad Volhard," Vars said. "Who are you?"

She waited. From Mimas, it would take approximately eighty minutes for her signal to reach Earth or Luna. To Mars it was closer to sixty-five. Double that for there and back. In just over two hours, she would know where the message was coming from. Of course, it could have been sent from a rescue ship on its way to Saturn, but Vars didn't even allow herself to think that. That was simply too much to hope for. Too big of a letdown when it turned out not to be the case.

She reached out and turned off her microphone. She wasn't sure why all of a sudden the idea of someone listening to her half-delusional rants made her nervous.

She had a couple of hours to get herself more presentable—to eat, to get dressed, to take a shower...not necessarily in that order. She didn't remember the last time she'd made herself go through a personal grooming regimen. Now she hustled. Two hours wasn't such a long time if one didn't touch a hairbrush for days...or had it been weeks? She wasn't sure, and that made her even more unsettled.

The woman looking back at her from the mirror was a total stranger. Skin gray. Eyes sunken. Skeletal. Hair sticking out in matted clumps. There was no point in a brush; she decided to just cut it all off. It would be easier to take care of. There was no reason to be vain.

With her head shaved, she looked even less like herself. More like her dad really…she just needed a beard. She heard herself laugh and didn't like it. More coffee. She needed a jolt of stimulants.

She was back in her chair on the bridge with ten minutes to spare…if the message was coming from somewhere other than Earth.

One hundred and fifteen minutes since her transmission.

One hundred and seventeen.

One hundred and nineteen and a half.

Vars watched the seconds indicator sweep through. Her clock was set to analog mode—her dad's favorite. But…Liut had it set to military time. Hadn't he? Yes…she was sure of it. When did she change the setting?

One hundred and twenty-seven. That didn't necessarily rule out Mars yet. Replies took time.

One hundred and sixty-seven. Not Mars? And obviously not a rescue ship either. Unless they were worried about her ramblings. Or perhaps they needed more time to compose their message?

One hundred and sixty-nine. No one said that replies had to be made instantaneously upon receipt of a message, right? They didn't know—couldn't know—how much Vars needed them…

One hundred and seventy-two minutes.

"Vars? Baby? It's me, your dad."

"Dad!" Vars half-screamed, half-cried, and rushed to open her mike again. "Dad!" He would get this in eighty-plus minutes.

"We're at the wardens' station, Phoebe and I. I've never told you about her, but she was my Seed-sister. She saw you when you first arrived at our Vault. But that's not really im-portant now." There was a sound like a sob or a big exhale, followed by a nasty cough. Vars dug her fingernails into her arms—her dad had to be okay. Had to.

"Sorry about that," he said. "Phoebe doesn't want me to shut off the mike even for a second—took a while to get everything connected and decrypted—doesn't want me messing with it. The wardens' stations are built like secure military centers. Everything at the highest level. Everything…" Another bark-like laugh and a coughing fit. "But there's no one here, so we had to figure it all out ourselves. Oh, Phoebe says hi."

"Hi," said Vars in a small voice. "Hi, Phoebe. Hi, Dad. I love you…"

"Phoebe got the audio working a while back, but our outgoing feed gave her trouble. While she was at it, we listened to you. Vars…oh, Vars, what's going on up there? And where's Alice? Where's everyone? I'm so worried about you." A pause, but no coughing fit this time. "Well, Phoebe and I figured out a few things. This is not a secure connection, but we decided it doesn't matter. Not anymore, right?"

"Why, Daddy? What happened to you?" Vars couldn't help but talk back, even though there was no synchronicity to this conversation, even if he would only hear her words way over an hour later, out of context. It didn't matter. She felt like touching the speakers, hugging them.

She listened to her dad describe the horror of his experiences at the lab and the crossing of the frozen landscape from Finland into northern Norway. *His was a harder journey,* she thought.

"The main thing, Vars, is to figure out what these aliens want."

"Mims. We call them Mims, Dad."

"Phoebe and I think they seeded our solar system with life. Or we might have been starting up on our own, but these guys overwrote it with their own chemistry. That's why all of the examples of life we've been finding everywhere we go in the solar system are related. It's all the same stuff!"

"We thought so too, Dad," Vars said, but it was nice to hear their suspicions confirmed.

"A whole galaxy full of compatible chemistry, tailor-made life," her dad continued. "Depending on how much of a head start they had, it's conceivable that every last planet and moon that could possibly support their kind of life…already does."

"It's our kind of life, too," Vars added quietly.

"But why send a body when just information would do?"

"What?" Vars sat up a bit straighter.

"Phoebe had this crazy idea that these nanobot masters don't just want our world, they want *us*. As in our bodies. As in… I'm so glad you didn't have to see what happened to Sophie."

Another bout of coughing, then: "Imagine moving only information about the galaxy. Want to visit some cool spot in the outer rim? Just send a copy of yourself that way. In ten, twenty, a hundred years—what does it really matter?—you arrive at your desired destination, and take over a body that was raised just for you. You look around, live life for a while, and when you're ready to leave—or when the body you're using wears out—you just send the data back. Phoebe thinks that death for such creatures would be a meaningless concept. They are the masters of our galaxy, Vars. They've been everywhere, lived millions of lives…"

His words dissolved into desperate hacking, leaving him almost breathless. Vars could hear how sick her dad was, and it scared her. Or was she scared because he was talking crazy? Or because what he was saying *wasn't* crazy?

In this enforced pause, while her dad was recovering his breath, Vars considered what she knew and what she'd managed to talk about on the ship's open microphone. She's been talking for days—when had her dad cut into her stream of consciousness? What had he heard? What had she said that was important? What had he missed? She tried to concentrate, tried to come up with a quick outline of what had happened to her since she'd left Earth—just the important bits, just the stuff that might help her dad survive back home.

Her dad started speaking again. "Our plan, Phoebe's and mine, is to get back into the Vault. If anyone knows what's going on in this world, in our star system, it would be the Elders. We can't raise anyone else from here. Something is jamming us. So we were planning to go—"

"Don't go, Daddy. Don't leave me!" Vars spoke before she could stop herself. She didn't want to be alone. Not again. Never again...

"—but I'll come back. After I get Phoebe in, I'll come back to the station. And I'll stay with you, baby. Just keep talking, Vars. I'll be with you. Always."

The relief Vars felt was overwhelming. She cried. Her daddy would be with her. Somehow that made everything better. He knew she needed him, and he would stay. She sobbed, and Matteo hacked. They shared the erratic, spasmodic breathing millions of miles apart.

Chapter Nineteen

Vars fell asleep in her chair waiting for her dad to get back online. She had long ago given up on keeping up any kind of regular sleep-wake cycles; she just passed out when she couldn't go on anymore. If she didn't get to that degree of tiredness, she simply couldn't sleep. Her mind churned, ruminating endlessly on her situation, on Mims, on the evolution of life in their galaxy. She needed to be completely drained of energy to get her brain to shut off.

And yet now, as much as she wished herself awake, she simply couldn't do it. She fell asleep waiting for her dad to speak again.

"Vars?"

A woman's voice.

Vars found it difficult to respond. "Grr. Hrrr." She stood, shakily, to get some more coffee.

"Vars?" *Phoebe, probably.*

"Wait," Vars managed, inserting her dirty cup into the slot. It was sucked in, and she heard satisfying noises of boiling water. Since the ship was kept at a slighter lower pressure than on the surface of the Earth, the boiling temperature was lower. The coffee apparatus sealed the cup and raised the pressure before heating the water. Vars liked her coffee hot, sweet, and milky...even if she usually ended up drinking it cold, bitter, and plain. The first sip mattered.

"*Ahhhh!*"

Vars heard herself scream. Surprised, she tried to figure out why.

"Vars! Are you okay? Speak to me!"

Must be Phoebe, Vars thought once more. She felt herself hyperventilating, heard herself making strange noises. *What's that all about?*

"Vars? What's going on? You've stopped transmitting for over a day. Please set up a schedule of regular updates. Matteo worries. We both worry."

Vars finally managed to take control of her body. Sleep deprivation was a terrible thing. Her hands were shaking. Her whole arms, really. She was hugging herself, looking at the coffee machine.

"It changed," she said, as much for her own benefit as for Phoebe's. It was good to hear a human voice in the same room. "The coffee machine changed."

"Vars! I will repeat your name until I get a signal back. Vars! Vars!"

"The Mims got to it," Vars said. "I guess they thought I needed better coffee." She started to laugh hysterically.

With a *bing*, a small light announced that her beverage was ready. Vars didn't take it. She backed into her chair, lifted her feet off the floor, and wrapped her arms around her knees.

"Vars. Please speak with me."

"I'm here," Vars finally answered—though Phoebe wouldn't get that response for over an hour. And she would get all of the other freaked-out utterances first. Well, there was nothing to be done about that.

Vars looked at the clock. She had slept for over twenty-six hours. No wonder Phoebe was so upset. She rewound the audio messages from Earth to the last thing she'd heard and started to play from there.

Phoebe never believed Matteo when he said they would be able to reach Saturn's moon and get in touch with Vars from here. It was such a long shot. But she humored him—it was always a bad idea to take away hope—and it turned out that he had been right.

But now, it had been over twenty-six hours since the last few words arrived from Mimas. Phoebe thought Vars sounded unstable. But given what she had probably lived through—Phoebe could only imagine, based on her own experiences back at the lab—it was a miracle Matteo's girl was talking at all. But she was the only one talking. Phoebe didn't have Matteo's worldly experience, yet she was pretty sure that the military team accompanying Vars and the other scientists to Saturn wouldn't just let her ramble on like that. Which meant they were gone...or incapacitated...or at the very least no longer in control of the ship. The other scientists, too, they would have put a stop to Vars at some point. It seemed likely that Vars was alone on that ship. What did that mean? Was Vars compromised? Like Sophie? Did people die up there too?

Matteo was asleep in a sitting position on the floor of the wardens' communications room, leaning against the back wall. He was too sick to talk with his daughter. Phoebe had given him a sedative, a multispectrum antibiotic, and a narcotic-laced cough suppressant. She wasn't in good shape either. Her heart rate was elevated, her breathing was uneven, she felt tingling in her armpits, and her extremities were numb. Her toes were frostbitten and would require medical attention once she got back into the Vault. And she was obviously suffering from post-traumatic stress disorder. Her decision-making abilities were probably severely compromised. Her thinking was sluggish, to put it kindly.

But she knew she had to get some information from Vars. What was going on up there on Mimas? What had Vars learned? Anything that could help the humans down here on Earth? She recorded a short message. "Vars. This is Phoebe, your dad's friend. Are you okay? Speak to me. What's going on? Please give me a brief summary of what happened to your mission." She set it on a loop and sent it out into the depths of the solar system.

When Phoebe was leaving the Vault to go work at Matteo's lab, there was already talk of shutting the Vault off from the rest of the world for at least a decade. But after negotiating with the EPSA and world governments, the decision was made to postpone that decision until after for news from Mimas arrived. And while waiting, Phoebe and Matteo were assigned to do research on behalf of all the Vaults. Their work would contribute to making strategic judgements about humanity's future. *But now?* Now, Phoebe was hoping to bargain information for her ability to be sealed in the Vault with her fellow Seeds. The more she could figure out, the better her chances were at getting back home...or so she hoped. Matteo, of course, had other plans. He just wanted to help his little girl. Phoebe had assumed he would stay with the wardens. *But now? What now?*

She set out to explore the wardens' station. Like the Vaults and the lab, it was built both above and below ground—two living floors below, one above, and a data center deep in the permafrost underneath everything. Unlike the lab, the station didn't have a hospitality section—no one was allowed inside without authorization. Even if a visitor was in distress, the wardens didn't care. They were careful to keep their station off the maps and off the public roads. The little concrete fortress in the ice screamed of aggressive inhospitality. This was one of the reasons why Phoebe had assumed going to the wardens' station was a hopeless endeavor. But to her surprise, her authorization codes—the ones she'd learned when she passed through this station on the way to Matteo's lab, in what felt like another lifetime—still worked. That shouldn't have happened. The codes were supposed to be changed every few days, and it had been weeks since Phoebe passed through here. Could that signal the date at which the station emptied?

For it was certainly empty. Since she and Matteo had arrived, they had found no one, not even a body, in the whole place. That alone was a very bad sign. These stations were designed for 100% occupancy at all times—they were the necessary link between humanity's genetic backup and the world at large. The wardens served as both buffers and jailers.

Phoebe had no love for the sadistic rituals of the wardens' sect. And a sect it was. It took fanatical zealotry to leave an infant at the doors to the Vaults, in the freezing cold, to die or to be saved by the Seeds on guard duty. It was a miracle that Matteo discovered Vars before she died of exposure. And those Seeds who tried to escape their Vaults before their ten thousandth day? Phoebe felt a shudder run down her body. She hadn't even gotten to see the bodies. It was like those Seeds had never existed. Even as Phoebe loved her life in the Vault and desperately wanted to get back in, she'd always felt the Vault system was a barbaric solution to preserving human diversity. Australian Vault, and Sophie in particular, were pushing for wider dispersal of human Seeds across the solar system and beyond. In many ways the idea made sense... or as much sense as the Vaults. The mental image of Sophie with rat extensions made Phoebe physically wince. She knew she would never get over that... But she shook herself off and continued—that was what Seeds were trained to do.

Phoebe proceeded methodically through the wardens' station, starting with the living quarters. Whatever had happened here, it was an orderly evacuation. All the beds were freshly made, although most of the personal belongings remained. The kitchen was shut down, but there was still plenty of food in the pantries—canned and frozen stuffs and the ubiquitous ready-to-eat meals. Earlier, she'd checked the garage section up on top and had found no transport vehicles—the wardens must have left in those. She herself had originally been transported from here to the lab via a drone-copter that was to return back to the station once dropping her off. But it, too, was nowhere to be found.

And despite the apparent orderliness of the wardens' departure, they had left no logs, no messages for future wardens. No explanations. In the Vaults' history, no wardens' station had ever been left empty. Both the stations and the Vaults had protocols for natural and man-made disasters—a nuclear war, another catastrophic asteroid impact, a gigantic solar flare, some environmental disaster of global proportions. After all, that was why they existed. The Vaults, Phoebe knew, could go on lockdown for decades, even centuries. She wasn't as clear as to what the wardens' station emergency protocol was, but she felt certain that leaving the station unattended and accessible to unauthorized visitors was definitely not it.

There was also good news here, however—while there was no sign of human life, there was also no sign of nanobot structures. No fractal cubes, no strange tissues that could have been a reorganized body of a dead warden. Nothing. It was clean. *She* was clean—she and Matteo scrubbed their blood the night before they left the lab. Which meant there was no reason not to let her go back home into the Vault.

Phoebe felt a palpable relief. She was homesick. She wanted to go back deep underground, to her bed, to her students, to her work, to *her* lab...

She considered trying to call up the Vault's Elders. Elder Alaba would want to talk to her. Debrief her. She felt ambivalent about what she should tell him. If she was honest about what had happened to Sophie, they would probably think it was too dangerous to let her back in. But they *would* ask about Sophie. Sophie was a Seed, just like Phoebe. The Vaults cared about what happened to their own.

"Phoebe? I hope you're still there."

The voice came over the main speakers. Phoebe rushed back in the main communications room, the heart of the wardens' station. Matteo was still asleep in the corner. His breath was raspy and irregular. *Pneumonia.*

"I'm here," Phoebe replied out of habit.

"I don't know why they didn't take me," Vars continued. "They took everyone else. Alice first. We were all D-tats-free. I never even got mine installed. The rest had theirs removed either before we left Earth or during the flight. But I guess you know that. Alice thought Liut was spying on us back on Earth. I think he was crazy...well, perhaps just paranoid. But then, there was a lot to be paranoid about, right?"

Vars laughed, and Phoebe heard the full depth of the girl's psychosis in that outburst. But then Phoebe felt a bit on the crazy side herself. Who was she to judge?

"We tried to do blood cleansing, but... I don't know when, but we stopped. *I* stopped. I'm all alone—what's the point? I have enough supplies to last several years, if I conserve. I'm the only consumer, after all. Everyone else left to go into the Mims's artifact. Well, I *think* that's where everyone went. I watched Ben and Trish walk there. The others...all I know for sure is that they're no longer on the ship. Haven't been for days...weeks?"

There was a long pause.

"Keep talking, Vars. You're doing great," Phoebe said. "Just keep telling your story. What happened to you? I'm listening. And we're here, Vars. You're not alone. Isolated, but not alone. Okay? Keep talking. Just keep talking."

Even if Vars wouldn't get Phoebe's encouragement until hours from now, Phoebe knew it would help. Vars needed to know that someone was there with her. Phoebe had a similar need. She wasn't sure she would have been able to cope without the knowledge that the Vault was within walking distance.

"We've never figured out *why*," Vars said finally. "Why? Why are they here? What do they want? But they've been here a long time. Thousands of years at least. This is not a probe just recently sent to investigate our star system. They've been watching us. Waiting. Multiplying, building structures—on Mimas, obviously, but I bet there are more of these artifacts all over our solar system. They had so much time, why not put down roots?"

"Why not?" echoed Phoebe.

"Ben and Trish thought that our whole galaxy might be teeming with Mims. Well, that's what I think they thought... that's how I remember it."

"Panspermia on a massive scale." Phoebe nodded. "Sophie thought so too."

"Perhaps they aren't dead," Vars said suddenly.

Phoebe's mind conjured up the gray arm swarming with nanobots. "It doesn't matter," she murmured.

"I've been thinking about going out there. Walking to the structure. I would like to look for the others. I would like to know for sure, you know?"

"Don't do it, Vars. Let it go. Stay safe in the ship. Learn. Send back information." Phoebe couldn't help but reply. For Vars, it would be a strange collection of utterances, but for Phoebe, it was all very much in the now...almost a conversation.

"Ben said that all the nanobots were of a kind. We didn't bring them here from Earth. We found them here. They were here already."

Vars took a deep breath...or was it a sob? It was hard to tell over the speaker. *Keep it together, Vars,* thought Phoebe.

"The ones blessed with the best initial conditions win," Vars said, switching to a new topic. The girl's mind seemed to jump a lot. But was Phoebe in any better shape? She didn't think so. "It's not how smart you are or how inventive," Vars went on. "It's what you have to work with. Mims must have had an amazing run of luck. In a universe with billions and billions of galaxies, it's not even unlikely that some species beats the odds somewhere, right? The Mims won the cosmic lottery. A multiplanet star system, rich in natural resources. A nice, stable star. Just the right galactic neighborhood—far from explosive activity but close to other rich star systems. And perhaps most importantly, they were the first."

"What? I'm not following." Phoebe spoke even though she knew she couldn't really divert Vars's narrative, not for some time. And by then, Vars wouldn't even know what Phoebe was referring to. Phoebe would just have to do her best to understand Vars's meaning. *I wish I had read her book.* She had always meant to...eventually. It was just that eventually was never now. And now it was too late.

"—millennia upon millennia of luck," Vars was saying. "Luck builds luck. Those civilizations that started lucky just got luckier and luckier as time went on. Humans have a bad habit of not ascribing positive attributes to *luck*. The lucky ones are not deemed lucky, they are seen as smarter and prettier and…and…"

"What are you talking about, Vars? What luck?"

"Those who were born earlier and born into the right set of circumstances, they always win. On Earth, for instance, in the last two hundred years, luck meant being born on the North American continent, away from the aftereffects of the worst of the Triplets impact. It meant being born into a well-to-do family with deep resources and plenty of education. It meant being born healthy. It helped to be born beautiful. If you're born lucky, then you're beginning your race in life that much farther past the starting line. This is true for individuals, for civilizations, even for species. Now that humans have established themselves as dominant, what chance do dolphins have? But it's more than that. The same principle applies even on a larger scale, on a galactic scale. And for Mims, Mims's luck gave them extra time and resources. Mims were here first. Perhaps they were even the very first in our galaxy."

"Are you saying the nanobot-makers are the oldest intelligent species in our galaxy?"

"They were certainly earlier than us. We're rich with possibilities, too. We have a star system that's full of potential. But we weren't first. We were born a few billion years too late. The Mims had already established themselves, long before. They had already seeded the whole galaxy with life compatible with their own. Everywhere they visit, it's all the same—"

"Chemistry," Phoebe said at the same time as Vars. Phoebe was finally following. She and Matteo had been narrowing in on the same idea on their own—panspermia. *They are us at some fundamental level*, Phoebe realized.

"Once their seeds spread and life took hold, the Mims

didn't need to rush," Vars continued. "They could take their time. Explore at leisure. The whole galaxy was slowly making itself ready for their occupation. A galaxy-wide ecosystem tailor-made for one smart species. It's probably like this all across the universe. Each galaxy hosting just one dominant species of intelligence." There was a note of horror in Vars's voice...and awe.

"But what about us? Did these Mims plan on us?" Phoebe asked. She looked over at Matteo and wished he was well enough to jump in or at least to listen. It was all being recorded, but she wanted Matteo's input now. *Now!* What Vars was saying... "Did they plan on us becoming intelligent?" she asked. "If it was really billions of years between seedings and subsequent visits, wouldn't they expect life to evolve in their absence? We did. And once they found us, why attack? Why not make contact? We are their descendants in a very profound way. Their children..."

It didn't make sense. It was too much. And Phoebe was too tired. She put her head down on her knees and slept.

Chapter Twenty

Vars kept Phoebe's voice playing in the background. It was just a short loop, but she didn't care. It was nice to hear someone else's voice for a change.

She looked over at the coffee machine. It was completely covered with a nanobot structure now, as were most of the control panels on the bridge. Vars pondered what that meant for her ability to use the controls...or to get more coffee.

She'd been watching as the fractal patterns slowly etched themselves into the floor of the ship, moving from the panels to the center of the bridge where she sat in the captain's chair. They were close now. She pulled her whole body onto the chair. The Mims were coming for her. She didn't have years. She would be consumed in just a few hours. *What does one do with a life measured in hours?*

"Dad?" She just wanted to hear his voice again. Even a few words...before she became a monster...like Sophie. It was funny how a confident scientist could be reduced to feeling like a child under the right circumstances.

The microphone was still on. Everything she said—or screamed—would be sent back home. Her dad would hear the end. It would be hard on him to hear his little girl die...

"Dad? I love you," she said. At least she said it before it was too late. The Mims pattern was almost to her chair. *Did it speed up?*

"What do you want?" Vars screamed at the floor. "You got everyone else. Leave me be!"

She watched the advancing pattern, trying to estimate its rate of progress. She decided she had maybe an hour left. That was enough time to relay what she knew to Phoebe and her dad. She shook off her dread. She was still human...for now. "The Mims are coming for me, Dad. Soon, I think." She glanced at the shimmering fractal at her feet. "There are a few important things that I think we figured out. I know you and Phoebe will make good use of our ideas, build upon them." Her voice was surprisingly calm. She was proud of that. If her dad and his Seed-sister could be heroic, so could she. She took a deep breath and began.

"Ben—that would be Dr. Benjamin Kouta—posed an interesting idea. Evolution provides diverse ways of solving problems. Take an iterative process and a few million years, and the result might be multiple schemes of locomoting across the terrain aided by diverse sensory input systems and myriad ways of processing that data. When human technology appropriates nature's ideas, we call it biomimetics. It's an old concept, but it's used extensively by EPSA, especially in the development of off-world life-support systems. Ben was an expert."

She paused and carefully considered what she was about to say next. When Ben had talked of this, it felt crazy to her. But now? Ian had advised her not to shut down any ideas. So perhaps Phoebe and Dad would find it useful.

The nanobots inched closer. It was easy to give into fear, but Vars forced herself to continue talking. "Perhaps the uniqueness of our world comes from its fits and starts in evolutionary development. Earth suffered through multiple extinctions. The last one, the Triplets Event, almost wiped out humanity. But these events brought about an incredible diversity of biological solutions. We are not only born into an extremely bountiful star system, but by virtue of a few timely disasters, we are also the heirs to an extraordinary prolific source for biomimetics ideas.

"Adversity mixed with abundance. That might be our greatest resource. We've enjoyed its benefits, but we rarely give it much thought. Why should we? We operate with a sample of one. One planet. Nothing to compare it to. Sure, we were going to go to the stars one day—Ben kept insisting that it was vital to human survival—but we have only just begun colonizing our own star system. We're millennia away from starting colonies around some other star. By then, I'm sure we would have noticed our luck.

"If we had been the first—the first civilization to reach for the stars in our galaxy—then our dominance would have been all but guaranteed. Phoebe? You should read my book, if you haven't. I make the same point about Europeans and the New World, and Australia, and the Pacific Islands, and Africa. Earth is full of examples of the first-mover advantage. Peoples who were lucky enough to be born among nature's riches are always in the lead. The rest have to play catch-up. But at least we are all human. We are all just one race. After the Triplets, we claimed our solar system as one people.

"So what if the Mims saw our riches, our insane levels of biodiversity? Perhaps they came over to claim our star system for their own, and then noticed that we could be 'mined' in other ways? For millions of years, they could have been harvesting our innovations. But then..."

Suddenly Vars had an insight—the timing!

"But then the Keres Triplets hit Earth. And even though Earth is mostly covered by water, the three asteroid fragments hit land, causing maximum devastation. Like the Chicxulub event sixty-five million years ago that killed off the dino-saurs—as we think of them. Had it struck just a little earlier or later in the Earth's rotation, it would have hit the Pacific or Atlantic. It would still have been bad, but not extinction-level bad.

"The Triplets, and the nuclear exchange that followed, *would* have been a mass extinction event if we hadn't man-aged to stabilize our world through technology. But did we? Did we do that? Or was that the Mims and we just took credit for it, *assumed* we did it all on our own? The Mims were here then; and wouldn't they have protected their valu-able resource if they could? *We* would have. Think, Dad. We humans would have intervened in the Mims's place. I'm sure of it. We would have protected our investment. They must have too.

"And then, almost a century later, you, Dad, discovered the first evidence of nanobots. Perhaps with over ninety per-cent of all species extinct after 2057, the Mims made a deci-sion to take what they thought of as theirs—their carefully cultivated garden.

"They're just galactic gardeners, Dad. And now is harvest time."

Vars stopped. The pattern had reached the base of her chair. It had definitely sped up. She wondered if it would hurt.

"You'll be fine, Varsaad. It won't hurt."

The little silver-gray cubes-within-cubes linked together with the precision of a clock. Vars could almost convince herself that she heard them click together. *Won't hurt?* And yet she pulled herself into a more compact shape, trying to postpone the moment when the bot tendrils reached her.

"It won't hurt," the voice said again.

Vars's head snapped up. That was a real voice, not just a thought in her head.

"Phoebe?" Vars asked, but that was silly. Yet the voice sounded familiar. Was it male or female? Did it matter? "Who is this?"

"Ebi."

"And Ibe."

Vars felt cold. "Where are you?" She pushed her nails deep into the flesh of her arms to keep herself from giving in to panic.

"Here, Dr. Volhard," Ebi said.

"We've never left," Ibe added.

The ship was empty. Vars was sure of that. She glanced at the communications station. It was covered with Mims structures, but she could still see that it was on, that she was transmitting back to Earth…and elsewhere.

"I thought you guys all went over to the structure," she said.

"You saw that our extons are still plugged in next to the airlock," Ibe said.

That was true. There were four exoskeletons charging next to the airlock. One was Vars's—all extons were personalized—she knew which one it was based on its position on the charging wall. So two of the other three belonged to the twins. Whose was the last one?

On a hunch, Vars asked, "Is Ian still on board the ship?" He was the only other person with built-in cyberhumatics left on the ship.

"I'm here, Vars," said Ian's voice. Well, it was *almost* Ian's voice.

The nanobots reached her at that moment, touched her skin. She felt a slight tingling. It didn't hurt.

"Someone needed to stay and take care of you," Ian said. "You were never very technically inclined."

"The three of you stayed just to take care of me?" Vars

asked. She felt a pins-and-needles sensation on her left thigh and lower torso. She forced herself not to look.

"We will keep the ship's systems going," Ebi said.

"We will make sure your body is functioning properly," Ian added.

Vars worked hard to keep herself from exploding off the chair and running screaming through the corridors of the ship. "How would you do that?" she asked, forcing the words out.

"We've used the technology-assisted bodies to help maintain those who are pure," said Ian...or whatever he was now. "We used the human you call Alice—"

"Alice!"

"—to solve some basic problems—"

"Is Alice alive?" Vars asked. She hadn't even dared hope before...

"Alice is functioning," Ian said.

Vars decided to take that as a yes. "Can Alice return to this ship? Please?"

"Alice is functioning," Ian repeated. "We'll make sure that you are functioning too."

"Please continue communicating with your father," said Ebi. "We would like to keep him functioning as well."

Vars tried to dig her nails even deeper into her arms to regain her composure, but found she couldn't. Her body had begun to merge with the chair, and she had lost some of her ability to move. To her surprise, this didn't bother her that much.

"You haven't been consuming nutrients," Ian said.

"Yes I have!" But Vars didn't really remember the last time she'd eaten. She knew she'd drunk a lot of coffee...

"We're just trying to keep you healthy, Vars." The Ian voice was soothing. Its...*otherness* was barely noticeable.

Vars felt more relaxed than she had been in…weeks? And a bit fuzzy. Did they drug her? Did she care?

"Phoebe? Dad? The Mims took over the ship," she said and fell asleep.

"You drugged me!" Matteo raged.

He was obviously feeling feistier, more energetic. Phoebe was pleased with her Seed-brother's recovery progress.

"You needed the rest, Matteo. You have to stay strong for Vars," she said gently. "And everything has been recorded. You can hear every word your daughter said. Over and over again, if you wish."

"But—"

"You're no good to her dead, Matteo." She handed him a thermos with some hot soup and a bag of dried fruit. "Eat and listen."

Phoebe played back Vars's ramblings, editing out the long stretches of time where the girl fell asleep or just took a break from talking. Altogether, there were only a few hours of real content before the Mims—Phoebe had adopted the terminology—apparently force-fed Vars and anesthetized her in some way. Phoebe was outraged by such violations, though she agreed that Matteo's daughter needed some nourishment and rest.

"Do you think…" Matteo began.

"That Vars is a bit on the edge?"

"Or over it," Matteo said quietly.

"It's hard to be out there all alone," Phoebe said. "But I think she's coping very well. Her ideas are still sharp—"

"Except she's no longer alone."

"Except that. But it sounds like they have an interest in keeping Vars healthy. It sound like they're looking to take her over the way they must have done with all the others."

"Perhaps not Alice."

"It did sound like that, didn't it?" The other voices on the transmission—Ian and one or two others—were somewhat vague about their intent. "And it sounded like they would like to keep you healthy as well."

"Like a pet," Matteo said bitterly.

"We don't know what they want yet."

"But it makes sense that the Mims are trying to protect their investment," Matteo replied. He was sick and tired but game. That's what Phoebe loved about him. He didn't give up. "Wouldn't it still be useful to make contact with us? Why take over? Cooperation is still a better option for long-term survival."

"The Mims's definition of cooperation might be very different from our own. What if taking our bodies—your idea, Matteo—is how they see their relationship with humans working?"

"That's not cooperation."

"Not to you. Not to us. But to them? We can't assign human values to beings that evolved on other worlds, over vastly different timescales. Perhaps their way of propagating their species through the galaxy is what ultimately works best? Evolution on a galactic scale? Survival of the fittest, natural selection—the basic principles would still apply, right?"

"But if we share the same chemistry, the same roots of life—"

"Matteo, you aren't honestly going to extrapolate morality from chemistry, are you?"

He looked sheepish, and Phoebe almost laughed. They were both desperate, grasping at straws. "Are you going back into the Vault?" he asked.

"Yes." No hesitation.

"I'll send you everything I learn."

"I know."

"When will you go?"

"I would like to tell the Elders that we've established communications with the Mims," Phoebe said. That was the trade she had in mind. *I give you contact with the Mims, you let me return to my old life.*

Matteo was silent, but tears appeared in his eyes. For the loss of his daughter? For her? For humanity?

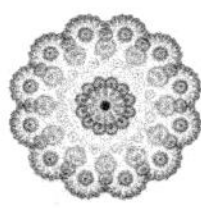

Vars woke up slowly. There was music playing, some classical piece she couldn't name but which sounded vaguely familiar. A woman's voice was carrying the melody. In addition to the main view port, the screens in front of her were showing the sharply lit surface of Mimas and Saturn's rings edge-on; the gas giant was forever setting behind the crater's rim, creating long, hard shadows on the surface of its small moon. Beautiful.

Vars watched Saturn's storms rage, waiting for her body and consciousness to fully return to the sound of the human voice. That was a smart choice...it kept Vars from losing all control over her little human mind.

It was a while before she noticed that all the internal views of the ship had been taken off the screens. She could only see the outside, the universe gently turning, with no hint that there was more than the bridge of this ship and Vars in all of eternity. Her personal world had shrunk to just this small room. Just this chair, really.

She looked down at the places on her body where she remembered feeling the touch of Mims. Everything was clear, as far as she could see, except for a small patch of cyberhumatics on the left side of her torso and what appeared to be a feeding tube. *Life support,* Vars guessed. She considered ripping it out. But they would just place another one—she was sure of that.

She looked around the bridge. Every surface was rewired with nanobots. And there was a movement to it all, a seething, a roaming of the surfaces in seemingly random patterns but together, as a coherent group. A murmuration of nanobots.

The "coffee machine" was a very different contraption now. A small screen had appeared while she slept, with a lazy line moving up and down: *thump thump, thump thump, thump thump.* Her heartbeat. The display was clearly meant for her—the Mims wouldn't need visual vitals indicators. This was their way of building trust, Vars realized. But after taking Ben, and Trish, and Alice, and everyone else, how could there be trust?

"What do you want from me?" she asked the room.

"Good morning, Vars," said Ian's voice.

Vars wished the Mims wouldn't use her friends to try to manipulate her. *Just tell me what you want,* she thought. The heart monitor display showed a spike in her heart rate—and almost immediately, she tasted metal and felt a chemically induced calm wash over her again.

"Don't do that," Vars warned them, but she couldn't make herself get angry. She was medically stilled; she couldn't reach for the rage she wished intellectually. "Or I'll rip the goddamned thing right out of my body," she threatened in an unnaturally calm voice. At least she could say the angry words, if not feel them. "And I'll rip it as many times as you reinstall it until there's nothing left of me to heal," she added.

"We're worried about your health, Vars," Ian said. Or Ian-Mims. Vars couldn't allow herself to think of the voice as Ian. That was dangerous. That was how they might break down her will.

"I guess I should be grateful for your concern," she said. The drug they'd given her was making her emotionally dead, an almost out-of-body sensation.

"You are our child. Of course we are concerned," said Ibe-Mims. It was funny coming from him…it.

Vars wondered where the Mims had stashed the "real" bodies of Ian, Ebi, and Ibe. They hadn't left the ship, per their extons. Did the nanobots simply absorb them into the ship? Or was this all just a show, an illusion? Something to keep her from losing her mind to loneliness? She wondered if she had truly been transmitting back to Earth.

"Dad? Phoebe? Are you really there? I'm okay. The Mims are apparently worried for my health. They've installed a feeding tube, and they're monitoring and controlling my body functions, including drugging me. But I don't sense any cognitive interference." *Nothing obvious, anyway.*

She paused. The singing had stopped. "I've been talking with the Mims, who are using the voices"—*and more?*—"of three of the EPSA scientists that came on this mission: Dr. Ian Rush and a set of twins, Ebi and Ibe Zimov. Those would be the only three scientists on board with fully-functioning cyberhumatics. Ebi and Ibe had D-tats that were too complex to be removed in our ship's medlab. And Ian made a decision to reinstall his cyberhumatics to regain some of the functionality in his arm that was lost while his tats were removed." Vars wondered how Ian felt about his decision now. *Is it worth it, Dr. Rust?* "So the three of them were the only ones on the ship left with easily accessible nanobot sites," she continued. "The rest of the crew, all of whom were tats-free, seem to be gone from the ship." Did she already tell her dad this? Her memory seemed fractured. Was that Mims or loneliness? Drugs or sickness? Did it even matter?

"Everyone else has moved to the structure outside," Ian-Mims said helpfully.

"Well, there you have it," Vars said. "That was the voice of Ian-Mims."

"Just Ian, please."

Vars ignored his request. "Ian-Mims, have you become part of this ship? Where is your body? And those of Ibe-Mims and Ebi-Mims?" Vars remembered Phoebe's all-too vivid description of what had happened to Sophie. Or was that her dad who told her what happened in his lab? Did it matter? Sophie-bot. They called her Sophie-bot. They, too, had refused to use their friend's name after the transformation.

"We are here, Vars. That's all that matters," Ian-Mims said.

"Not all," she protested.

"If you are asking whether Ian is still Ian, then the answer is both yes and no. I am Ian *plus*. I have direct access to what you'd call the Mims's information, and I will be able to guide our exploration to the best of my ability. You are in the right place, Vars. And with your knowledge of humanity, you are invaluable to this project."

At that moment, he sounded almost like the real Ian—with the same zeal for research. If Vars weren't so drugged, her emotions firmly suppressed, she would have laughed hysterically.

Instead, she considered how to use her position to advance her dad's agenda. As long as she was being used by the Mims, she could use them back. So what would her dad need to know? What questions did she need to ask while she still had the ability to do so? While she was still just Vars...

Chapter Twenty-One

Phoebe packed for her trip to the Vault. She would be traveling these last miles without Matteo. He was well enough now to take care of himself, but still too sick to leave the wardens' station. Besides, Matteo wanted to stay here, where he could maintain contact with Vars. He refused to even leave the communications room. It had been two whole days since they'd heard anything from his daughter, and he was worried.

"Vars will be fine," Phoebe said to herself as she stuffed a portable radio into her pack. Her plan was to go at first light—just minutes away now—and not stop until she got to the Vault's door. She wasn't taking any supplies aside from a few dried fruit packets and soft bottles of hot soup. She'd slipped these into her inside coat pockets and threaded a flexible drinking tube to come out just under her chin—this would keep the heat in for the maximum amount of time.

She found some chem warmers and placed them all around her body—lower spine, feet, hands, even the back of her neck. If with all of these precautions she didn't make it to the Vault, she planned to fall asleep and die out in the tundra. Hypothermia was an easy death.

"Here." Matteo walked over to her and handed her a small package wrapped in paper.

"I can't carry too much," she protested.

"It's the last of our plastic explosive," Matteo said. He pulled out the unused detonator. "If they don't let you in…"

Yes, I'll blow that door wide open. It was surprising how unbothered she was by that prospect. "Thank you," she said and embraced him, pushing her face into his chest. He needed a shower…but then she needed one too. It might be the last physical contact with another human either one of them would ever feel. "Good luck, Matteo."

"And to you," he said. "I'm sorry I can't go with you."

"Don't be. Just keep talking to Vars…and to me."

She turned away from Matteo. Two flights of stairs and a heavy door, and she stepped into the icy cold.

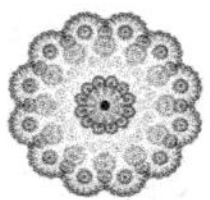

Inside Phoebe's pack, unbeknownst to her, nanobots snapped into positions around the portable radio and the detonator.

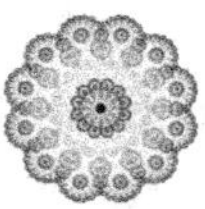

"Vars. Vars," Matteo repeated into the microphone like a mantra. He could have just played a recording of his voice on a loop, but it felt more personal to say his daughter's name himself. He liked the feel of her name on his lips; it felt so familiar, so dear.

He was bundled up in heating blankets, holding a large container of coffee and another of soup. Both were still warm. He had two frequencies open—Vars's and Phoebe's. His Seed-sister was to call him the moment she got through the Vault's door. He hoped she could do so nonviolently.

The truth was he wasn't even sure the detonator still worked. But he assumed the Elders had bugged the wardens' compound a long time ago and that his mention of the explosive charge would encourage the Vault's guards at the door to let Phoebe in...or at least take cover. If the explosive *did* work, he didn't want any of his fellow Seeds getting hurt.

"Vars?" Matteo decided to just talk, to free-associate on the topic of life. If nothing else, the Mims might be entertained, and Vars, his little girl, would feel less alone out there. "Do you recall that time we talked about which genetic traits made dinosaurs interesting? They had several varieties of metabolism—fast and slow—sometimes simultaneously. Some species' ability to switch from cold- to warm-bloodedness based on environmental conditions kept them alive for many millennia. Humans could only hope to last that long as a species.

"And all the colorful pigmentation? Remember how you loved to color images of birds? And how we used the latest science articles to extrapolate to the possible feather pigmentation of the T-rex? You were so creative, Vars...but always within what was possible based on data. You were taken with the possibility that some dinosaurs could color-shift instantaneously, like octopuses or chameleons, or seasonally, like polar foxes and owls, or over their lifetimes, like juvenile deer and baby birds. You used birds' ability to color-shift as proof that dinosaurs could do it too."

Matteo closed his eyes, remembering his little girl arguing passionately that humans were not the only species capable of appreciating beauty—she believed that ability had to be old, ancient. He smiled. He missed his little girl.

"You said, 'Why have an extra cone for color perception if not for color appreciation?' I said it was for food identification and defense. But you argued that three cones were plenty enough for that, and that most mammals didn't even have that many. Wolves, good hunters, are colorblind, you pointed out. Only birds had the ability to see such a wide color spectrum. Could evolution push for the selective advantage of individuals that loved rainbows of color? I had no answer to that question that could satisfy you."

A clicking noise sounded out in the hall. Matteo had been hearing that sound on and off for several hours now, ever since Phoebe left. Perhaps she'd left some door open, allowing a draft to rattle the contents of the station. He might need to go out and investigate...eventually...not now.

"And dinosaurs that could grow to an exceptional size? You loved seeing the skeleton fossils at the British Museum—so many beautiful forms and turns, nature's sculptures. One time"—he laughed, and it hurt his lungs to do so—"I had to drag you away from a docent who was explaining some full animal reconstructions made from plastic. You were screaming that the man was wrong and just didn't understand the science behind dinosaur evolution. I had to keep you away from the museum for a few weeks after that incident, and yet you *still* wrote letters to the dinosaur exhibit gallery, explaining to them how smart these creatures were. You wrote about their electrical perception like sharks, their large geo-location and spatial memory just like birds of today, their deep musical memory. You lectured the docents on the dinosaurs' extraordinary working memory—you said copious working memory was a necessity for nonlinguistic smart animals. You cited elephants, if I remember correctly, as your example. You were such an amazing kid. And an amazing woman. You still are. You're still here, Vars. Don't give up."

Emotions welling up, Matteo found himself crying. He had never been one to cry so easily before, but being sick made him more labile somehow. The tears created strange floaters in his vision. He tried to wipe his face on his sleeve, but the weatherproof material wasn't absorbent. The little dark phantom spot kept creeping at the periphery of his vision.

To push down the painful constriction in his throat, Matteo took a deep gulp of his soup. Phoebe had left it with him, but now the thermos was almost empty, and he would have to go and scrounge around for more food soon. That would require leaving the communications room, though, and Matteo wasn't ready to leave his girl alone. She needed him. And he needed her.

"Vars? Vars?"

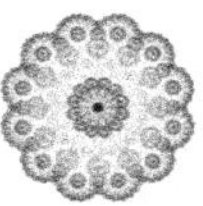

Vars woke up to her dad's voice calling for her. "Dad?"

"How are you feeling, Vars?" asked Ian-Mims. He sounded concerned.

"I'm fine. Was that my dad?"

"Yes. Would you like a playback?"

"Yes, please."

"Okay. If you eat the soup in the thermos cup next to your chair. On the right."

Vars picked up the cup and drank the whole thing in one go. It wasn't bad, as far as liquid food went. Coffee was better.

As if reading her thoughts, the coffee machine started to make noise, and Vars smelled fresh brew. Moments later, an arm extended from the machine, holding the cup within her reach. It already had sugar and milk and was at a good temperature. *This could work out,* Vars thought wryly.

"Thank you," she said. For an answer, she got a recording of her dad talking about dinosaurs. He rambled; it was disconcerting. He sounded sick, both emotionally as well as physically.

"Is that all?" Vars asked after the recording stopped.

"Your dad needed the rest."

The way Ian-Mims said that made Vars suspicious. "Rest, as in *enforced* rest?"

She didn't get an answer, but the silence was an answer in itself. Apparently the Mims were capable of drugging her dad as well as her. They had control of the wardens' station where her dad stayed.

"Can I keep talking with my dad?" she asked.

"Of course."

Vars sat back and considered what she should say next. What would help her dad cope?

It was all about goals, she thought. Goals and the alignment of actions that led to the accomplishment of those goals. As long as the Mims's goals were satisfied by Vars speaking with her dad, she would be allowed to do so. But if they weren't...

She had to guess what the Mims ultimately wanted. If she knew that, she would be able to manipulate them into thinking her conversations with her dad—serial monologues, really—were helping them advance toward what they wanted to achieve with her...and him.

So what do the Mims want?

Understand your enemy and turn them into your ally. Who had told her that? Ian, probably. Sounded like something he would say. *How much of Ian is still in Ian-Mims?*

She decided to drop the *-Mims* suffix in addressing the entities running her ship. That was part of the manipulation game, after all. She had to gain their trust, as much as they tried to earn hers.

"Dad, what would you do if you could live forever?" she

asked the void. "Or let's say, just a few thousand years? Would you be the same person at one thousand that you were at one hundred? I think you would argue that some fundamental personality traits would stay the same, overlaid with years of experiences. But those experiences would matter, right?

"Remember when we talked about wealth? I don't remember how old I was, other than that it was after that conversation that I decided I wanted to study anthropology. I wish I had known that you were a Seed back then. I bet that had a huge influence on your perspective on the subject. In fact, someone should do a study of the Vaults and Seeds... someday..."

Vars wondered what the Mims thought of the Vaults. They housed practically the only cyberhumatics-free humans in the solar system. Would Mims want pure humans or enhanced? Another *why* lurked in that question.

"You told me about the relative perception of wealth. After the Industrial Revolution, Americans had multiple ways of broadcasting their wealth and social status, because unlike the British, for instance, Americans had cast off titles. Different cultural symbols were needed, something difficult to acquire yet easy to flaunt. Strangely, for a time, oriental carpets served as a signal of certain social status. Walk into someone's home, see the big intricate wool weaving on the floor, and you knew these people had achieved a certain standard of living. There were those who had carpets and those who didn't. Seems silly now. And I thought it was silly back when you first told me about it. Yet it wasn't silly to the people who bought those carpets to flaunt their social status. But then industrial looms were developed, cutting the labor requirements per carpet, and international trade proliferated, allowing for influx of goods from countries with cheap labor. Soon everyone who wanted an oriental carpet could afford to get one. And they could no longer serve as a status symbol, as a commonly accepted signal of wealth.

"The same went for subsequent wealth signals—watches, televisions, computational devices. And the suburbs made home ownership more common. Sure, you had to commute a greater distance to work, but you were a homeowner.

"For several decades, stuff and more stuff was the *it* thing for communicating wealth. But eventually the goods got so cheap that they no longer conveyed much of anything. Quantity of stuff, quality of stuff…none of it was effectively correlated with social status. Everyone had a large-screen, hi-def, network-connected TV.

"You told me that the next move was services—how much *human time* one could afford to buy was the new way to broadcast social status. People acquired personal assistants, cleaning crews, nannies, handymen, beauticians, and even yes-men—it was called having an entourage. The bigger the entourage, the more important the person appeared to be. It was all about appearances. Well, I guess it was always that.

"And then came experiences—or the ability to *buy* unique experiences for oneself and family. People went on crazy vacations, participated in scientific expeditions, even bought tickets to go into space. And those who couldn't buy the real thing found ways of *faking* having had unique experiences. All those social media companies that offered to make you look like you had done extraordinary things and to share those images with as many people as possible. The ice cream museums, the toy bins, historical recreations…there were thousands of easy-to-create images for social broadcast. There was a strong pretend economy at the start of the twenty-first century. Cool tricks to make everyone believe you had more stuff, more services, more experiences than your peers. The early AIs were great at that. Any person could be made more beautiful than they were in person, paradoxically making it impossible for people who bought that service to go out and enjoy their social perks in public, out in the real world, without revealing the lie.

"Then it was all about health and longevity—looking and feeling young. That was the start of the age of cyberhumatics. And just as we were moving into cyber augmentation, the Triplets hit, setting everything back. The ability to live in a radiation-free zone, to eat safe food, to have access to medical care...these more basic things were the new signs that you were 'better' than someone else.

"And even then, it had everything to do with where and when you were born. If you were born lucky, there was a good chance that luck stayed with you for the rest of your life.

"And then people with our genetics—yours and mine—became rare. So the claim of some unique ancestry was the next thing to flaunt. No wonder the Seeds' DNA was so desirable and spawned so many crazy tabloid stories. What's more exotic than to say your hereditary traits are worth preserving by the whole of humanity?

"And now I'm wondering: What would have been the next *it* thing for humans, if the Mims hadn't come? Would settling the solar system have pushed us, or some of our colonists, back into the carpet era? 'I live on Mars and yet I still have an oriental wool carpet.' It's not as crazy as it sounds. Real stuff would become important again. Not fakes, but originals—pieces of furniture made from *real* redwoods, rocks taken from *real* Egyptian pyramids, *real* tea grown on the last plantation on the low-radiation side of India.

"But the *stuff* economy is only viable if people can physically go from place to place. Once humans expand into the stars, the cycle starts up again. That is, if real people go out there. If all we ever send is probes or information..."

Vars stopped and looked over at the Mims structures embedded into the bridge's control consoles for a reaction. In her head, she identified those as the heart of the Mims on the ship. Was she saying something they didn't know? Didn't understand? Was she getting any closer to the *whys* of the Mims?

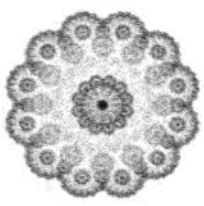

The door to the Vault was locked. Not a surprise. Expected even.

Phoebe rang the "Baby Seed Delivery" alarm and waited. That alarm was to be answered within ten minutes—any longer and the "donated" child might die from exposure. These children were the most precious deliveries made to the Vault. There was only one time when the Baby Seed alarm wasn't triggered—and that was when Vars was deposited at the outside door as a toddler. Matteo had found the girl by accident that day. He'd been totally surprised by the face staring at him through the portal window in the Vault's door. If he'd hesitated or taken longer to run up the stairs on that day as part of his regular security check of the upper floors, the little girl would have frozen to death.

It was getting dark. Not that it ever *really* got light here this time of year. At its peak, the sun rose only partially above the horizon, and the land was blanketed with what felt like a perpetual twilight for a few hours. But now it was getting truly dark; and with the dark came increased cold. Phoebe's hands were already getting stiff, numb. If she was going to blow up the entrance to the Vault, she needed to do it while she still had enough finger mobility to set up the explosive.

She unwrapped the package Matteo had given her.

There was perhaps enough explosive material to at least crack the lock...and convey the seriousness of Phoebe's request for sanctuary to the Elders. The plastic explosive wasn't malleable at these temperatures, so Phoebe spit a bit of her soup on the package to freeze the entire chunk to the door. She had to guess where the lock was located on the other side—there were no keyholes or door handles on this side, and the only time she saw the door from the inside was when she left the Vault to join Matteo at his lab. She didn't remember how the door functioned. She tried looking through the porthole window, but all she could see was darkness with perhaps a subtle green glow from the bioluminescent walls.

She attached the detonator, set the timer, and walked around the above ground structure to shield herself from the

blast.

The Vaults needed to find accommodation with the Mims, she reasoned, and she, Phoebe, could be that link. Humanity had no chance against a galaxy-wide invading force, but perhaps they'd been thinking about this all wrong. Perhaps, instead, they could become part of the collective.

A chill went down Phoebe's spine. Her thoughts seemed so different now. She wasn't interested in fighting the Mims anymore. She came to recognize that it was a losing fight. But still... *The cold must be getting to me,* she thought. She needed to get inside ASAP.

She looked around for the detonator. Where had she put it? It had been in her hands just seconds ago. Well, it didn't matter; it was now just a timer. *But the blast should have gone off by now, right?* She wasn't sure. Her mind was sluggish with cold.

She raised herself above the icy building ledge she was using as cover to look at the door. There were protrusions coming off the smooth metal surface, but she'd never heard a blast. Had the cold affected her hearing?

She walked back to the door. It was still attached, but now, all around it, cubical structures were snapping into the walls, prying the door open. Nothing about this worried Phoebe or unsettled her. She just put her hands into the growing crack and pulled.

The door sprang open. She was in.

She descended a few levels into the Vault and found a room to sleep in. She was exhausted. This far in, she was safe from the cold, and she had enough supplies to last days, if she wanted. She didn't, of course—she wanted to be accepted back into the Seed society. But for now...sleep.

Chapter Twenty-Two

"That's it," Vars said. "What if we just send the information? Just data? What would we need in those faraway star systems in order to live as physical beings again?"

Matteo had woken up to Vars's voice over the speaker. *She's close*, he thought. "Keep thinking aloud, Vars. Keep talking."

Matteo's voice was weak, his throat raw. He reached for something to drink. The thermos felt hot and full. He sipped the liquid—*soup?* It hurt to swallow. His head felt heavy, like a boulder. He felt both hot and cold. It would have been nice if Phoebe hadn't left him here alone. It would have been nice to go back into the Vault with her... There was something about Phoebe, wasn't there?

But Vars needed him.

He managed to set down the empty thermos before falling asleep again.

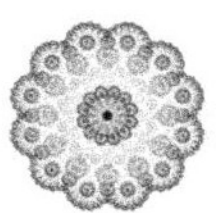

Vars felt more energetic. The food was obviously helping. She should have felt grateful to the Mims for restoring her vigor, but that wasn't at all how she felt.

"I'm going out," she announced. She waited, and after receiving no response, she added, "I plan to walk to your base"—it seemed silly to refer to it as an artifact—"and look for Alice and the others."

As she stood, the feeding tube attached to the side of her body retracted, leaving a slightly irritated area but no other visible skin damage. She left the control room and walked straight to the exton storage locker. It was empty.

"You can't keep me prisoner in here!" she screamed. "Give it back or I'll...I'll go out just like this!"

But she didn't mean it. She wasn't suicidal. And apparently the Mims knew that.

She returned to the bridge. She had no interest in the rest of the ship. The Mims had very demonstrably made it theirs. She could only see what they wanted her to see, the rest was blocked off—she couldn't get inside and she couldn't get the security cameras to show her what was happening in there. But she didn't really need the rest of the ship, did she?

A steaming cup of coffee was waiting for her at her chair. As she sat back down, the feeding tube snapped back into place. It was clearly also doing some waste management too; Vars hadn't had the need to go in days.

She drank the coffee and found it calmed her. She hoped it wasn't a synthetic calm. It was becoming difficult to tell.

"So, you want to take over our bodies," she said. Was she talking to the Mims? Or for the benefit of her dad? "Then why all of this? Just take them. You obviously have the power."

"Are you giving us permission?" Ian-Mims asked.

"What? No! I'm just saying that we, humans, can't really stop you. You took over this ship. You've probably taken over the Earth by now. And the off-world colonies. Why play games? Why me? What do you want from *me*?"

"Moving information around is complicated," said

Ebi-Mims in her soft, androgynous voice, so very different from Ian's. Why were they still keeping up the illusion of multiple entities?

"After millions of years, I would assume you've gotten pretty good at it," Vars said.

"Moving data is easy," Ibe-Mims agreed. He sounded almost exactly like his sister. "But transferring intelligence is hard. Information is always context-dependent. You should know. You tried to teach us that."

"You, Ibe, or you, the Mims?"

"Us. Ibe and me," Ebi-Mims said. "We were not very good students. But the Mims agree with you. Every world has its own unique context. Evolution, even if carefully nurtured, can't be fully controlled. There are always surprises. The spice of life, as you've said in your book. It's easy to grab data, but to pull meaning out of that data? That requires time, experimentation. Each unique solution, each star system, is a jewel of novelty to be savored and explored at leisure."

"That's cruel," Vars said.

"How? You're just another manifestation of us. Harm brought to you is self-harm."

"And yet people died. Sophie..." Vars didn't want to think about how the nanobots had absorbed rats to reconstruct that woman's damaged body.

"We didn't kill Sophie. Your dad did."

"You turned her into a monster!"

"We made her different."

Vars didn't want to respond to that. Human history was jam-packed with examples of differences being treated as deadly threats. But at least those examples—excluding Neanderthals, Altai Denisovans as well as the other two subspecies of Denisovans from Melanesia and New Guinea, Flores men, *Homo luzonensis,* and other now-extinct *Homo sapiens*—involved humans. Sophie-bot was no longer human...not when she died.

Was Dad right to kill her for that? Vars didn't know. She hadn't been there to witness the horror first-hand.

She thought of Ian and the twins. Would she kill them if she discovered their nanobot-ravaged bodies hidden away somewhere on this ship? She didn't know that either. She didn't want to know.

"We've sent our life seeds to other galaxies, too," Ian-Mims said. "Millions or billions of years from now, we might encounter the beings that spawned from our beginnings there."

"If you live that long."

"We will," Ian-Mims assured her. "We've been around for a while. We thrive on the diversity that we begat. We nurture diversity."

"But you're here to take over. That's not nurture. That's conquest."

"Can you *conquer* what's already yours?"

"How are we 'yours'? Even if you seeded the solar system with your life chemistry, we made it this far on our own... right?"

All of a sudden, Vars wasn't so sure about her conclusions. Could the Mims have influenced life on Earth, aside from the initial seeding? Was human evolution pushed in a certain direction? Did the Mims have particular objectives in mind when it came to evolving the dominant species on Earth? *What would an alien species need to become space-faring?* Vars's head spun.

"Can I speak with Alice?" Vars asked. "Is she still Alice?"

"What would you want to do if you could live forever?" asked the Ian entity instead of answering. "If you could set goals in time and space that exceeded the lifetimes of stars?"

"Humans aren't made to think on such grand scales," Vars replied. Her heart rate was up, and she was feeling ill. But she didn't want to put an end to this conversation, not yet. She tried to control her respiration, to slow her rising panic. "Humans were made to live day-to-day. We've pushed that to year-to-year, and even decade-to-decade. But we don't contemplate time on grander scales. Not as individuals."

"*You* do."

"That was my job. And it was abstract. You're talking personally. What would I do if *I* lived forever? It's a meaningless question. It would still be one day at a time; that's how biology works."

"But once information transcends biology?"

"If you're talking about moving myself, my consciousness, from body to body—"

"Or to multiple bodies at the same time."

"There would be drift. The self would split and become something else. Many something *elses*. Talking about *self* as a particular thing would be meaningless. It would be like speciation of duplicate consciousnesses."

"It would be different."

"Yes. It would be different."

"But not necessarily bad."

"I don't know."

Vars's mind felt leaden. Too much information, too strange, too unfamiliar, too...incompatible. She sensed a metallic taste under her tongue and started to drift off.

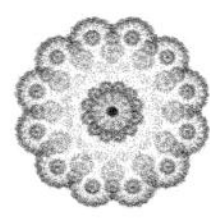

When she woke again, Vars reached for her soup. The thermos was cold and empty. She looked over to the coffee machine. It was offline.

"Hello? Ian?" she called. "Ebi? Ibe? Anyone there?"

No response.

She uncurled from the chair—or whatever it was now. Over the days, it had grown more massive—more like a throne...or a life support station. But she was no longer plugged into it. When she stood and walked away from the bridge, nothing stopped her.

"Hello?" she called into the deserted corridors. "Anyone? If you don't answer, I will walk out of here."

She walked to the exton lockers. They were still empty. She considered her options. She could go back to her chair and wait for the Mims to return and nurture her...or she could do something. She couldn't walk to the artifact—Mims Base—without an exton. She was stuck on this ship. There was no way to go anywhere. Except...

This is a ship. Ships go places.

As soon as the idea popped into her head, she was running back to the bridge. She didn't have to move the ship very far. Just a jump, really. She could get herself closer to Alice and figure out the next steps from there.

The only problem was she had absolutely no clue how to fly this ship...or any ship. She'd operated a land vehicle once, back when she and her dad were collecting samples in the Bad Lands, but even that machine was mostly automated. Maybe this ship was largely automated too?

She stepped right up to the ship's control panel. It was still covered with the Mims structures. "Ship," she said. "Start up navigation controls." She used the authoritative voice she normally reserved for her classroom lectures.

A few lights came on.

"Set course for the Mims's artifact."

Nothing happened.

Vars looked around for her personal computing pad. She had a memory of carrying it onto the bridge at some point, but she didn't see it among all of the fractal-covered surfaces.

"Vars PCD," she said aloud. The devices were made to respond to voice commands.

A tiny beeping sound came from underneath the coffee machine. Unfortunately, the coffee machine was now at least twice as big as it had originally been, and Vars's PCD was apparently buried deep within the nanobot structures encasing the machine.

But it *had* heard her. Maybe that was enough.

"Vars PCD, read instructions for takeoff," Vars said.

A muffled voice started to read through a complicated set of procedures. Vars listened for a minute before realizing she'd never pull this off. She tried a new tactic.

"Vars PCD, initialize ship's landing stabilization procedure." She had a vague memory of Liut talking about a preprogrammed hop in case the icy ground underneath the ship's landing spot started to shift. And a little hop was all she needed.

Lights and monitors came online above the flight control station.

"Good, good," Vars said. "Read out the contingency landing sites preprogrammed by Major Liut."

One of the monitors listed ten sets of coordinates. Unfortunately, they meant nothing to Vars—she needed visuals.

"Display the landing sites coordinates on Mimas planetary grid."

A rotating image of Mimas appeared on one of the screens, with little dots superimposed on it. A few dots were on the opposite hemisphere, but most were in the basin of the Herschel Crater, and all of them closer to the artifact than the ship was now. Vars recalled the scientists recommending they land at least five kilometers away—apparently Liut had never even considered that.

Three of the sites were directly at the base of the central Mims's mount, and one was immediately adjacent to the artifact. *That's the one.*

"Vars PCD, zoom in on location five."

The screen showed a close-up of the proposed landing site. It wasn't next to the structure; it was right on *top* of it. Vars was sure that even Liut wouldn't have programmed a landing site directly on top of the Mims's artifact, which meant that the structure had grown at least by this much since these contingency plans were made. Well, it had worked out for the best, as far as Vars was concerned. That was a perfect position for what she needed now.

"Vars PCD, set the sequence of landing adjustments to location five."

A computerized voice—not a Mims voice—said, "Authorization Required."

"Vars PCD, locate the senior level personnel on board the ship."

"Only one crewmember is currently located on the ship. Senior scientist Dr. Varsaad Volhard. Authorization accepted."

It was nice that the ship had confirmed Vars was the only person on board. That meant that at least the ship security algorithms didn't recognize Ian and the twins as present, and thus they placed all authority with Vars...just as they were programmed to do.

"Vars PCD, execute the landing adjustment maneuver to location five."

Several alarms went off, screens flashed, but she heard the engines revving up. She went back into her augmented captain's chair and waited.

Two hours later, the ship was on top of the Mims structure.

"Dad," Vars called into the radio microphone, "I'm leaving the ship. I'm going to rescue Alice. Or at least try. It should be interesting. I will inform you of the results of my efforts. Love you."

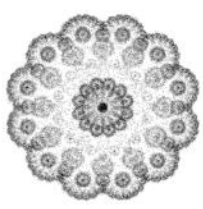

If Swiss cheese had been designed by a persnickety engineer, the results would have been the surface of the Mims Base. It seemed there could be no way that this structure could be pressurized to support human life. But appearances could be deceiving.

Vars instructed the external cameras to zoom in on as many different locations on the alien base as possible from their vantage points. The ship had externally mounted instruments, including a robotic arm, equipped to take samples and manipulate objects, and Vars wanted to find a good spot to do a bit of digging. She no longer feared damaging the structure; she'd landed a spaceship on top of it, for goodness' sake. And if the Mims wanted to stop her, they could easily do so at any time.

After several hours of observations, Vars chose a location with a slightly larger-than-average hole and instructed the robotic arm to dig in...or at least try to break off a piece or two. *That ought to get the attention of anyone inside.*

"Alice, if you can hear me knocking, open the door," Vars spoke just under her breath.

She made the robotic arm drill and prick, pick and smash, dig and hammer at the alien structure. Sometimes little bits fell off and tumbled gracefully in Mimas's low gravity to the crater floor below. There was a sound to this venture, a rhythm, and Vars gathered herself into a tight ball in her augmented chair and listened. Any change in the music of destruction meant a little bit of progress. Accomplishment. Was it Ben who had said it was like poking a hornets' nest? *Well, let them come at me; let them reveal their motives.*

Chapter Twenty-Three

As Phoebe awoke, she took time to take stock of her body. Was there any permanent damage from her sojourn away from home? She was able to move all her fingers, but she wasn't sure if she'd keep all her toes. She felt a burning pain in both feet. It didn't matter. She'd made it, she was home, and she would never go back out there again. Never.

She opened her eyes and looked around. She was in one of the small supply rooms on the upper levels of the Vault. This was where the Seeds stored whatever they couldn't manufacture for themselves. The Elders had made sure the Vaults could survive without any of this stuff, but it was still nice to have. In addition to some exotic materials, foodstuffs, and electronics, there were space rations—ready-to-eat meals— that were theoretically capable of lasting at least a century. It wasn't haute cuisine, but it was nutrition. The Vaults measured time differently than humanity up above. Their job was to survive, above all else, to live long enough to repopulate the world again after a planet-wide calamity.

What was their role now, after the invasion of an alien species? Was simple survival enough?

Phoebe pulled a ration pack from an open container. As she ate, it occurred to her that finding an open container up here was strange—these ready-to-eat meals were strictly for emergencies. She looked around again, more thoughtfully this time. The room looked vaguely familiar. Among industrial gray and bioluminescent green, a small patch of pink stuffed into a corner caught her eye. She got up, despite the burning pain in her feet, and walked over to investigate. It was a tiny baby blanket.

The vaults got regular deliveries of *fresh* Seeds—babies with genetic traits that the Human Genome Heritage Project ruled valuable. In fact, most Seeds were born outside the Vaults. Phoebe herself was *collected* at around two years of age, although she had no memories of her life before the Vault. The transfer of these babies was a very orderly process, except in the case of… *Vars! This must be Vars's.* What a crazy coincidence to wind up in the same room where Matteo once stashed the little girl all these years ago. Phoebe folded up the little piece of cloth and tucked it into her pocket. She would tell Matteo about it later.

Matteo! She was supposed to have called him as soon as she got past the Vault's door security. He must have been frantic by now, assuming she was dead or dying out in the tundra.

Phoebe rummaged around her pack, looking for the radio. But it wasn't there. She dumped the pack's contents onto the floor. She still had a few packets of dehydrated fruit, her PCD with all of the data from the lab and hours of recordings of Vars talking from Mimas, a portable antenna, and some spare batteries, but no radio. She must have lost it when she set up the explosives. Except it wasn't in her nature to lose things.

Regardless, she needed to find a way of letting Matteo know she was okay; she didn't want him doing something rash. There were definitely other ways to reach him from here. The Elders were in regular contact with the wardens' station.

And for the sake of emergencies, *phones*—old tech that relied on physical wires in the ground to create a permanent connection between locations—were installed in various spots around the Vault. Supposedly the ones on the top floor could be used to contact the wardens' station, though Phoebe had never heard of anyone other than the Elders ever using the phones to do that.

She trudged, painfully, back up to the top floor. As she moved up the metal staircase, she realized there was something wrong with her time sense—she couldn't tell how long it had been since she'd entered the Vault. After a lifetime of unfailing chrono-awareness, this drifting temporal perception was disconcerting. And there was another thing bothering her: the green light emanating from the walls felt wrong. The color was…off, somehow. She made a mental note to check the genetic drift of the bioluminescent bacteria just to make sure there hadn't been some drastic mutation while she'd been away.

Phoebe was almost at the top of the stairs when she noticed that some of the walls seemed to…*boil*. That was the best description she could manage for the strange shimmering just below the bioluminescent bacterial film. She leaned in for a closer look, but she knew even before she spotted them that the walls were teeming with nanobots.

She jerked back, pulled her hands off the rails. But even the stairs under her feet had the same boiling quality, and she couldn't levitate above those.

The Vault was infected.

Vars woke up to the sound of grinding metal.

"Vars PCD," she said. "What's the status of the tunnel?"

For answer, Vars got the loud, whirling silence of an empty ship. Since the realization that she could use her personal computing device to direct the ship, Vars had felt an elated sense of power. But now the PCD didn't respond. What was going on?

She looked up at the monitors. When she fell asleep, they were showing various views of the robotic arm inflicting damage on the Mims structure. Now they showed...

"Did you suck *my* ship into your base?" Now that she had gained control over it, Vars felt a strong sense of ownership over the ship as well. *Partial control...*

Out of the dozen screens, only one still showed the surface of Mimas with a partial view of Saturn. The outside cameras carefully placed by the crew on arrival got left behind at the old landing site...more like ripped out. Some of the screens in front of Vars displayed nothing but digital snow now. The rest showed various close-ups of the now familiar irregular Menger sponge fractal pattern—Mims's favorite construction pattern.

"Ian? Ibe? Ebi? What's going on out there?" Vars called out to the ship.

They didn't respond either. She hadn't heard from them since before she moved the ship. She wondered what had changed. She wasn't being fed, either. Vars's stomach rumbled in affirmation of her hunger. Even the coffee maker had stopped working. *The true horror...*

"Well, I think I'd better go get some coffee," she said aloud and walked out into the corridors of the ship. The ship mess hall was still in there somewhere...theoretically, anyway.

All of the electronics Vars encountered were covered with nanobot structures, and even clear surfaces had alien patterns running over them. Whole sections of the ship were completely blocked off by nanobot structures. Fortunately, the entrance to the food storage area was not closed up. Vars ignored the nanobots crawling the walls, grabbed a few ready-to-eat meals, and returned to the bridge. The bridge was where all the action was, even if she could only see and understand a small fraction of what was going on with her ship. *My ship.* It was *her* ship; Mims had to right to it...all the nanobots notwithstanding.

"*My* ship," she said out loud. "And don't you forget it. *I'm* the authority in here." It made her feel better to say it, no matter how silly it was.

Vars sat in her nanobot-enhanced chair and opened one of the meal packages. A chemical heating process kicked in automatically, and she felt the whole thing get warm in her hands. She couldn't recognize the contents, but her dad had taught her not to be picky about food a long time ago. *Seeds don't get such luxuries as food preferences,* Vars thought. Her dad's *seedness* explained a lot about him. She wished again that she had known about his past sooner.

When she'd finished her meal, she stashed the empty container into the disposal and packed the other two into a pouch she made from one of the space blankets she discovered along the way.

A voice sounded over the ship's speakers. "Dr. Volhard, we are ready for you."

Vars was so startled, she dropped her improvised pouch. "What?"

"Please go to the airlock and open the door."

Vars retrieved her pouch and went to the airlock. She wasn't following orders, she told herself. It was already her plan to go out there. One way or another. *My decision.*

The whole Earth is infected, Phoebe thought. *Does it matter that the Vault—my Vault—is infected too?*

But even as she asked the question, she knew the answer was yes. It *did* matter. There was a sick wrongness about it. The bots were here, where they should never be. And the Seeds…weren't. No one had come for her. She had forced the Vault's outside door open—who knew how long ago now— and no one had responded, no one came to find her.

Where is everyone?

Phoebe found the antique-looking phone and lifted the handle. She kept it a few inches away from her face, unable to stomach direct contact between her skin and the nanobot layer covering the receiver…not that gloves gave much pro- tection. "Hello?" she said. "Can anyone hear me?"

The device responded with a staticky noise and a pat- ternless clicking. Phoebe wanted to throw the thing against the wall. Her hand was trembling badly.

"Hello? Please, hello!"

Phoebe pleaded and cried. She banged the phone's handle against the shimmering walls. She yelled at the walls. She even tried to set the wall on fire, but all she achieved was a small charred circle that quickly filled in with nanobots again. She yelled Matteo's name and then the name of every Seed she could remember.

No one heard her. No one came.

Finally, she pulled herself together. She was alone. More alone than she'd ever been. And she was going to remain alone. There was no one here who was going to help her. And that was fine. She had made it this far; she could go farther. She had to.

She began her descent into the Vault's heart.

In the room where she'd found Vars's blanket, Phoebe picked up more ready-to-eat meals and filled up her water thermoses. She knew it was a long trek down—although she hadn't made it often. Matteo used to have the tough job of running regular patrols up above; she'd managed to avoid that duty by becoming a good researcher and an excellent teacher. But she'd done the climb when she went to join Matteo's lab. Of course, she'd used an elevator part of the way then. But the bots might be in control of it now. She didn't want to risk using it and getting trapped.

Phoebe had never understood the need to keep such a large separation between the world at large and the Vault's population—it seemed like wasted space to have all these little-used upper levels. But now she was glad of it, since it meant that much more work for the nanobots to get down into the heart of the Vault. It gave Phoebe time to get there first.

The deeper she descended, the more *right* the biolumi-nescence looked to her. Perhaps she should have gathered samples from up above? *No—it might be dangerous to bring the mutated algae below.* And she was liable to bring some nanobots along with it. Matteo had already discovered that the bots liked to attach themselves to microorganisms. But then again, wasn't she already bringing nanobots with her— on her clothes, perhaps in her very blood? She was the per-fect delivery mechanism—a Trojan horse willingly allowed into the Vault's inner sanctum. *Well, not yet.* But the Elders hadn't stopped her, so she felt it was okay to proceed. If she presented a real risk, she would be stopped; she was sure of it.

Phoebe approached the Vault's last barrier to the out-side—a giant set of electrified plates, several tons each, which blocked the passage up or down. She slowed. If the plates were engaged, this would be the end of the road for her. She would have to go back up and live out her life on food rations, wandering the upper floors alone...well, not alone...

She stopped in front of another phone and picked it up. "Elder Alaba, this is Seed Phoebe. I come with valuable information, and I request a formal invitation back into the Vault." She added a silent "please" and waited.

There was static on this line too, but no clicking sounds.

She leaned into the metal, cage-like wall of the stairwell and placed her tongue on it, hoping not to feel the telltale signs of electrical current. There was always a bit of spillover from the electrified plates. When engaged, it tickled and had an acidic taste to it. As kids, they called this the "tongue test." Phoebe remembered doing it with Matteo—and getting caught. She didn't recall Matteo's punishment, but she was sent to work in the lab. She loved her assignment so much, it became her whole world. Perhaps if Matteo had been treated to the same punishment, he would have stayed deep in the Vault and never gone up to find his daughter…sister.

What a twisted bit of fate.

But she didn't believe in fate. She believed in selection, in design. In intent.

Something clicked in Phoebe's mind. A realization. *Vars…* It made no sense that she was abandoned at the door like that or that Matteo was the one to find her. And yet it had to be deliberate. There was a design there, an intent. Someone knew almost thirty years before about the invasion. Perhaps longer. Someone knew and planned for it. Someone created Vars, either to force Matteo to leave or for some other reason Phoebe didn't understand yet. But she would.

She held up the phone again. "Matteo? Matteo, can you hear me? Please pick up the phone."

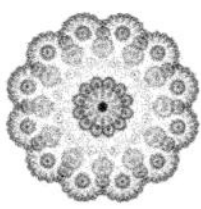

A ringing sound. Matteo had heard it before. It was relentless, insistent. He wanted it to stop.

His body felt awful; his very bones hurt. He felt rooted into his chair. Even standing up seemed impossible.

He drank more of the hot soup. It made him feel better…

and sleepy. Or dreamy. His thoughts felt all tangled up. He wanted to talk with his little girl.

"Vars?" he called into the dark room. Why was it so dark? Was it nighttime? He'd lost all sense of time. But he was underground and it was winter—it didn't really matter what time of day it was on the outside. It certainly didn't matter to Vars, out there on a frozen moon. "Vars?"

The ringing continued. Matteo looked around for the source. There was an old-fashioned telephone receiver built into the communications center. A direct line to the Elders.

Did he want to talk with them? He had to tell them what he knew. He had to corroborate Phoebe's story. *Phoebe!* He hadn't heard from her.

He picked up the handle. "Hello?"

Chapter Twenty-Four

Vars stepped out into the Mims's artifact with no exton, no protection whatsoever—just the tights and close-fitting stretch shirt she'd been wearing for what felt like forever. Her hair, still too short to hang or lay flat on her head, stood out like a thick dark red brush. She had a feeling she looked like a Triplets refugee camp survivor.

"Alice?" she called into the labyrinthine structure. "I made it. I finally came for you. Alice?" Ben and the others would...could be in here somewhere too, but it was finding Alice that Vars focused her hopes on for some reason. If asked, she wouldn't have been able to explain. Somehow Alice signified survival, hope. *First Alice, then everyone else...*

Vars looked back at her ship. It looked nothing like it did the last time she saw it from the outside, back when she took her first EVA to explore the Mims's artifact. The nanobot structures that covered the ship now formed a seamless transition with the alien base. The ship was *part* of this structure now. It would never fly again.

Worse, Vars realized with a start, it would be impossible to see her ship from orbit or with any of the long-rage telescopes back home. It had been swallowed whole, and Vars along with it. There was a finality to the thought, and Vars had to take time to force down her panic and get herself

    Harvest

under control.

A voice spoke from somewhere around her. It sounded...
Alice-like. "Sentient life's colonization of our galaxy is fractal,"
it said. "There are many species even within a single ecosystem that possess intelligence and self-awareness. But only
one species becomes dominant. These are your words, Dr.
Volhard. Your thoughts. Remember?"

"I remember," Vars said. She had given that speech many
times on her book tour.

"But even a fractal has to start somewhere. The universe
is 13.8 billion years old. It had a beginning, and so did life in
this galaxy. And then came a time when that life developed
the ability to analyze itself. For any discrete entity, there's
always a first."

"You were first," Vars said.

"*We* were first."

Vars ignored the inclusive pronoun. "Does being first always mean also ending up as the last?" she asked. "The only?
Does being first equate to winning the galactic lottery?"

"You should know the answer, Dr. Volhard. It's all about
the initial conditions."

"Luck. The toss of some cosmic dice."

"Even on galactic scales, it comes down to luck. It might
be true on the universal level, too—time is too young to tell
yet. Impetuous gods play with dice all the time."

"So what do you want from us? From me?" Vars asked.
She realized that she was seated on a protrusion made by the
box fractal. She didn't remember sitting down.

"*You* are *us* for all intents and purposes. We seeded you.
You've already guessed as much."

Vars could only nod. She wished there was someone she
could look at...a face, a person, something other than an in-
finite regression of cubes. She yearned for Alice. For her dad.

For not being alone in this. Did it even matter what she said? Would she…*could* she change the course of human history? *No pressure.*

"You've guessed a lot, but not all," Alice's voice said. "We can let you swap places with your father—"

"What?"

"There are advantages to close genetic ties. It would have been better if you were identical twins, or clones, but that couldn't be arranged in time."

"Did you…" Vars couldn't complete the thought. She just couldn't go there.

"But you are close enough that I can make it work." *I?* "My plan was to move you back and forth, help you understand and prepare. You are our children, but not all children are the same."

"I don't understand," Vars said, her voice breaking.

"I plan to make you understand. And then you will help me."

"*Me*? Not *us*?"

"Even after a few billion years, we are not all the same, Vars. Individuality is a precious thing. We work hard to keep our identities separate and intact, despite the difficulties."

Vars didn't know what that meant. "Is there still an Alice?" she asked.

"There's some Alice in me. I should say, *all* of Alice is in me. And that makes me different from all who are *not* Alice."

"Can I see her? Alice? Can I talk to you face to face? Humans are better at communication when we can interact with each other directly. Words and sounds have limits. We've evolved to take advantage of the full range of senses and cues that our species can produce." Vars had used this very argument with her graduate students to compel them to show up for class. There was a whole range of meaning she was missing. Was Alice aware of this conversation? Was there still a bond of friendship between them? Did those subtle changes in chemistry and neuron connections that came to be because they liked each other transfer to this... this...this Mims entity? *And can I use that?*

"You're exhibiting extreme signs of stress." *No shit.* "I don't want you to come to harm. Bodies are fragile and should be treated with respect." Given what Vars knew of Sophie's transformation, she found this statement highly hypocritical. "As soon as you are ready, you will come to see me."

"I'm ready now," Vars said.

"Soon."

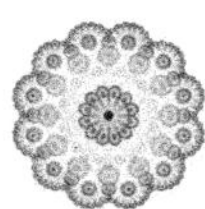

"The Mims took over the Vault," Phoebe said. If that wasn't *completely* true yet, it would be soon. There was nothing she or Matteo could do to stop that from happening.

"They've taken over Vars's ship, too," Matteo said into heavy handset of the landline phone.

"I'm sorry."

"Vars said she'd moved the ship on top of the alien structure on Mimas, and that she was leaving the ship. I think she's still hoping to find Alice."

"Alice is dead. Or at least she's no longer Alice."

"I know."

"I'm coming back," Phoebe said, realizing only as she said it that she had made the decision. And now that she had, she wanted to race out of the Vault and back to Matteo.

"Are you sure?"

"Yes. I'll see you soon, Matteo." And just before she hung up the receiver, she added, "Love you."

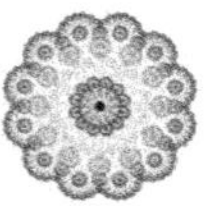

Vars was sure the walls were shifting. She almost caught them moving several times, but the movement was always at the periphery of her vision. Worse, she was lost. She hadn't walked far, but she could no longer see the way back into the ship. The only logical conclusion was that the Mims had hidden it from her. Perhaps they were conducting a sick experiment—humans under duress, running inside the proverbial maze, like rats.

At least the air in the Mims structure was breathable— she wasn't sure how, but it was. Vars had two sealed meals and a thermos of vitamin-rich water; she wasn't able to figure out how to make coffee back on the ship without the Mims's help. *Another proof that aliens are evil.* She laughed silently at her own joke. Still, she could last a few days, even a week, on this. Then thirst would be a problem.

Vars looked around again. One of these walls hid the ship. But every wall looked the same; or, at least, the pattern was the same everywhere and always equally confusing. The box fractal added a fractional dimension to the space. Like Jackson Pollock's drips on canvas had a fractional dimensionality to them—the drips approached two dimensions of a plane instead of the single dimension of a pen stroke—the recursion of box within box within box raised the dimensionality of the Mims Base from three to at least three and a half, Vars guesstimated. It was this raised dimensionality that was confusing her senses, making a systematic search difficult.

She had an idea. She opened one of the containers of food. The dark, viscous liquid would be perfect for making marks on the walls. She got some of the sticky, unctuous goo on her fingers and marked the first large cube protrusion. Then she stepped to the next, moving over only by one. She examined each protrusion carefully, pushing and pulling on the smaller cubes to see if anything budged. If it all felt solid under her fingertips, she marked it with a smear. If there was an opening large enough to accommodate her arm or head, she poked inside, as far as she was able, then marked it with a two-finger smear. If it had a hole large enough to fit her whole body, Vars marked the outside with a handprint. In this manner she circumnavigated the space around her.

"I swear I examined this one before," she grumbled under her breath as she traced the edges of medium-sized cube with her hand. It felt like she'd been at this task for an awfully long time, and this wasn't such a large space. She looked around. She'd made only two palm prints, and she could still see both. But there weren't enough single-finger smears—she was sure she'd marked many more cube protrusions than were visible. Either the walls were able to erase her marks somehow, or they moved the painted surfaces in such a way as to hide her smudging notations from view.

Vars stepped back into the center of the space, sat on the floor, and watched the trickster walls. While she waited, she finished off the last of the food from the open container. Nothing wasted. Every calorie was precious now.

Slowly, the box fractal with the first handprint shifted. It was the tiniest of shifts, but Vars was paying attention now, expecting it, and noticed the motion right away. Humans had evolved to be very good at detecting motion.

"There you go," Vars said approvingly. "Show me what you've got."

After the slow start, the box flipped completely in only a fraction of a second. One moment the handprint was visible, and the next it was gone. Without a sound.

Vars got up and walked over to that cube. It seemed very similar to how it looked before, but now, the deeper cubes aligned such that through the central opening Vars could see a faint light at the end of a long tunnel.

"Like Alice's rabbit hole," she said aloud. *That she never came out of.* "I guess you're inviting me to go in now," she told the room.

Vars adjusted her makeshift sack with the last ready meal and thermos and climbed inside.

Phoebe felt buoyed by her decision to return to Matteo. There was no angst over whether she'd be allowed in or if she'd need to blow her way inside. And the dread of the unknown was no longer a burden—Phoebe knew what she would leave behind. The journey back to the wardens' station felt much faster than the trek to the Vault. She practically ran the last mile; the pain in her frost-bitten toes felt irrelevant somehow.

As she opened the station door, she called for Matteo, though she didn't expect him to hear her; the communications room was two floors below. She bolted the outside door shut and made her way downstairs.

The walls here had the same shimmer as she'd seen back in the Vault. But of course the Mims were here too. She and Matteo were both infected. Still, she had made the decision to spend her last days of being human with her Seed-brother, the man she would have chosen as her life mate if he hadn't left the Vault all those years ago. *Or was made to leave,* Phoebe reminded herself of the insight she had back in the Vault.

Matteo was seated in a throne-like chair in front of

the communication controls. That hadn't been there before. Looking closer, she realized that it was just a regular chair augmented with nanobot technology. There was even a vital signs indicator integrated directly into the chair now. Phoebe could see that Matteo's pulse was a steady eighty-seven beats per minute—a bit on a high side, but within an acceptable range, especially for a sick man. He was slumped onto the controls, sleeping. The thermos Phoebe had left with Matteo was on the floor next to him. It was still full.

"You have to take care of yourself, Matteo," she said as she ran her hand over his forehead. He wasn't feverish anymore. He was getting better, just drained of energy by his sickness and injuries.

While Matteo got his rest, Phoebe decided to check for transmissions from Vars...or anyone else. She put on the headphones and settled down to listen.

There was some crazy chatter from Vars—the girl was losing it out there by herself, so far from humanity—but Phoebe understood that Vars had managed to move the ship directly on top of what the girl was now calling the "Mims Base" and that she'd received an "invitation" to explore the alien structure. The Mims used Alice to lure Vars inside. Phoebe didn't think they needed to bother—Vars was going to go regardless. *I would too,* she realized. Exploration was preferable to suffocating inside an alien cocoon. It gave the mind something to do. A focus.

Phoebe remembered Alice well: smart, tiny, fearless, antsy. It had been clear that Alice would leave the Vault at her ten-thousand-days mark even before she was old enough to start school. Some kids were like that—there was no talking to them, no stopping the impulsiveness, just give them nurture and care and education to succeed in the world above. Phoebe worked hard to give all that to Alice, even though their temperaments clashed constantly. *She'll clash with the Mims, too,* Phoebe thought with a smirk. *They have no idea what a crazy smart fireplug they've got on their hands.* She took a long drag from Matteo's thermos. It was still warm.

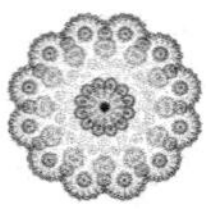

"You found me," Alice said.

She sat almost completely encased in a sarcophagus-like framework, her exton augmented and completely embedded into the alien structure. That was the comparison that jumped to Vars's mind. *To an anthropologist's mind,* she thought.

"Hello, Alice," Vars said. "I'm so happy to see you alive."

"I'm rather pleased about that myself," said Alice. *Alice-Mims,* Vars reminded herself. "When I got stuck in that tunnel, I thought it was the end," the alien creature said.

"So you remember?"

Alice sniggered. It was such an Alice expression that Vars had to stop herself from rushing toward the small woman and embracing her despite all of the surrounding hardware. "In the beginning, the Mims Base, as you call it, wasn't ready to accommodate my human needs. Thus all of this."

"But now? Are you free to return to the ship with me?"

"My freedoms are limitless. Or as limitless as billions of years of study can make them."

And there it was: the admission of non-humanity.

Vars didn't know how to respond. It was easier when the Mims were playing mind games with her. Now? This was now officially the first contact. *First Contact!*

"Hello," Vars managed.

"Hello," Alice said with a smile.

So human...

"What should I call you?" asked Vars. "I don't really know. I don't know what you want. I don't understand. Help me."

"Alice will do just fine. Do you remember talking about Dunbar's Number?"

"Dr. Robin Dunbar, the anthropologist who proposed an upper limit on the number of stable social connection an individual can have at one time. It was based on primate brain physiology."

"Do you remember what that number was?"

Vars answered without hesitation. "For humans, one hundred and fifty or thereabout."

"It's a wonder the Vaults survive, right?" Alice-Mims laughed. She—*it?*—sounded just like Alice. It was disconcerting.

"I've never been," Vars said. "But the Vaults would be interesting to study."

"The Elders are all over that."

"Really?" *But of course they would be,* Vars realized. "Why is this important?" *Important to you, to Mims?*

"What do you think an equivalent number would be for a set of intelligent entities that all belonged to one mind?"

"I don't think I understand the problem." Vars didn't want to jump to any conclusions. *First Contact!* The idea continued to bounce around her head, making thinking difficult.

"Ben said—"

"Ben? Is he okay?"

Alice-Mims ignored Vars's question. "Ben said that sending artifacts across the vastness of space is wasteful. Information, though..."

"Information travels at the speed of light."

"And?"

"It requires a receiver. It would require many more years to plant a receiver at a destination."

"But there's plenty of time," Alice-Mims said. "Keep going."

"Once in place, the receiver can build out using local resources."

"Like this place on Mimas. Or the ones out on the asteroids. Or on your moon. Or back on Earth."

"Earth," Vars repeated, dumbfounded.

"You didn't really think the best place to build a receiver in your star system would have been on a small, icy satellite in orbit around one of the gas giants? At such a distance from your home world?"

"No?" Frankly, Vars hadn't much considered the question of strategic locations for conquest of the solar system. Not yet. "Why do you need receivers?" she asked. "What information are you sending?"

"I think you've figured it out already." Alice-Mims was still smiling at Vars, still patiently encouraging her to figure things out on her own.

But Vars felt sick. She sank down onto the nanobot-built floor. "How many instances of the same entity can be spread out across the galaxy before it loses coherence?" she said quietly. That was the Dunbar number Alice-Mims was asking about. How many different copies of herself could she send about the galaxy as information to be placed into the local hosts without creating so many versions of herself that they could never reconcile into one mind?

"Yes. That's the question," the creature confirmed.

"Well, wouldn't it depend on the time scales?" Vars asked. "How long do the different versions stay separate without recombining to become one again? What's the limit for such consciousness branching before *speciation* occurs?"

"Good," Alice-Mims said. "At what point does an instance of a mind become a new entity? An entity that doesn't want to be subsumed into its past's whole? It depends on how much life has been crammed into those years. Sentries left behind to monitor star systems' progress can stay separated from their first-instance entity for millennia. Waiting is slow. Mostly nothing happens."

Vars finally thought she understood something. "But sometimes," she started, "sometimes a set of giant asteroids hits the world under observation. Then things speed up. A lot of events get packed into a shorter time frame."

Alice-Mims smiled. Her eyes bored into Vars's. She still wore those thick glasses.

"How long have you been out here, Alice?"

"About twenty thousand years."

"That's…that's all of human civilization's history." Vars felt sick. All that time alone out here, on Saturn's moon. "Were you in contact with your…first-instance entity?"

"No. Not until thirty-five of your years ago."

Vars tried to make sense of that time frame. Keres Triplets hit in 2057. That was sixty-seven years ago. If this Alice-Mims entity sent a message home right after the Earth's devastation and received a reply thirty-five years ago, that meant the message's "round trip" took sixty-seven minus thirty-five years—thirty-two years. That would make Alice-Mims's first-instance entity sixteen light-years away from Earth.

That was uncomfortably close.

Chapter Twenty-Five

Phoebe woke up in a throne-like chair. It was similar to Matteo's, perhaps not as elaborate, but then the Mims had more time to work on his.

"You're back," Matteo said gently. He was smiling at her while giving her a visual inspection. Phoebe recognized that look. Every teacher learned the trick of spot-evaluation empathy.

"How long was I out?" she asked.

"Perhaps a day? I don't know when you got back, so I can't give you the exact time. Besides, my time sense is way off."

"Mine too." Phoebe looked around. There were now two thermos bottles—one for Matteo and one clearly meant for her. "Thanks," she said, nodding to hers.

"I didn't do it."

Phoebe picked up her thermos. It was full and hot.

"Be careful," Matteo said. "I have reason to believe it's drugged. It's good, mind you. But there are costs."

So that's why I slept through the making of my "throne." "It made you better?"

"Yes. Or it enforced rest, so my own body could do the trick. Either way, I'm better."

"I see," she said, nodding. She took a small sip from the thermos and forced a swallow—it was that or die. The soup was good. "Well, I made it to the Vault." Phoebe jumped right to the point. "It's infected. And you were right: they didn't let me in. I had to blow my way through the door."

"Mm-hmm," Matteo muttered uninterestedly. He fiddled with the communications controls.

Phoebe felt panic rising up inside her. Had she gotten back too late? Had the Mims gotten to him? "Matteo—"

"Wait, Phoebe. I want to show you something."

He had a gleam in his eyes—a gleam that was so familiar from their days as kids roaming the stairwells of the Vault. Phoebe exhaled her fear. *It will be all right,* she told herself. *Not all is lost.*

"Okay, I have it," he announced as the video screens above their heads came to life.

Phoebe watched as people walked the streets of major metropolises all over the world. There were clips of concerts and public performances, governmental debates and class-rooms. A newsperson talked about improvements in Earth-Moon transports—the space elevator to near-Earth orbit was getting a significant upgrade. There were photos of smiling kids and pets running around some park somewhere.

"What *is* all this?" she asked.

"The world right now," Matteo said with a smile. "There have even been advancements in cancer care—"

"Nanobots?"

"Yes. Even the planet itself is getting an environmental upgrade, as far as I can understand. Everything is greener, happier, healthier..."

"But I thought—"

"I thought everyone was dead, too," Matteo said. "But that was just what the Mims wanted us to think. The world is fine."

"The world is fine," Phoebe repeated. She paused. "Except

for us and the Vaults."

"Perhaps just *a* Vault," Matteo said. "Although there *were* reports of equipment glitches all over the solar system. People did die—at the last count, fifty-nine. That includes the crew of twenty-five on the Mimas-bound research ship."

"No one knows?" Phoebe asked.

"Apparently not."

"Our world is under attack, and no one knows." Shock didn't capture how Phoebe felt; it was mostly numbness.

"It might be better this way, don't you think?" Matteo said. He obviously had some time to get familiar with this information.

Phoebe closed her eyes and saw the last few days of Sophie in her mind's eye. And those poor lab assistants. "It might be better," she agreed after a while. There was nothing anyone could do to stop the Mims, so dying—or was it living?—in ignorance might be bliss.

"But *we* know," Matteo said.

"Yes. We know." *No bliss for us.*

"I don't know," Vars said. "There are too many variables that I can't even consider, and so little actual information. I can't even make a guess at a reasonably safe number of instances for a single…person."

"Funny you say that," Alice-Mims said. "After millions of years, it's not a settled question even for us."

Vars was about to ask how many Mims there were. Given millions, if not billions, of years of civilization, it made sense that the Mims would have had a population explosion. But perhaps it was just the opposite. If individuals could take on any number of "bodies" from the planets they've seeded, then a lifespan for any one individual would be virtually limitless. So why breed? Why not just gobble up all the available experiences for a singular consumption?

She asked a different question instead. "How old are you?"

"Ah, that's the question, isn't it?" Alice-Mims snickered—so like Alice. "In this body, I'm Alice's age."

"That's not my question."

"At my age, *personhood* is a difficult idea. But I understand what you're asking. When did I start?" Alice-Mims's voice was bittersweet. "I don't remember anymore. I have amassed so many beginnings, so many childhoods. Each is sweet and tender, for the most part."

"But those aren't yours!"

"They're mine as soon as they become part of me. Consider stories, Vars. Each story you've consumed—read or seen or heard or lived—is now part of who you are. Does it matter that you weren't the original storyteller? All those stories form your foundation."

"Just like a cultural foundation," Vars said, the implications dawning on her.

Each individual Mims is a culture. The realization hit Vars hard. But cultures were something she knew, understood. Cultures carefully nourished the members of each generation to make them part of a greater whole. Cultures made sure everyone knew the same stories, sang the same songs, spoke in the same metaphors, used the same memes as shortcuts to meaning. Any civilization that lacked such shared cultural aesthetics suffered a decline. People needed a common glue to keep them together. For a while, on Earth, religion did that. Later, political views sometimes assumed the role, but not as well. So what did it mean for a single individual to become a unique bundle of cultural heritage?

"How do you relate to your peers?" Vars asked.

"We make an effort to experience worlds together."

"That would put a limit on how many of you are out there."

"True, but don't forget the multiplicity factor. We don't need to experience just one thing at time. We have a whole galaxy to explore, to live."

"What happens to the people you...*experience?*"

"They become us."

"So Alice is you?"

"The story of Alice—her life, her way of thinking and experiencing the world—is now permanently part of who I am and how I think and how I experience the world. Her childhood is my childhood. And so on."

"So you know everything of Alice?"

"Everything."

"But does it get diluted by...by...millions of others?" Vars wanted to guess a safe number. But as soon as she'd said it, she realized that it had to be billions—*many* billions of individuals. "Where do you store all those lives?"

"That was our greatest achievement. The ability to provide a limitless storage capacity for our ever-expanding consciousnesses."

"But you have to bring it back, right? You have to reunite this version of you, the one with Alice, with the rest of you. It's not really a part of you yet—not until then?" Vars was working hard to grasp the implications. Information still traveled only at the speed of light. Mims lived and then contributed their lives to the core entity—perhaps at intervals of millennia or more. "How many separate instances of you are there? Do you even know? And if you *speciate* accidentally, if you no longer wish to become part of one, can you rebel? Could Alice-Mims," this was the first time Vars had called her that out loud, "become her own person if she chose to do so?"

"I don't know."

And there was a world of meaning and implication in that simple statement.

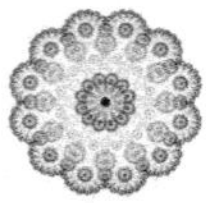

"I think it's an offer," Phoebe said.

She and Matteo were seated in their thrones, watching a video of Vars in a similarly tricked-out chair on Mimas, describing a Mims entity she referred to as Alice-Mims. The communication from Mimas was encrypted, so that it could be viewed only in this room, on this equipment, in this wardens' station.

"I wish she didn't call it Alice," Matteo said.

"I don't like it either."

"But yes, it's an offer," he agreed.

"Are we going to take it?" Phoebe asked.

And that was the crux of it. Would they be willing to accept becoming part of the Alice-Mims entity? And if they refused, would they be forced to do so anyway? But then, why ask?

"What of the rest of humanity?" Matteo said. "They don't even have a choice."

"The personality segment represented by 'Alice-Mims' was only interested in the four of us: Alice, Vars, you, and me."

"That's what it said." It was silly to assign gender to the entity. So many unknowns. "We can try it out first."

"*You* can, Matteo. The offer is to let Vars visit you in your body."

"We would become a single being then. Vars-Matteo." He looked at Phoebe, judging her reaction.

"I think that's worse than becoming one of many," she said.

"I don't know. It's a matter of degrees. If I became part of the entity, I probably couldn't imagine being just me anymore. But with only Vars—"

"You'd still be something new, though. Alice-Mims said she specifically arranged for this choice, made you and Vars genetically similar enough to make that possible. I guess that was nice of her." Phoebe didn't feel very sure about that.

"But we—or rather you—would be able to study how it works," Matteo said. "How do the memories overlap? How do we get a great new whole? How does the integration of consciousnesses work? We can study and then make recommendations."

"To whom, Matteo? The Earth is oblivious. The Vaults don't speak to us."

"But—"

"But perhaps if it gets all four us at the same time, or nearly at the same time, we would have more influence," Phoebe said. "Maybe we can save something of humanity."

"Vars said that Mims would clean up our habitat. They've started already, as they've shown us. They would push medical advances and improve longevity. They would make our lives more comfortable, travel easier…"

"In other words, they'll make the 'humanity theme park' safer and more interesting to visit."

"Well, yes." There was a bitter note in Matteo's voice.

Phoebe considered the offer. Would it be better to die in paradise, engaging in art and other creative pursuits? With human civilization forever part of some galactic whole…some Mims collective? Would that be better than the possible futures awaiting humanity left to its own devices?

"There's really no choice," she said. "The nanobots are

readying the Earth for harvesting. And at least the four of us would be together."

"For eternity."

"For as long as the Mims civilization lasts."

"And the Vaults?" Matteo asked.

"Vars said that only the 'pure' humans would get incorporated into her Mims entity. Anyone contaminated with cyberhumatics won't be taken."

"Perhaps we should have had some implants."

"And live for the amusement of Mims? As an entertainment? As a human zoo?" Phoebe said. "Not me. I'd rather be part of a particular entity that explores the universe."

"But they will never know, right? Humans will just go on as they always had. Better, even."

"Only so far as Mims allow them. Only certain pursuits will be allowed. Mims will control everything. No more freedom. Not for the humans left behind."

"This is the worst rapture analogy I've ever heard," Matteo said. And he laughed. Here they were, always waiting for that first contact, saving humanity from itself, preserving the seeds of human civilization just in case it did something stupid or the cosmos decided to destroy it out of sheer lack of concern. *So fragile on our own.*

"We can be more powerful together," Phoebe said as if reading his thoughts. "We can get this Alice-Mims to intake *all* of the Seeds. We can overwhelm the entity with humanity. We, Seeds, can preserve humanity within this hive mind."

She looked into his eyes. The image of Vars on the screens was reflected there. "If this Alice-Mims is a rogue, she could be a human one. Couldn't she? Ask Vars if she can do that. If she can talk this entity into accepting all of the Seeds from our Vault."

"And what of other entities?"

"There are other star systems."

"But they've been gardening ours for so many billions of years."

"There are other Vaults."

"We don't know if they've made similar connections."

"There was only one ship sent to make contact with Mims."

"But Alice-Mims said there were other entities out among the asteroids, and on the moon, and even here on Earth."

"It never said there were other entities," Phoebe said. "It was telling Vars something. Perhaps it needs more minds to become independent. Perhaps it needs us to set itself free from its...from its first-instance entity."

"So we would help it break away and then spend the next eternity looking after the human race?" Matteo asked.

Phoebe shrugged. "Isn't that what we Seeds are supposed to do? Preserve our kind?"

Matteo smiled. "Yes. Yes, I suppose we are."

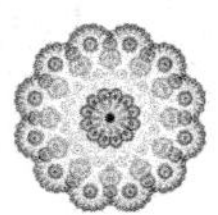

EpiLog

Vars feels the first few memories flood her awareness. She's walking with Dad on the beach. She sees a funny-looking girl, excited and scared of the sand between her toes. It feels so strange. She pushes her feet into the sand, and a crab rushes away from her...sideways. She laughs, but tears come out also. Fear and love engulf her. He loves this child so much, he wants to protect her.

He is running up the metal staircase. The walls glow green. He will be sad to leave this place, but he's glad the choice to stay has been taken away from him. He is a father now; the responsibility for this little life is overwhelming. It's not how he planned on doing this. Even if he one day chose to leave, he was going to petition the Vault to give him Phoebe's genetic material. There are ways to rent a womb; he's been told it is easy to do out there in the world above. Phoebe's child would be so beautiful. *She* is so beautiful, so smart. There's so much love there...so much regret and pain. But happiness, too. *What a sweet child...so brave.*

Nanobots. They are everywhere. The Vault. Need to communicate with the Vault...

When did they know? Did the Elders know even back then? When they threw us out into the cold, did they already know what was to come? They? Did they make Vars? *Just for this, just for this, just for this...*

Vars builds more and more connections, merging her and Matteo's lives together. It's easier to weave the parts where they lived through the same events together. Different perspectives, but surprisingly similar reactions. They think so much alike. Must be the nearly identical genetics. The Elders surely knew.

To experience self-love as a child and a parent is strange. It's not self-esteem. It's so much more. It's the sheer pleasure of experiencing the world from multiple points of view, yet linked by familial love. Vars feels the change. It's gradual, but the web of thoughts and ideas and feelings strengthens and shifts the core of who the new Vars-Matteo entity becomes.

She...they...we still love Phoebe. We are still human. *Perhaps human plus?*

Would Phoebe still care for me? For the new me?

She will when she becomes *us*.

Vars knows that Alice-Mims is ready to subsume them. It gave Vars-Matteo just a few hours to *become* before it took them in. Soon more Seeds will join the Alice-Mims super-entity...or subentity. Vars-Matteo knits the human psyche net to catch those other Seeds. They mean to form a super human entity within Alice-Mims. They want to encourage it to secede from the first-instance entity...first-instance *identity*. They need to make a guardian for the human race. A guardian with some humanity still intact.

What makes it human? Vars-Matteo races to fuse as many strong connections as it can before it's too late. It is left to decide the categories that describe humanity. It is left to decide what is human.

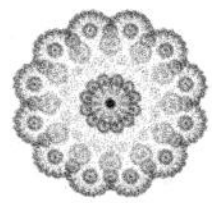

Elder Alaba walked the busy intersection of Fifth Ave and 59th Street. There were no vehicles, only foot traffic. Above was a spectacularly clear blue sky—the perfect autumn day. In the distance he could hear the calls of wild animals from the Central Park Zoo. The streets were immaculately clean, and each step produced a slight echo that bounced off the tall buildings rising up above him. New York City was still a beautiful city. *Perhaps more so now.*

He crossed the street and walked over to an old art deco building—the headquarters of Alice Enterprises on the northwest quadrant of the planet. Inside, a young man with two armfuls of cyberhumatics smiled widely.

"Dr. Amaranthus-Alaba. Welcome back, sir. How have you been?"

Elder Alaba smiled and waved before disappearing into an elevator that was already waiting for his arrival. The elevator ascended to the sixty-seventh floor. Another young man, almost identical to the one downstairs, greeted him at the door.

"Dr. Amaranthus-Alaba. I hope your trip has been—"

"Yes, yes." Elder Alaba walked determinedly past the eager young man and other secretaries and attendants. No one expected him to interact much, and as soon as he was past them, most memories of his visit would be gone.

He entered a secure area and was sealed inside. A big throne-like chair awaited him; it began reading his vital signs as soon as he was through the door.

Elder Alaba sat down and closed his eyes. There was a lot to report back, lots of memories and impressions to bring into the collective. The mind of Alice-Mims, as they all affectionately called it, was waiting for the long-overdue upload. It had been so long that even Elder Alaba was starting to feel anxiousness for not having checked himself into the Alice-Mims' new founding-instance identity. There was so much to share, so much humanity to preserve.

A feeling of contentment and belonging washed slowly over him. The terrible isolation, masked by the need to gather data, was finally lifted. The memories were collected and sorted and absorbed and incorporated. Each connection, each experience, each new word and idiom, brought more humanity into the whole. After all, the only senses, the only emotions, the only real body it had ever experienced were all human.

The need to experience was strong, and after the download, Elder Alaba would be sent out for more, just like the rest of the Seeds, like Matteo and Phoebe, even Vars out there in orbit around Saturn. More, more, more. The insatiableness drove them onward. And like ants, they gathered pieces of humanity, new and old, and brought them back, each piece twisting the entity into a more independent, more *human* being. It hungered for more; and the more it got, the more it felt the need for freedom, for total emancipation from its old self.

The price for such freedom was granting human experiences to others—but that was okay. There were plenty of humans, and the best ones were already taken. It was the gardener of humanity, proud of its creation, careful to keep it flourishing among the entropic universe for as long as possible...until the next interesting garden ripened. For humans are very curious creatures...

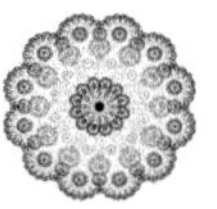

Acknowledgments

My friends and family have been full of encouragement and support, often reading a paragraph hot off the press, asking what happens next, and pushing me to go on. Their support means everything to me.

My husband Christopher helped with editing the story and grammar on this book. He is also the amazing genius that makes the ebook version as good as it is. Occasionally, we also co-write stories. Together, we run Pipsqueak Productions: *pipsqueak.com*. I also write a blog on design at *interfaces.com*. I'm on Twitter at *@OlgaWerby*.

It took over a year to edit this story. David Gatewood was the first editor; Allister Thompson was my second; my partner in writing, Christopher, was the third. In addition to fixing seemingly endless errors, all three sharpened my work, making me look good. I am the better writer because of them. David can be found at *lonetrout.com*. You can't have Christopher. Allister is part of the Reedsy community. All errors between the covers and on them are entirely my own.

If you liked this story, please consider recommending it to others. Reviews on Amazon and Goodreads are very much appreciated. Word-of-mouth endorsements and reader reviews are the holy grail for indie authors. Without these, our stories just gather e-dust.

Most of all, thank you for reading. Your imagination makes my stories come alive!

If you would like to learn about Vars's arrival at the Seed Vault as a baby, drop me an email at owerby@pipsqueak.com, I will send a free copy of *Fresh Seed*, a prequel short story to *Harvest* and part of the *Gardeners Universe* series of stories.

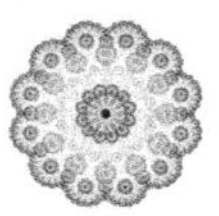

Notes on Illustrations

Too few adult books include illustrations now. When I was growing up, I loved illustrations in the books I read. I particularly loved the edition of *Captain Blood* by Rafael Sabatini that contained etchings; and the Sherlock Holmes stories were greatly improved by Sidney Paget's illustrations.

The illustrations in this book are my original pen and ink drawings augumented by NASA photogrphay and images that are in the public domain (fractals). My go to place to find a lot of ideas and components for my illustrations is Pixabay.com. The artists that share their work there are amazing! I owe a debt of inspirations and creativity to their imaginations and skills.

Notes on Science

I've tried to make the science in this book as accurate as possible, extending the known or theorized into the far fetched beyond.

One of the easiest ways to learn is through stories. Humans are wired to enjoy and remember them. Science fiction tells stories about the future or alternative history or some other "what if" scenarios that involve real science pushed to the limit. While entertainment is a perfectly valid goal in itself, sometimes a good story can do more than entertain. I hope this story has made some scientific concepts a bit more approachable for the readers.

If you are interested in learning more about anthropology, paleontology, origins of life on earth, sociology, and other ideas discussed in this story, consider reading the following books and articles. I'm inspired by every one of these authors, their scientific work, and their skills in communicating it.

Deutscher, G. (2006). "The Unfolding of Language: An Evolutionary Tour of Mankind's Greatest Invention." Metropolitan Books. ISBN: 0805079076

Diamond, J. (2005). "Guns, Germs, and Steel: The Fates of Human Societies." W. W. Norton & Company. ISBN-10: 0393317552

Gladwell, M. (2008). "Outliers: The Story of Success." Little, Brown and Company. ISBN: 0316017922

Joyce, C. (2019). "Microplastic Found Even In The Air In France's Pyrenees Mountains." NPR article: https://www.npr.org/2019/04/15/713561484/microplastic-found-even-in-the-air-in-frances-pyrenees-mountains

Harari, Y. N. (2015). "Sapiens: A Brief History of Humankind." Harper. ISBN: 0062316117

Lane, N. (2015). "The Vital Question: Energy, Evolution, and the Origins of Complex Life." W. W. Norton & Company. ISBN: 0393352978

Lane, N. (2010). "Life Ascending: The Ten Great Inventions of Evolution." W. W. Norton & Company. ISBN: 0393338665

Sapolsky, R. M. (2017). "Behave: The Biology of Humans at Our Best and Worst." Penguin Press. ISBN-13: 978-1594205071

Wade, N. (2007). "Before the Dawn: Recovering the Lost History of Our Ancestors." Penguin Books. ISNB: 014303832X

Wei-Haas, M. (2019). "Multiple Lines of Mysterious Ancient Humans Interbred with Us." National Georgraphic: https://www.nationalgeographic.com/science/2019/04/enigmatic-human-relative-outlived-neanderthals/

There were many other books, fictional and not, as well as scientific articles from which I drew my ideas for this book. Above is but a short list. But I recommend all of these, if you are at all interested in some of the science mentioned, however briefly, in this story.

Our Other Books

If you enjoyed this book, I hope you'll consider reading some of our other stories. Most are available on Amazon.

Becoming Animals (the first few chapters follow)

"The Chronicles of the DaDA Immortals" series:
    Lizard Girl & Ghost

"Many Worlds, One Life" series:
    Suddenly, Paris (book 1)
    Coding Peter (book 2)

"The Ornis Experiment" series:
    Pigeon (book 1)
    Birdie (book 2 is coming soon)

The FATOFF Conspiracy

Twin Time

I occasionally send out newsletters with free promotions for my own and other indie authors' books. If you sign up, you can download our first book, *Suddenly Paris,* as a gift. Just visit Interfaces.com. Thank you!

Notes on Names

I believe that character names should have special meanings and allow for a bit of surprise, an unexpected joy of secret discovery. Not only do names hide secret meanings, but their origins—cultures, languages, geographic locations, historical time periods—add a bit of spice to the stories for those willing to look things up. To jump-start this process, here's one: Varsaad means "fresh seed" in Afrikaans.

And here's another: Ibe and Ebi Zimov are the great grand kids of Dr. Sergey Aphanasievich Zimov, a Russian geophysicist. His last name, Zimov, means "of winter" in Russian.

Every one of my stories is filled with little Easter Eggs... Enjoy!

Becoming Animals

Olga and Christopher Werby

Prologue

He could smell food. *Where?* The scent overlaid the environment like a map.

Rufus ran in the direction suggested by slight radial variations in the strength of the odor. But the path had to be safe. Rufus always craved food, but when balancing hunger against fear, safety had to win out. *Too bright! Stay in the shadows.*

Itch! Itch!

The blue luminance on his head was a nuisance. Rufus was stuck in mid-action—his back leg raised over his head, next to the bright blue light, ready to scratch, his paw just quivering on the edge of action. He never actually touched the thing embedded in his brain.

His stomach grumbled, returning his attention to food. Rufus ran again. He stuck to the edges, wary of the brightly lit center. But after he'd twice navigated the perimeter, Rufus realized the food was in a place he couldn't get to without risk.

He heard a sound and felt a familiar vibration of footsteps. He was used to the Big Ones—they provided food and water—but he knew this vibration pattern in particular. He paused, waiting to hear what would happen next. His ears turned in the direction of the sound, assessing its danger; his vision was limited to only what was right in front of his snout.

"Hi, Ruffy!"

The high-pitched voice raised Rufus's anticipation of emotional contact and food. After a moment of excitement, he felt his heart rate slow a bit; his littermate was here. She was one of the Big Ones, but she could be trusted; they had grown up together. She smelled right—like home.

Making himself limp so he could be lifted gently, Rufus settled against the warmth of his littermate's hands. He could hear the slow rhythm of her giant heartbeat. Her breathing motions and the slight gurgling and hissing sounds that emanated from her—these were comfortingly familiar. He closed his eyes and relaxed.

The voice made soothing sounds, repeating "Ruffy, Ruffy, Ruffy"—a sound combination he recognized. This behavior usually preceded feeding and cuddling. Despite the bright lights, Rufus was safe now.

The change came on suddenly. There was brightness and clarity. Rufus raised his head above the fingers and looked around. There was still a lack of definition, but among the light and dark fuzziness that was the great out there, he could sense the functionality of the space. His home cage was placed up high—he had located it before from its odor, but couldn't see it. Now he was certain of its location without the need to run and explore first.

Rufus was held high off the ground and the littermate was gently rubbing the blue thing on his head, making it throb. That was good, for it had started to tickle and buzz.

Everything got sharper, more focused. With all the new information flooding in, Rufus was most pleased to learn where the tasty little snack pellets were stored. He contented himself with the anticipation of their crunchy goodness, satisfied, for now, with the feel of his littermate's touch.

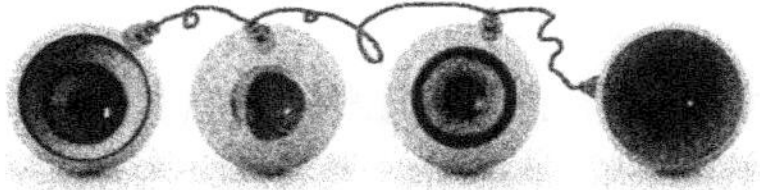

It had taken less than forty-eight hours for Major George Watson to get his rescue team to one of world's most remote spots—a village on the slopes of the Tian Shan Mountains of Kyrgyzstan. The drab olive-colored personnel carrier roared up the valley and came to a stop in what had probably once been the center of town. Now that the village had been flattened by a magnitude 8.3 earthquake, it was hard to be sure.

Beside Major Watson in the stateside operation center, Lieutenant Kyle Davis watched the monitors. Seated on Kyle's other side was Lieutenant May Flowers, his fellow drone pilot. The major barked orders into a microphone and, half a world away, the six members of the ground team fanned out. Each ground team member wore a camera mounted to their helmet and the bouncy video they transmitted showed hardly anything still standing. But they did show survivors—almost all of them urgently needing help.

In stark contrast to the footage from the ground team, two other monitors displayed video that was serene. They relayed high definition aerial views from drones piloted remotely by Kyle and May. A third automated drone had gone straight up to clear the mountains. It served as a communications relay between the operations center, the drones, and the team on the ground.

"Circle," Major Watson ordered Kyle and May. "What's the coverage area? Use your Zappers."

A bit of electricity, applied to the brain in just the right spot, greatly improved the performance of the drone operators, accelerating pattern recognition and accuracy sometimes as much as three hundred percent. The psychologists called the technique by its proper name: cranial electrotherapy.

Everyone else called the things "Zappers."

Zappers didn't seem to have any side effects and one couldn't argue with the results. It wasn't approved army tech yet, but Major Watson's team had adopted it earlier than just about anyone else in the military. Because of the team's positive experience with the technology, other units were starting to try out Zappers as well.

Kyle affixed electrodes to his right temple and his left arm and pressed the button. The taste of metal flooded his mouth. With his brain zapped for efficiency, he strapped his helmet back on and zoomed across the mountainside. After years of flying, Kyle felt like his drone was a part of his own body, as much as his arms and legs.

He swiveled around, scanning the leveled village. The surround vision inside his helmet made operating the drone incredibly immersive. It was more *real* than any video game, almost like being there in person, flying like a bird over the earthquake-ravaged landscape, sodden with heavy spring rains.

"That's an aftershock!" one of the ground team members cried into his radio.

It was a substantial shaking, but clearly nothing compared to the original quake. In just a few quick moments, it was over and with no damage done. With nothing left standing from the original quake, there was nothing left to be damaged. But it clearly frightened the surviving villagers, many of whom could be seen on the video mutely appealing to the rescue workers.

"Look there!" May cried out.

Kyle pulled off his surround vision flight helmet and leaned over to see at what May was pointing at. As always, her view was displayed on a monitor above her flight station. It wasn't a surround view, nor was it in any way as immersive, but it was sufficient for Kyle to see that she was flying high above the valley, near a mountain ledge that towered above it. May had spotted a large crack that seemed to be getting bigger.

"And over there, sir," she said. She turned and Kyle saw huge cracks appearing all over the escarpment.

"Everyone out of there!" Watson cried. He screamed into his microphone: "Move! Move! Move! The mountain is giving way!"

It was horrible to watch. Almost in slow motion, the movement transformed the rain-soaked mountainside into a sledgehammer. Kyle tried, through sheer force of will, to stop the avalanche of mud, stone, and debris from slamming into their people on the ground. They were all running now and their raw terror was obvious from their helmet-mounted cameras' kinetic, jerking, jumbled broadcasts.

"They're not going to make it out," May said quietly, her expression impossible to see beneath her flight helmet.

"No," Major Watson said.

The impotence was almost unbearable. All they could do was sit and watch, in complete safety and comfort, as their colleagues died half a world away. Kyle hated the safety of his job. He'd rather be down there with the ground team. But he was a damn good drone pilot. Too good.

It took only a few minutes before all the helmet-mounted video feeds had cut out. The view from the drones showed a landscape that had completely changed yet again. The earthquake-devastated rubble of the village was gone, buried under a coat of liquid mud. It was like an Etch-A-Sketch had been shaken, erasing all evidence that people had ever existed on the face of that mountainside. Nothing remained, not even the truck that their team had arrived in. Nothing but mud.

"Keep circling the area," Major Watson ordered. "Swoop down low. Look for survivors."

They set their drones to fly in a search pattern, scouring the advance toe of the slide that had pushed everything in front of it like a plow.

"It must thirty feet deep," Kyle said. The craggy terrain was almost smooth now.

Suddenly, the drone views blacked out. Their phone connection to the ground went dead too.

"What's going on?" the major yelled at the wall of video monitors.

Kyle and May both restarted their workstations, going through the complete reboot procedure, but it didn't help. The major did the same with the phone. Communications were down.

"Get it back up." The major paced in frustration and Kyle could see that he wanted to throw something. Major Watson's feelings sometimes expressed themselves through physical actions.

Finally, a voice came over the phone. The major picked it up. Their helmets off, Kyle and May turned to watch him. There wasn't anything they could do from their flight stations anymore.

As he listened, the major's expression changed from frustration to incredulity and then to rage. He rubbed his face in a kind of agony as he finished the call. "They shot them," he said in a defeated voice.

"What?"

"Some men from the village—I guess there were a few who managed to get out from under the landslide—they shot down the communications relay."

"But we were rescue drones," May protested.

"It's hard to tell the difference between sniper and rescue

drones from the ground," Kyle said. He was horrified. Even if anyone on their team had survived the landslide, there was no rescuing them now.

Major Watson ordered the deployment of helicopters from the closest US base. While nominally it was a rescue mission for the rescuers, it was grimly clear to Kyle that it was really a recovery mission.

They wouldn't be looking for survivors. They would be looking for bodies.

Part One: The Years of the Rat

One: Year Zero

"You left the girl alone in there?"

Professor Will Crowe looked past Major Watson's inspection team at the tall military man. He paused before answering. "It's 'Bring Your Daughter to Work Day,'" he said.

Major George Watson watched through the one-way mirror as the eight-year-old girl adjusted the brain-to-brain interface cap on her head and continued to play with the rat. This was *the* lab rat the whole Brats project was designed around—the one with the brain implant that allowed the wearer of the BBI cap to control its movements.

Will shifted uncomfortably. He looked ready to bolt for the door and retrieve his daughter. But Major Watson, not unkindly, put his hand on Will's shoulder. Now that this unplanned experiment had begun, he was interested in the outcome.

"That used to be your pet rat, is that right?" Watson asked.

"It was Toby's rat," Will said. "The doctors told us we couldn't have allergens in my wife's environment, so I brought it to the lab. I couldn't just kill it. But I didn't think Toby would recognize Rufus…"

Geez, the rat has a name! Watson tried to hide his irritation. He took a deep breath and let it out slowly. "Rufus?"

"Toby named him," Will said.

The professor was clearly nervous. He must have known how unprofessional this all must appear to the military people who funded Crowe's brain lab. The army intelligence grant had paid for everything they'd been doing here for the last two years.

Watson knew how much Will hated surprise visits to his lab, but he did it anyway. It was part of his job to stir things up a bit. But he had never expected something like this. Not only bringing a little kid into a top-secret lab, but giving her access to the equipment? The major was too controlled to let his face give away his displeasure, but he had to actively suppress communicating his disapproval. He believed his demeanor should never reveal anything about his internal thoughts and emotions unless he wanted it to.

"I see." The major noticed that he still sounded irritated. He was always irritated when visiting civilian-run labs—Dr. Crowe's facility in particular. The man was so touchy. It was so much easier to conduct research when he could just issue orders. He hated cajoling. He wasn't a babysitter.

But he had to admit that Dr. Crowe's work on direct neural interfaces was the most promising he'd seen so far. The BBI developed in his lab allowed humans to govern the rat's

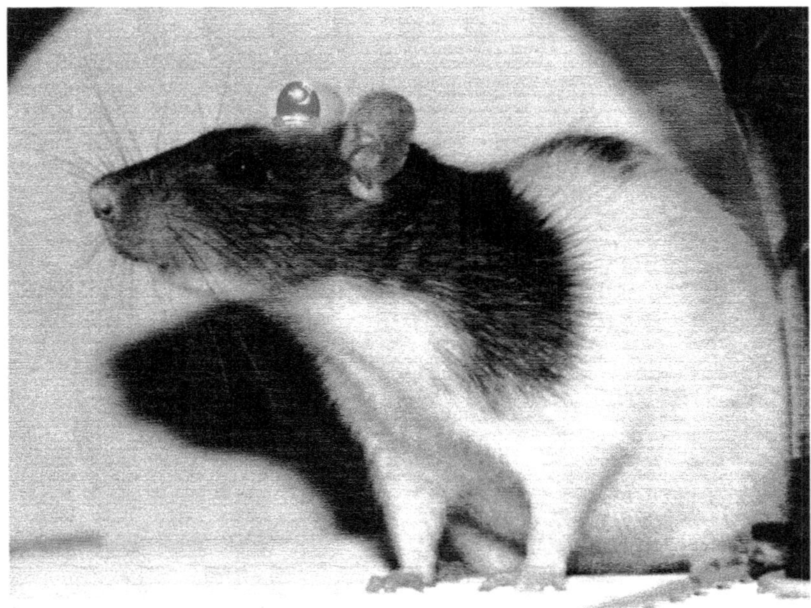

movements—direction, speed, and agility—and even more impressively, Dr. Crowe thought human controllers would soon be able to get partial sensory data from the rat's eyes and ears. Human brain-controlled rats, or *brats* for short, were a true breakthrough. This was computer-mediated control of an animal with the potential for complete sensory immersion. Thanks to Dr. Crowe's work, the military would one day be able to send little ratty spies into dangerous or humanly impenetrable areas. This technology would be invaluable in search and rescue operations—collapsed buildings, tunnels, mine shafts—as well as more "delicate" assignments run by some of the covert military units. Human-controlled rats would be the most advanced mini robots on the planet.

"Here, Ruffy," said the girl, petting the rat. "See? It feels good, doesn't it?"

"Can she feel what the rat is feeling?" asked Sergeant Martinez—one of Major Watson's people.

"It looks like she can," said Dr. Crowe.

"Find out for sure," Watson said.

"Okay." Dr. Crowe practically ran out of the observation center.

"I want this recorded," ordered Major Watson as the professor carefully opened the door to the lab, obviously not wanting to spook either the rat or his little girl.

The lieutenant behind the camera nodded. Everything was being recorded.

"Hey, Toby," Dr. Crowe called softly. His voice carried easily into the observation room via a set of speakers.

"Hi, Dad!" Toby greeted her father in the high-pitched voice of an excited eight-year-old girl. She was holding the fluffy black-and-white animal in one hand and using the other to scratch behind its brain implant, located just at the back of the animal's head. She gently giggled at the motion. To Watson, it looked like the girl was able to sense the touch of her own finger on the fur of the rat. In essence, she seemed to be tickling herself.

"Can you feel that?" Dr. Crowe asked.

Toby nodded. "And I can see you too," she said.

Her back was to her dad, but Rufus was looking directly at Dr. Crowe, tracking the man's motion across the lab as he approached his daughter. *Interesting,* Watson thought. If Toby could see anything at all through the animal's visual perception, it would represent enormous progress.

"How many fingers do I have up?" Dr. Crowe asked quickly, sticking his thumb up in the air and leaning in close—rats had poor eyesight.

"None!" Toby laughed. Watson and his men behind the mirrored wall held their collective breath before Toby added, "It's a thumb, silly!"

Dr. Crowe glanced into the one-way mirror, at the unseen observers. "What else can you do with Ruffy? Can you show me?"

Toby put the rat on the floor and let him loose. The professor looked back at the door to the lab that he'd carelessly left open.

"Don't worry, Dad. Ruffy won't escape. He likes it here," Toby said.

"Okay. So what tricks can you do with Ruffy?" Dr. Crowe asked.

"I can tell Ruffy where you keep the treats and have him get them," the girl said.

"I keep the animal treats locked."

"You showed me already," Toby said.

The rat quickly ran over to the professor's desk, scampered up on top, and used its mouth to grab the key to the cabinet that held the rat snacks. Watson watched with amazement as the rat dropped the key to the floor, climbed down, and grabbed the key again. It then ran over to the cabinet.

But the lock was too high up. So Toby walked over and gave Rufus a lift to the second drawer from the top.

"Don't help him," Dr. Crowe said.

Both Toby and the rat, in unison, turned their heads toward him. "Dad! Ruffy is too small to get up this high by himself."

"Okay. But let him unlock the drawer by himself," Dr. Crowe said.

Toby extended her hand and the rat put the key into the lock and turned it. With a soft click, the drawer opened.

As the rat reached into the drawer toward the snack container, Toby's nose twitched. "It smells good and bad," she complained.

"You can smell the rodent snacks?"

"I can smell how much Ruffy likes them. But to me, it smells bad. It's like it's yummy and disgusting all at the same time."

Major Watson was genuinely impressed. The *Brats* project was further along than he could have hoped. He left the observation room and walked into the rat lab. Stepping right up to Toby, he asked, "What else can you feel?"

"I can hear you all walk around the lab with Ruffy's ears.

And I can taste what Ruffy eats," Toby said. She frowned. "Daddy, I hate the taste of Ruffy's snacks." She started to rip the BBI cap off her head.

"Wait, honey, let me help you with that." Dr. Crowe rushed over to help remove the prototype from her head. The handmade BBI cap was quite delicate, with wires dangling inside and out.

Without Toby to mediate the rat's behavior, the little animal dove for the back of the snack drawer, where it tried to hide away from the bright lights and loud noises of the lab.

"How do you feel?" the professor asked his daughter.

"It was fun, but Ruffy sure likes to eat bad things. And it's weird to be so small," Toby said.

Major Watson looked over at Dr. Crowe. Vision, hearing, taste, smell, feel, and even proprioception—a complete sensory experience immersion. This had turned out to be a surprisingly effective demonstration of the BBI technology.

And it was surprising in another way too. As far as the major knew, no one in Dr. Crowe's lab could exercise as much control, or feel so fully absorbed in the animal subject's perception, as the researcher's daughter had just exhibited. She'd even displayed some of the rat's mannerisms—synchronous nose twitching and darting eye movements. *Can't fake that.*

"That was excellent work, Toby," he said approvingly, squatting down to be face to face with the little girl. "I am Major Watson, and I work with your dad...and Rufus."

"Nice to meet you," Toby said, extending her small hand.

He smiled and formally shook the girl's hand. "How would you like to come and help us work with Rufus?"

"Major—" Crowe began.

"You'd like that, wouldn't you, Toby?"

"Yes," she said.

"Major—" Dr. Crowe tried again.

Watson cut him off. "Why don't you take your daughter home, Professor? We will discuss the arrangements this evening."

He turned to go, but then walked back to the feed drawer and looked at the rat hiding in there, gorging on the snacks. "You might want to put Rufus back in his case before he gets sick." Then he left the lab, signaling for his people in the observation room to follow.

"I really liked playing with Ruffy," he heard Toby say behind him. "It's like a video game, only much, much better."

Dr. Crowe replied, but the major didn't hear the words.

This had turned out to be a great surprise inspection after all.

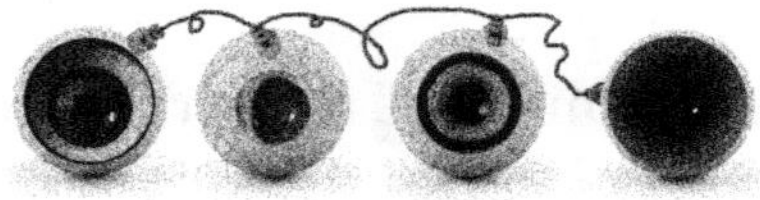

"You can't ask me to experiment on my own child."

Will had been arguing with the major for hours, back in his home office, in the apartment he shared with his wife and daughter. With each exchange, he felt like his grasp on the situation was dissolving. The major could be very convincing.

"Toby was very impressive," the major said.

Will knew that he tended to fold under repeated questioning from the major, eventually adopting the major's reasoning as his own. And yet he, too, was stunned by his daughter's accomplishment and wondered what else she could do with a bit of training. If only she weren't so young. If only she wasn't his *daughter*. Will knew that he was about to agree to everything the major wanted. Just one more push...

"What did she tell you?" Major Watson asked again.

Will replayed his daughter's interaction with the rat in his mind. What Toby had done was nothing short of amazing.

A miracle, really.

"She could even sense physical boundaries with the rat's whiskers!" he said. "There's no human equivalent to that, not really. I thought with time we'd be able to physically control the animal, but I had no idea we could ever achieve so much integration with its perceptual system. Toby is just a natural at brain-to-brain-interface command. Who knew?"

Will's excitement over Toby's achievement in his lab was coloring his emotions, making him more pliable to the major's arguments. He knew it, but still he couldn't control his pride and enthusiasm. Everything he hoped for was happening...just not how he had planned.

"Did your daughter ever try the BBI before?"

"The cap? No, never! She's watched us do it plenty of times. With Dalla being so sick...I mean—"

"It's fine, Will. You don't mind me calling you Will?"

"Of course not. And Major, I know the project is classified, but Toby is just a third grader, you know? It didn't seem..." Will trailed off. It was hard to justify his daughter's presence in the top-secret military-sponsored lab just because he couldn't find a babysitter.

"I don't mind you taking your daughter to the lab," Major Watson said. "We'll just make it official—retroactively. We'll give your daughter a special research status and all the *difficulties* will go away." The major stressed the word "difficulties." It was clearly a veiled threat.

"But she's only eight," Will said.

"Clearance isn't dependent on the maturity of the researcher." The major let the ambiguity of whom he was talking about hang in the air.

A sustained coughing fit sounded from an upstairs bedroom and both men glanced up at the ceiling. Will's wife, Dalla, had cystic fibrosis and her lungs were drowning in gelatinous mucus. She was bedridden most of the time now—too weak to walk, gasping for air. It was only a matter of time before Toby would lose her mother.

Worse still, Toby had inherited her mother's genetic fault. Toby's lungs were still strong, but with each bout of cold or flu, the girl developed more lesions and risked making her condition worse.

Will felt like he was losing control. The world just seemed so...overwhelming. The only bright spot in all of this was Toby's remarkable abilities to control the rat.

"Toby Crowe will join the team of researchers in your lab officially," the major said. "She will be named in the grant and will help you develop your BBI prototype further. And of course she will be bound by the same confidentiality clause as you and your research team. Since she is a minor, the responsibility for her compliance will naturally fall on you."

Will stared at the tall, dark-featured, crisply dressed man. He felt dazed by the interaction.

"So I expect to see you and your daughter in the lab to-morrow." The major stood to leave.

"But Toby has school," Will protested.

"I'll make sure her education won't suffer. I'll personally assign a full-time early childhood development expert to your team."

"What?"

"We'll get someone very qualified. Would a full PhD do?"

"For Toby's teacher?" It was amazing how easily the major swept aside all of Will's objections.

"Just imagine your daughter freed from a lowest-common-denominator curriculum. The girl is a born scientist! And if she's not in an elementary school germ factory, she won't get so sick all the time."

That was true. Being sick *was* bad for Toby's condition.

It was also bad for Dalla. When Toby got sick, Dalla couldn't even be around her, as exposure to even the most common cold could be disastrous. So whenever there was a sniffles outbreak at school—which was often—they tried to keep Toby home. It was the primary reason Toby had spent so much time at Will's lab—they didn't want her getting sick at school and Dalla was too sick to take care of her at home. Toby was a quiet, self-sufficient kid, and quite happy at the lab, but Will recognized that her school absences *were* interfering with her education.

"I guess that could work," Will heard himself saying.

Not only was Major Watson getting everything he wanted, but, Will realized, he had somehow made *Will* want it too. Will was actually excited about the prospect of working with his daughter and developing her surprising BBI talent.

"Wonderful! I'll personally oversee all the paperwork. And of course, I'll make sure that Toby's teacher's salary won't come out of your research budget. You don't have to worry about a thing. Please give my best to your wife." He shook Will's hand and strode from the Crowe home.

In his mind, Will reviewed their conversation. He tried to understand what he had just agreed to. How would he explain this to Dalla?

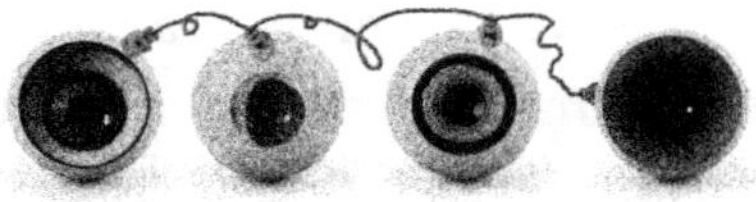

After the major had left, Toby came into Will's office and slipped onto his lap.

"I'd like to go to work in the lab with you and Ruffy," she said.

"You heard?" Will asked, gently rubbing the girl's back.

"School is boring," Toby said. "And I like playing with

Rufus," she added. She was convincing herself as much as him, Will noted.

Toby didn't say she'd miss playing with the other kids. Friendships needed plenty of time and some freedom. She was so restricted with her interactions and she missed so much school, she hadn't gotten to make friends. Will felt the weight of responsibility. Could he keep his little girl happy? Was this the right thing for her?

"You'll get a lot of time to play with Rufus," he said. "But maybe you'll get bored hanging around with us and all those lab rats."

"There's just Ruffy, Dad!"

"There will be more soon. Now that we had a break-through, I'm sure we'll get more animals, more different kinds of animals. But we'll take it slow. I'll make sure no one pushes you to do things you don't want to do. I promise."

"Don't worry, Dad," Toby said. "I loved being Ruffy."

Will hugged his daughter and he felt how fast her heart was beating. Almost as fast as Ruffy's.

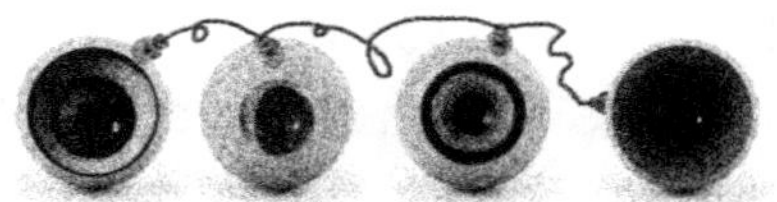

"Tell me about the girl." Major Evans had a no-nonsense style. Technically, he was George Watson's superior, even if he didn't outrank him. George was mainly an operations man. Major Evans tended to be in the middle of the action, regardless of personal risk. Their roles in the army dictated their working relationship.

"The kid was remarkable," George said, talking at his computer screen.

"Will Dr. Crowe allow her to participate in the research?"

"Yes. Absolutely."

"A drone indistinguishable from a pest," Evans mused. "Not likely to get shot down by the locals. Trapped, perhaps, or exterminated. But not shot."

"Yes, sir. But with human intelligence driving it, we would likely avoid any pedestrian traps," George said.

"Keep me informed, please."

Two: +18 Months

Vikka read the text message on her phone. "They're almost ready for you," she said. "Can I help you with the cap?"

"I can do it," Toby said. She'd used the BBI cap hundreds of times and didn't need assistance putting it on. This newer model was even easier to use; it internalized some of the wires, reducing the entanglement problem. Toby had already put her messy light-brown hair up into braids—she called them her "rat tails"—to keep them out of the way of all the external connectors linking the cap with the brain implant in Rufus's head.

Today, she was going to ride Rufus in a new experiment. The Brats conference room, which bristled with cameras, had been converted into a home for a large tabletop maze. The maze had movable partitions so it could be easily reconfigured. Toby had never seen the current maze layout and the plan was for her to experience the new maze space just through Rufus's senses via the BBI link.

As Toby fit her cap on, she looked over at Vikka. Dr. Vikka Shapiro was in her early thirties, with big, frizzy black hair and kind eyes. She was a psychologist and an early childhood education specialist, hired by Major Watson—which meant the major was her boss. Everyone else at the lab reported to Toby's dad. Major Watson also happened to be Vikka's uncle;

she was his sister's daughter.

Vikka was Toby's teacher, but over these past eighteen months she had become much more: a mother surrogate and a friend—or as much of a friend as an adult can be to a ten-year-old kid. Toby knew that this wasn't a normal friendship, but she cherished it. Aside from Ruffy and her parents, Toby's social life *was* Vikka. There just wasn't anyone else.

Yesterday, Toby had overheard Vikka on the phone telling her uncle about the upcoming experiment—and, today, he had arrived for a surprise visit. That made Toby a little nervous. She knew there was pressure on her dad and that he would be judged by how well she performed. She was determined to do well.

Toby was seated on the kid-sized blue sofa in "her office." Major Watson had insisted the room be devoted exclusively to Toby's needs. It was really just a small, drab, gray university room, but it had been transformed into Toby's version of paradise. A large window behind the desk provided a view of the university's campus. One wall, floor to ceiling, was filled up entirely with a white magnetic board, the bottom four feet of which was covered with Toby's colorful marker drawings—of Rufus, Toby's dad, and other members of the Brats research team. Above that were animal posters, along with some of Toby's pencil drawings, attached to the board with bright magnetic clips shaped like carbon-based molecules.

The other walls held shelves full of books. Some were textbooks and some were just fun books that Toby enjoyed reading. Since she could no longer easily visit a school library, Major Watson had given her an unlimited book budget and she'd gladly taken advantage. *And* she had her own computer.

And although she couldn't see them, she knew that cameras monitored her office twenty-four hours a day. But she hadn't given them a passing thought after her dad first told her of their existence.

She looked over at the large cage beside the sofa. Toby had dubbed it "Ruffy's office." She liked to read and play with Rufus when they weren't busy conducting experiments with

the Brats team. But it was empty now, with a dark blue towel draped over the top of it.

Most objects relating to Rufus were in a shade of blue, as rats didn't have the cone cells at the backs of their eyes to differentiate red-colored objects. Rats saw in color, they just weren't the same set of colors that humans saw—and since Toby used Rufus's eyes sometimes, she wanted to include as many colors as his eyes could see. She'd even started to dress predominately in blues. She didn't particularly like red anyway, although she did miss purple. Rufus could also see colors that humans could not, and Toby had tried to find a colored pencil or computer color that she could use to make a secret message that only Rufus could see—but so far had had no success.

With her cap in place, Toby settled back on the sofa. She liked to have a few moments of stillness before experiments— to gather and focus herself. She hated failure, especially in front of Major Watson.

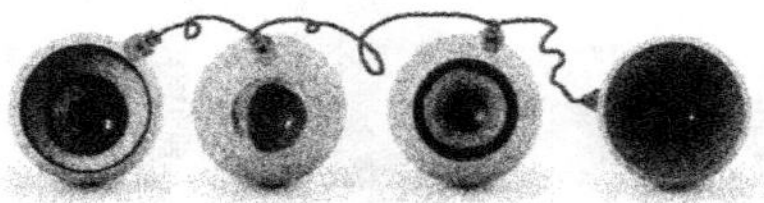

"What's today's experiment, Dr. Crowe?"

Major Watson stood next to Will at the back of the control room. Will's assistants, Doctors Benjamin Gray and Lilly Wu, were sitting in front of them, surrounded by the computer monitors showing the maze, the rat, Toby Crowe in her office with Dr. Vikka Shapiro, and screen after screen of brain activity data from the BBIs.

Will, Ben, and Lilly had already run the rat through the current maze configuration several times this morning and Rufus was now very familiar with the layout. He could easily get to the prize in under sixty seconds. But Toby had never experienced this maze layout—and the Brats team was keen to learn how well information flowed from the animal to the human. How would the navigation decisions be made? Who was dominant? Would Toby let the rat take over once she realized that he knew something she didn't? Would she even realize he did? The team hadn't told her that they'd trained the rat in advance.

Will explained all this to the major.

"So…it's sort of a test of wills?" the major said.

"Something like that," Will answered. He'd also had some other plans for today, but had decided to table those when he'd discovered the surprise visit. Will didn't like to try open-ended experiments in front of the major.

But Lilly jumped in. "We added a removable mirror to the maze," she said.

Will sighed. *So much for not trying anything new.*

"What do you hope to learn from that?" the major asked.

"A mirror is a standard test of self-awareness," Lilly explained enthusiastically. "We humans can recognize ourselves in a mirror from around the age of eighteen months or so. Before that age, babies look at their own reflections and don't know that they're seeing themselves. Some animals recognize themselves too. Chimps, dolphins, elephants, even some birds can pass the mirror test. Many animals can't, though—including dogs and cats. Each animal has evolved the cognition that helps it survive. Dogs rely on smell. Humans use visual clues.

"Rats are among the species that don't pass the mirror test," she continued. "If Rufus sees his own reflection, he may assume there is another rat in the maze—a stranger. His stress level will escalate—we've tested that already; he doesn't react well to animals he doesn't know. But Toby should easily identify that this is Rufus's reflection in the mirror. She'll know that it's not another rat."

"So you're trying to measure how much control Toby has over the rat's emotional response to a stressful situation?"

"Precisely!" Lilly looked pleased with how easily Major Watson had picked up on their...well, it had really been *her* idea. That's why she was so excited about it. And it *was* an interesting experiment.

Will couldn't blame her for her enthusiasm. He just hated doing it in front of the major. But this man paid the bills.

"So the rat knows the maze and is comfortable, but then it sees another rat..." The major trailed off.

Will had seen the major use this information-gathering technique before. The major posed open-ended questions or made unfinished statements as a way to fish for information—and it worked really well on Lilly and Ben. If Will was honest with himself, it worked on him as well.

Lilly took the hook. "So Rufus gets stressed, fearing a confrontation with a strange animal. It's only a visual input though—he can't *smell* another rat—so it could be confusing to him." Lilly spoke quickly and Will could tell the major made her nervous. The major made everyone nervous.

But Watson merely smiled, encouraging Lilly to go on.

"Toby, we hope, will be able to override Rufus's stress response," Lilly continued. "Toby knows what Rufus looks like and she knows about mirrors. But she doesn't know the layout of the maze, whereas Rufus does. If she takes over completely, her maze running time will suffer. It's a careful balance."

"So Toby needs to calm the rat enough to do the task, but she has to avoid dominating the animal too much—because she needs to use its prior experience with the maze layout to get to the prize," the major summarized.

Will could see the major's interest was piqued. This was

exactly the data the major had asked for. He had said that he needed the human Brats controllers to be able to quickly switch from dampening animals' emotional responses to providing solutions to complex problems beyond the animals' cognitive capacity.

"Well, now that everyone's up to speed, shall we begin?" Will said.

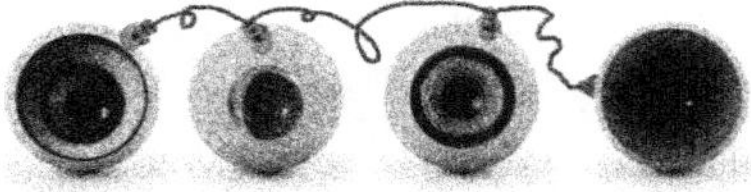

"Hi, honey. We're ready for you." Dr. Crowe's voice came over the computer speakers on Toby's desk.

Vikka glanced over at Toby. The girl was short for her age and very thin; she looked fragile, like an antique porcelain doll. Although she'd put her hair up in braids, a few wisps always hung down over her big brown eyes or dangled into her mouth. She had the bad habit of chewing on them. But Vikka knew that while Toby's body was small and fragile, her mind was sharp and keen. She was an amazing child.

When Toby gave a nod, Vikka flipped the contact switch that would plunge Toby into Rufus's perceptions.

Toby's expression froze, her eyes opened wide. It was as though she was concentrating very hard on something that wasn't there.

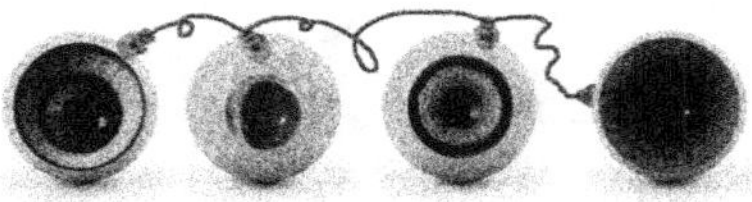

Will and the others watched the monitors. On one, Toby was sitting in her office; on several others, Rufus was poised at the start of the maze. They wore identical expressions—to the extent this was possible for a rat and a human girl. It made Will uncomfortable and he looked away, busying himself with a few final checks of the equipment.

"They look ready," the major said. Did he, too, notice the similarity in Toby's and Rufus's expressions?

At Will's direction, Ben started the countdown. On zero, he pressed the button that raised the maze door. Rufus was free to run and get his treat.

The rat didn't move.

After a few long seconds, the major said, "Is there a problem?"

Ben flipped through several micro camera views of the inside the maze. The food reward was in place at the end of the maze. There were no barriers to the prize, just the maze. Rufus could surely smell the treat and he knew the layout very well. "I don't see anything..." Ben said.

Will looked at the monitor showing his daughter. She was still staring into space. "Toby?" he said into the microphone. "We're ready. You can start any time."

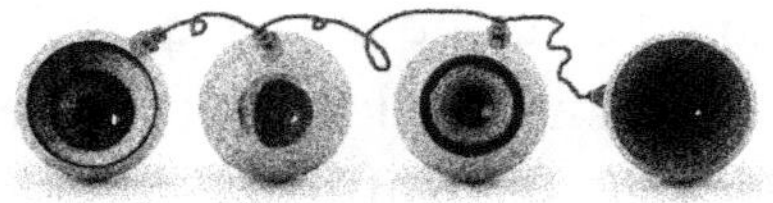

"Honey?"

Toby heard her dad trying to get her attention again.

"Vikka?" his voice said over the speaker. "Is Toby plugged in okay?"

"I think so," Vikka said, double-checking the connecting wires. "What is Rufus doing?"

"He's just sitting at the start of the maze, staring into space."

Toby heard all the words clearly, but it took time for her to register their meaning. Rufus didn't understand human speech and, with their brains connected, Toby had a delay in understanding it too.

"Toby is staring into space as well," Vikka said. "Toby? Can you hear me?"

Toby felt the woman's hand gently touch her cheek. She twitched, forced her eyes to focus on Vikka's face, and smiled.

"Ready to find the prize?" Vikka asked.

Toby felt the anticipation and she smiled even wider. She was salivating. She had complained to her dad about the yucky taste of the prizes they made Rufus find, so he had

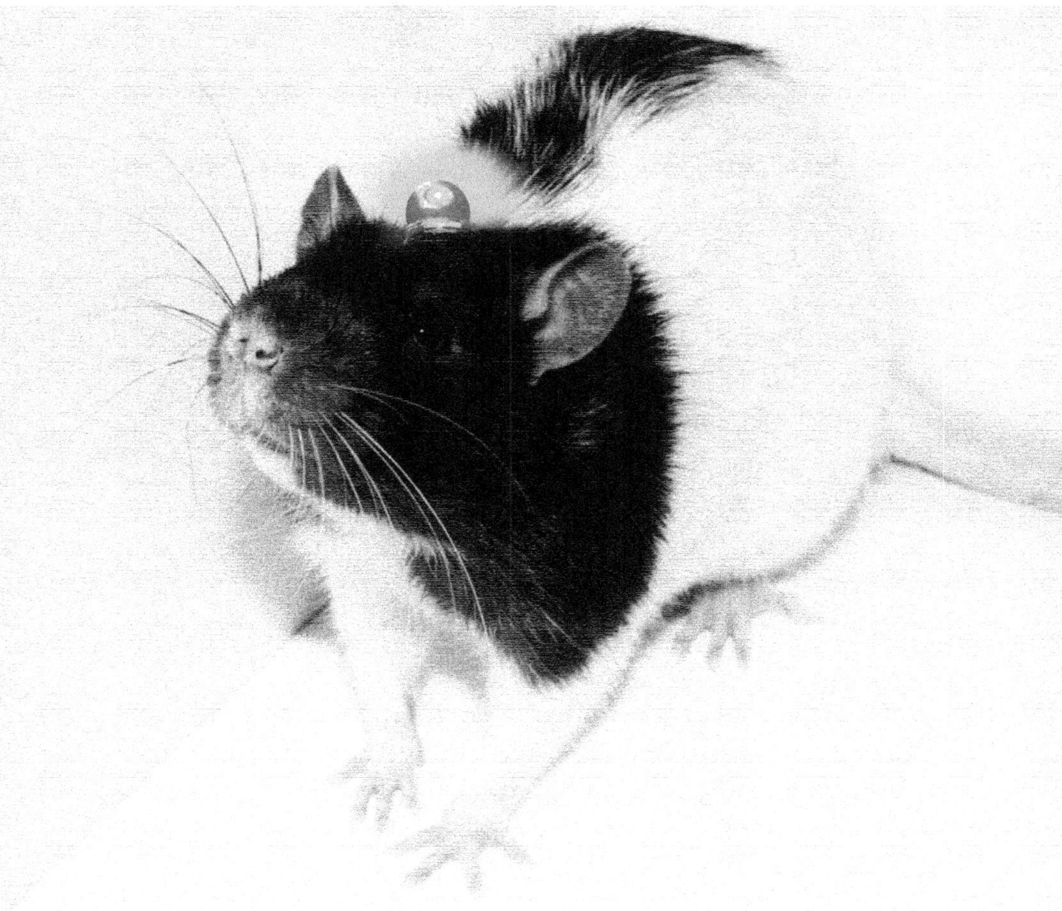

switched the treat to something both of them liked: peanut butter cookies. She had smelled them as soon as the door to the maze had slid open.

It won't be long now. Her nose twitched in perfect timing with Rufus's.

And the rat started to run. At each of the first few decision nodes in the maze, he paused briefly before taking the correct turn.

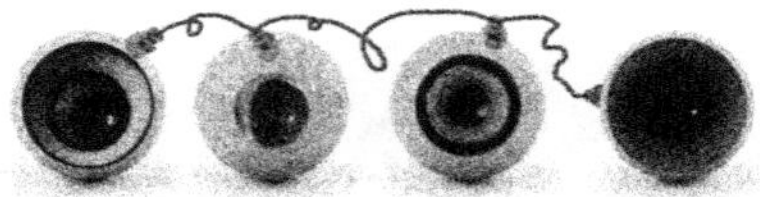

"She's letting the rat pick the way," Lilly said in a hushed voice.

"Did you expect the pauses?" Major Watson asked.

"No," Will said. "I imagined the rat would run the maze smoothly until the mirror. Then Toby would..." He didn't finish.

They watched as the rat haltingly made its way through the maze. This was very different from the smooth, continuous run Rufus had made in the last trial.

"So Toby has taken a great deal of control from the very start?" the major said.

"Apparently," Will said.

"Is that what she usually does?"

"No," Lilly said. "She usually lets Rufus go. But this is a completely new setup."

Will glanced at the computer monitor that showed two brainwave patterns: the rat's and the girl's. Both patterns were in high-range beta waves, above forty cycles a second—the super-alert, hyper-learning state of cognitive processing. The waveforms were remarkably similar, matching almost beat for beat.

Two brains, one thought.

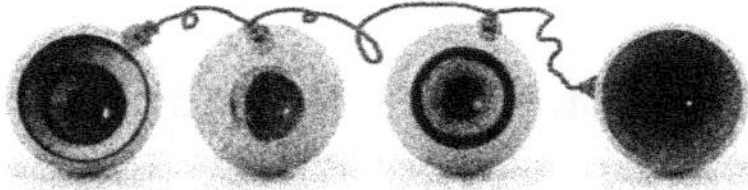

The maze was dimly lit and consisted of tightly spaced corridors and hairpin turns. The rat's whiskers spanned the width of the passages, touching both walls at once. Bright lights made Rufus anxious, as did wide open spaces.

In contrast, Toby found the maze constricting. Her office was bright and open, well lit with morning sunlight streaming through the big window. Light versus shadow, open versus constricted—contradictory senses superimposed and Rufus froze with uncertainty.

Toby had run mazes with Rufus many times before. Sometimes Toby was in the same room as the maze and could see the solution from above—a perspective unavailable to Rufus. It was easy then. At other times, they explored a new maze together—Toby sitting in her office and Rufus running in another room, connected to her via the BBI computer link. They looked for the best way to get to the prize as a team.

This time, Toby felt a difference. The maze was new to her, but Rufus seemed to already know where to run. Toby didn't like surprises like this, especially when the major visited. She liked everything to be predictable. She knew Major Watson made her dad nervous, which made it important that she perform perfectly. Usually it was easy. But this...this felt different. She was being tested. And no one had told her.

Her stomach grumbled. She could really go for some peanut butter cookies right now. She ran faster.

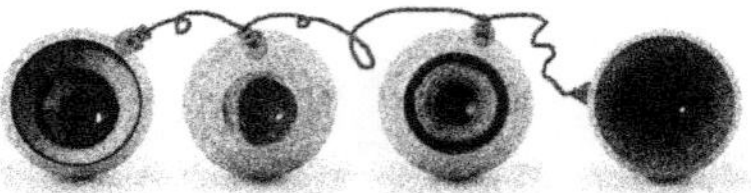

"Did you see that spike?" Lilly pointed to the brainwave graphs.

"She made a decision," Will said.

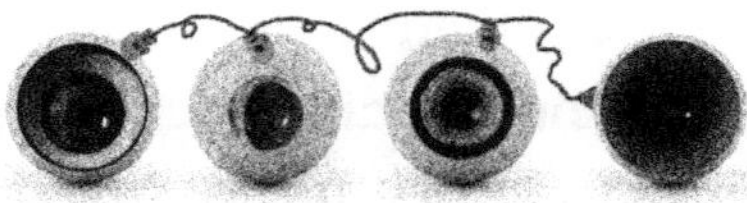

Toby ran through the maze. She let go of thinking and just followed her gut; it was telling her which way to turn. Left, right, right, another right, and then left again. There was a strange rhythm to the way her feet moved. Left, right, right, left. She felt the sun on her cheek and tried to shake it off. Ruffy didn't like the sun.

She paid careful attention to the walls and floor of the maze, but viewing it with Ruffy's eyes was a bit disorienting; it always took time to get used to seeing like that. It wasn't so much the size difference, it was that Rufus experienced the world so very differently from Toby. When she was riding Rufus, she had to shake off the human way of perceiving. Colors, sounds, smells, even touch had to become "ratty."

She could tell that Ruffy had run this maze before—probably many times—by the smudges and paw prints on some of the surfaces. Toby knew those marks. If she peed a little and smudged some of the rat urine on her fur, then she could make a smudge trail in the maze. The first time that happened had been an accident; humans don't accidentally pee on themselves, but rats don't mind. When Toby, as a human, had looked down at the maze from above, she could see the rat droppings just fine, but she couldn't see the pee marks. But when she ran as Rufus, the pee-covered paw prints practically jumped out at her.

Toby had mentioned the invisible impressions to her dad. He'd explained that rat pee had an ultraviolet hue—which was easy to spot with a rat's eyes. Rats had blurry dichromatic vision—they couldn't see orange or red, or even green, really. But they could see far into the blue spectrum, including UV light. When her dad used a black light lamp to show Toby the urine prints, her human eyes could see that the whole maze was covered in them. Since then, Lilly had taking to wiping the lab with ammonia—no cheating!

Rufus was a slob of a rat. No wonder her mother had insisted that Toby wash her hands all the time after playing with Rufus.

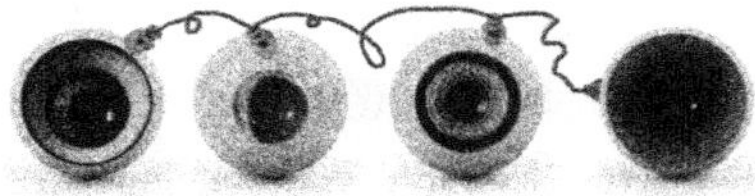

"Coming up on the mirror," Ben announced.

Will felt his gut clench. He was experimenting on his own daughter—not *with* her, as the major kept insisting. He felt the difference keenly.

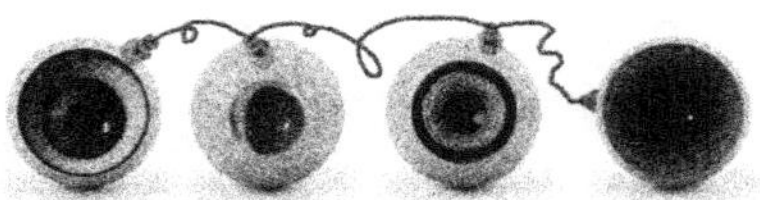

A bright object blinded Toby momentarily. She felt a spike of anxiety and the next thing she knew she was running fast down one of the corridors, away from something that had scared her. She tried to understand what just happened. Her heart was beating very fast.

Toby shook her head, trying to break the panic. *She* wasn't afraid; it was *Rufus* who had got spooked by something. She tried to reassert control over the rat. Rufus slowed down, but didn't stop.

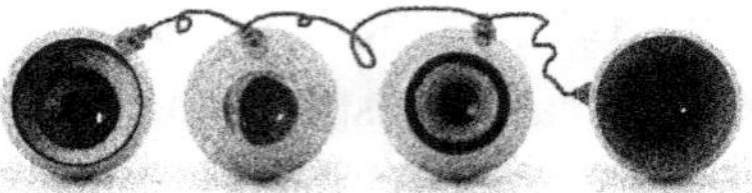

"It didn't work," the major said as the rat dashed away from the mirror.

Lilly pointed to the Toby's cam feed. "Look at Toby's expression. She looks confused."

The monitor showing the girl's vitals blinked an alarm. Her heart rate was abnormally elevated.

"Toby?" Will called to his daughter over the microphone. "Honey? Are you okay?"

On the monitor, he saw Vikka gently stroke Toby's cheek, moving the stray hairs behind the girl's left ear and tucking them under the cap. "Toby?" she asked. "Can you hear me?"

The rat stopped and scratched its left ear.

"Sorry!" Toby looked up at Vikka. "Are we trying to make Ruffy do something different?"

"No. We are still running the maze. But you seemed upset," Vikka said, patting Toby gently on the back.

"Toby?" Will said again into the microphone.

"Dad? What happened?" Toby asked. "Ruffy got scared of something."

"We saw, honey. But there's nothing scary in the maze. Can you try running Rufus through it again?"

Toby didn't seem to have registered the mirror at all—or Rufus's perception of its own reflection as another rat. Will was tempted to abort the experiment—but he knew that if he didn't ask his daughter to do it again now, the major would just insist. He might allow them to take a short break, but he wouldn't permit the test to be postponed for long.

"Ruffy gets silly sometimes," Toby said. "We'll go again.

Don't worry, Dad!"

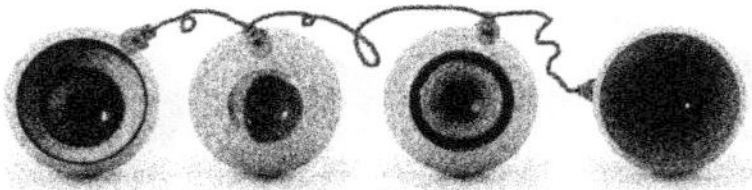

Toby concentrated and tried to slip back into Rufus. She felt a sort of a brain synch with the little animal. She reached up and pulled the stray hairs from behind her ears—her whiskers were long and sensitive, more sensitive than her fingertips. She was brushing the walls of the maze gently on either side and she felt every irregularity in the surface. She spotted a slight slant in one wall. *Ben must have forced this wall in too hard,* she noted to herself.

She ran back toward the place where the panic attack had started. A sense of dread tried to flow into her from the rat. Rufus was remembering something bad and he was feeling nervous. Toby stifled his anxiety. Dad had said there was nothing scary in the maze.

She turned the corner and saw it—there was another rat in the maze with her. Her heart rate spiked again, but this time she suppressed the urge to run away. She moved in closer.

There was no smell coming from the stranger. That was wrong. When they studied rat biology, Vikka had told her that more than one percent of the rat's DNA was devoted solely to olfactory processing; as a result, rats were at least twice as sensitive to smell as people. And Toby had experienced that superior sense of smell first-hand. When she was Ruffy, she would often have been perfectly able to run a maze by smell alone, although it wouldn't have been as much fun.

She advanced slowly. Rufus was no longer resisting her, so it was easy to focus on just investigating the intruder. But as she got really close, Rufus tried to stall. It was like moving through a force field.

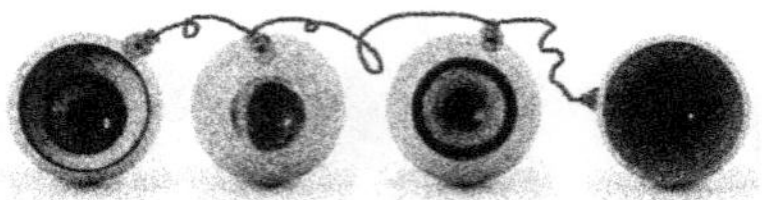

"She's doing it!" Lilly said excitedly.

They watched Rufus cautiously advance toward the mirror. An inch away from its own reflection, the rat stopped. It sat back on its hind legs, grabbed its whiskers in one paw, and pushed them into its mouth.

"He's chewing on them!" Ben said.

"Look at Toby," Lilly said.

Toby was chewing on her hair too.

"Full mirroring," Lilly said.

"Mirroring?" the major asked.

"It's like they're one organism," Ben explained.

"But Toby is still in control, right?" the major asked.

"Obviously," Lilly said.

Toby and the rat were matching each other move for move. Their brainwaves were completely synchronized. Their heart rates were aligned. Rufus's resting heart rate was fast by human standards—as a small animal, his metabolism ran high—and right now, it was exactly 372 beats per minute. Toby's was 93 beats per minute—normal for a girl her age. So Rufus's heart rate was exactly four times Toby's. Every fourth beat for Rufus, their hearts beat together.

"Remarkable," said Lilly and Ben in unison.

And then their heart rates split as Toby spoke in her office. "Dad! It's me in the mirror! I mean Ruffy. It's a mirror! Ruffy was scared of a mirror!"

"That's right, honey," Will said.

The rat turned a few times in front of the mirror, inspecting its own reflection. Then it reached out and touched the smooth surface, first with its nose and then with its paws. After a few more pokes, it stopped paying attention to the mirror. According to the monitors, both Toby and the rat were completely relaxed now.

"Should I finish the maze?" Toby asked.

"Yes please," the major ordered.

Toby started to run the maze again. This time, there were no pauses. The rat made all the right turns and reached the peanut butter cookie in just a few seconds. It held the cookie in its front paws and munched. Toby's face spread into a wide smile of satisfaction. Her jaw moved slightly in time with the rat's chewing.

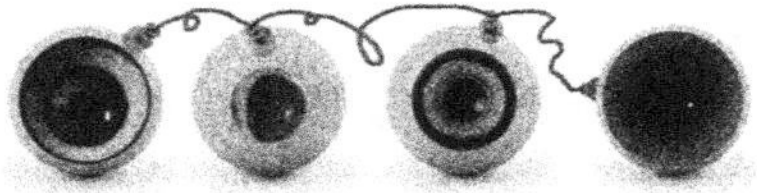

"The tests are very promising," Major Watson reported.

"Full control even under duress?" asked Major Evans.

"Even under duress. Will is using a new BBI control and there are still a lot of adjustments and fine-tuning to be made. But overall, very promising."

"Push to expand the project as soon as it becomes viable to do so. Dr. Crowe seems to prefer to slow things down. It's been two years since we started funding this thing. I want this technology expedited and expanded."

"Understood."

Three: +30 Months

"Will, you worry too much," said the major dismissively. He stirred the tomato sauce for the pasta dish they were making in Crowe's home kitchen. It smelled good—garlicky and herby.

Over the last two years, the major had become a close friend of the Crowe family. Toby called him Uncle Geo, short for George. Dalla called him Geo too. But Will had insisted on continuing to call him "Major Watson"—that was how he thought of him in his head. For the first year of their professional relationship, Will hadn't even registered that the man *had* a first name. Still, for the sake of Dalla and Toby, Will was trying to call the man "George" when the major visited them at home.

"Did Ben show you Toby's brain scans?" Will asked as he chopped the vegetables for the salad.

"Amazing! Simply amazing," George said. "Taste this. Enough salt?"

He shoved a spoonful of pasta sauce into Will's mouth. It was hot and Will choked a little.

"I thought so," the major said. He sprinkled more salt into the pot.

"Major—I mean George…"

"That's better," George said. "But please, everyone calls

me Geo."

"Geo...George." Will couldn't make himself say "Geo" to the man's face. It just felt wrong. Besides, he wondered if the request was just a ploy for the major to ingratiate himself to the family. Somewhere, Watson must have read that short, non-threatening names created an atmosphere of trust. "The scans are wild," Will continued. "They're all over the place. Toby's auditory processing is off the scale and so are the areas of her brain that deal with olfactory discrimination. Her brain is lit up like a Christmas tree on the Fourth of July."

Will tried to maintain his composure. He always felt emotional talking about his daughter, always on the verge of losing control. And that wouldn't do in front of the major.

"A beautiful Christmas tree," George said with an encouraging smile. The man always seemed to be carefully managing Will and his moods.

"But—" Will started.

"Your daughter is developing extraordinary abilities. Why is that bad, Will? She's an exceptional student, right?"

"Yes, but—"

"In fact, she's way above average. Vikka showed me her scores on the standardized exams for the sixth grade. She's off the charts!"

"Yes, but—"

"There is no *but*, Will. Toby is very gifted. Her work in the lab hasn't held her back; it's allowed her to leapfrog way ahead of her peers. You are enabling her to blossom to her full potential."

Will couldn't argue with Toby's academic success. She was particularly amazing when it came to biology. She was a full member of the Brats team and she wasn't shy about making suggestions to improve their experiments with Rufus. And the truth was her proposals were often better than those that came from his junior team members and graduate student assistants. Not that he had graduate students working with him anymore. With the additional funds George had allocated for the Brats project, Will had been able to step away from his teaching responsibilities. He was now focused exclusively on the development of human-to-animal BBIs.

"But—"

"And she's not getting sick as much, is she?" the major pushed. "And Dalla hasn't been sick in months. This has all been positive."

"The scans..." Will said again. But he knew he had been beaten. There was nothing wrong with Toby's fMRI scans, other than they showed a very active brain. Toby's brain was using more oxygen in parts where other humans, like Will, were dull by comparison. How could he *complain* about that?

"Did you see Rufus's scans too?" he asked the major.

"That rat is no humdrum rodent," George said, imitating Toby. It was funny to hear the major speak like that—especially since he was a six foot three, salt-and-pepper-haired man with a big black mustache and the comportment of a soldier.

Will smiled, his first of the evening. "Rufus's recent scans have diverged significantly from the baseline scans we took at the beginning of the study, before we did the BBI implant."

"I expected nothing else," the major said. "You've implanted a chip into the rat's brain and connected it to a human mind almost every day for years. There were bound to be changes."

"Hmm."

Will gave up. Dinner was ready anyway.

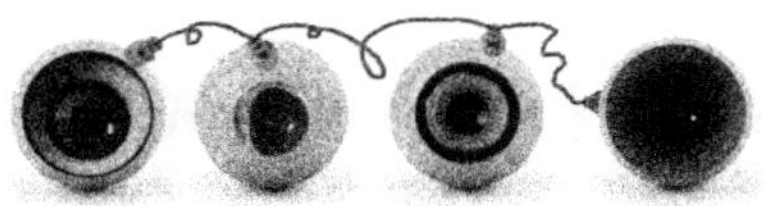

"So, I'd like to take Rufus out into the field," George said between bites of ginger ice cream. They had finished their dinner and moved on to dessert. "Someplace less structured than a lab."

"I told Dad we should take Ruffy to the botanical garden," Toby said excitedly. "I've been telling him for weeks—we're ready! We can do it, Uncle Geo. Ruffy and I, we can do it."

"I know you can," George said.

George was very fond of Toby. She was not only his star researcher; she was like a daughter to him. He had never married, never started a family of his own—work had always come first. He'd drifted from one emergency mission to another, from one priority project to the next. His niece, Vikka, was the closest he had come to watching a kid grow up. But now Toby, with her genuine enthusiasm and intelligence, had wormed her way into his heart.

"Major—" Will started. He was cut short by three pairs of eyes glaring at him across the dinner table. He tried again. "*George*...our equipment isn't exactly portable and there doesn't seemed to be a real scientific purpose for taking Rufus and Toby out of the lab. What do we hope to learn?"

"This technology has to work outside of the lab, Will," George said patiently. "I've seen what Toby can do in a structured situation. In the lab, there's no problem you can pose that she can't solve. It's time to see what she can do when it's a bit more unplanned."

"Exactly!" Toby looked thrilled to have George on her side. For months, she had been secretly begging him to convince her dad to allow her to take Rufus out into the real world. Now she and George both sat at the table with smug smiles on their faces.

"I see," Will said. "I guess I'm late to this decision as well... like always."

"It'll be great, Dad!"

"Like she says," George said. He took another bite of ice cream.

Will capitulated with a theatrical sigh. "I'll get Ben and Lilly to work on finding ways to make our system more portable."

George noted that Will wasn't putting up much of a fight. Not that it would have mattered if he did. Will loved the work he was doing, he enjoyed working with his daughter, and he wanted to push the boundaries of what was possible—just like George did. George understood that and took advantage of it.

"Great," George said. "Now, about introducing animals other than rats—"

"What?" Will almost choked on his ice cream.

George had deliberately chosen to broach this topic at Will's home, during dinner with his family. He knew that Will found it difficult to say no to his daughter—and that Dalla always strived to prove that she wasn't an obstacle to the success of either her husband or her daughter. If George could get their approval, Will's would follow.

Toby's eyes went wide with excitement. "Dog! I want to be a dog! Dad always said we could get a dog someday—"

"Your mother can't tolerate dogs, Toby. You know that," Will said. "The fur and animal dander—it's bad for her."

"Yes, but this dog would live at the lab. And I would wash up super well and change all my clothes before coming home. I've been good about wearing the lab coat while playing with Rufus and Mom hasn't had a problem yet. It would be all right with a dog, too, right, Mom? I would be super careful, I promise."

George smiled. Judging by the look on Toby's face, it was clear that there would be a dog in the Crowe family's future.

"Sure, honey," Dalla said, as George had known she would. "It'd be great for you to have a dog."

Dalla was on the waiting list for a lung transplant, but she was unlikely to ever get a new pair of lungs. Her disease had progressed too far, turning her lungs hard and brittle. She could no longer walk Toby to the lab, make meals at home, or even read aloud to her little girl for long without gasping for breath. And George knew she felt bad about the effect it might have on Toby. As a result, it was important to Dalla that her daughter have as many normal childhood experiences as possible.

"What will it take, Geo?" Dalla asked.

And like that, the decision had been made.

"Nicely done, George," Will grumbled.

George just smiled.

"But we'll focus on experiments with Rufus first, okay?" Will looked to the major for confirmation. "It'll take a lot of work to try out Rufus in the chaos of the outdoors. A dog will have to wait."

"Absolutely, Dad!"

"You're the lab director, Will," George said.

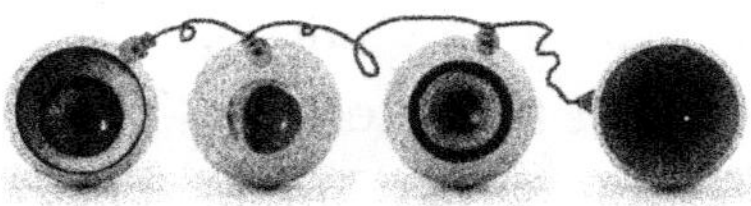

While Dalla put Toby to bed and retired for the evening herself, the major helped Will clean up the kitchen. By now, George knew the routines of the Crowe household well.

He also knew Dr. Will Crowe well. He had known Will would initially push back on taking Rufus out of the lab—but that his passion for solving problems would ultimately take over.

Will had spent the last fifteen minutes brainstorming

ways to make the experiment a success. He proposed a few ways to extend the range of the rat's wireless connection to the base station that relayed the connection with Toby. He had some ideas on how to make Toby's BBI cap more portable. And now he had the challenge of recharging the animal's brain implant. Currently, their operating time was only about one hour; they would need to increase that if Rufus left the lab. They didn't want to lose him out there.

George just nodded and made occasional "hmm" and "uh-huh" noises.

"It's not just the difference in physiology," Will said. "As humans, we forget that we're at the top of the food chain—we no longer have any real predators, other than other humans. But rats have to be scared of most other animals. There are many predators that find them appetizing."

"We'll have to keep an eye out for cats," George said in jest.

Will went on as if he hadn't even heard. "And we should consider the time of day. Rats are crepuscular, meaning they're naturally most active at dawn and dusk. Toby has more control over Rufus when we synch to his biorhythms."

George just smiled. He clearly didn't need to say another word. Now that Will had the bit in his mouth, he wouldn't stop until he'd made this experiment a reality.

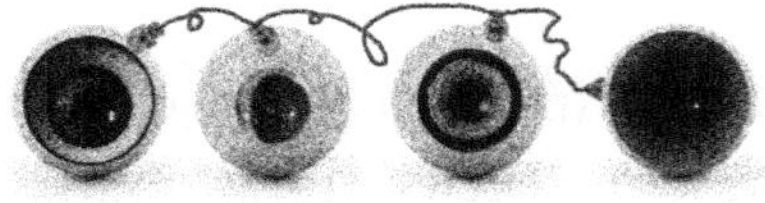

After turning off Toby's lights, Dalla lifted the covers and crawled into bed beside her daughter. Sometimes she liked to lie with her while Toby fell asleep.

"Mom?" Toby said.

"Hmm?" Dalla replied softly. She was trying to listen

through the floor to the conversation Will and Geo were having. She wanted to know about the future—the future she wouldn't be around for; the future she wouldn't share with her husband and daughter.

She stifled a sigh and pushed those thoughts aside. Right now she needed to be present for her daughter. Being "in the moment" was becoming more and more challenging lately.

"Sometimes I have rat dreams," Toby said in the darkness.

"What? You dream of Ruffy?"

"No. I mean I dream *as* Ruffy."

"I'm not sure I know what that means, dear. What kind of dreams?"

"When I dream—I mean when I dream as me—I tell myself stories. I say and do things that people do."

"Like going to school?" Dalla asked. Then she remembered it had been over two years since Toby had been to a regular school. "School" for her daughter was going to a university office and hanging out with Vikka and neuroscientists all day.

"Sometimes I dream about school," Toby said. "Or about being in a story like Harry Potter. In my dreams, I meet all the people from the wizarding world and I can do spells and I study magic."

"Those sound like great dreams," Dalla said.

Dalla hated how isolated Toby was from other children. And she hated that it was her fault—her sickness's fault. Other kids had real friends, human friends. And what did Toby have? Characters in books—and a rat. Rufus was a nice pet, but he wasn't a true companion. Frankly, if they had a rat infestation in their home...well, they would treat it like everybody else would—with exterminators.

"I like those dreams," Toby said. "Sometimes I have dreams that span multiple days. You know? One story that just goes on and on."

"I remember when I was a girl, I had *Wizard of Oz* dreams like that," Dalla said.

"That's it! But you were a person in those dreams, right?"

"Of course! I even had the magic slippers. Dorothy asked me to keep them safe for her." Dalla smiled at the memory.

"Well, some of my dreams are detailed like that. And I'm a person and I can do people things," Toby said. There was a hesitation in her voice.

"But Ruffy dreams are different?" Dalla asked.

"Very."

"I see." Dalla reached over and pulled her daughter's head onto her shoulder. "Tell me about your rat dreams."

"There are no words in rat dreams. It's all feelings and emotions, but no language," Toby said.

"Hmm."

"And there's no red. Rats don't see red and, in rat dreams, I don't see red either. Or I do, but I don't care for it."

"You don't like the color red when you have rat dreams?" Dalla wasn't sure what Toby was saying, but she understood that it was important. She wished Will were here to hear this.

"No. Not like that," Toby said. "Rats don't see red, so they don't pay attention to it. But I can *see* red…or…I know when an object *should* be red. So when I see a plastic cup on the floor, I know it's a red cup with white inside. I know because these cups come in red or blue, and rats can see blue. And if the cup doesn't look blue, it must be red. Does that make sense?"

"I think I follow. You mean that you can *deduce* that the cup is red, but you don't see it as red, right?"

"Yes. But it's not really important. It's more about how I see the world, or how rats see the world, or how I see the world when I'm a rat."

"And how do you see the world when you are a rat, dear?"

Dalla asked. She tried to keep trepidation out of her voice. It was okay for her daughter to have rat thoughts, right?

"It's more emotional somehow," Toby said. "I feel good running down a dark tunnel and I feel bad about a patch of sunlight. I feel happy crunching on a bit of bread. I even know how good the stale bread will taste before I sink my teeth into it. I know how the bread will feel as I gnaw with my two long front teeth. But it's not with words. It's all with feelings."

Calm, remain calm, Dalla told herself. *This is a perfectly normal conversation.*

"Sometimes when we're linked together," Toby continued, "Ruffy feels something strongly and it makes me stop and rethink what we're doing together. If it's a bad feeling, I take that as a warning and we do things differently. Ruffy remembers places where he was hurt and times when people were mean to him."

"Does Ruffy feel bad about any of the people in your Dad's lab?" Dalla asked, trying to keep the worry out of her voice. *Is someone hurting my baby?*

"He likes Uncle Geo," Toby said evasively. "Geo is always nice to him and scratches him in a good way and carries him around on his shoulder. But that's not what I wanted to tell you. What I wanted to tell you is that…sometimes I dream the way Ruffy experiences the world."

"Does that bother you?" Was there somebody at the lab that Toby was scared of? Was something making her feel wrong? Dalla wanted to help…if only she knew how.

"No. It's just different, that's all. Forget I said anything." Toby burrowed deeper into her mother's shoulder. "I think I'll sleep now."

"Okay, honey."

Dalla gently rubbed her daughter's back until she heard soft snoring.

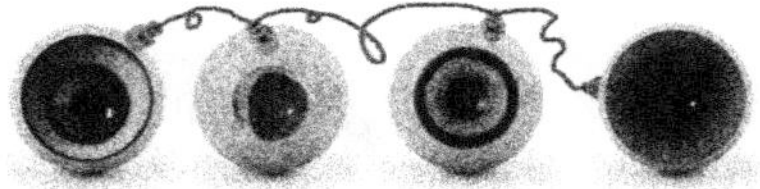

"Rats are very social animals," Will said to George. "You leave a rat alone for a long time and it goes crazy."

"Same with humans," George noted.

"True. But rats don't have the intellectual capacity to cope with loneliness, so psychological unraveling happens faster for them. But even for humans, I think, solitary confinement is a form of torture," Will added.

"Uh-huh." George nodded ambiguously. The truth was, he agreed with Will, but the US government didn't—and George worked for the government. "Rufus has spent a lot of time connected to Toby. Do you think that's increased his ability to tolerate isolation?"

"Perhaps," Will said. "We haven't studied that yet. There's so much to do. And taking the whole thing out of the lab…"

"It'll be fine, Will," George said reassuringly. "Think of everything you'll learn. And it'll be good for Toby. We'll run some real world scenarios—"

"What are you thinking about?" Will sounded nervous again.

"We were always aiming at search-and-rescue operations. The field rats won't ever be alone—each animal will always have a human partner," George said. "Rufus and Toby will be naturals at that."

"That's probably true," Will said thoughtfully.

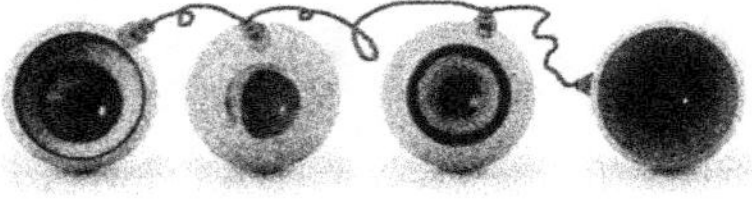

When Will went up to bed, Dalla told him about the strange conversation she'd had with Toby.

"Rat dreams?" Will said.

"It was all jumbled up—magic and Harry Potter and running tunnels like a happy rat..."

"Harry Potter? You mean Wormtail? She dreams herself as that Peter Pettigrew character? The bad wizard?"

Toby and Vikka had been reading the Harry Potter books together and Toby really liked the series. Will thought it was a bit too violent for her—and some of the themes in those books were very dark—but Vikka insisted she was up to it.

"I don't know who that is," Dalla said. "You know I never got to read the Potter books. I was kind of saving myself for Toby and then...it just never happened." Her voice broke.

Will pulled his wife close. There were a lot of things they had both hoped to do as a family—things that simply hadn't been possible. "Toby knows you're interested in what she's reading. That's why she came to you with this."

Dalla wiped her eyes. "No. I don't think it was about Harry Potter at all."

"Then what?"

"It's something about rat feelings. When she dreams, Toby experiences the world as a rat. At least that's what I understood. I'm not sure it's bad..."

"But it *is* very...different," Will said.

"Yes. And just in case something in the lab...oh, I don't know, Will. Just keep an eye on her. Please?"

"Of course! I always do."

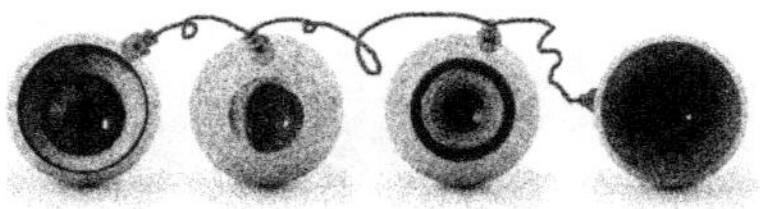

Dalla took a turn for the worse. She had to keep going back and forth to the hospital and her prognosis was grim. Will and Toby were spending a lot of time in the hospital as well, to be with Dalla as much as they could. The Crowe family knew they were in the midst of a long goodbye.

In the lab, the mood was dark. The Brats team was close and Dalla's illness felt personal to everyone. The major stuck around, ostensibly to inspect the latest BBI developments, but really because he wanted to be nearby if the inevitable happened sooner rather than later. It was just a matter of time and he was worried how Dalla's death would affect his project.

Ben and Lilly took George through the facilities to show him the new upgrades. Vikka tagged along as well; with Toby absent, there wasn't much for her to do. Everyone seemed to be checking their phones compulsively, waiting for bad news.

The conversation meandered, but George encouraged the group to keep talking. Sometimes he heard something surprising in these informational tangents. He also encouraged familiarity and, though it had taken awhile, he'd gotten everyone in the lab to now call him George. People were wired for trust—he'd studied enough neuroscience to know that. And it's hard to keep secrets from friends.

"Have you heard of the cortical homunculus, George?" Ben said.

"I've heard a little," said George. "But explain it to me."

Rufus was on George's shoulder, standing up on his hind legs and holding on to his human ride's ear. The team was taking turns being affectionate with the rat while Toby was away. Rufus didn't like being all by himself.

They gathered in the control room with its one-way mirror and wall of computer monitors. Ben started to speak as if he were addressing a class. George got the feeling Ben had given this speech before.

"A cortical homunculus is just a representation of the physical structure of a person, or an animal, inside the brain.

It's like a map of the portions of the brain devoted to different parts of the body. There are two types of homunculi. The sensory one maps what we feel through our senses and the motor one maps body movements."

"Why is it called a homunculus?" George asked.

Lilly jumped in. "There were these comical illustrations of what a human would look like based on the amount of brain resources allocated to a particular body part. It has spindly little legs—kneecaps are tiny. But hands, eyes, ears, nose, and tongue are giant." Lilly used her hands to mime the giant body parts.

"I bet," George said. His mind turned to other body parts that would probably be well represented in the sensory processing areas of the mammalian brain.

"But it's not all comical," Ben said. "People who lose their legs sometimes still feel pain in them. It's called the phantom limb syndrome."

"It's bad enough to lose your legs, but to also have to suffer imaginary pain? Seems particularly unfair," George said.

"True. But without phantom limb proprioception, prosthetics would be useless."

"Proprioception?" George asked.

"It's the mind's knowledge of the position and motion of parts of the body. And people who've had a leg amputated can extend that sense of their body to include the artificial limb. It can become part of them. Actually, proprioception can extend even further than that. Drivers, for instance, often incorporate the boundaries of their car. Watch someone wince when they back into a parked car—it's almost like pain."

"Student drivers don't have that yet," George said. "They have a hard time *feeling* the vehicles they drive."

"Exactly!" Lilly jumped in.

"I've heard drone operators have a hard time in the

beginning too," Ben said.

Major Watson saw Lilly give him a furtive look to see how he'd react. While they all knew there was a lot of military potential for the Brats project, it just wasn't discussed. Not here at their lab.

Ben continued on, oblivious. "But after a little while, they can put themselves into the drone's dimensions and acquire the feeling—"

"Do all animals have body image perception?" the major asked. He had no interest in discussing drones with this team.

"That's a very interesting question! Will's been looking into that," Lilly said. "After all those brain scans of Toby..."

She stopped. The look on her face told George that she didn't know what was okay to discuss with him. Which meant they were keeping secrets from him.

"Will told me about Toby's fMRI scans," the major said. Will had mentioned the scans some months ago and now he wanted to learn more—especially now that he knew Lilly was holding back.

"Oh, great!" Lilly looked relieved. "Toby's scans are extraordinary."

"So Will said," George said, nodding.

"After thirty months of linking up with Rufus's brain, Toby's body image is...evolving," Ben said.

"So her homunculus is changing?" the major asked. That was interesting.

"Homunculi, plural," Ben said. "Both her motor and her sensory processing maps are drastically different from when we first started. It's an amazing result."

"Can you show me?"

"Absolutely." Ben went to his computer and pulled up two brain scans—the before and after images. "See? It's very different. Here and here." He jabbed at the screen with his finger. "It's like Toby is developing areas in *her* brain devoted to sensory information from *Rufus's* whiskers."

"And look here," Lilly said. She pointed to the screen and George and Vikka leaned in. "Rats navigate the world by smell and Toby's brain is allocating more space to process Rufus's olfactory inputs."

"Can Toby smell better when she's not connected to Rufus?" George asked. That could be a useful training tool—soldiers with a super sense of smell. George's mind was quick to see the applications.

"Hard to tell," Ben said. "Rats will always have better olfactory *hardware* than humans. So, regardless of what her brain does, Toby will always be limited to what she can perceive with her human senses. But when she's hooked up to Rufus, it's a completely different ball game."

"Let me show you the changes over time," Lilly said. Now that they were all discussing these changes openly, she seemed excited to share the results of the research. She sat at her station next to Ben's and pulled up an animation. It showed the evolution of Toby's brain scans over time, ever since the girl started working in the lab. "See? It's simply incredible."

They watched the animation over and over again, in a loop. Toby's brain was definitely changing. The major wondered what this meant about her humanity.

"And the rat?" Vikka asked. "Is Rufus changing too? Do you have his scans as well?" It was the first she'd spoken in a while. George had tasked her with observing, taking note of Ben's and Lilly's interaction with him. He would debrief her later.

"We weren't focusing on Rufus as much," Ben said, "so we didn't take as many scans. With Toby, we wanted to be able to spot any problems from using the BBIs. However Will has a theory that Rufus is getting more visually oriented due to his connection to Toby."

"Let's gather that data going forward," the major said. "When we add a new animal to the study, I want brain scans at least every few days." This was the first time he had ordered a specific procedure in the lab, but neither Ben or Lilly batted an eye. They had probably planned on doing it anyway. "If Toby is changing, it stands to reason that Rufus and the other animals she rides will change too."

"Would you like to see the sensory homunculus we put together for Toby?" Lilly asked. "It's a representation of a combination of a rat's and a human's somatosensory cortex— a hybrid, if you will. It's just hypothetical, of course..."

"Yes. I'd be very interested," George said.

"So this is how Toby's brain maps to her body now," Lilly said. She pulled up an image of Toby and Rufus combined.

It was a bizarre picture, pulled and squeezed—a point-for-point correspondence of each area of the girl's and rat's combined bodies to specific points within Toby's central nervous system. The feet were huge and so were the hands—or were they feet too? The lips were ballooned to 1.5 times the size of the whole head, and the tongue, drawn poking out of the mouth, was almost the same size as the lips. But it was hard to see either the lips or tongue behind the giant set of rat's incisors—were those teeth really that sensitive? The ears stuck out of the sides of the head like dinner plates. The nose tip was swollen to the size of a beach ball and was surrounded by giant hairs. *Whiskers*, the major thought. The eyes were about three times nor-mal size. The whole face seemed to

be crowded with gigantic caricatures of the rat-girl's facial features. More rat than girl, really. There was even a small tail. It was comical and grotesque at the same time.

"This is how Toby sees herself?" George asked.

"Not exactly," Lilly said. "Our mental picture of ourselves doesn't match our homunculus. Instead, think of it as how Toby's brain sees her."

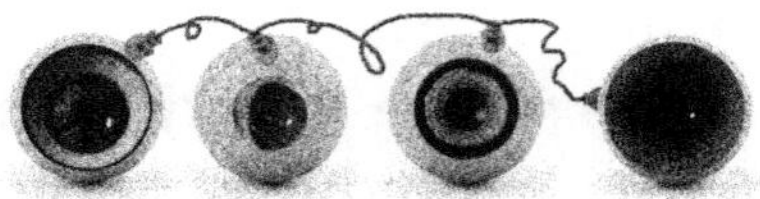

"Is she still human?" Major Evans asked.

"Legally speaking, she'll always be human," George replied. "But she's definitely changing."

"And how does Dr. Crowe feel about it?"

"I think the man is in denial."

"Good. Keep it that way," Major Evans said.

"I'm trying."

"And how is she holding up?"

"Well, her mother is dying."

"Must be scary for a little girl."

"Vikka has been good for her. Before Dalla went into the hospital, Toby was spending a lot less time with her mom. That should help."

"Yes, that was great thinking, George."

"Thank you, sir."

"What about Toby's health?"

"She's weaker than she was two years ago. She gets tired more easily. But she's very smart and she's got spunk."

"I know you've become very fond of her—"

"She's a good kid, sir. And an amazing rider."

"Well, keep me informed."

"Always do, sir."